JUST
DESSERTS

PAMELA G. HOBBS

POOLBEG

Published 2020
by Poolbeg Press Ltd.
123 Grange Hill, Baldoyle,
Dublin 13, Ireland
Email: poolbeg@poolbeg.com

A catalogue record for this book is available from the British Library.

ISBN 978178199-349-1

www.poolbeg.com

ABOUT THE AUTHOR

A native of Dalkey, County Dublin, Pamela made use of the local children's library from the age of seven every Tuesday and Friday afternoon on her way home from school. By thirteen she was penning her own stories, though very few ever got finished. Her dream as a child was to write and illustrate her own books and to that end, she attended the National College of Art and Design studying visual communications. Although she still uses her visual side, nowadays she definitely spends more time at the laptop than the easel.

Being a winner in the Novel Fair 2015 gained Pamela both confidence and experience from being around other writers. She was subsequently selected for 'Date With An Agent' (The International Literary Festival, Dublin) in 2016, 2017 and 2018. These events gave Pamela invaluable contacts and also the impetus to write her first short story, "Time Heals", which was shortlisted for the Colm Tobin International Short Story Award, May (2017), part of the Wexford Literary Festival. She is a member of the online writing group indulgeinwriting.ie

As an adult education teacher in Kilkenny, Pamela's days are busy, challenging and fulfilling. Her evenings are spent in another world altogether – that of romance and intrigue. It doesn't matter if she is reading or writing, her favourite motto is, 'Life can be tough – find your happy ending wherever you can.'

Pamela, her husband and two sons lived in the United States, on both coasts, for twelve years and she wore many hats – florist, office manager, call centre supervisor and colour specialist for a children's clothing company. Before moving to Oregon, she wrote articles predominately focusing on Irish immigration for a well-known Irish paper in Philadelphia.

Pamela has included many Americans in her writing and she likes to focus on the numerous family connections the Irish have with the USA.

ACKNOWLEDGEMENTS

With thanks to the sisterhood – Melissa, the Donegal addition, smart, talented and beautiful – you are most definitely "our wain".

And to Paige, the American addition – equally smart, talented and beautiful – whose mothering to our beloved and precious Lyra Maeve is a shining example to all mamas. Thank you, Redmond and Matthew, for your excellent choice in partners.

Thank you to big sister Jane, wordsmith extraordinaire, for the title – it hits all the spots. To Claire Dean, my extremely patient and long-suffering editor. To Mary D, for the fabulous trip to Edinburgh, what a delightful way to do research! And of course to Johnny, best husband ever.

DEDICATION

To all who are burdened,
speak the truth, when you are ready,
for it holds both power and grace.

ALSO BY PAMELA G. HOBBS

Family Affairs
(The Fitzgerald Family series Book 1)

Roman Holiday
(The Fitzgerald Family series Book 2)

Chapter 1

"Go away."

Ali didn't bother turning round on hearing the slight sound. She knew her brother would have come back to check on her and she simply couldn't face more questions. Not much point since she didn't have any answers.

Or at least none that would satisfy her detective brother, Flynn.

She stared blankly out the large, grubby window of the open-plan loft area she'd recently finished converting. Despite the mess and chaos behind her, all she could focus on was that she needed a new bottle of Windolene. She reached forwards and dragged her finger lightly through the dust. The grey, slightly sticky residue on her fingertip made her unaccountably sad. Stupid, really, considering the damage and mayhem the bastards had left in their wake.

Again.

How was she expected to answer any of Flynn's queries when she'd no clue why she'd been targeted for yet another break-in? Some feckers had it in for her, or maybe they didn't realise *she* was now owner–occupier of the building and they actually wanted the previous owner . . . Well, no point telling Flynn that – Super Detective would have checked that off the list the first time, several weeks ago.

Ali sighed. Her shoulders remained hunched as she wrapped her arms around her body in an effort to ward off the trembles threatening to invade. She would *not* give in to this. Sure, it would mean upping the security and that would cost, but hey, this was her dream and knock after knock wouldn't swipe her off her feet.

She was made of sterner stuff. Everyone said so.

Hadn't she owned and run a restaurant in the heart of Dublin for four years – and successfully, too, one might add? But by last year she'd just slowly burned out. *No staying power?* It might appear that way. While it may be someone else's idea of heaven, she knew in her heart that the daily grind of cheffing and the pressure to keep the menu fresh and interesting just wasn't her bag any more.

Had it ever been? Funny that, she couldn't remember. She'd chosen cooking as a career early on. Enjoyed the creativity and challenge. The stress and the success. The control. The rewards. Not the financial ones – those were *way* too hard to come by – but the reviews. People returning time and time again because they loved her food, that was a high she wouldn't easily forget. But there were other highs awaiting her, she was sure of it. She just had to focus on the future. Doing something else. Changing direction. Blocking the past, forging ahead.

She was good at that. Too damn good.

A throat cleared. *Shit.* She'd forgotten Flynn was waiting for her and God, she didn't need this right now. Fuss, fuss, questions, more fuss. Bracing herself on the window sill, she continued to stare at the greyness before her.

"I'm fine. Leave me alone. Just go."

"I am afraid I can't do that."

Ali felt a tingle through her entire body. That wasn't

Flynn's voice. This one had that odd accent – one she recognised. One she would rather never hear again.

Liar.

Sometimes the universe was a bitch.

She turned and studied the man standing, still and silent, a couple of metres away. The tingle began thrumming as she took in his height, his breadth, his short dark hair and weird pale eyes. High, sharp cheekbones angled across his face and his mouth – *well, his mouth was presently immobile, like the rest of him, but the lips were pure sin. Full, firm and so fucking kissable there should be a law.*

"Well, if it isn't my old pal Scotty," she drawled. "What are you doing here?"

He didn't even blink. She remembered that about him. It was freaky at first, but then you realised, of course he blinked – it was just a less overt process than on most and after a while you kinda forgot about it. He remained motionless, but his eyes were pinned to hers.

"Ms Fitzgerald," he paused. "May I have a few moments of your time, if you are not too busy?"

He did that thing of his. Spoke in an odd, formal way. *Deliberate. Precise. Polite.*

"No, MacScot, you may not have *any* moments of my time. You've made it super clear you don't *want* my time and, as you can patently see, I'm up to my tonsils in the clean-up."

His jaw clenched. *Good.* She hoped he was as irritated as hell. She hoped he was pissed. That little tic, towards the back of his gorgeous clean-shaven jaw, was kicking into action. *Excellent.*

"You have been staring out of the window, not cleaning, so I assume you do have some available time," he said in

3

that strange, somewhat gravelly voice. "Perhaps we could sit for a minute or two and talk about what happened."

"For fuck's sake," Ali snapped, "what's there to say? I've been broken into, my space vandalised with spray paint, my new tables carved up. And all I can say is I'm bloody grateful the ovens haven't arrived, or that would probably be another fucking expense." She huffed out a breath. "At least the windows aren't smashed this time but Christ, the insurers won't touch me with a bargepole after this fiasco."

She rolled her left shoulder, easing the beginnings of an ache. Knowing it would hurt like a bitch later if she didn't put some ice on it, she chose to ignore it. She had a male person to get rid of, pronto.

He moved slowly, calmly, to gather two stools from their upturned positions on the floor and casually set them to rights. He sat, never taking his eyes from her, and rested his hands, loosely clasped in front, like he didn't have a care in the world.

"Please, sit." He motioned to the vacant stool.

He wasn't going to leave, that much was obvious. She might as well get this over with.

"Fine," she grunted. And sat.

Detective Gabe Mackenzie gritted his teeth as Alice Fitzgerald practically threw herself onto the seat. She was one stubborn, angry woman. He didn't blame her for the anger. Who wouldn't be if their property was partly destroyed, their workplace invaded – and for the second time in only a few weeks. Something was off about this. Broken glass was one thing, but this vandalism was more personal. More specific than just random thugs blowing off steam. It was beginning to present as very personal. Towards Ali Fitzgerald.

That, he would not tolerate.

"Tell me what happened when you arrived this morning. What did you see? Notice? Anything out of the ordinary as you approached the building." He reached into his jacket pocket and took out a small notebook and pen.

Ali raised her eyebrows. "Can't you just read Flynn's notes? I've already gone through this with him *and* the garda who arrived on the scene. Two other people have this info, Outlander, ask them."

He kept silent, waiting her out, his eyes trained on hers, watching for her thoughts to shift, change, focus. Recall.

"You're a pain in the ass, you know that, right?" Ali folded her arms tightly across her chest.

Defensive. A little afraid or maybe just chilly. Probably both.

She wore a faded khaki long-sleeved T-shirt and beige cargo pants. Her boots were steel-tipped, at a guess, and he assumed the socks she wore beneath were industrial strength with moisture wick for comfort. Nothing about this thin, almost scrawny woman seated before him was remotely "girly". She presented as tough as the footwear she preferred. She had cropped, spiky bleached-blonde hair, eyebrows that were dark and dangerous-looking and, right now, eyes that spat sapphire-blue chips at him. Her face was narrow and pale with dark circles beneath those sooty-lashed eyes. She was both uncomfortably engaging and dangerously attractive.

His belly squeezed. His skin heated. He *hated* his visceral reaction to her. Resented it. Resented his co-worker, Fitzgerald, for sending him to deal with his younger sister.

"I'm too close to it," Flynn had said. That didn't fly with Gabe at all. Flynn looked out for his family. Always.

"Fine," Ali said without an ounce of enthusiasm.

She'd finally understood Gabe wasn't going to respond to her previous jibe. At least not outwardly.

She began recounting the morning, and about her arrival at the building – the loft – that was to house her cooking school. He knew a bit about her situation from Flynn's report on the first break-in. Ali had leased her restaurant in Temple Bar to new chefs and had stepped back to follow a different path. She'd appeared on a TV cooking show while managing the restaurant and a major TV company had offered Ali her own show. It was a huge risk, but she'd jumped at the opportunity. Under her own conditions and stipulations, of course. Then, she'd bought this building with the help of an inheritance from her grandmother and began planning.

It wasn't going to be competition-style like *The Great British Bake Off* model, Flynn had told him – she was going to *teach* the uninitiated *how* to bake. *God help them*, was all Gabe could think. He'd had a "run-in" with Ali Fitzgerald at her brother Devlin's wedding at Christmas and the memory of that encounter invaded his dreams. Frequently. Things had not gone well. And she had, in the end, left him in a huff. But before that, dancing with her – or rather being dragged onto and then off the dance floor – had been . . . *surreal*.

He knew how to dance. You don't come from the Mackenzie clan without being initiated into dance at an early age – not just the Highland fling-type but actual waltzing and, indeed, the good old jive. It was an expected outcome of being a member of an ancient family who had responsibilities towards hundreds of people – of tenants on their land and other landowners in their own vicinity – even if that was hundreds of miles' radius. So dancing, catching on to how her family danced and the routine they had going, that wasn't an issue. Touching her, on the other hand, had been. The second she'd grabbed his hand and pulled him after her he knew he was in trouble – not deep-in yet, but trouble nonetheless. He'd felt the touch of her skin all the way up his arm – every sensation playing along his nerves.

He didn't like it one bit.

When the dance had ended and everyone broke into little groups laughing and chatting, she'd grabbed a whiskey from a passing waiter, downed it in one and hauled him over to a dark corner. He'd let her, of course. He could have stopped her at any moment – they both knew that. She'd slammed him against the wall, snatched a bunch of his shirt front for leverage and, on tiptoe, fused her mouth to his. He'd seen it coming – and had just an instant to bank down the bubble of feeling rising in his chest before simply letting her kiss him. It nearly killed him to remain passive, not to respond. Not to shove his hand into her scrappy blonde hair, hold her in place and devour her.

But no. That would not do.

For reasons too many to count – the main few being she was his co-worker's sister and he was already alarmingly attracted to her after only a couple of very brief public encounters. Really, she was too tipsy to know what she was doing and, well, other than his own overloaded baggage, she was not for the likes of him. When she'd pulled back from the kiss, stared at him with eyes now hard as ice chips, he'd let her berate him. He knew he'd hurt her pride and he'd do it again, to save her from himself in as many ways as he could. As many times as he had to.

"Well," she'd said, the chill in her eyes infusing her voice, "you don't kiss worth shit. I'm wasting my time. So long, Scotland." And she'd spun on her beautiful slender feet and sashayed off in the direction of the bar.

Ali rubbed her hands over her mouth and on up, pushing the heels of her hands firmly into her eye sockets. Drained, she leaned forwards, elbows on her knees, feet planted on the ground slightly apart.

"That's it," she told the man patiently writing everything down in his leather notebook, old school. "I seriously haven't a clue why I'm being targeted." She paused, her chin tilting. "I assume I *am* being targeted?"

"It certainly appears that way," he said, his mouth tightening. "I will contact the television production team and see if they can shed any light on the situation."

"What would *they* have to do with anything?" Ali asked. "I'm the owner of this place – I'd have bought it with or without the show," she insisted.

He raised an eyebrow, patently not believing her. "But the ultimate decision was, I was informed, based on the fact that filming would take place here, correct?"

"Brothers are a pain in the arse," Ali announced. "Did he *inform* you the producers won't delay shooting or change the deadline despite the mess here?" She stood up, strode about the room and kicked at a fallen stool. "They'll just make us film in the studio instead." She kicked the stool again. "I'm not filming in a fucking studio. It's here or nowhere."

Wearily, she bent over and uprighted the bashed stool, slumping into a sitting position on the polished wood. She gazed across at the detective, taking in more details of how he looked. He sat so still and was apparently lost in thought as she let her eyes wander up and down his strong frame. He was lean and fit – that, she knew from his dance moves and when she'd plastered herself along his body in a shameless attempt to get him to respond to her kiss. It had been hard not to feel the muscles of steel beneath his shirt.

Oh! the mortification.

But Ali refused to do mortification for more than mere seconds, so she decided he was either slow on the uptake, clueless in general or "gender ambivalent". She was pretty sure he wasn't gay – even gay men had been known to respond to Ali when she was on form. Well, maybe not actually respond, because, duh, gay, but they sure appreciated her. This tall hunk of Scottish manhood had pretty much ignored her. And she didn't for one second think he was either slow or clueless on any level. Ergo, he was just not attracted to her. Not a great tick in her ego box but hey, she *would* move on.

As her eyes lazily wandered over his form, she was struck by the contrast of his skin colour with the collar of his white shirt. Her eyes flew to his hands, resting loosely on his knees, the notepad now tucked away. Again, the stark contrast with the white cuffs. How come she'd not noticed this before? He was really quite tanned, an almost *café au lait* colour. Warmth spread up her belly as an image of those strong, tanned fingers splayed across her pale stomach came unbidden to her mind. She shook her head. That image had no place in her thoughts – *that line of thought . . . image? A hiding to nowhere.*

9

She stood up. "I'm going to make a few calls and then start the clean-up. You . . . " she said, pointing her finger, doing a twirl-round motion, "can go elsewhere. We're done here."

"Actually, we are done here when I say we are," he countered quietly. "As it happens, I have nowhere in particular I need to be, so I will help you."

As he spoke he shrugged out of his jacket, walked to a chair with a back and carefully hung his jacket around the curve. He then opened the buttons of his cuffs and began, carefully and methodically, to fold up his sleeves. Ali stared at him in shock.

"You're not staying here," she spluttered. "You'll . . . you'll get in the way," she finished helplessly, knowing this was a very bad idea.

She needed him gone. Now. *Oh, fuck, the damn forearms were on view. That gorgeous skin colour, dusted with dark hair, and his now flexing muscles, they ought to be outlawed.*

"Where is your first aid kit?"

"My what?" Ali spluttered, totally thrown by his question.

"You have one, I presume? If not, I can collect some supplies from my jeep." Without waiting for a reply, he began opening cupboards above and below the sink area, bending to search the dark spaces.

"Ah," he said, pulling out the green plastic box. "This should do."

Opening it, he examined the contents and laid some supplies out on the worktop. He turned, washed his hands under running water, using the soap from in the dispenser for a good lather, and dried them efficiently with some paper towel.

"Take off your shirt, please," he said in a "don't mess with me" voice.

Ali gaped at him, incredulous. For many reasons. *How the fuck dare he tell her what to do and how the fuck did he know she was hurting?*

She was, in fact, speechless. But only for a nanosecond. Ali didn't "do" speechless.

"You can't order me about telling me what to do! I'm not taking my shirt off for you, or anyone else, for that matter, so you can forget it," she announced.

"You are hurt," he said calmly, evenly. "I want to help you. Take off your shirt – let me see to the cut or graze and then we can get back to the matter at hand. This is not open to negotiation."

What could she do? What would *he* do if she refused? *Damn it to hell.* Her shoulder was stinging and uncomfortable, not to mention at an angle, she already knew, that was difficult to reach. When she'd gone flying down the steps earlier, knocked sideways by the door flinging open, she'd felt the wrench in her shoulder and had tried to reach for it. Bloody impossible.

Slowly and with, she admitted to herself, some degree of discomfort, she hauled off her long-sleeved T-shirt and presented her back to him.

"No funny business," she growled.

With more gentleness than she had thought possible, he eased back the strap of her vest top then carefully cleaned and bandaged the nasty graze. It stung, no question about that, and he was probably right, it would have got nasty if left alone.

"Your skin was broken and there was some blood, but it is clean. And I have applied some antiseptic cream and a covering. It should be fine. You may bruise, but I would suggest arnica rather than ice for now."

He tidied away the supplies as Ali shrugged back into her top.

"Thanks, Doc," she mumbled ungraciously. Then felt shit for being so crass. "I mean it, thank you."

He nodded once then began bending and righting the various fallen stools – *and double damn if every time he bent forwards, the fabric of his dark grey trousers tightened delightfully over his very fine ass.* He turned his head to capture her gaze and, embarrassingly, she had to jerk her eyes away. But not before he raised an enquiring eyebrow though wisely kept silent.

"Fuck it," she snapped. "Suit yourself. Looks like you'll do it no matter what I say. You are seriously bossy and controlly, you know that, right?" She hauled her phone from her trouser pocket. "I'm phoning a couple of pals who'll help with sanding the tabletops. Knock yourself out."

She knew she was being a brat, especially since he'd just played doctor, but God, this was difficult. Right now, she was pissed with herself for allowing him to get to her, with him for not leaving and with the whole fucking situation for screwing up her life. Again.

They worked flat out for about four hours. Bren and Gerry arrived with sanders for the tables. Friends from school, they ran a carpentry business, not, as often joked, an ice-cream empire. If they were paid a cent for every time someone asked "Oh, like the ice cream?" they'd be rich as Croesus. But they took it with good humour. They were horrified at the state of the beautiful oak tops now gauged out with, according to the police, a chisel. A regular woodworking tool. Maybe their specialists would be able to match it, as they'd taken moulds before they left.

Being a Sunday, Bren and Gerry had the time and were kind enough not to ask for payment. "Just a few beers and maybe an autograph from your famous sister-in-law," was the request. That, she could do.

Frankie, her brother Dev's wife, aka Francesca Jones, was a famous movie star and model. Their wedding at Christmas was supposed to have been a "small, intimate affair" with several hundred nearest and dearest. *Well, yeah, that didn't happen.* Word got out and the paparazzi turned up and begged for photos. The happy couple obliged, and Ali and Molly, the youngest Fitzgerald, had been bombarded with requests for autographs ever since. It wasn't the worst thing that could happen, so the sisters did what they could for those who dared to ask.

The noise level increased and dust particles permeated the air until eventually the sanders were turned off and everything settled. At that point the unwanted but, it turned out, very handy detective started to mop – *like he actually knew what he was doing, for Christ's sake.* Ali took a moment from wiping the tables free of dust to gawk. He used strong, steady, even strokes and managed to cover quite a large area very quickly, efficiently cleaning and rinsing the mop as he went. His tie was off, the tail end hanging from his back pocket, and the top two buttons of his once crisp shirt were undone.

He absolutely should not *have looked as fricking manly as he did.*

Ali knew she was grumbling internally but really, what chance had she got? Hot and sweaty, her long-sleeved T-shirt had long been stripped off and she worked swiftly from counter to counter in her white, albeit slightly bloodstained, vest top. She hadn't bothered with a bra that morning because in all honesty, there was barely anything to fit into one, so what was the point? And comfort was high on Ali's list of life's pleasures. The bandage itched in places but only a little, so it was a small price to pay.

Bren packed up the sanders, and they all stopped to take a breath and check the progress. It was good. They'd done well. Really well. The long worktables looked fresh and clean – granted, they'd need to be oiled again, but the ugly words and nasty gashes were gone, revealing a beautiful natural pattern in the oak. The stools were clean and stacked, the spilled drawers all returned, replenished, to their places and the floors were now spotless. Ali heaved a sigh and wiped a dusty hand across her forehead.

"Thanks a million, lads, that's brilliant. Good as new."

She smiled at her old school friends and they shrugged it off.

"No hassle, Ali," Gerry said, "just repaying the favour."

She looked at him enquiringly.

"Remember when we called on you to whip up a brunch for potential clients for that big job we were tendering? At a few hours' notice? Well, payback in this instance isn't a bitch but a pleasure."

Ali did remember. She'd refused any payment for her time – just took cash for the groceries – and had been happy to help. The friend card turned out to be a sweet deal sometimes.

Gerry walked over to her and gave her a big hug.

"We're happy to help, right, Bren?"

"Sure, Ali, any time. But, Christ, I'm parched. Have you anything stronger than water?" he asked hopefully.

"Funny you should ask," Ali grinned. She cocked her head to one side on hearing the outside door slam followed by footsteps on the stairs. "Big brother is arriving with supplies."

Chapter 2

With two six-packs of beer clutched to his chest, the newly minted bridegroom sauntered into the loft space. If ever a phrase was apt, this brother really did look as bright and shiny as a new penny.

"Like what you've done with the place," he quipped, grinning at his younger sister as he placed the bottles and cans on one of the long tables.

Devlin Fitzgerald was dark-haired, a touch under six foot and, as far as Gabe could see, in fighting-fit shape. Dev had the same deep blue eyes as two of his sisters while, if his detective skills were on point, he'd swear Molly, and his own colleague Flynn, had an almost pale turquoise colour. They were, collectively, an attractive bunch, the Fitzgeralds, and as Dev enveloped Ali in a big hug, he figured an affectionate one, too.

"I'm so sorry this has happened again, Ali. It sucks. Any updates?" Dev turned his head to catch Gabe's eye and walked towards him, hand outstretched. "Hey," he said. "We met briefly at the wedding, right? Detective Mackenzie? You work with Flynn, I think."

Dev's handshake was firm, cool, but his eyes were taking measure. Gabe didn't mind. He preferred to size someone up himself, in his own time, and he respected that trait in others.

"Congratulations, again. And belated apologies for

turning up unannounced. It was work-related." Gabe returned the handshake and met the blue eyes straight on before indicating the open space with a tilt of his head. "We are checking all angles here. Flynn assigned me to this case."

"Did he now?" Dev asked. "Why isn't he doing it himself?"

"Conflict of interest, I believe."

"Nah, that can't be it. He was all over the deal when Frankie was in trouble last summer and he totally got involved in Caro's shit." Dev shook his head. "It's something else."

Gabe was reluctant. "I really cannot say."

"Huh," Dev mumbled and turned to greet the two helpers. "Lads, you two are brill for coming over and helping the brat out. Really appreciate it. My parents do, too." He shook each of their hands and slapping Bren on the back, urged him towards the beer. "Help yourselves," he said, twisting the cap off a tall brown bottle.

"What ya got?" Gerry asked. "Hope it's not some fancy microbrew shite," he laughed. "Give me a solid can of Guinness any day, man."

"Well, you're in luck, my friend," Dev grinned. "I happen to have both the shite you're hoping to avoid and some of the black." He pulled a can from its plastic ring wrapper and handed it over.

Ali moved over, snagged a brown bottle, snapped it open and took a drink. Her long, pale neck moved, swallowing, catching Gabe's eye. He was captivated by the sight. Bren moved into his line of vision to grab a beer, breaking the spell, and when the view was clear again, Ali had the bottle nestled against her cheek. Her eyes were downcast but a second later, they lifted and clashed with his own. Gabe stilled, awaiting the ready barb, the snarky comment, the jeer, but she surprised him. With a half-smile, *a beautiful little curve of her mouth*, she waggled her bottle in the age-old gesture of "You want some?"

Gabe blinked. His gut was stuck on the smile. *The soft, mobile turn of her lips. The pale pink hue of . . .*

"Yo, Highlander!" she called, all softness gone in a flash. "You want a beer?"

"No," he cleared his throat. Tried again. "No, thank you. I will take a water, if you have one?"

"See the big, shiny steel fridge by the far counter? There should be both still and sparkling in there. Knock yourself out." She put her bottle down and, bracing her arms behind her, hoisted herself up onto the freshly sanded tabletop.

Oh, hell.

All that did was push her small, perfect breasts out.

With determined steps, he turned from that sight and walked unhurriedly to select a bottle of water.

Dev propped one hip against the table while Gerry and Bren pulled up stools. Gabe twisted the cap from his bottle, drank deep and replaced the lid. Holding the bottle between his fingers, he folded his arms across his chest and leaned back against the countertop, content to let the friends chat among themselves, catching up, puzzling over the break-ins and cheering Ali on for her upcoming show.

Gabe didn't join in. He had nothing to contribute. He didn't know them – although he made a mental note to run backgrounds on the two men sitting in Ali's kitchen, happily sipping beer. That did not, in Gabe's mind, preclude them from nefarious deeds. He knew Dev wouldn't hurt a hair on her head, and hot-tempered and rash though his reputation was, he always put family first.

The fingerprint crew were long gone and hopefully working round the clock to find some matches in the system. Gabe was curious as to why Ali Fitzgerald was being targeted. On the surface, she wasn't a threat to anyone. She owned this building outright, had left her own restaurant without any bad blood, and the tenants and chefs seemed equally delighted with their new set-up. No obvious motivation, so no obvious suspects. Yet . . . the pertinent term was, *obvious*.

Ali Fitzgerald's life was about to become an open book, whether she liked it or not. Gabe rather assumed it would be the latter.

"Thanks a mill. You were amazing," Ali called one last time as she closed the door behind Bren and Gerry. Dev had left a few minutes earlier having given her the third degree on safety first, blah blah blah. That happened after he'd inadvertently bumped against her shoulder and she'd winced. His rant had her eyes glazing over as he'd rattled on about her minding herself. But, she had to admit, brothers could come in useful.

Following the beer break they'd all worked for another hour, Dev joining in with some heavy lifting and furniture manoeuvring, and her loft space-cum-TV kitchen was back to what passed as normal. Or at least to what she'd planned as the day-to-day layout. Accepting that it might change when the show started was hard for Ali. She liked, *needed* things to be as she made them. This new change of career had practically overwhelmed her with worry – so much *change*, so many new avenues to explore. It was, she knew, a fantastic opportunity – hence she'd taken it, she wasn't an idiot – but, God, in her heart she was a scared and anxious mess. All the what-ifs, all the maybes, all the I can'ts lurked just below a very thin surface.

She placed her hands on the heavy wooden door and sighed deeply.

"Pizza?"

The sound of the Scotsman's voice in her space made her shoulders tense. If he wasn't so . . . so . . . *him*, it would be easier. She'd no problem with men in general. They even came in useful at times – for example today, with the heavy lifting and sanding. Or on a lonely evening when the batteries in her favourite toy were dead, or when she could use a sweaty workout. But here, his voice, that odd mixture of accents – actually, it wasn't even that, it was the *sound* of his voice. It made her skin prickle and she wasn't yet sure if that was a good thing.

"Sure," she replied, "I could eat. But you don't have to stay. I mean . . . " She realised she sounded ungrateful. "I mean, I can get my own as you probably have somewhere to be."

Ignoring her, he took out his phone, dialled, ordered and hung up. She glared at him. She couldn't help it.

"You don't even know what I like. Maybe I hate olives or mushrooms or whatever else you asked for." She faced him with her hands fisted on her hips. "You're very bossy."

"That is rich, coming from you. But no, I am not bossy. You will note I haven't ordered *you* to do anything. I simply ordered some food. I requested that each topping was only on half a pizza, so if you didn't like my choices you could eat from the other side."

Feeling the chill from the evening air now she'd stopped her manual labour, Ali reached for her T-shirt. She knew he watched her every move. *Christ – were her nipples on alert?* But when she pulled her head awkwardly through the neck opening, she saw his eyes were in fact on her face, not her body.

"What?" she demanded. "Have I dirt on my face or something? Quit staring. You're freaking me out."

He said nothing as he walked purposefully towards her. His legs were long, the fabric of his trousers clinging to the muscles of his thighs as he moved. His shirt was smudged with a few streaks of dirt, but he seemed oblivious. She stood her ground, determined not to let him invade her space without her permission. He stopped slightly in front of her and pulled a handkerchief out of his pocket.

A real one. Not a Kleenex tissue. *Who the fuck carries those around any more? Granddads, that's who.* But Gabe Mackenzie was not, in any shape or form, a granddad. He stretched forwards, fabric in hand, and gently rubbed at her cheek. Then he stepped back, holding out the material. Sure enough, a big, dusty mess was visible.

"There was indeed something on your face," he acknowledged.

And damn but she felt stupid, disappointed that it was merely that that had caused his intent gaze. *The man sure knew how to clean and medicate, so he must be a neat freak, as well.* Good that she found this out now – she

21

absolutely didn't want to find anything, other than the look of him, remotely attractive. And neat freaks were a no-no. *Check. That was settled.*

He turned and wandered to the counter and began opening and closing drawers. He found knives and forks and some plates. He placed them opposite each other on the table and set two stools in position. Then he put another beer next to Ali's place and a fresh bottle of water next to his own.

"I am considering why all this wasn't pulled out and smashed when the intruders were cutting up your tables," he mused. "Perhaps they were disturbed."

"That did occur to me," she admitted, "but dishes and cutlery are easily replaced. I had to call in favours for the tables. But, huh, I think I may have interrupted them." Ali put a hand to her throat and felt her breath quicken.

"I was wondering when you were going to explain your shoulder." He waited, patient as a freaking saint. This man was *no* saint.

"Did Flynn not tell you?" Ali asked, sidestepping the comment.

"I would like *you* to tell me. I am unable to help if I do not know the whole story. All of it," he finished firmly.

Ali sucked in a breath to steady her nerves. Nerves she really wished were not in evidence.

"I arrived shortly before nine this morning. Are you sure Flynn didn't fill you in?"

He continued to watch her, unblinking.

"Fine! As I reached the top of the stairs, the door flew open and I was shoved backwards down the steps. I think there were two men, but I can't be sure. It all happened so fast."

The detective found his notebook and wrote briefly before flipping it closed.

"You could have been seriously hurt," he said.

"Nah, I know how to fall and as soon as I got pushed, I went into auto mode and let myself go. It's hard to do but easier on the body. Hence only a bash on one shoulder."

"You may well have been the one to interrupt them, or it could have been something else entirely and just poor timing. Intruders get spooked easily. Especially amateurs."

Ali looked about the now clean space.

"Didn't look like an amateur job to me," she grumbled. "The place was a fucking disaster when I came in."

"What happened after you fell?"

"I didn't fall," Ali protested immediately. "I was pushed. There *is* a difference."

The detective tilted his head slightly, watching her. She felt uncomfortable under his gaze and hopped up onto her stool, reaching for her beer.

"God, you're relentless. I was stunned for a moment as the two feckers hurtled down the steps and ran off. I didn't see a car or motorbikes. They just ran. And then I came up here and phoned the cops."

She paused as a shiver ran through her, the memory of it all too bloody real. She took a drink.

At a hammering on the door, the bottle connected with her teeth as she flinched in surprise – *ouch* – but Gabe merely walked to the door, opened it, took the pizza, paid the delivery person, closed the door quietly and returned to the table. All of his movements were steady and calm.

Most irritating.

Ali shoved her free hand into the back pocket of her pants and tugged out some crumpled notes.

"Here," she said, "I owe you for the food."

"No, you do not."

"I do," she insisted. "It's the least I can do considering you stayed and helped all afternoon." She put the money on the table and pushed it in his direction.

"No," he said again, "you do not. Already taken care of. Now eat."

He glanced down at the pizza box he was opening and her arguments flew out of the window. *Oh. My. God!* The fragrance of melting cheese, pepperoni, mushrooms and whatever else he'd ordered was just too much. Her stomach let out an extremely loud rumble and damn! if she didn't see his mouth twitch. Just a bit. She reached for a slice and, folding it longways, devoured it.

"*Mmm.* Delish," she groaned. "God, I was starving."

Sauce dribbled down her chin and as she scrubbed at it with the heel of her hand, a paper napkin appeared in her line of vision. She snatched it churlishly and caught the sauce before it landed on her chest.

"Thanks."

Fuck. That was the second time he'd cleaned her up. Or at least proffered cleaning supplies. *He must think I'm a bloody teenager.*

Or a holy show of a mess.

Probably that one.

She reached for another slice and studied him across the table. He'd placed three slices on the plate and was picking up the first when he paused, his eyes meeting hers. There was silence for a moment – no longer than a moment, but it felt . . . charged. Ali felt mesmerised by those pale eyes – green, she realised – and couldn't look away. *Shit*, she could feel a blush edge into her cheeks.

She hadn't blushed for years. But still, she was enthralled. He blinked then, unhurriedly, as if he were a camera shutter on slow, capturing a second for all eternity. He cleared his throat, put the pizza in his mouth, turning from her gaze, and the spell was broken.

Weird and crazy. Ali could feel her breath hitch, felt her chest rise and fall – whether in agitation or excitement, she couldn't tell. One thing she knew for certain: she didn't like it. She'd made a play for this man before, had been soundly refused, and she was *so* not ever going there again.

"Passion," Gabe said.

Ali spat out the mouthful of beer she'd been swallowing. Coughing, she blinked furiously at him, using the scrunched-up paper napkin to mop up her spills.

"Excuse me?" she gasped.

"Passion," he repeated. "As in crime of. I have been thinking." He got up from his stool and began walking about her space. He'd been turning over the details of the upheaval and vandalism in his head and had reached a logical conclusion. "I think the vicious, destructive carving into of your beautiful oak tables, or countertops, was a crime of passion."

He turned and looked at Ali, who sat there, a frown forming between her sooty-lashed eyes. She was shaking her head.

"No way," she argued.

Of course she did. She pretty much disagreed with everything he said. *As if on purpose. To be difficult.*

"If it was a crime of passion, wouldn't they have yanked everything from the drawers and smashed plates and done more graffiti?"

"Not necessarily. This was very specific. And very deliberate. Although we tend to think of passion as a heated frenzy, there was a coldness, a hatred in the passion that drove someone to carve up your pride and joy."

He stopped speaking. He had to. Even as he uttered the words "heated frenzy", he could have cut out his tongue. He'd heard the involuntary gasp from Ali and the images flashing in his own mind of her heat, her frenzy, her passion nearly had him stuttering, his mouth had gone so dry.

He *needed* to stop speaking. Stop using words that were too visceral for his brain to separate from his body. Or rather, his body's desires. All afternoon he'd been conscious of her every move, her husky laugh as she bantered back and forth with the men, then watching her eyes darken as she savoured her food, her tongue as it licked at the sauce on her lips . . .

He should have ordered sandwiches. Something boring and not remotely sexy when eaten. Brown bread and ham. *Lettuce would have worked. Nothing vaguely enticing about eating lettuce. Everyone knew that.* But no, he'd ordered Italian food – the food of love. Sexy food. *Idiot.*

He cleared his throat. "Anyway . . . " He paused, not sure what to say next. He was never not sure.

"You're wrong," Ali said, pushing away her half-eaten second slice. "About the passion, I mean. I'm not the sort to instil passion in anyone. Haven't been for a long time. And I don't want to be," she added rather fiercely.

Gabe took a breath. There was no air in his lungs. *She thought she didn't instil passion? Was she blind? Did she have a mirror?* He needed to divert from letting his body think about passion. Or at least *that* kind.

"It can be a form of hatred, too. Jealousy. Injustice. Revenge," he said into the silence.

Ali let out a snort. "Great. Now someone just hates me as opposed to feeling love and passion for me. Super. I'm thrilled. Or, wait . . . " She glared at him. "Maybe it's some vigilante looking for justice or revenge, for God knows what. Jesus! I'm not sure what insults me more."

"I am not explaining myself well."

"Ya think?"

Gabe walked to the large expanse of window. It was dark outside, and the twinkling lights of the dock and the ships looked slightly blurry behind the still-dusty windows. He leaned one arm against the window frame, angling his body so he could see her reflection behind him. Her shoulders hunched, her slender arms wrapped about her body, she looked an unhappy mixture between angry and . . . *lost*. His gut tightened.

"What I mean is, I may have an idea of where to start looking. I can delve into your recent past and begin to narrow down anyone who may hold a grudge, or who feels hard done by because of something you may have inadvertently done."

"So, what you're really saying is it's my own fault."

Her tone was flat, steady. Deadly.

"That is *not* what I said."

Gabe ran a hand over the back of his neck as tension built within him. *What the hell was wrong with him?* He was never this clumsy or gauche when doing his job. It *was* her fault, but not in the way she meant. He was thrown by her.

Off-kilter. Off his game. But he still had work to do. He tried again.

27

"You are hiding something from me and I thought we had established that I need the whole story, Ali, not merely what you choose to relate to Flynn to keep him appeased. You have my complete confidence unless your safety is at risk." He kept his eyes on hers as she blushed but, to give her her due, she didn't look away. "Trust me. Talk to me."

Ali glared at him. If her eyes could spit tacks, they'd be landing squarely at his chest. She took a breath and looking out of the window, began speaking.

"Ever since the first break-in, weeks ago now, I've had several . . . well, a number of incidents, let's say, where I felt uneasy. In danger, even." She turned her head to look at him. "I told Flynn most of this. And I know he'll freak out and guard me like a baby." She sighed and resumed her vacant stare out through the glass. "Twice, I've been knocked off my bike. The first time seemed like a complete accident – another bike swerved into me from round a corner. I felt it was his fault, like he was aiming for me, but I was unharmed and he just cycled off as I picked myself up.

"The second time, I was cycling along a quiet road and a car door opened into my bike as I was going past. I was flung to the ground and my ass hit the tarmac with some force. I thought my wrist was sprained but it was just bruised." She turned back to him again. "And the bastard just drove off! He didn't even get out of the car, just peeled off down the road."

Gabe reached for his notebook again and began writing. "Go on," he said steadily.

"One of the nights I was taking the DART – it was wet and late, and I was hurrying. The steps of the overpass at the station were slippery and I fell headlong down the second half of them."

"Fell?"

Ali squirmed. "It felt like someone shoved me. Hard. But I've no proof. There were several people jostling in a group behind and they seemed horrified and helped me up. Nothing was too badly hurt – just my bloody pride."

"Go on," he urged.

"This is going to sound stupid, but as I lay on the ground, somewhat winded, I saw a man in dark clothes backing away, staring at me on the ground but obviously wanting to leave, too. Even then I thought that was weird. But I figured he was maybe just voyeuristic. Flynn knows this, which is why he's now threatening to get someone to watch me. It sucks."

"I see." More writing in the notepad. "Back to the car incident for a moment. Did you get his licence plate? Make of car?"

"I gave all that to Big Brother. I didn't get the whole number, but it was a VW Golf, dark grey, with a D-reg, so not much there."

"And?"

"Argh. You're a pain!"

"I am doing my job," Gabe corrected.

"At least three times since that there's been someone lurking around my house and I think . . . " She hesitated, then straightening her shoulders, she continued. "No, I *know* someone's been following me." She whirled round to face him. "I'm not imagining things, I swear. I didn't cycle for several days as my wrist was too sore, plus my bike needed a new wheel, but I'd hear footsteps on my way home from the DART station at night and when I'd turn, nothing. No one there. It was creeping me the fuck out."

"Did you go to the hospital about your wrist?"

"Just to my GP. They strapped it and told me to rest it for a while."

"There will be a record of this at their surgery, then." He made more notes, then added, "I do not believe you are imagining things. You should always listen to your instincts. They are your natural protection."

She snorted. "Yeah, right, what age do they kick in? Oh, never mind. I also know someone went through my rubbish and definitely tried to break in via my front door. There were gouges next to the lock and wood chippings on the ground."

"And you did not see fit to tell your brother this?" Gabe raised an eyebrow at her, incredulous at her cavalier attitude.

"Have you met my brother? Would *you* tell him? I've had the locks changed and even installed an alarm."

She looked vaguely sheepish when she said this and Gabe just sighed.

"You forget to set it, don't you?"

She looked away. It was acknowledgement enough. He stood up straight, turned to meet strained eyes and took a breath.

"We can continue this tomorrow," he said quietly, closing his notebook. "We are both tired. Have you a lift home?"

She gathered the pizza boxes and put them in the fridge then started flicking out lights. She reached for his discarded jacket and practically threw it at him.

"I don't need a lift – I've got my bike. It's good as new."

And she held open the door, *rather pointedly*, he

thought. Sighing, he knew when to take a step back and moved towards the door.

"I will walk you down," he said.

"No need."

"Nevertheless."

He remained as she locked up then followed her down the flight of steps and out to the alley. There were good outside security lights, he noted, and her bike was chained to a railing directly under a street lamp. He waited while she unlocked it and settled her leg over the bar. It was a man's racer. He wasn't surprised.

"Helmet?"

She gave him a look.

He sighed again. "Here . . . " He handed her a card with his contact details. "Take this, keep it safe. Use it if you need me, day or night. I will come by in the morning about ten and we will discuss strategy," he began.

She raised a hand to halt him.

"I'm so not interested in your strategy right now. Revenge, injustice or the downright malice aforethought – it's all the fucking same to me. My place was still wrecked. I've still been hurt or targeted or whatever. Go home, Dr Scot. Your genius brain probably needs time to recharge. I know mine does."

She took the proffered card, didn't even glance at it and stuffed it in her back pocket. Then off she cycled. She didn't glance back or wave or say goodbye. She just peddled away.

He had his work cut out, that was for damn sure.

Chapter 3

It was close to 4 a.m. when Ali woke, rearing upright in bed, heart racing and sweat covering her body. The thundering beat in her chest was uncomfortable and as loud in her ears as any fast bass riff.

"*Fuck*," she groaned.

Wrapping her arms around her legs, she rested her head on her knees and tried to slow her breathing. This was nothing new. She knew the drill. It would pass – it always did. Just sometimes the terror took a little longer to leave her brain *and* her body. Sleep therapy, that's what she'd been told to use. *Hah! Yeah, that was never going to happen.* She didn't need to learn *how* to fall asleep – that wasn't the issue. She needed to know how *not* to dream. She needed fucking oblivion.

She reached for the glass of water on her bedside table and drank deeply. She rolled the cool glass across her forehead, chanting her own mantra in a low whisper: *not real, all in my head – not real, all in my head – not real . . .* She replaced the glass and flopped back on her pillows, truly exhausted.

It didn't require a degree in rocket science to know why her effing nightmare was back. The stress from the previous day was enough to put anyone on edge.

Ali was no exception.

But she was pissed at herself. She should have taken a

sleeping pill, should have remembered what stress did to her – especially when she was considered the victim and a prime target. *Been there, got that T-shirt.* A few weeks previously, after the first break-in, the nightmare had returned and now, here she was again.

"Not exactly on a good learning curve, are you?" she asked herself aloud in the quiet, dark room.

Flipping over, she half lay on her stomach, her oversized T-shirt around her hips, and tucked her pillow at an angle beneath her head.

It had been a long day. And an even longer evening. Images of the tall Scot floated into her head. *A fine specimen of a man, no doubts on that score.* She remembered the way the strong woven fabric of his shirt had stretched across his broad shoulders as he'd swept her floor for the third time, the way his trousers had hugged his ass as he bent to sweep up the debris. The way he'd tucked his tie into his shirt about midway down his chest so it wouldn't get tangled before taking it off and stuffing it in his back pocket. It had looked sexy. She'd no clue why, just that it had a sexy vibe, and she remembered thinking that at the time. Embarrassingly, she'd thought a lot of things about him were sexy. The way he'd tended to her so gently when he'd realised she was hurt. That was sexy, for God's sake. And it shouldn't have been.

And she didn't even like him. Not really. He was bossy. And weird. And strangely awkward. *No, that wasn't true – he was just different. Too damn calm, for one thing. Who speaks in a calm, measured tone all the time? Who remains quietly in control and then stays to help clean up? What was that about?* No one asked him to stay – she certainly hadn't wanted him there.

But . . . he *had* stayed and had been of tremendous help – quietly and calmly doing so many chores they all rolled into one. And of course then he'd given her the third degree. But even at that he'd not been aggressive or intrusive. Just steady.

She needed to get the "skinny" on him from Flynn. Pronto. She'd asked before, after the very first time they'd met – just before Dev and Frankie's wedding. The papers on her new workspace had just been signed and she'd headed back to Temple Bar to her old restaurant for a celebratory drink. Molly and a few friends had swung by to say hi and congratulate her on the new adventure, and then Flynn had walked in . . .

Accompanied by Gabe Mackenzie.

He'd worn an overcoat in tweed and raindrops from the normal December weather liberally sprinkled his shoulders. His dark hair, brushed back from his forehead, was sleek and shiny from the rain. His eyes had panned the room and as the two men had made their way towards Ali's noisy table, she'd latched on to his gaze.

For a second, a split second, her world had gone completely still and her heart had given one hard thump in her chest. Then Flynn had enveloped her in a hug and Detective Gabe Mackenzie had been introduced briefly. His large hand had held hers in a firm clasp for mere moments but Ali, lying in her bed in the early dawn several months later, still felt his touch. She'd made some inane comment about wearing tweed in the rain and how as a Scot he ought to know better, and he, in that freaking calm manner, had simply said the fabric was treated and it protected him like a rain jacket.

He hadn't made small talk – in fact, he'd barely talked

at all. Just sipped an orange juice and let his eyes wander the bar and tables. He'd been so damn comfortable in his own skin, so immensely self-contained that Ali had felt the urge to ruffle his feathers. But they'd left before she'd had a chance and the next time they'd met was at the wedding – with her woeful attempt to kiss him, which had gone so awry. She wouldn't be making *that* mistake again.

She punched her pillow and let her eyes drift shut with the image of a strong-shaped mouth, quirking ever so slightly at the side, stuck firmly in her mind.

"You've got your assignments," Flynn told his team, "now go do the work. Call me if anything unusual turns up, otherwise deal with it."

He nodded a dismissal to the group of select detectives and they gathered sundry belongings then began to troop out.

"Mackenzie," he called, "stay back."

Gabe stopped, turned and raised his eyes to meet Fitzgerald's.

"What do you need?"

Flynn closed a file in his hand, placed it on the table and reached for another. He held it aloft.

"My sister's case," he said, "any leads?"

Gabe rubbed a tired hand over his face. He'd slept badly, for way too many reasons, and wasn't as refreshed as he liked to be. Even his yoga and meditation routine earlier hadn't done its customary job.

"No leads," he began, "but I do have a plan that I hope you will sanction."

Flynn pulled out a chair and indicated that Gabe take the one opposite.

"Let's hear it." He sat back, folding his arms.

"Your sister may not like it," Gabe started, ignoring Flynn's instant snort, "but I believe it may garner some results."

"You can be damn sure she won't like it," Flynn agreed. "She'll hate anything that's presented as a possible solution, mostly because she doesn't want to believe there *is* a problem. Or, indeed, that *she* is the problem." He caught Gabe's raised eyebrow. "And no, I don't actually mean her . . . " he corrected. "But the issue remains that she's being targeted and you, my friend, are charged with finding out who."

"I intend to shadow her for the next few days and grill her on all of her movements, all of her relationships, all of her encounters, planned or otherwise, since she signed up for the TV show."

The head detective sat back in his chair. "You believe it's connected? To the show?"

"I do."

"Because?"

Gabe leaned forwards slightly, clasping his hands loosely in front of him, elbows resting on his knees. "Motivation," he said calmly. "It is both a crime of passion *and* opportunity."

It was Flynn's turn to raise an eyebrow.

"If the perpetrator had planned it out, in the cold light of day, then way more serious, expensive damage would have been done. This guy, if it *is* a male, is pissed off. Angry. Jealous. And is lashing out in a childish temper." Gabe looked down at the file on the table and flipped it open.

"The first incident was straight after the show's

announcement." Gabe indicated some dates and cross-checks. "Followed by the two different bike incidents and the DART station scenario. And this latest one was right after the contestants were revealed."

He scrubbed a hand across the back of his neck, frustrated. Then he filled Flynn in on the stalker issues and the attempted break-in, thankful Ali hadn't, after all, insisted on confidentiality. Flynn frowned and began writing in a jotter on the desk.

"It is a place to start," Gabe said, "and I will *not* let her out of my sight. Starting today."

Flynn snorted again trying, unsuccessfully, to turn it into a cough.

"Good luck with that, man. Rather you than me. I love the spitfire dearly, but I'm almost pleased I'm lead on another case and can't take on Ali's, too – besides it being bad form to work on a family member's case."

Gabe looked steadily at Flynn. He knew about Frankie and Caro and wasn't pretending otherwise.

"Oh, all right, that's not it at all. Ali can be a bit head-wrecking, and amazing and talented though she is, I'm just . . . Look, I'm just grateful you're here and can help." He stood and buttoned his jacket. "I'll get someone posted to her apartment, even for a few days, just to see if there are any more attempts on her home. This is getting more worrying by the moment and it's also perhaps bigger than we first suspected. Keep me informed," he said, "every step of the way."

And when he and Gabe exchanged handshakes, Gabe knew, despite Flynn's easy dismissal of her situation, that this sibling was deeply concerned.

"Count on it," he said and gathering up the file, he

left the building to make his way to Ms Fitzgerald's and lay out his plan.

He was under no illusion that it would go well.

He was right.

When Gabe walked into her workspace an hour later, he could tell she hadn't had a restful night. He silently took in her tired eyes and the pinched mouth and sighed. *No, this wasn't going to go well. For either of them.*

"Why are you here?" she snapped, cradling a cup of something hot.

No, definitely not a good start.

"I said I would be here. We need to discuss strategy. And before you say anything, your brother, the detective one, agrees with my suggested plan of action."

"I'm pretty sure you know you can shove your strategy where the sun don't shine." She took a drink and turned to a flask on the counter behind her. She held it up. "Want a coffee while I'm bitching at you?"

A smile tugged at the corner of his mouth. He wouldn't let it out, of course, but damn if he didn't find her amusing.

"That would be nice, unless you have any herbal tea?"

She let out a choked snort. "Herbal tea? What are you? Ninety? Jeez, Scotty, man up and take a real brew."

She reached for an enamel mug and poured the dark brown steaming liquid with a steady hand. *She can hold her nerve, that one,* he thought as he took the mug. *It was strong – lumberjack strong – and hmm . . . surprisingly not bitter.*

"That is actually quite good," he said. "I don't usually have caffeine this late in the day."

This time she laughed out loud. "Late in the day? It's fucking ten thirty. In the *morning*, Granddad!" She shook her head in obvious disgust. "You need to get out more."

"And so, here I am." He took another sip and placed the mug on the table. "We need to have a conversation, Ali. And *you* need to listen to what I have to say – all the way through – before you toss it out. Can you do that?"

She eyed him steadily over the rim of her cup and sighed deeply. "Yeah," she agreed none too readily. "I can do that. I don't have much choice, do I?"

"Not really, I am afraid, no."

Gabe wasn't going to lie to her. He wouldn't sugar-coat things, either – it wasn't his way. But if he could, he'd be thoughtful and patient. He knew these were simple kindnesses that were often lacking when dealing with the victim of a crime, no matter how minor that crime might appear to be.

He put his leather backpack on the ground and pulled up a stool. She moved round to the other side of the long table and sat almost opposite him. For a moment she stared past him out of the large window behind him.

"Windolene," she muttered. "I forgot the bloody Windolene." She blinked rapidly, shook out her shoulders and focused on him. Alert now. Ready. "Strategise away."

"Fuck, no," Ali ground out. "This is a joke, right? Did Flynn set you up to this? I'm going to murder him."

She rose from her stool and began pacing. What was the lunatic thinking? *Shadow* her? He was stark raving mad if he thought she'd get on board with that one. An officer driving by her house every so often she could handle. But this?

He waited till she paused and turned before he spoke again.

"You did agree to hear me out. The whole way out. Are you not a woman of your word?"

That rat bastard. How did he know that was the one thing that really pissed her off – when people said one thing and did another? It was sneaky and deceitful, and she hated it – two-faced liars didn't interest her. Ever. *And, fuck him, he was right.* She'd promised to listen and yet the second he'd mentioned his plan, she'd gone off on a tirade. And yet again, he'd remained as still as stone. *Weirdo.*

She strode back to the stool and sat.

"You're right. Sorry," she said, "go on."

He blinked slowly on hearing her apology and stared straight at her for a long moment before continuing.

"I expect you to do all the usual errands, meetings, social events and family business as normal. All of your TV production meetings. And . . . " he paused, ensuring she was looking at him, "any dates you are supposed to go on. No," he continued, ignoring her derisive snort, "I will not be *on* your dates with you, but I will be in the background, so I will expect you to keep them family-friendly."

Ali shook her head. "You really are loco, aren't you? How do you think it'll work, eh? I have a bazillion things to do over the next week or so before filming actually begins and will absolutely *not* have time to babysit you. And for the record, I don't date."

"I can assure you I do not need or want a babysitter. You won't even know I am there. I will literally be your shadow and silent as the grave."

She could well believe the silent part. He wasn't

exactly a chatterbox on a good day. But the whole plan still bugged her.

"Why? What will all this get you? What's done is done, surely. You can't un-vandalise my place. You can't make those bike incidents disappear. Or my lock not get picked."

"I will be taking note of every interaction, watching every person you speak to, engage with. Most people have a 'tell', something that gives them away when they are trying to hide something else. I am good at that. At noticing and disseminating."

Gabe picked up the mug of cooled coffee and took a sip. Grimacing, he put it back, reached into his backpack and took out a bottle of water. He watched her as he unscrewed the cap.

"Will you do something for me?" he asked.

"Depends." If Gabe had been an eye-roller, she knew this would have been the perfect time. He was so easy.

"Close your eyes and let your mind wander back to the first bike incident. Let it play in your mind as if you were watching a film."

"Are you nuts? The last thing I want to do is go back over it."

"I did not say that it would be easy. I thought you might be strong enough to do this. It is perfectly fine if you are not."

He was playing the old reverse psychology card. But damn! she hated being called weak.

"Ha. I'm as strong as they come. Sure, I'll do your hypno shit. Bring it on."

Gabe walked round behind her and placed his hands on her shoulders, careful to avoid her graze. She flinched automatically and he raised them immediately.

"Apologies. I should have told you I would be touching you. May I?"

Ali swore under her breath. His touch felt different to yesterday. Just as gentle but not necessary. Softer. She was going barmy thinking like this.

"Go ahead," she grunted. "Just no handsy shit."

There was silence for several moments as he simply rested his palms lightly but firmly on her shoulders.

"Close your eyes," he said.

He inched his hands up her neck and onto her head. He placed his middle fingers at each temple and spread his hands over her head, massaging his thumbs into the back of her skull.

"Think of the route you took that day. Think of the weather, the time of day, the feel of the breeze on your face as you peddled."

He continued talking in a soft, low tone, his hands making her feel light-headed and shaky all at once. And yet a calmness came over her. She could feel her shoulders relax as she did as he asked. He kept talking and talking. Asking question after question, about incident after incident, and all the time his hands made magic on her head. Soothing, exploring, pressing and circling . . .

"Fuck!" Ali jerked back and jumped off the stool. "What the hell just happened?" she demanded.

Gabe was standing next to the counter drinking a glass of water as if he'd been running a marathon. Ali felt both drained and, weirdly, elated.

"Seriously, Doctor Voodoo, what did you do? What did I say? Did I fall asleep?"

"No. Not exactly," he said, turning on the tap and refilling his glass.

"What exactly? Tell me! You're freaking me out."

"You made some interesting observations. You have a very linear thought pattern and you are aware of way more than you think."

"What the *fuck* did I say?" she yelled.

He sighed. A deep, down-to-the-belly sigh, and she realised he was as exhausted as she felt. *Huh.*

"You saw a man, mid twenties, mid height with black hair and swarthy skin. That was your word." He caught her gaze. "You were very thorough. And we can assume it was the same person, or one of them, who knocked you down the steps at the DART station and again yesterday morning, as he had, according to you, the same physical characteristics.

"You didn't see the man in the car, but you did see the whole number plate, which we will run through the system back at the station."

There was silence for several minutes. Ali was pondering all he'd said, all she'd apparently said and none of which she recalled. It was like he'd put some kind of spell on her, if she believed in that shit.

"Thoughts?" he asked.

Ali sneered at him. "Including me now, are we? How kind." But she leaned forwards, elbows on the table, her hands entwined. "You think it's someone I know, don't you?"

"I do."

"You're wrong. No friend of mine would do this to me," she insisted. She was sure of it. She had good, loyal friends. "And going by that description, I definitely don't know him."

"I didn't say the person was a friend. Or even that the dark-haired man is the one in charge. Maybe he is an underling. The mastermind, whether male or female, may in fact be a mere acquaintance or co-worker, a delivery person. The swarthy man is a bungler and ergo, not the person in charge. For that we can be grateful. But there were *two* here yesterday. That we know."

Gabe took another drink and Ali studied him. He was wearing a different jacket, shirt and tie: *boring, ordinary, normal.* Only he didn't look any of those things. Not even a bit. He looked worn out and why the hell did that not make him uber unattractive? So bloody unfair. His shiny dark hair fell down over his forehead, although short everywhere else, and he brushed it back absently. Maybe it was the high, chiselled cheekbones or the slant of dark brow over those freaky-coloured eyes, but he got away with the hairdo.

Somehow.

His skin, that lovely creamy mocha colour, was completely blemish-free and had no hint of a beard. He must shave really closely. *And his mouth? Well, that deserved a little dialogue all of its own.* It was ridiculously even in the lip department – about the same thickness top and bottom but, more importantly, it looked firm. Strong. And a lovely soft pink.

Shit – she had mothballs in her head, as her granny used to say. Lip colour was *not* a thing with her. She usually noticed if, a) a guy had a decent set of teeth, and b) if his lips appeared in any way kissable. Kissing wasn't really her bag, anyway. She liked to get straight to the point. Down to business, so to speak. Who needed wet, slobbery lips and tongues doing the nasty? Not her. But she hadn't seen his teeth yet – at least not in a smile. She wondered, very briefly, if she could ask him to "open up", like at the dentist, so she could check out the pearly whites.

Probably not. He most likely thought her a pain in the ass and she didn't need to fuel that fire. Maybe she could make him laugh. *Maybe not.* She hadn't seen one smile from him. But in all fairness, they weren't really in a smiling situation. But she was pretty sure she'd seen a tiny quirk, so assumed there was a sense of humour in there somewhere. Casting her mind back to the night of Dev's wedding, she still couldn't summon the image of this tall, dark, oddly handsome man smiling. *Bugger.*

"Do you ever smile?" The words were out before she could get her brain to put a halt on her mouth. Shit. *Moron.*

Gabe Mackenzie just looked at her and . . . *nope, no smile forthcoming. Not a glimmer.*

She huffed out a breath. "Never mind. It was a stretch." She returned his look. "So, you believe that if you follow me around, you'll magically figure out which asshole did this to my building, to me?"

"No magic needed," he said, "just deduction and intuition. And facts."

"And how are you going to get these mysterious facts? Ask?"

"That is usually a good place to start," he agreed. "I won't get in your way. I am good at what I do."

"Yeah, yeah, so you said. Nothing wrong with your ego, is there?" Ali slid down off her stool again to pace about her space.

"Not a thing. I don't lie to myself and I certainly will not lie to you," he said in a measured tone.

Huh. Imagine that, Ali thought. *A man who trusts in himself implicitly and who actually believes he doesn't lie . . . What have we before us, a paragon?*

"Well, don't make promises you can't keep, Mac. I won't be happy."

"You are already not happy. I will do my utmost not to add to that burden."

He stood, too, and began to gather his belongings. For some reason Ali didn't want to explore too deeply, she found herself wishing he really was telling the truth. That he wouldn't lie. That he wouldn't add to her misery. Maybe it was his rather formal turn of phrase. Or his stillness. Or his general self-contained demeanour. But she suddenly, fiercely, wanted it to be true.

A good, honest man. Hmm. Jury's out.

"Right, then," she said, all business, "I've got to go to the warehouse in Ballymun. It's on the north side of Dublin, in case you don't know it. I need to collect more supplies. The TV company's paying, so it should be, for me at least, an enjoyable spending spree. How do you want to play this?"

He shoved a hand into his pocket and pulled out a set of keys.

"I will drive," he said.

"Good," she replied, "I'm not sure my bike's crossbar would hold you."

And she headed out of the door.

New experiences are good, he reminded himself grimly as he pushed a large trolley down yet another aisle. Stepping outside one's comfort zone is a form of growth, he'd heard rumoured. God knew he'd had thousands of experiences outside his comfort zone on a regular basis – such was the nature of his work – but this? This mindless, unending aisle after aisle of kitchen supplies?

This was a whole new level of discomfort.

Ali, on the other hand, was in flying form. Anyone seeing her now would never believe she'd been traumatised mere hours before. She practically skipped along each aisle, picking up, studying, returning or tossing an item into the trolley. She was like the proverbial child in a sweet shop, only her sugar high was technical and gadget-oriented. If the products hadn't seemed so . . . dull, so completely unnecessary to his own admittedly limited kitchen skills, he may almost have enjoyed himself. Not the warehouse or the products, but the woman.

She was wearing faded jeans and work boots. Her jumper was oversized and a deep blue – he was sure it had some fancy name, but to him it was the blue of an Oklahoma summer sky, as he remembered them from his early childhood when visiting his mother's family. It hung off her left shoulder and she was, thankfully, wearing another one of the white vest tops underneath.

The bandage was gone from her left shoulder. He should have checked to see if it needed replacing, though obviously she didn't think so. The jumper covered her rear – when she was standing – but when she bent down, limber as an athlete, the soft, worn fabric stretched across her bottom in the way that was, to his mind, irritatingly distracting. *Why couldn't she wear a jacket like a normal person?*

Simple answer: there was nothing normal about Ali Fitzgerald. Even if he hadn't listened to her smart mouth and heard her cheeky banter with others, he recognised the steel barrier she'd erected round herself as a shield from pain. From the moment he'd first seen her – her bright, sharp face slightly flushed with pleasure the night she'd signed for the building space – his senses had been on high alert. Disgusted with his lack of control, he'd banked those feelings down almost immediately, but not before the shadows of distress had simmered about her. Anger, hurt and betrayal were singing out to him and he hated it.

He hated that he'd seen it, felt it. He knew better than to let that in. He *knew* better, *damn it*. And even though he'd quickly shut it down, those mists from her past were like veils draped across her shoulders, holding her imprisoned in their gossamer threads.

If he was to survive this case, body *and* soul intact, he needed to remember his own rules. No messing with the "special abilities", no unlocking of his unusual talents. None. It was too difficult. Too risky. The rare times he used his powers, the rare times he let his real self out, he'd ended up battered and broken. Exhausted. The small, useful side of that huge mountain within had helped on certain police cases in the past and that was enough. More than enough. He didn't owe anyone more than that. And that's how it had to remain. For his own sanity.

Ali Fitzgerald and her complicated life needed to be put very securely in a box. And the key discarded in a mire so deep it would never be found.

Chapter 4

Paint.

They needed paint, and lots of it. Yesterday, Ali had purposefully avoided focusing on the walls. All those awful marks and streaks. She knew those letters formed words and some had even landed in her brain, but she'd refused to absorb them. Enough going on dealing with the tables and the mess on the floor. But today she needed to deal with that conundrum – an actual other day – and the letters, the words, had to be faced. Somehow, it had been understood that no one mention the crude, hurtful words. Perhaps they knew she needed time. The reality was she needed the tables sanded first so the dust would settle before painting.

Ali was nothing if not practical.

And so a stop at Paintworld, en route from the heaven that was the Kitchen Keeper warehouse, became a thing. She glanced at the stone face that was Gabe Mackenzie sitting beside her, carefully concentrating on driving. Carefully not paying her any mind. Well, that was just fine. She didn't need his brand of attention. He was already going to be way too much in her life over the next few days without . . . more.

"There, there's a space."

She pointed to a gap in the lines of parked cars and then twisted to glare at Gabe as he kept driving. He didn't spare her a glance, just smoothly turned at the end of the section and cruised up the next, to slide neatly into a spot almost directly opposite the entrance. *It figured.*

"Are you looking for a specific shade?" he asked as Ali picked up several colour charts when they were inside. "Or are you going with the ecru again?"

Ali turned and stared at him.

"How do you even know ecru is a colour? Or that it's on my walls?" She held up a hand. "Wait. I don't want to hear. I don't want to know your history of colour palettes, but since you obviously have a weird eye, take these and pick one." She shoved a bunch of strips of paper into his hands. "I'm going to get rollers and trays."

Ali turned the corner, scooting her trolley with one foot, the other pushing off the ground as she leaned on the handlebar, trying for some form of steerage. She found the shelves with all the extras and began sorting through some choices. A few moments later, Gabe appeared with two large buckets of paint and deposited them in the trolley.

"I chose a warm grey with a touch of taupe for the two walls needing the colour, but I think you should leave the ecru on the other wall as it will be a nice contrast."

Sincerely flabbergasted at this very odd man, she said, "How do you know how much I'll need?"

"I did the math."

"Of course you did."

Christ! he was one strange dude.

She picked up a cellophane-wrapped tray and stopped, aware he was staring at her.

"What?"

"Don't you have all these supplies from your previous paint job?"

She sighed. "I suppose you're one of those neat freaks who washes every roller, tray and brush and tenderly wraps them up for future use." She paused to glare at him. His steady eyes gave nothing away. "Fuck. You are, aren't you?" Heaving a sigh, she plopped her booty into the trolley. "Well, no bleeding surprise there. *I'm* not, as you can clearly see. And no judgements, please. I have other talents."

He cleared his throat. "I wouldn't say my storage of supplies involves tenderness, but I do wash and prepare and store them correctly. I buy quality and keep it for its expected lifetime. And I am not judging. Your talents appear to be many and varied."

"I bet you wear overalls and never get paint on yourself, either," she muttered as she took her place in the queue for the cashier.

"Not overalls, no."

Was he blushing? Surely not?

"But I do keep an old set of clothing to use. I understood most people do that."

Ali snorted. "Oh, God, and I assume you use masking tape and everything," she chuckled, a vision in her head of this highly uptight specimen up a ladder, strong, muscular arms raised as he masked the ceiling.

Unbidden, her image also included an old, worn T-shirt pulling from ancient, faded jeans and exposing a flat yet ripped stomach. *Gah! That wouldn't do.* Fortunately, the queue moved forwards and she focused on the cashier as she paid for her purchases.

The drive back was spent in relative silence and Ali was glad of it. She absolutely did *not* need to think of Scotty MacScot in any way other than the buttoned-up cold fish he was. She made him swing by an Aldi so she could run in for a couple of bars of dark chocolate infused with mint.

"You *so* don't want to know," she said, smiling benignly at his raised eyebrow. "Wait, where are we going?"

Ali peered out of the window of his jeep, noticing they were on a different route to the loft space.

"I am swinging by my apartment to collect some extra clothing to wear while painting," he answered smoothly.

"You really don't have to," Ali muttered ungratefully.

"Regardless," he said.

"What does that even mean? Regardless? Regardless of what? My wishes? My feelings? What?" Ali turned in her seat to glare at him, arms folded tightly across her chest.

"In this particular instance it means that even if you do not want me painting in your space, I will be doing it anyway. Ali . . . " He speared her with a quick look. "You are under my protection. I thought that was clear. Where you go, I go. What you do, I do. Within reason," he added as she snorted.

"But," she protested, "I . . . never mind."

Turning back to gaze out of the window, she knew it was hopeless. He was hopeless. He wouldn't listen and the sooner this enforced *togetherness* was over the better. She sighed.

Gabe got out of his car and with a promise to be quick, he took the steps to his apartment two at a time and unlocked the door. The house was an old Georgian three-storey on a quiet street in Rathgar and his flat was accessed via an outside staircase at the side of the building. It was temporary, he knew that, but space and place, setting and surroundings, were important to him.

He left his front door open and hurried to his bedroom. The high ceilings relaxed him and calmed his mind when he sat in either the living area or the kitchen, or even lying on his bed. His furniture was simple. It had been overstuffed with all manner of chairs, dressers, tables and free-standing closets, none of which he needed, so he'd stored a lot of the pieces, at his own expense, in order to have the clarity he needed when he walked through the front door.

He'd even enjoyed choosing a few second-hand pieces at local auctions – something he'd never envisioned doing before. He'd covered the walls in a pale grey matt paint and added window blinds in cream. The curtains that the landlady had left were a genuine eyesore and now lived in plastic sacks in the spare room wardrobe. Sure, doing up this place had required an outlay of cash with no chance of a return, but it had seemed . . . necessary, somehow. Gabe had long ago learned to trust his gut when it came to certain decisions and when he'd walked through the door several months earlier, he'd known he'd be here a while.

The wardrobe in his bedroom was deep and some rummaging was necessary before he located the old, worn cargo pants and long-sleeved grey marl T-shirt that sported minor spatters of paint. He stripped to his boxers and was buttoning the fly of his trousers, when a sound from his doorway had him spinning round.

"This is . . . nice." Ali waved a hand in the general direction of the interior of his flat as she propped her shoulder against the door frame.

Gabe grunted. The light from the hall skylight haloed

her spiky bleached hair and if it wasn't laughable, he'd swear she had the look of an angel – *an avenging one, anyway.*

"I asked you to stay in the car," Gabe said, gritting his teeth as he pulled on his T-shirt.

"You *told* me to stay in the car. In case you haven't figured it out yet, I don't take direction well."

She quirked an eyebrow as she spoke and pushing away from the door, she strolled into his space, owning it.

Gabe blinked. *Great. Just great.*

As he watched her wander about, her work boots thudding on the bare wood floorboards, all he could see was him lying in his bed later, this vision before him playing in his head. She was in his head enough already – he certainly didn't need this stunt to augment that fact. He sighed.

"Out," he said, pointing to the door as he picked up trainers and socks and a sweatshirt. "I would rather you wait in the living area."

He punctuated this remark by heading there himself and sitting on his leather couch, where he finished dressing and laced his shoes. Ali strolled in behind him, made her way to the long Georgian sash windows and peered out. She absently ran a finger against the glass and looked at it. She turned to him.

"Do you have Windolene?"

"Pardon me?"

"I bet you do, or your landlord may have left you some." She peered at her finger again and twisted it in his direction. "See? Clean as a whistle. You must be very domesticated."

It didn't sound like a compliment, Gabe thought as he

tipped his head towards his kitchen. And almost wished he hadn't cleaned those windows last week.

"Under the sink."

"I knew it."

"So, Springsteen or ABBA?"

Ali fiddled with Spotify as Gabe lay out some groundsheets he'd collected from his spare room before they'd driven back to the loft.

"May I have another option?"

He didn't turn round, but she took in the view anyway. *Hmm. Yup. He filled those pants out admirably well.* Long legs and strong thighs were still pretty obvious, even covered in faded khaki, *and as for that grey T-shirt . . . it hugged his body really nicely. Shit.* He should really stick to the boring trousers and buttoned-up shirts because this Gabe, slightly ruffled and casual, was veering towards seriously *hot*. Not on her agenda. *No way. Virtual head slap, Ali.*

"Not unless I agree with it."

Ali took her painting and cleaning playlists seriously. They needed a balance between belt-out-loud rock or pop tunes, or belt-out-loud emotional ballads. Springsteen and ABBA covered all those bases.

"How about some Count Basie or Django Reinhardt?"

"Christ, Granddad, this is the twenty-first century. Get with it. Choose."

Gabe straightened the dust sheet and moved a ladder towards the wall before popping the lid on a can of paint with a screwdriver. He rested his hands on his hips, glaring at her.

"We should start with ABBA to get us moving and

add Bruce later to kick-start us when we are flagging," he suggested.

Ali stared. *Huh. That was actually a good plan. He probably did some kind of mathematical equation in his brain to figure that out,* Ali suspected. He took everything so seriously. She hadn't seen one smile crack his face. She needed to work on that. Purely for research. To make sure he was human.

"ABBA it is," she agreed and set up the *ABBA Gold* list, cranking it up to fill the high-ceilinged loft with the first strains of "Dancing Queen".

It was a bit of a no-brainer that she'd use the roller and Mr Uptight and Serious would do the edges. And yes, she'd expected him to pull out a roll of masking tape, but he surprised her.

"I have a steady hand," he explained as he climbed the ladder to cut in the edges where the walls joined the ceiling.

Ali shrugged, not really believing him, but she figured she'd give him the benefit of the doubt and all, considering he was helping, and instead set up her roller and tray on the opposite wall so they could swap later. Her singing voice wasn't great, but its lack of prowess or ability to hold a tune didn't stop her enjoyment. And if – as she sang the words, many incorrect – she let her mind wander to the image of the Scot stripped to his waist in his bedroom, that merely kept her focused.

Because, dear God Almighty, admitting she didn't take direction well had been, although true, a cover-up. Ali had been stunned when she'd wandered into his flat. Bored waiting in his car, she'd hightailed it up the steps and into his small foyer. The open door to the large living space had beckoned and Ali was all for adventures.

The space had been a surprise. Large and airy with the generous high ceilings and intricate mouldings, it should have been cold. *It wasn't.* A large leather sofa was the main piece of furniture and an old, marked oak table sat low in front of it. Several stacks of books lay in neat piles. *No surprise there.* What was a shock were the scattered woven rugs in different strong colours, both along the back of the couch and a few folded neatly like cushions along the seat. Jewel tones of deep turquoise and aubergine, saffron and jade. More rugs were folded and stacked on two leather chairs on the other side of the coffee table. These were patterned – plaids and bold stripes.

Well now. Ali had backed out and wandered along the polished wooden hallway to an open door where she could hear rustling. She came to a halt when she caught a glimpse of the tall, almost naked man. His broad shoulders rippled as he moved, every sinew dancing and catching the light. His back tapered to a trim waist and what was remarkable to Ali in that moment was the colour of his skin. She'd already become aware of it previously, when noticing the varying contrasts against his white shirt, but this – in all its manly glory – this was a sight to behold. *Mocha? Café au lait?* She didn't know the terms – she just knew the beauty of it.

When he turned on hearing her – probably her instinctive hum of approval – she almost gasped aloud. His body was so well formed he looked like he'd stepped from the pages of *Athlete Monthly. Well-defined pecs, ridges for days, dark, perfectly shaped nipples, those oh-so-sexy V-muscles inside leading south and,* as he stretched his arms to slide into the T-shirt, *a well-formed "inny" belly button.*

And not one ounce of hair.

She smirked, remembering, and maybe hmmed a bit more.

"Hey, Scotty," Ali called over her shoulder as she applied fresh paint to her roller and placed it against the wall, "shave or wax?"

There was no response, only the ending strains of "Super Trouper". As the melody for "I Have a Dream" started, Ali turned to repeat her question. He was motionless, paintbrush poised as he looked at her in puzzlement.

"What on *earth* are you talking about?" he asked.

"Ha. You know. I saw your chest earlier and as a matter of research, I just wanted to know which camp you fall into, shave or wax?"

Ali struggled not to grin at the look on his face. It was priceless. Haughty. Arrogant.

"Why is this any concern of yours?" he said. "And what research?"

"Well," Ali said, turning back to her wall so he wouldn't see her smile, "most guys I know who are hairless, wax. Do they wax in Scotland?"

"Why would any man in his right mind wax their chest? Or shave it? Is that really a *thing* young men do?"

He sounded like he was actually pondering the situation and very definitely finding it wanting.

"Yes, Pops, they do. It's the fashion. Don't you watch TV?"

"No. I do not. Or at least only the news and some sport."

Ali added more paint. "You still haven't answered. And don't say it's not my business. I know it's not. But I've seen the 'goods', so to speak, so I'm just curious. I'll tell my body hair secrets if you tell yours."

She stole a peek at him then and, *no, it couldn't be . . . It looked like he was blushing. Yay!* She counted that as a win. And she also stored away the fact that he seemed remarkably shy.

Gabe cleared his throat. He shouldn't answer her. It was none of her business, as she'd just admitted, and it was a highly inappropriate thing to be discussing. She was his subject, his client, in a way. Personal conversations weren't supposed to happen. He could feel heat rise in his face as he lied to himself. Of course personal conversations were going to happen. He was going to be digging and hunting for all manner of personal things about her. Sure, it was in order to keep her safe by finding the culprit of the damage, but it still felt like an intrusion.

He cleared his throat again. "I have very little body hair," he admitted. "It is hereditary."

"I thought all Scots were hairy mountainy men."

"I am only half Scottish."

"Huh. What's the other half?"

Gabe paused, focusing on an edge of trim. He dipped his brush carefully into the container in his right hand and turned his attention back to the corner slot where he was working.

"I am half Osage Nation."

There was silence and Gabe wondered, as ABBA continued to sing about the winner taking it all, if Ali had heard him. He stole a look at her, cross with himself for sharing such personal information about himself. If she hadn't heard, he certainly wasn't going to repeat it.

She put her roller down and looked up at him. "Huh," she said. "Cool." And went back to her wall.

Huh? He shares a deeply private part of his blood and she says *huh*. That would, as the saying goes, teach him.

They painted for some time. Just over seventy-seven minutes, in fact, stopping as the last beat of "Waterloo" rang out. Ali had sung along to several of the hits and Gabe had found himself doing the same. Except he sang inside himself. He knew better than to let his voice be heard.

"Break," Ali called as she arched her back and rested her roller against the sink. "I need water, carbs and chocolate."

She headed to the fridge and Gabe stood up from his crouched position along the skirting boards. He looked about at their handiwork. His trim of the room was just about complete and Ali had covered most of the wall space in the two separate colours chosen earlier. Gabe reached for some cling film to wrap round his brush to protect it from drying out while they took their much-needed rest. Ali was scrolling through her phone as Gabe took a couple of bottles of water from the fridge and put them on the table. He also pulled out some leftover pizza and the bar of chocolate and rested them side by side.

"All the food groups," he said as Ali reached over absently, intent on her screen, and plucked a slice of pizza from the foil.

"Thanks," she said distractedly and ate.

Gabe opened both water bottles and unwrapped the chocolate. He rolled his slice of pizza and took a bite.

"So," Ali said, "are your people from Missouri, Arkansas, Kansas or Oklahoma?"

She was going there, after all. Now, he had to decide whether to shut it down or open up. Shutting down made most sense. He knew that.

"Oklahoma," he offered, not listening to sense.

"Have you been?"

"Yes."

"I wonder, how I can keep up with you? You're such a veritable mine of information." Ali put down her unfinished pizza slice and snapped off two squares of chocolate.

"I answered your question."

"That you did, oh talkative one. Hey," she continued, "is that your Osage name? Chatty? Or maybe the Osage equivalent of Talkie? Or Blabbermouth?"

Gabe tried hard to keep his mouth from twitching.

"Our names are intended to be apt, not ironic. But they are not for sharing."

"Spoilsport. Well, I'm going to think of a name for you."

"I believe I have heard you call me many names already," Gabe offered as he packed away their food remains, tossing some foil in the bin.

"Sure, but now I have a whole other selection to choose from: Talking Little, Silent Bear, Quiet Warrior, Noiseless Newt."

He let out a snort – he couldn't help it.

"Noiseless Newt?"

Ali grinned. "I'm only messing with you. Wanted to know if you were paying attention."

"I always pay attention."

Ali was silent at that, her eyes resting on his. The moment stretched and he realised how true it was. He did pay attention. To her. Everything about her commanded his attention. And not just for the job at hand, but for her safety. *Who was he kidding?* He paid attention to the way her eyes narrowed in concentration when she was busy, that her shoulders seemed unnaturally tense a lot of the time. He noticed how she ate really slowly and consumed very little. He noticed how her clothes fit her body. He wished he didn't notice that. He wanted to notice it more.

Ali dropped her eyes from his gaze and brushed her hands against her trousers. "Time to switch," she said, business-like. "You do my trim side and I'll roller yours."

And now he was thinking of rolling *with* her, over and over, on the floor, in a bed . . .

Gabe got a grip, released a breath he'd been unaware he'd been holding and gladly switched places. As he painted, his thoughts dwelled on her case. His gut told him her life wasn't in danger. If it was, she'd be dead by now. Whoever was pulling the strings would have been impatient with the "swarthy" man's ineptitude and finished the job. No. This was about making things difficult for her, halting her progress. Her show was due to get under way within a couple of weeks and this damage – the vandalism and the personal assaults – was certainly a way to delay that. Or to stop it.

The question was, why?

Chapter 5

The meeting was set for 9 a.m. and Ali was running late. It had been another of those nights. Waking sweat-drenched from a nightmare she couldn't remember and then lying there in frustration as she tried to force her mind and body to relax. It had been an unsuccessful attempt. She'd got up and showered at six thirty and then, in typical fashion, had become immersed in writing new recipes as she ate cold toast and sipped hot coffee. Suddenly, it was eight forty and the studio was a good half-hour away by bike.

She texted the show's producer to explain she'd be late but was startled when her doorbell rang.

"Shit!" Her phone hit the floor as she stumbled to open the front door.

He was wearing a grey suit and tie today, a snow-white shirt, almost blinding against his skin. His damp hair was brushed back from his face and his expression was as stern and unsmiling as ever.

"Are you ready?"

"Jesus, Scotty the Silent, you gave me a heart attack. What are you doing here?"

"You have a meeting at the studio at nine. I am here to take you there. Are you ready?"

Ali stared at him, a million snarky things at the ready to say. For once, she shut up – she needed him and his jeep to get there on time.

"Give me a sec," she said. "Start the car."

She whirled back inside, grabbed her phone and jacket, caught a glimpse of herself in the mirror and thought *fuck it*, then slammed the door behind her.

The studio was modern and impressive and full of steel and shiny wood. The conference room where Ali was to discuss things with the producer, director and various staff was bright and cheerful. Coffee and tea were set up on a sideboard, and plates of warm muffins and fresh doughnuts were centred on the long table.

"Wait. You *can't* come in here," Ali hissed as they approached the table.

"I can, and I will. Where you go, I go. That is the deal I made with your brother."

"Flynn didn't mean *everywhere*, surely? The producer won't want you in the room."

Ali nodded in the direction of the tall, thin man pouring tea into a china cup. Marc Bewley was an up-and-coming TV executive and in demand by many of the peripheral stations, as well as RTÉ, the main broadcasting channel.

"Your producer is not of any concern to me, unless he is involved in the vandalism of your loft. Which seems unlikely. But one never knows what people will do." His voice was cool and even, and with an "Excuse me," he went to speak briefly with Mr Bewley.

A hurried conversation ensued, and Marc looked over and back at Ali, who had the inkling to bite on her nails, a habit she'd shed years earlier. She hated being the focus of their attention, however briefly. Odd, she knew, for someone about to go on nationwide TV.

But that was different.

The producer nodded once, and her bodyguard returned to her side and took a seat next to hers.

"I am just here to watch and listen," he said, for her ears only, as he handed her a cup of coffee. "Forget I am even in the room."

Ali took a deep, steadying breath. *You couldn't forget the large Scot was in the room! His presence was . . . unmistakable.* He folded his lean body into the chair and rested his hands loosely on his lap, leaning back, relaxed and at ease. Ali, on the other hand, felt as if she were wound tight as a bow. She was eager to know how the producer and his crew would take the minor delay owing to the location damage. She really hoped they wouldn't suggest a studio. Her whole buy-in to the concept of the show was because it was her place, her kitchen and her "classroom", not something staged and fake.

Marc Bewley cleared his throat, said a breezy good morning and the meeting began.

It was interesting, Gabe noted, how Ali was able to hold her own with the TV people, give her views and concerns, tangle with them over problems and offer solutions, all without swearing once. He wondered if it was just himself who brought out her guttermouth. He almost wished it was. At least it was a reaction.

She was knowledgeable about her subject – that in itself wasn't a surprise – but that she was able to introduce angles and options to what, Gabe suspected, were new areas of work for her, intrigued him. She was way more intelligent, way more observant than she liked to let on. *Was it deliberate? Or habit?* It would be a challenge to find out. It also made him realise she may in fact know more about her vandals than she supposed. He could work on that.

He studied each of the staff members around the table. Some were connected with the actual show, some were outliers – they dealt with external tasks and any complications. He listened and observed – as he'd told Ali he would – and not one of them tugged at his gut, his instinct. The perpetrators weren't in the room.

He could feel no ill towards Ali – quite the reverse, in fact. He would wager, were he a gambling man, that several of the men and at least one of the women, in particular the make-up artist, would like a chance to get to know Ali a *lot* better. She appeared oblivious to their overtures. Even when the meeting was over and three men vied for her attention, Ali simply gathered up her notebook, indicated with a jerk of her head that she was ready to leave and strode out of the door.

Interesting.

"Where to?" Gabe turned on the engine and waited as Ali strapped in.

Ali heaved a sigh. "Seriously? This shit again?"

Gabe continued to wait, silent, hands easy on the wheel.

"Fine," she snapped. "It's your funeral."

She gave him directions to Blackrock village and he followed her into a small shopping centre with some exclusive boutiques.

"Are you going clothes shopping?" Gabe asked with a barely repressed shudder.

"Oh, don't you want to come with me? Help me choose some clothing for the show? If you play your cards right, I'll even let you help me choose my new lingerie."

Her grin was almost feral and Gabe had to give her the round.

"Betty from wardrobe said she would select your clothes for each episode," he ventured in the vain hope that the next few hours wouldn't find him sitting on a chair outside various changing rooms.

"Well, Betty from wardrobe has been misinformed. I choose what I wear, no one else, and if you'd been paying attention, as you were supposed to, you'd have heard me insist on that."

He had heard. But he'd been hoping he'd been incorrect. This wasn't what he was paid to do. Babysitting a client as she went about her day was one thing, her *working* day, but clothes shopping? This was a new level of hell.

"So . . . " Ali glanced at him. "I'm trying to decide between retro girly a lá late fifties, early sixties. You know, like Sandra Dee, all full skirts and cute preppy blouses or . . . " She paused dramatically. "Or go all Mary Quant – geometric design tube mini and an overdose of black liner. Thoughts?" she asked as she flipped through a line of clothing in a well-lit shop.

"I don't know who either of those people are," Gabe admitted. "Do you have to dress like somebody? Can you not just be yourself? Wear your own clothes, or at least clothes that *are* you?"

Ali blinked at him, stilling. "Why do you think they'd let me be myself?" she asked, her eyes clouding slightly. "Don't you think they'll want a brighter, sharper, prettier me onscreen?"

"But why? Are you not who they wanted?"

"God, you're clueless," Ali said, and actually reached up and patted his face.

Turning suddenly, she pulled on his arm and dragged him from the shop.

"Where now?"

"I . . ."

She looked crestfallen and bewildered, not a look he'd ever seen on her before. He felt a wave of tenderness wash over him as he realised she wasn't nearly as tough as she liked everyone to believe.

"Come with me." Gabe took off, assuming she'd react positively to his brisk, no-nonsense tone. "I need a coffee. And we need to talk about this show of yours."

"Yes, sir!"

He could feel the snark down to his toes and thought, distractedly, *that's better.*

His chai latte produced a snort as they sat opposite each other on soft leather chairs.

"This," she said, indicating her extra-shot flat white, "is coffee. What you're drinking is just flavoured water and not in a good way."

They both sipped in silence for a moment and then Gabe leaned forwards, elbows resting on his knees, and asked, "How did you get the show?"

"I won it."

"As a prize?"

"No. Yes. Sort of. It's complicated." Ali held her cup in both hands as Gabe sat back in his chair.

"Tell me," he said. "Uncomplicate it. And start at the beginning."

"Is this research for my case?" Her voice was wary.

"It might turn out that way. Humour me."

* * *

She did. She both humoured him and did her best to simplify her story. She began by telling him about her few guest appearances on an afternoon cooking show – a serendipitous result of some great reviews of her restaurant in the weekend paper's food supplement and the fact that one of her biggest foodie fans happened to be a TV producer. She told him how she'd ended up always doing desserts on those shows, more by default than design. Viewers texted the show, liking her open, honest style, they said. Ali shrugged as she told him about her fan base growing and how they wanted her on the show a couple of afternoons a week. The audience felt, she said, as if she were teaching them, step by step. The producers saw an opportunity. Cooking shows were very popular and so were competitions. They decided to marry the two.

"They told me I was going to get my own show, teaching the uninitiated how to bake, but they didn't want it to appear to be too easy a transition from guest to host. So, in order to generate more excitement for the new show, and give me some gravitas, they invented a competition, between myself and four other chefs. We had to bake on the afternoon slot, against each other, and the winner would get their own show."

"But you were already the winner, correct?"

"Yeah. That part sucked, because the other four didn't know that. They thought they were in with a shot, not knowing the judging was a scam, of sorts. In fairness, the judges did tell the producer afterwards they'd have picked me, anyway. And they kept their comments really close to the line – I didn't win every bake. But the others didn't realise it was a set-up and I certainly didn't tell them. What?" She glared at him, at his stony face. "I didn't ask for that. That's the way TV works, seemingly. You'd be horrified at how manipulative 'reality' TV can be. I know I was. But I want the show. I wanted out of the restaurant business per se and this was a good, financially viable way to do it."

"I didn't say a word."

"You didn't have to. I can see your judgy face loud and clear." Ali scrubbed her hands over her face. "I get it. It doesn't feel . . . ethical. I know that. But I didn't do anything wrong, not really, and yeah, I know I'm justifying this, but it was my show or no show and at least the others got recognition, right? And I already sort of have a plan to fix it. To feel less crappy about it. Oh, all right, Mr Judge and Jury, to ease my conscience."

"A plan."

"Yes. Jeez. Way to sound supportive."

"I don't mean to sound anything. Please, go ahead. Tell me your plan."

Ali flopped back in her chair, the fight draining from her. She could admit to residual guilt, to feeling like maybe, just maybe, she had in fact cheated. But she was determined that her fellow contestants would get something, other than their faces and talents, on that one-hour show, to make up for their loss.

"I'm intending to invite each of the other chefs from the contest back on my show as regular guests. They're good bakers, to be fair, but the audience for the afternoon show had already, by their response to the programme, picked me. I'm going to include my competitors in the new show as much as I can – well, as much as the producer will let me. I think it'll be good TV – and maybe the students can mark us on *our* bakes or something. I haven't figured it all out yet, but I'll definitely be involving them."

The notebook was out of his jacket pocket and with his dark eyes on hers, he said, "Names?"

Ali gave him the four names and contact details of each of the other chefs.

"You're going to investigate them, aren't you? It can't be any of them. It was just a competition. They didn't know it was mine to win. And anyway, I knew them from before. Dublin and its cheffing and baking community are small. Some would say too small."

"Even so. Many people do not like to lose. Would you agree that most creative people, like chefs, are competitive, at least in the kitchen? That they want to be the best. Are you?"

Ali sighed. *He was right, damn him.* Of course they weren't just competitive, they could be vicious. All chefs wanted to be the best at what they did. For their food to be the most sought-after, enjoyed, celebrated. She wasn't any different. Nothing made her happier than the satisfaction and enjoyment from those she fed.

In baking, she'd found a new level of pleasure. To create a pastry or a cake of perfection, a blend of sweet and tart to delight the palate . . . that was the holy grail. And she knew she was really good at it. Maybe not world class – she was still learning and it was a lifetime commitment for all bakers, she understood that. Ask any long-time baker and they said they never stopped learning new things. But she knew she could pass on her skills in a simple and easy way – and *that* was what made her just the right presenter for this show. And she wasn't letting some fuckers who'd vandalised and damaged her property get in her way.

She straightened her spine. "You know what? Do it. Check them out. And anyone else you think may be a suspect. Knock yourself out. I'm not letting these bastards beat me. Marc Bewley agreed to give me one more week before filming, so you'd better catch the culprits by then. I absolutely can't stop once the filming gets under way. I've been told, in no uncertain terms, that no more delays will be tolerated, even if it's not my fault. So," she said, hauling herself to her feet, "get to it. Go detect. Be a Hardy Boy or a Columbo or whoever. Just do it." She carried her empty cup to the counter and caught his stern face looking at her. "Or maybe you could be Rebus. He's Scottish, right?" Ali called out a goodbye to the barista and shook her head in despair. "You haven't a clue who I'm talking about, do you, Caveman?"

The very handsome, puzzled caveman shook his head. "Not even a little bit," he admitted.

But Ali was sure she saw the slightest twitch to his lips. All was not lost.

They shopped. Not in swanky boutiques for the likes of "ladies who lunch" but in Urban Outfitters and Gap, COS and Massimo Dutti. Ali bought fresh shirts, all white, but the cut varied from loose and practical, to fitted and stylish. Her trousers she kept to simple grey or black workout gear – expensive, well made and great fabric – basically, seriously good leggings but pliable for movement and comfort. She already had a ton of fabric aprons but, for the hell of it, and because she was still within the allowed TV budget, she bought more.

She was saving them on shoes and dresses, she figured, and knew that within a few weeks they'd be getting offers from fashion houses to dress her. That was the dumbest thing Ali had ever heard, but she wasn't going to look a gift horse in the mouth. Nor was she dressing up in some fancy rig-out – *no, sir*. She was taking the Scot's advice and dressing as much like herself as she could. Satisfied and exhausted, they headed back to the car park, stored the numerous bags and boxes, then drove back to her apartment.

Ali was temporarily living in her older sister Caro's former home – a first-floor flat on a quiet street in Dún Laoghaire bought by Caro several years earlier. Ali and her siblings had each received an endowment from their grandmother and had chosen many different ways to utilise their funds. Ali had purchased the restaurant in Temple Bar that she was now leasing. She used live over it but wanted a complete change so micromanaging wouldn't set in. Caro was living in Rome with her son, Toby, and was likely never returning to this two-bedroomed apartment. Wherever Caro ended up, Ali doubted it would include this space.

They brought the packages inside and Ali flipped on lights then stowed the bundles in the spare bedroom – Toby's old room. She turned to her shopping partner and watched as he took in the simple serviceable furniture, the mismatch of styles and patterns.

"It's not much but it's home, for now," she said. "I'm making food. You're welcome to stay."

She turned towards the kitchen, not waiting for his

reply, and began taking out produce from the fridge and packages from the larder.

"Feeding me is not part of my detail," he said, his large shoulder leaning on the door frame. "I can go."

"Suit yourself," Ali replied offhandedly.

But damn, she realised, *she wanted him to stay*. She wanted to show this tall, weirdly odd man that she was *good* at something. Obviously he knew, intellectually, that she must be a good chef, but she wanted him to experience her talent. She wasn't sure why that mattered to her, just that it did. She was absolutely not begging him to stay, though. Ali didn't beg anyone for anything. Ever. Even thinking those words brought a flash of nerves skimming up her body.

"If it makes any difference to your taste buds, I'm keeping it simple and just doing eggs and greens."

The light eyes met hers unwaveringly. Not blinking, merely looking. Moments passed and Ali couldn't tear her gaze from his. She could almost hear him thinking. Considering. Assessing. He was probably going to say no, he was such a stickler for protocol. And there was a guard outside, one of Flynn's men already on duty in an unmarked car. They'd acknowledged him on the way in. There was no need for this man to stay. To share her table. She wanted him to go – *she wished fervently that he'd stay* – but she wasn't about to analyse that abrupt change of heart.

"Thank you for the invitation," he said. "How may I help?"

Ali handed him a whisk.

Chapter 6

It wasn't *just* eggs and greens. It was the fluffiest, tastiest omelette Gabe had ever eaten. Filled with home-made pesto, wilted spinach, sweet tomatoes and a variety of cheeses served with an equally colourful salad, it was heaven on a plate.

Folding his napkin neatly next to his cleared plate, Gabe said, "That was a revelation. Thank you." He lifted his water glass, tilting it in her direction as a toast. "Congratulations, Chef."

Ali took a drink from her wine glass, eyeing him over the rim. "All in a day's work, Scotty. Nothing too special."

"I think you know all too well that your cooking is excellent."

Gabe rose from the table and collected the plates. He scraped Ali's leftovers in the bin and she watched as he placed them in the dishwasher but didn't say anything. He wondered, briefly, if she'd rearrange them after he was gone. He knew he would, in her shoes. Maybe she wasn't as control-oriented as he was. Or not in this area, anyway. He felt waves of *tightness* coming from her and wondered at it. What a contradiction Ali Fitzgerald was turning out to be. Sharp, sarcastic and at times rude, but she was also . . . more.

Gabe had been waiting outside the dressing room in one of the shops – the name escaped him – and he'd heard Ali talking to another woman in the communal space. The woman had asked Ali's opinion on a garment she was considering. Ali, in that sharp, sarcastic, rude way had been brutally honest. "No," she'd said. "The colour is dreadful on you. With your skin tone you should never wear *that* shade of blue." As the woman had protested, saying the assistant had said it was all the rage and in style, Ali had snorted, "Of course she did, she's on commission. No. You need to wear a softer blue, more of a Wedgewood. Trust me." The woman had retrieved the other colour from the sales clerk and was apparently stunned at the difference. And very thankful.

When the customer had sailed past Gabe with her new purchase, she'd been beaming. Ali's honesty, her time, had been a huge boost to the woman's confidence. Gabe had mentioned the incident to Ali in the car on their way to the flat.

"Well, of course I told her the truth." Ali had been horrified to imagine a different version of the story, one where she simply said, "That's lovely on you." She continued, "No woman should ever let another woman out in shite clothes. That's not what the sisterhood is all about."

Gabe took a fresh glass of water from Ali and followed her into the living area. He sat in a large leather chair, comfortable and creaky, and very definitely old. She switched on the gas fire and turned to the stereo system. Hands on her hips, she studied the selection of CDs, replacing one after the other until she held just two.

"Are you looking for something specific?"

"You'll see," she said mysteriously. She loaded them into the slot and without a backwards glance, headed to the kitchen. "I'll bring you dessert in a moment," she called out behind her.

As the room warmed up, the strains of Miles Davis filled the space. Gabe stretched his legs out in front of him, loosening his tie. Relaxing for the first time in days, he closed his eyes and let the sounds of cool jazz drift over him. While the music tended to one side of his brain, the other remained on the enigmatic woman in the kitchen.

Every movement she made was efficient and capable. She walked with purpose and intent, speed and flexibility. She was obviously fit from her cycling and her lean frame appeared strong. Why, then, did Gabe feel waves of vulnerability every time she was near him? He kept that part of his mind closed off for a reason, but somehow her aura was seeping in. He either needed to open up and take a proper look, or shut it down completely. Neither situation made him remotely comfortable. He hadn't tapped into his "gift" for some time and certainly not for anything or anyone who wasn't work-related. Wasn't Ali work-related? Suddenly, his wish to know more about what made her tick was so far from work-related that he could feel a flush of sexual heat rising on his body.

That had got to stop. Ali Fitzgerald was not for him.

He shifted in the chair, trying to find a more comfortable position owing to his body's reaction to the vision of Ali now fixed in his brain.

"Here, try this."

Ali handed Gabe a plate with a triangular slice of lemon tart. It had a drizzle of raspberry coulis artistically arranged in a stripe across the filling and onto the shiny white plate, with a sprig of mint and a dollop of whipped cream next to it.

"Oh," he said. "I mean, thank you. This looks delicious."

Embarrassed at his gaucheness, he sat upright and took the proffered fork. The first bite was an explosion of flavour. *Sharp. Sweet. Crisp. Moist. This dessert had it all.* Gabe closed his eyes and savoured every nuance.

"You really are very talented," he said when he'd swallowed most of his slice.

"Thanks," Ali said, but her cheeks were tinged with pink.

His comment had pleased her. He was surprised. Surely everyone told her how amazing she was at this? Her talents in the kitchen were already recognised in the Dublin area and soon, her specific baking skills would be known nationwide. And maybe beyond, depending on the success of the show.

He could tell this meant a lot to her. This was a shot at a new direction for her career and he was determined to ensure she got it. That she would be safe to enjoy it. It was his job to make it so. And to do that properly, he had to stop all the static energy that was circling him, energy that had nothing to do with his heritage and everything to do with this woman, and all the emotions that reared and clung whenever he was near her. That she was a bundle of unsettled, complicated feelings he was in no doubt. That it was up to him to help with those? Of that, he was equally sure, she was totally off limits.

In every way.

He rose to his feet, straightening his tie.

Clearing his throat, he said, "I appreciate the food. I have to go."

Ali raised her eyebrow. "You okay?"

"Absolutely. Yes. I am fine. Yes." *Christ,* he sounded

like he was having a brain freeze. He never fumbled his words. He also usually spoke deliberately and precisely. "Apologies. I mean that yes, everything is okay. I must leave now."

Yes, because that sentence was *so* much clearer than the last.

Sighing, he turned towards the hall, aware that Ali was right behind him. Not only frustrated with himself, he was also frustrated with her for no reason other than she was there behind him, temptation personified, and with this entire situation. Even if he actually felt like he could test this weird, uncomfortable feeling that he was getting used to having when around Ali, he knew there was no way he could act on it – not while she was his case. His responsibility. And probably not anyway, without the case. She was Flynn's sister. Off limits. All men knew the sisters were off limits. It was a code. Despite his many areas of social ignorance, Gabe knew this one. And he was not about to break it.

He turned as he opened the door. "Lock this behind me," he said calmly, his brain functioning again. "I know JJ is outside, but do it anyway."

Ali folded her arms over her chest, her gaze on his.

"Hand me your phone," he said, acting on instinct.

She reached into her back pocket and handed it over. Gabe quickly keyed in his number and handed it back, nodding firmly.

"Now, since I am pretty sure you 'mislaid' the card I gave you on day one, here is my contact information. You may call me if you think of anything else about the other chefs, or anyone who may have a grudge against you—"

"We've been over this," she interrupted.

"Please," he said simply. "Just know I am at the end of the phone. JJ can of course help with watching your home and general surveillance, but I am interested in the recall of events and conversations. Let them play in your head and call or text if anything comes to you. Goodnight." And without waiting to see her reaction, he pulled the door shut behind him.

Fuck him, anyway. Ali shoved the duvet down from her overheated body, her legs twisting in the cotton fabric. All she could see was the damn Highlander. When she'd brought in the lemon tart to feed him dessert, her heart had almost stopped at the sight of the tall, rangy man stretched out in her leather armchair. A sight so rarely, so *never* seen in her living space that she'd nearly dropped the plate. *His long legs encased in dark grey fabric, crossed casually at the ankles. His shoes – a polished, well-worn black leather – looking large and out of place.*

He'd tucked his hands up behind his head in a pose so at home, so *natural*, that Ali had found it hard to reconcile the alert man from dinner and shopping and everything else with this physical specimen of ease and what came across as effortlessness. She knew that wasn't true. She knew he'd be on his feet in an instant, ready to do business, do battle. She didn't doubt that for a second. But right then, watching his dark lashes create shadows on chiselled cheekbones, his usually firm mouth relaxed with a tiny hint of a curve as he listened in apparent pleasure to some smooth jazz, that was a special moment. Ali had wanted to capture the visual in her brain, in her heart, and look at it later to wonder why it affected her so much.

80

Well, later had arrived in the form of a very frustrating dream. She'd replayed that scene in her mind, but everything had been heightened – the light in the room darker but with a glow from the fire throwing shadows over every plane of his strong body. In her dream, a blessed relief from her recent nightmares, he'd been shirtless – the scene from his room yesterday combining rather perfectly with tonight in her living room. In her dream, she hadn't stopped to let her eyes wander. She'd crossed to him, no plate of tart in sight, and kneeled by his chair, letting the palm of her hand smooth over the muscles of his chest and abdomen. His skin had been hot and alive beneath her fingers – and his groan of approval had her skimming her thumb over dark, erect nipples.

He liked her touch. He liked how her hands felt against his skin. And she grew bold and let her lips cover the places where her fingers had trailed. Slowly, his eyes had opened and caught hers in an unbreakable connection.

"Yes," he'd whispered, "take what you want, what you need. I am yours."

She'd gasped her surprise as his hand had snaked out and caught her wrist, holding her firm. Gripping her tightly.

Because suddenly it wasn't the Scot's gorgeous sensuous tones, but a harsher voice, a meaner sound. A different pair of eyes focused on her. *Oh, no. No . . . !*

"You know where I want this hand, don't you?"

Ali woke with a jolt, her own hand pressing on her rapid heartbeat, gasps of air whooshing from her chest. *In time,* she thought, *I stopped it in time. It's okay. I'm okay.* Her dream had started to turn ugly, but she'd stopped it.

Fuck him, she murmured again, wondering which him she even meant, and threw back the bedding to go and get a drink of water. *Maybe that's what I should be doing,* she thought. *Maybe I need to get laid so I can get Scotty MacHighlands out of my head.* Or in this case, back in.

She poured a glass of water in the kitchen and drank in deep gulps. All was quiet and still outside. The small back garden was eerily motionless. But what had she expected? A gang of youths holed up preparing to invade her home?

She walked through to the living space, noticing the beams from the street lights casting shadows across the floor. *She was safe, she was fine, she was cool and in control. JJ was outside doing his duty. All was well.*

A sudden *clang* and *crash* from the back of the house had her whirling, a hand to her throat. She darted to the kitchen window in time to see Smokey, the neighbour's cat, scamper away from an overturned bin in the garden. The pulse in her neck began to slow as Ali took long, deep breaths and leaned back against the dresser. *Okay.* Perhaps not as cool as she'd been pretending to herself.

Ali pushed away from the dresser and hurried back to her bedroom. She climbed back into bed, pulled the duvet up around her and sat with her back to the headboard, pillows tucked snugly about her. She reached for her phone and scrolled. Her lips quirked as she found him in her contacts. He'd entered himself as Scotty MacOsage. She opened a text box:

Ali: Hey. You awake?
S MacO: I am now.

Ali: Shit. I thought you were like an Indian ninja and never slept.

S MacO: It's fine. I sleep lightly. How may I help you?

Ali: Are you in customer service? You sound like you are. And I'm sorry – my political correctness is shitty. I shouldn't have used the word Indian, right?

S MacO: I am not insulted. Do you need help?

Ali: No. Or maybe. Anyway, I was thinking I'd ask the other competition chefs over to the loft on Thursday for a chat – a lunch to discuss the possibility of them coming on the show and you could, you know, vet them. What do you think?

S MacO: Interesting proposition. Do you have to ask the producers first?

Ali: Screw them. This is just my way of sounding the others out. If they like the idea I'll take it to Bewley. No point me getting the okay from him and the chefs then refuse – I'd look like an idiot.

S MacO: As long as the chefs know it is just a concept at the moment, I don't see why it wouldn't work. And you are right. I can get a feel for their personalities.

Ali: Thanks. Are you sure you don't mind me texting at this hour? It's just I thought about it and figured you should know – in case you had to change your schedule or something.

S MacO: You can text me any time. And if I am awake, I will respond. But promise me that if you are ever in trouble, actual trouble, you will phone. That way I will know it is serious and I will answer

right away. Agreed?
Ali: *Agreed. And thanks for agreeing to come over for the lunch, too. You're probably going to tell me you'll read their auras or something!*

The small dots indicating Gabe was typing paused and Ali waited, wondering how he'd take her joke. The dots started jumping again and then paused once more. That went on for several moments and she was beginning to wonder if he was writing a tome. Finally, a message popped up:

S MacO: *Why would you think that?*

Ali snorted. It took him that long to reply with *that* question? Had she somehow touched a nerve? *Do Native Americans read auras?* She wasn't even sure what that meant. She'd only been poking fun at him.

Ali: *Keep your shirt on, Highlander. I'm only messing with you. But now we're on the subject, what are you wearing?*
S MacO: *Excuse me?*
Ali: *You saw my text . . . Are you in your PJs? Or are you stretched out in bed, naked as a jay bird? I felt I should ask as "middle of the night texting" should always be just a little risqué, don't you think?*

Ali chuckled as she imagined Mr Strait-Laced reading that. She really enjoyed throwing him off guard. It was only fair. He did it to her all the time – though, she was pretty sure, completely unintentionally. His whole manner, his delivery – so old-fashioned and often clipped

– it reminded her of an old western TV star from the sixties. She wondered briefly where he'd gone to school. Where he'd learned that way of speaking. It was . . . charming. It threw her off. It kept her on edge, but not in a bad way. She wanted to make him lose his cool. To make him break his mould. She wondered if she could.

S MacO: As I am not a regular participant of "middle of the night" texting, I really couldn't comment on the extent of how risqué one should be. Ali: I'm still waiting for an answer . . .

The three little dots danced before her eyes again – starting, stopping. She held her breath. This could go badly. He could just shut her down. He'd be perfectly within his rights to do so, she knew that. But something just egged her on . . . A message appeared:

S MacO: The latter.

Oh. Dear. Lord. Ali swallowed, her throat suddenly dry. The image in her brain was . . . hot. So damn hot. *His long torso all tanned and muscly, shaped and sculpted . . .* Her phone binged again:

S MacO: You?

Well, shit. The man had balls, she'd give him that. And it served her right. A part of her had wanted him to shut her down, to call a halt. To remind her of their professional relationship. To remind her of her brother. Of how grossly inappropriate her question had been. She squirmed in bed, heat flowing to various normally dormant body parts.

Ali: Same.

Her phone stayed "silent" for several long minutes. Then:

S MacO: I will be in touch about the time on Thursday. Alex will be your bodyguard tomorrow. Go to sleep, Ali.

And he switched off from the conversation.

Unfortunately, sleep was the last thing on Ali's mind now, thanks to knowing he was naked in that big bed – a bed she'd seen and could all too vividly remember. *Only one thing for it.* She reached into her bedside table and grabbed her favourite toy. She sure hoped it was well charged – it was about to get a serious workout.

Gabe let the water stream over his body, its strong spray hot and pulsating. He groaned and ran his fingers through his hair. He'd known a literal cold shower wouldn't work, so he didn't even try. *How could it after that conversation?* He was no saint. He may have remarkable constraint in many ways, but he was still a man. Ali's question had been awkward enough and God knows why he'd answered it – and then asked his own question. He'd been a tired fool. Too sleep-deprived to make sound decisions. That was on him.

But, holy fuck. Ali naked in her bed? That slim, lithe creature swallowed up in a duvet all breathy and alone?

Too much. Too much of a vision for any man.

He'd just made it to the shower, his hand hard around himself, getting release the only way he could as the water poured over his tight skin. He felt on fire as he stroked himself – hard, fast, efficient. He needed her out of his head. He needed to stop imagining her beautiful body beneath his, *over his, wrapped around his.*

Gabe rarely swore. It wasn't the way he was raised, by either parent. His mother had never cursed in her life – it wasn't how she operated, how she communicated. She was always thoughtful and correct. Always polite and restrained. He'd never seen her really angry. Everything about her was contained. Compartmentalised. He himself spoke English in a variety of ways – always to suit the situation. In Scotland, or when speaking to family members from his paternal home, he fell into a natural burr. In Oklahoma, he allowed his American twang to emerge. And on the job, he spoke as neutrally as possible. But cursing was *not* his style.

His father, a hot-headed bull of a man, also, surprisingly, rarely swore. He had a fantastic command of the English language and preferred to show off his linguistic talents by using a variety of colourful phrases to get his point across. Plus, as he always said, he couldn't expect his tenants to respect him if he was using gutter language, as he called it.

Gabe used muse quietly over that, knowing full well that many of those men and women who owed their livelihoods to his father would have far preferred him to swear up a storm in words they could at least understand than wax lyrical in a ridiculously poetic manner. But his father was unlikely to change now.

87

Gabe had practised swearing as a teenager. Of course he had. And he became quite good at it. But spending time with men and women from various cultures throughout his adult life had found him referring back to his parents' ways. It didn't bother him when others swore, he admitted to himself as he shut down the shower and towelled off, that hearing Ali swear was tantalising and, *fuck it*, sexy as hell. He wanted her to use certain words, screamed out loud, as he slid in and out of her body. God, he was an animal. He was filled with lust for the young woman in his care and there was nothing, *nothing*, right about that. He had to get a grip on his galloping libido. Otherwise he was going to have to remove himself from the case. He was going to have to face Flynn.

Fuck, no.

That was not *going to happen.*

Chapter 7

Gabe parked his car and drew a long breath. He hadn't spoken to Ali since their night-time texting. He'd chickened out and sent one of his officers to observe from the background as she went about her business. It was just too much. How could he face her after being so unprofessional? What right did he have to make personal remarks to her? None was the answer to that. He knew she'd had her new ovens installed the previous day and had even given his "stand-in" some freshly baked goods. He wouldn't have minded some scones. *Petty, much?*

Letting out his breath and repeating the slow in and out process several more times helped to centre and calm him. He knew that once he entered her space and met those other competitors he'd have his senses on high alert, and that required supreme focus from him. Focus hadn't been his strong point around Ali Fitzgerald since meeting her and that had to change.

The room was filled with chatter and music. It was distracting and, at first, uncomfortable. Gabe opened his mind and tuned in – not to the actual sounds but to the atmosphere. He glanced about and spotted Ali near the centre island, a large meat cleaver waving about. *She could do damage with that,* he thought, and was strangely comforted by the thought. And he'd bet she wouldn't be afraid to use it, either.

She wore one of her new oversized, crisp white shirts belted at the waist with a swatch of brightly coloured fabric. When she stepped away from the counter to the fridge, he saw she was wearing black skin-tight leggings and flat black shoes. Audrey Hepburn sprang to mind – that gamine look suited Ali to a T. He wondered, *did she even know who Audrey Hepburn was?* He was showing his years, he mused as he wandered into the space. This might be the one area he could beat her in so-called modern pop culture.

"Hey, Jay Bird," Ali called out, smirking at him. "Everyone, this is one of the 'minders' Flynn has set on me. He's dark and dangerous, so don't get on his bad side. Just call him Scotty."

The grin she threw in is direction had his stomach clench even tighter. The Jay Bird reference had set it on fire as the forbidden images disregarded their allotted compartment in his brain and came flooding in. Nodding shortly at the hostess, Gabe walked about offering a hand to shake and noting each person's name. He was, of course, also cataloguing a myriad of other things, but he'd sort those out later.

Karl Murray was a wiry and nervy thirty-something. As handshakes went, it was unspectacular. Karl worked in a local restaurant doing nights only and admitted he'd really wanted the daytime gig. He'd worked in a kitchen with Ali several years earlier when they were both working their way up. He missed his daughter as he slept during the day and had to be in to prep things by 4.30 p.m. each day. Gabe opened his mind and listened inside to Karl's "noise". It was rumbling but not dangerous. It seemed Karl also had a penchant for a decidedly large selection of illegal drugs. And money problems. Maybe he was more desperate than he seemed.

Mary Rochford was a tall, striking woman in her early forties. She was business-like and professional as she told Gabe about her catering business and how much she thrived on the demand of it all. Ali had encountered her when Mary had put out a call for extra pies and tarts for a high-profile function and they'd hit it off immediately. Her cheekbones were tinged a delicate pink and her short dark hair had an aubergine hue. She was sharp and direct. These were not traits that bothered Gabe – everyone, regardless of gender, needed to be sharp in this cut-throat profession. He felt an odd sort of contentment float about her and instinctively struck her from his "to be watched" list. He wasn't concerned that it was a rash decision. He knew to listen to his gut.

The other two former competitors were in deep conversation as he approached them. Gabe swallowed, his throat suddenly itchy and dry. *Something wasn't right.* Instead of interrupting their intense discussion, he veered to the fridge and took a bottle of water. Uncapping it, he caught Ali's interested gaze. She gave him a "well?" look and he shook his head slightly. Her eye-roll was almost funny.

"Okay, everyone, *à table*, or in this case, à countertop."

Ali had set up the island space in a charmingly mismatched way. Each plate was a different colour, each set of cutlery a different style and each table mat a different pattern. It should have looked garish and crass but, because she had innate style, it didn't. The food was delicious. Shrimp tossed in garlic butter over angel hair pasta, green salads with baby Roma tomatoes, walnuts and feta, crusty bread to be torn apart and lathered with either butter or olive oil.

As each guest sat down to eat, appreciative noises and questions flew around the space. Chef questions that went over Gabe's head. Cooking times. Local sourcing. Age of the oil. *That was a thing?* He just bought the extra virgin olive oil in the shop and didn't think much about it. That was obviously sacrilege.

A fruity and light Pinot Grigio was served, but he stuck to sparkling water and focused on the job at hand. The two other chefs he hadn't met were to his left and began a long discourse, to the gathering in general, on the topic of Slow Food, promoting local produce and traditional cooking. It went over Gabe's head but allowed him the opportunity to listen closely to what wasn't being said.

Mel Carney, maybe fifty, the speaker, was short and rotund. He sported a long ponytail and several tattoos up his arms. He let off an agitated vibe that was heavily dosed with insecurity. And he had a habit of rubbing his nose rather frequently. Mel and Ali had also both shared a kitchen – in Temple Bar, when Ali had been in charge and running her own establishment. He was a great baker, according to himself, and he deserved to be the winner of the competition – no offence to Ali intended. None taken, Gabe agreed.

Blaine Whitehead, the fourth chef, was almost as tall as Gabe and although thin, was exuding strength and had only met Ali a few months earlier through a mutual friend. So, no history there, Gabe mused. Ergo, maybe no loyalty.

As the conversation dipped and swung from one to the other, Gabe discovered that Mel was from Belfast –

the accent was strong – and Blaine was from down under. His Australian delivery was brazen and loud. But he seemed taken with Ali and repeatedly tried to touch her, her arm, her shoulder, her back as he sidled up next to her.

To the untrained eye, Ali enjoyed the attention. But Gabe's eye was nothing if not trained. She hated it. The subtle movements that drew her away from his hands were infinitesimal but definite.

Her jaw tight, her lower eyelids raised, Ali called out brightly, "Dessert time!" and turned to gather platters from a sideboard.

Gabe began collecting plates and the others followed his lead. He organised the dishwasher and turned to find Ali looking directly at him.

"Feel free to rearrange," he said.

"You're good," she allowed and nodded. "Strategic. And space-smart. I like it."

He straightened, absurdly pleased. *I feel like I got a cookie from the teacher*, he mused as he helped to hand out small plates for dessert. *This is ridiculous.* But there was nothing ridiculous or quirky about the display of sweetness before them on the counter. Ali had done herself proud. A traditional pavlova filled with cream and berries – so simple but perfect. A pear and almond tart. Easy, she said, for beginners, but it looked like it would fit right in in a Parisian patisserie with its gloss and colour. She'd made Chantilly cream and had also served a bowl of fresh berries in case anyone preferred simple fruit and cream. Gabe watched her as she offered several selections to her guests and they all exchanged variations on the classic recipes.

Mel studied the pear tart. "Rather simple, don't you

think, Ali? Surely you want to challenge the students and you know, make good TV while they struggle?" He sniffed and wiped the end of his nose again.

"*Au contraire*," she said. "This show is about helping, not making someone who's never baked terrified of trying. Mary . . . " She turned to the tall woman, who appeared to be in a blissful state as she sampled the pavlova. "How long did it take you to get pastry exactly right, so you felt comfortable making it in a hurry for a surprise visitor?"

Mary swallowed, tapping her spoon against her chin. "Ah, let me see. I disagree with you, Mel. Pastry was my nemesis. It took me weeks. Karl?"

"I hear you. It's not easy. It requires confidence and practice. If your students master that, a whole world will open up to them. Pies, tarts, open shells. It will all be theirs. Good idea. I salute you." But his tone was a tad grudging.

"No ganache glaze or creating structures like the *Bake Off*?" Mel was incredulous.

Gabe had no idea what that was so stayed silent. Ali handed him a slice of pavlova and a spoon. He didn't have a sweet tooth and usually declined, but she threw him a look, so he obediently dug in.

Oh. Well now. The taste and texture that hit his tongue was staggering. *Soft, flaky, chewy like toffee. Berries that were both sharp and sweet. All the flavours.* He closed his eyes in pure ecstasy. He'd never tasted anything so decadent in his life. It was the lemon tart all over again but with a taste so different it was mind-boggling to the uninitiated.

The conversation between the other chefs continued but he realised, as he savoured his mouthful, that Ali was quiet. He opened his eyes to find her watching him. Intently. Nervously. *That was strange. She was the baker*

– the rising star. What on earth could make her nervous? She quirked her brow.

"It's . . . good. So good."

He didn't know the words to describe what he was tasting. How it made him feel. This was new to him. But, oddly, she seemed satisfied with that and with a slight smile, she turned back to her guests. Gabe inhaled the rest of the meringue and ventured a small slice of the pastry. More taste explosions. *Softer, gentler but no less flavoursome. Crisp pastry with solid yet moist pear and an overall hint of almond.* It was delicious.

The others were debating the merits of flaky over shortcrust for everyday use and they may as well have been discussing supernovas, for all that it meant to Gabe. He had a job to do and as he unobtrusively cleared and stacked plates, and wiped counters, and wrapped leftovers, he did what *he* did best.

He listened. And observed, discreetly.

Ali wiped her hands on the tea towel, hung it back on its peg and sat down wearily on the tall stool. The others had left and she was exhausted. She poured the last dregs from the coffee pot.

"So, Aura Man, what did you learn?"

She sipped on the almost cold brew as she studied the man across from her. *He was such an enigma.* He'd moved about her room calmly and quietly all afternoon as she and the other chefs chatted and argued over the best bakes for the show, most of them preferring their own versions over hers. Egos at large, she supposed. The tall Scot had barely spoken. But his presence, at least to her, *felt* huge.

She knew he enjoyed the food, the shrimp and salad,

but she'd been taken unawares at her own hesitancy when offering him her dessert. No idea why, but his pleasure at its flavour made her stomach flip and that was more concerning than anything. She knew he liked the lemon tart, but he'd barely sampled it before leaving. Ali watched him now as he pulled up a stool. He began rolling down his shirtsleeves and she rather wished he wouldn't – those forearms were a sight to behold. Not a body part she normally noticed, she was discovering that there were a lot of body parts, *his* body parts, that were annoyingly intriguing. Beguiling, even. *FFS*!

"They are an interesting collection of individuals, that is for sure," he began. "The only one who I genuinely feel we can remove from our list of antagonists is Mary. She has no malice towards you in any way. She is comfortable in her own skin and where she is at her stage of life."

"Does that mean the other three wish me harm?" *What an alarming thought.* "Is it because I'm female and I won over them?" she demanded, seriously pissed off. "Because if it is, those fuckers are *not* coming on my show. Jesus, it's the twenty-first century, for fuck's sake! Bloody boy children need to get over themselves. I mean, seriously, they can't hack a woman beating them? What the Jaysus does that say about *them*?"

And she was only getting started. Ali continued ranting about men, the size of their genitals, their brains – the same, in her opinion: tiny – their abilities as chefs, what they and their mothers could do with themselves, and several more-colourful epitaphs. Never one to hold back, she rose to her feet and had rounded the counter twice before she flopped back on the stool, rubbing her face with her hands in sheer frustration.

"I don't believe it has anything to do with your gender," he said calmly.

Ali glared at him. "So why did you let me rattle on?"

"It seemed like you had a lot on your mind, so I assumed you needed to remove it. Many of your points are valid. Many men are insecure in their new roles as the modern man. Mel, for example, feels completely emasculated by his wife. But that has nothing to do with you or your show. He simply feels he can never measure up – to anyone. He should practise Buddhism. Or yoga."

Scotty MacOsage reached for an orange and began methodically peeling it in one smooth, unbroken movement. Then he selected a napkin and placed the segments on it before offering them to Ali.

She'd been fascinated with his hands as they'd swiftly opened the fruit and she automatically took a piece, despite the fact that she rarely ate fresh fruit. A failing, she knew. *But we can't all be bloody perfect and eat super healthy all the time, although she did well, most of the time.* She glared at him again, resenting his control, his evenness. She felt like a jumbled mess inside and everything he did, every movement or gesture, was so weirdly calm that she wanted – really, really badly – to disrupt it. To ruffle it. To ruffle him.

"You seem awfully sure of yourself," she said grudgingly.

"Yes," he said. "I am."

"Why? I mean, how come?" She propped her chin in her hand, elbow on the smooth wooden surface. "Not the being sure of yourself part. What I really mean is how do you figure these people out? What's your trick?"

He looked at her in that way of his – unblinking, still.

"Trick?" His voice took on a soft yet steely edge.

She felt a shiver of unease skid down her spine at his tone. It sounded dangerous, despite its low volume.

"You know what I mean," she insisted.

"Trick?" he repeated. "Tricks are party magic, Ali. I do not trick people. I would never trick you."

"Jesus – sensitive, aren't you?"

And then she saw it. A slight flush on his high cheekbones. If she hadn't been staring at him so intently, she'd have missed it. He *was* sensitive about his "abilities", or whatever they were. And he didn't like being called on it, either. *Curious.*

"Okay. Fair enough. Not tricks. What, then? How do you read people? Flynn said you were originally brought over to be involved in some big secret kidnapping case and they now want to keep you for other covert work."

He stiffened. "Flynn needs to keep his mouth shut." A tic worked in his left jaw.

"Shit. Okay. He didn't tell me. I actually overheard a conversation he was having on the phone."

"Overheard?"

"You're like a frigging dog with a bone. Listened in then, all right? He had no clue I was sitting behind the wall. I'd slumped down exhausted after a workout and he was talking on the phone outside my open front door. He'd popped over for a chat about something, I can't remember what."

"I didn't know you worked out," was the only response.

"I don't. Hence the exhausted slump. I cycle, that's about it in the exercise scenario. I'm aerobically fit but can't lift weights for shit. But we diverge. How do you do whatever it is you do? Why did Flynn choose you for this case?"

"Your curiosity is admirable. Why Flynn chose me for

this assignment, I have no clue. All I will say is this. My grandmother and several more greats before her, on my father's side, all had what they referred to as the gift of sight. Usually the future." He heaved a sigh and rubbed his hand wearily over his jaw. He looked straight at her as he spoke. "Coupled with that, my mother has always had the ability to read people's feelings through touch. I appear to have got a version of that, too."

"Fuck."

"Indeed."

There was silence between them for a few moments as both absorbed the information. Ali was shaken. She figured it must be something in woo-woo territory, but hearing him say it . . . well, that was a reality she didn't want to acknowledge. It was scary. The very last thing she wanted was for him to read the shit-stir of a mess that was in her head.

"Do you see into everyone's head?"

"Absolutely not. I never intrude. Never. And if you must know, when Flynn calls on me to do some serious 'searching' for a crime scene, it is actually quite a challenge, internally, so I rarely do it for myself."

Ali reflected on what he was saying. But she needed to be sure.

"So, you don't know what I'm thinking right now, do you?"

A faint smile – oh so faint she almost missed it.

"I can imagine what you are thinking – it is what most people think if they discover what I can, on occasion, do. But it is not from my internal place of listening. I would just be hazarding a guess."

"Go on, then."

"You are most likely thinking that I am a freak of nature and not, in fact, to be trusted. You are probably thinking I am a secret thought-stealer and mind-reader. I am neither, but that never seems to appease anyone. Most people, when they know of my abilities, run a mile and never look back."

He blinked then. That solitary eye movement that had so fascinated her since she'd met him.

"I'm not most people," Ali said quietly.

"No."

He got up and found his jacket, shrugging easily into the navy wool. He walked round to stand in front of Ali as she sat at angles to the tall counter. He reached out and put his hands on her shoulders, gently. Firmly.

"I will never open my mind to yours unless it is for your safety or to do with the case. I give you my word. You can believe me or not, it will not change my behaviour. Thank you for today, for bringing everyone together. For giving me the chance to meet the others. I think it will bring forth merit. I am going back to the office to do some research on what I have discovered and I will be in touch." He squeezed her shoulders lightly and turned to go.

"What *did* you discover?" Ali asked, trying her best to ignore the heat where his hands had been.

"I will let you know in due course. JJ is on watch. You will be safe. Till next time," was his ambiguous reply and he shut the door behind him.

Ali wrapped her arms about her chest, a shiver running through her. Was one of the people who'd been here today responsible for damaging her property and causing havoc in her career? It was so hard to envisage. *Are people that crazy?* Of course they were, she answered her own speculation, but why her? She hadn't intentionally hurt anyone as far as she knew. Before they'd left she'd broached the subject of them coming on her show as guests and all had been enthusiastic and positive, so she had to go ahead with that, knowing one of them may, in fact, want to do her harm.

She walked over to the big window, now thankfully clear, clean and shining in the late afternoon light. Resting her forehead against the glass, she rubbed her hands over where his had been. She'd felt that touch to her bones. It hadn't been rough or overly strong, but she'd felt the warmth of his fingers as if they'd been digging into her flesh.

She'd also felt safe. That wasn't a feeling particularly relevant to Ali. She so rarely felt safe. *Not really. Not inside.* She shook her head as jitters began to take hold. She needed to go for a long cycle and lose herself in the speed and freedom of the two wheels beneath her.

She pulled back as splashes of rain hit the window. *Excellent.* Now she'd get soaked on her bike ride, but if she played her cards right, she'd end up at her parents' house just in time to scrounge some dinner. And a brandy. Her dad had the best brandy.

Gabe closed down his computer and collected together the pages of notes on the table into a neat pile. He stood, stretching his long limbs, and gazed about. It was dark outside and most of his colleagues were long gone. The night shift, skeleton crew that it was in his department, were settling in, powering up their machines and starting on their first coffees of the night.

Gabe's eyes focused in on Flynn's office. The frosted-glass compartment in the corner of the large workspace still had lights emanating from it, casting a soft glow in an otherwise bright room. Gabe frowned. *Did Flynn never go home?* Sure, he, himself, was still here at – he flipped his wrist over – 10.45 p.m., but Flynn never seemed to work regular hours.

Gabe walked over, tapped on the open door and entered. Flynn lifted his head from a stack of reports and grimaced.

"You, too?"

"Yes," Gabe admitted. "But at least I'm leaving now. How much longer will you be here tonight?"

"Another hour or so. What's up?" He pushed back in his chair and folded his arms across his chest.

Deceptively relaxed, thought Gabe. *That guy is always alert, always ready.*

"I have narrowed it down to two suspects. I need a warrant to search these properties . . . " Gabe handed over a sheet of paper with addresses printed on it. "And I need to dig a bit more into the finances of the second name." Another sheet of paper.

Flynn scanned the information. "Are you sure?"

"It is one or the other and I am leaning towards this one . . . " He tapped a finger on the left sheet. "I am going to make sure our suspect plays right into our hands."

"As long as my sister's safe, you can do it however you wish."

"She is safe. And she will be safe. I will not let anyone harm her. Not any more."

Flynn looked startled at that. "Any more?"

"I meant at all," Gabe corrected.

102

But as he left the building to head back to his apartment, he knew he *had* meant it. Without meaning to, without trying, without using any of his so-called gifts, he knew in his gut that Ali had been hurt and hurt badly at some stage in her life. He knew it was absolutely nothing to do with the case, absolutely none of his business.

But he was absolutely going to find out who was responsible.

The rain had settled in and was coming down in sheets by the time Mel Carney sidled down the appointed alleyway behind the pub. The Golden Goose was packed inside and crowds of smokers spilled out onto the pavement where the overhang kept them partially sheltered from the weather. He pulled his collar up against the elements and cursed the wait. He really wanted a hit and was testing himself to hold off till after the meet.

Bloody fecker, making him stand around as if he were Lord Almighty. It was late and dark and miserable, and he was getting seriously pissed off by the time the swanky car pulled to a halt. A tinted back window rolled down and a hand gestured Carney towards the vehicle. He shuffled forwards, cold, wet and now jittery.

"Have you my cash bonus?" he asked bluntly.

"All in good time, my dear fellow, all in good time." The voice that spoke from the depths of the car was cultured and educated, reeking of posh private schools from the south side of Dublin. "Up until now you have done precious little to earn a bonus, so I am not inclined to pay or reward you anything extra than what is accessible though the account set up for you and Garcia.

Tell me why I should indulge you since you have failed me so spectacularly."

Carney shuffled his feet but drew in a breath for confidence. "I'm in now – she's giving me a spot on the show. Well, all of us," he added in the interests of fairness. And fear that this man would find out he would not be alone. "But it was my idea," he lied happily, "asking her to include us so I can stay close to her." He shoved his hands in his jacket pockets as he tried for a nonchalance he was far from feeling.

"Ah, excellent. I will want regular reports as to what is going on. Garcia has proved almost as useless as yourself, but he has certain skills that may come in handy at a later stage." The man's voice was cool and controlled. Completely lacking in emotion.

"I'll keep you updated. I'll get Juan Garcia to pass on the info to you as I get it. No problem." He tried for bravado, unaware that he just didn't pull it off.

"And remember, Carney, if you are caught and questioned, you'd better stick to our prepared story about gambling and your nagging wife. And leave Juan Garcia and indeed my good self out of it. Or there will be consequences. Ones that will not appeal to you or your long-suffering spouse in any way. I trust I make myself clear?"

"You can trust me, I swear. But I did tell you I won't hurt Ali. I draw the line at that. She gave me a job when I needed one and while I'm happy to see her dreams of being a star thwarted, I won't cause her any harm. And you can't make me." He added that last bit defiantly and with more vigour than he'd shown so far.

"And aren't you the honourable gentleman?"

The voice was loaded with sarcasm, but Carney was

too agitated to recognise it. He wanted his reward and he wanted to go home. Now.

"You owe me. You said I'd get a bonus for extra. This is extra, me being close to her for the next few weeks. Pay up," he whinged and regretted it instantly as a heavy sigh emanated from the confines of the plush interior.

"Actually, I owe you nothing, you piece of scum. But I am pleased with the new development and expect every step she takes to be related back to me." A manicured, soft, fleshy hand appeared out of the open window, a brown package held towards Carney. "Your bonus and your *extras*, but don't expect me to deliver any more of that. All future engagements are to be via Garcia or by text on the phone I gave you. No more personal contact. And remember, you are on your own."

The hand withdrew, the window rolled up seamlessly and the car purred away.

Not much bloody use telling me to stay quiet – I've no fecking clue who you are, Mel Carney thought as he tore open the package and heaved a sigh of relief as he saw not only the wad of money but, more importantly, also the plastic sealed package that was his ticket to bliss.

Chapter 8

There were no more excuses, no more stalling, no more reasons to postpone. Her kitchen was ready. She was ready. Sure, the bastard who'd ransacked her place was still at large but, seemingly, Jay Bird had a plan – a trick up his sleeve to catch the guilty party – and Ali was just supposed to play along, all innocent and ignorant.

Yeah, well, fuck that.

She marched across the floor of the large, busy open-plan work area and with the slightest of knocks, she pushed Flynn's door wide open. *Oh, wouldn't you just know it.* Her brother wasn't alone.

"What? You need the boss to hold your hand, Jay Bird? To give you the green light? I demand to know what the state of play is." Ali threw herself into the chair next to the Scot's and glowered at him before turning that scowl on Flynn. "Tell me what's going down. If it concerns me, and it sure as shit does, then I've a right to know."

Her brother locked eyes briefly with his comrade. Sighing, he leaned forwards, his arms folded on his desk, and spoke.

"Mac wants the producer to do a selection of interviews with the morning chat shows talking about all that's happened." He caught Mackenzie's eye again and continued. "Basically, he'll say that in fact the vandalism has only heightened your fame and their dedication to you, then hopefully the perpetrator will be pissed off and make a final move. He'll most likely try to destroy your loft kitchen, but it won't happen, as we'll be ready for him. Catch him red-handed. No way out. Done."

Ali gaped at him and then turned to the silent figure next to her.

"That's a joke, right? You're definitely not putting Marc Bewley on TV singing my praises and making himself a target. Whoever is doing this to me could easily turn on those who support me. No effing way. He has kids, for fuck's sake."

"We don't think he'll be a target. We think it'll be the TV set," Flynn said steadily.

Or me. She kept that thought to herself, for now.

She straightened in her chair. "No. That's not acceptable. I'll do the interviews if necessary. And the bastard can come for me. I'm not letting some poxy producer deal with my shit. No way. It's either me or no one." She turned her fierce glare on both of them. "Got it?"

Flynn rubbed his hand behind his neck, frustration with her obvious in his every move. She didn't care. She was *not* backing down. Her way or no way. Seriously, who did these Neanderthals think they were, deciding what she could or couldn't do? That was so several millennia ago.

"Gabe can talk to the producers or hosts of the morning shows and arrange two interviews for tomorrow and Thursday. Your first filming is Friday, right?"

She nodded.

"Okay. But Mackenzie will be by your side till the creep makes his or her move. He'll tell you what kind of taunts to make, what simple but effective slurs you can use that will only be obvious to the actual culprit. It will go over others' heads." He turned to the still-silent man. "Do *not* leave her side. No more handing over your shifts to Alex or anyone else. It's you or no one."

Ali smirked at his unintentional repetition of her own determination to take control.

"So, Highlander, it's you and me against the world. How's that grab you? Hey, you leaving already? This was just getting interesting."

"Enough, Ali." Flynn tossed her a look as the big man rose from his seat. "Do you need anything?" he asked.

"No. I have it all in hand. I just need to tweak a few things now that your sister is . . . participating."

"You so want to say interfering, don't you, Doc?" Ali said.

"You do not want to hear what I actually want to say. Good manners, and your brother's presence, forbids it." He walked out of the room, closing the door sharply behind him.

"Hah! That's the equivalent of a temper tantrum for old Scotty MacScot," Ali snorted.

But she felt . . . *peeved.* Maybe a bit hurt. Perhaps he didn't want to spend time with her, even for work, even for her safety. She wished she knew why that sucked so much. Or, maybe she was simply overthinking things.

"You do know his name is actually Gabe Mackenzie, right?" her brother said sarcastically. "He's a highly decorated officer and has a brain that would put many of us to shame."

"Sure I do."

"So why do you insist on calling him anything but his name?"

"Where's the fun in that?"

Flynn sighed, but it was more of a soft laugh than an actual sound of weariness. "And Jay Bird? What's that about?"

Ali reared up from her seat and backed towards the door. "Trust me, brother, you do *not* want to know."

And she left, leaving the door wide open behind her to Flynn's frustrated, "Can you get the do . . . oh, never mind."

The shows went surprisingly well. Ali was prepared and the questions that the interviewer asked were leading. Which is what they wanted, Ali supposed.

"Yes," she agreed with the presenter, "my workspace was vandalised – twice, in fact – but it's obviously someone who has no clue who I am or who my family is." *Christ, she sounded like a twat,* but she knew that a sense of superiority was needed.

"And just *who* are you?"

She took a drink of water and laughed. "I am the person no one should mess with." She looked straight into the camera. "You can come at me as many times as you like, but nothing will stop me from doing my new show. Nothing and no one." She turned back to the presenter. "It's going to be great!" she enthused. "We have a great line-up of contestants – or students, I should say – and I'm intending to bring on my fellow competitors for guest slots, to add a bit of healthy rivalry to the mix."

"Is that wise?" The presenter knew his lines. "What if one of the former chefs, the ones you beat, is the person vandalising your premises?"

"Vigilante chefs?" She barked out a laugh. "Have you met these guys? No. They wouldn't. Not one them would actually have the balls – sorry, Mary – to be that audacious. They're chefs. Like me. Well, obviously not like me – I won!" she added, aiming for triumphant.

She felt even worse than she'd expected, mouthing off like that. She figured if Scotty thought one of them was responsible, she didn't mind hitting it home, but she did feel marginally bad for the others. The innocents. The ones who didn't carve into her oak counters or spray paint insults all over her walls. Or push her down the stairs. But needs must.

The following morning, she did another chat show with a similar line of questions and responses. Ali left the studio about 10 a.m. and headed straight to her loft. Leaning back on the closed door, she heaved a huge sigh. *Tomorrow. It would all happen tomorrow.* She'd point-blank refused to do rehearsals with the students. She knew her stuff and they didn't. That was the whole concept. The crew for her show would arrive in about two hours to start setting up lighting equipment and cameras plus all manner of paraphernalia, and all being well, they'd shoot the first two episodes tomorrow, two more on Monday and Tuesday, and every Monday and Tuesday after that till the season's collection was in the bag.

Peeling off the simple dress that Marc Bewley had insisted she wear for the TV chat show, she headed to the bathroom, where she kept a change of clothes. *Maybe I should move in here*, she thought as she had a quick shower. *It would be convenient.* On second thoughts, if the show was to take off, she'd constantly be tripping over work crews and TV people, and that was a step too far. She'd continue to stay in Caro's place and maybe, in time, buy her out.

She missed her big sister. There were reminders of her

and Toby in the flat and that pleased Ali no end, but she may have to redecorate, put her own stamp and style on things, if Caro really and truly moved to Rome. It was certainly on the cards.

After drying herself, she wandered back into the kitchen area and yelped in surprise. He was sitting on a stool, *cool as you like*, sipping a glass of water.

At her entrance, he eyed her thoughtfully and said, "You really ought to, a) actually remember to lock your door, and b) get dressed before wandering about in an open space."

Ali crossed her arms over her chest, having fortunately tucked the large fluffy towel about her before leaving the bathroom.

"And you ought to remember your manners and knock!" she snapped. "Jesus, JB, you nearly gave me a heart attack."

If anyone, thought Gabe, *was going to have a heart attack, it will be me.* She had no business wandering about in a towel – *one that hit her mid-thigh, showing off slim but shapely legs. And shoulders . . . God, her shoulders were still damp and her collarbone was begging to be licked – a little drop of water nestling in that dip in the centre.* He swallowed and shifted slightly on the stool to a more comfortable position as his body responded to the sight of a near-naked Ali.

"I did knock," he said somewhat hoarsely and cleared his throat. "But the shower obviously drowned it out. Since the door was unlocked, I thought I had better see if you were home or if there was, in fact, an intruder. My apologies for frightening you."

111

"You didn't frighten me," Ali said as she pulled up a stool beside him.

Oh. Not a good idea. The towel fell open between her thighs and the soft, dewy skin drew his eyes like a magnet. He shifted on the seat again.

"I just wasn't expecting anyone."

"All the more reason to lock the door. Especially after your performance on the show earlier."

He knew his tone sounded grim and it irritated him that she could make him feel unnerved.

"How do you think it went? Was I enough of a bitch?"

He heard, very clearly, the disgust in her tone.

"It was your idea to do it," he reminded her patiently.

"Fuck it, I know."

She leaned forwards, her towel doing all manner of seductive things that allowed him to see a hint of cleavage and a bigger expanse of skin on her upper legs. *This was not going well at all.*

"But I hate being such an obvious jerk, you know? I want the audience to *like* me. God," she groaned, "I sound pathetic."

Her head dropped into her hands and he instinctively stretched out his own hand to lay it gently on her shoulder. She froze. He could feel it. Instantly. He withdrew his hand immediately but, *damn*, he could feel the tingles on his fingers where they'd touched her, however briefly.

"You are not remotely pathetic," he said. "What you are is brave and forthright. You said nothing that anyone could consider rude or arrogant. No, that's a small untruth, you were a little rude and somewhat arrogant. But, more importantly, you sounded confident and self-assured. And ready to take on the bastard who hurt you, and the viewing public."

She looked up, straight into his eyes. Held them.

"You said bastard," she almost whispered. "I don't think I've ever heard you swear before."

"I swear," he said, keeping her eyes on his. "When it is needed. Or justified."

"And it's needed now?"

"I think so. It seems like you need reassurance and I don't want you second-guessing yourself. It is not you."

"Oh, it's me. At times. I just don't normally show it. You . . . " she paused. "You make me honest. And I don't like it," she grumbled.

"I don't like some of the things you make me, either, so we are quid pro quo," he said quietly, not really intending her to hear.

She cocked her head at that. "Oh? Expand, please."

"I think it would be better if I just go. You have crew arriving, don't you?"

"Chicken," she said, her eyes not leaving his. "Do I make you do or feel things? What kind? Good? Bad? Tell me."

"No, Ali. I need some sanity left when I am around you. Baring my soul will not, I assure you, help."

"But it would help me," she whispered. "I need to know that you don't think I'm a jerk or a selfish brat or whatever else I'm afraid you think of me. I can imagine all manner of juvenile offences I may have committed and right now, this minute, I need to hear something positive. Tell me."

There was a beat of silence as Gabe digested what she was asking. Ali needed him. Now. To help her feel better. It was his job, he reasoned as he stood from the stool.

His duty. He was, in fact, he concluded in some very unused section of his brain, obligated to help.

"How about I show you instead?"

Nudging her thighs apart, he stood between her legs and reached out to cup her face in his hands. Tilting her head, he stared into her eyes, his racing heart a secret he was glad she couldn't see.

"Tell me no," he said.

"Yes," she countered, her voice soft, barely there, but he heard it.

Slowly, so slowly she could pull back at any time, he leaned down to let his lips brush her cheeks, first one, then the other. He angled her head slightly and finally let his mouth show her everything. Slow and gentle, his lips touched hers, again and again. Soft, like thistledown. Even with that slightest of touches, the shot of need that speared his groin had him groan in the back of his throat.

Her lips parted and he took her mouth. One hand remained steady at her chin, the other cupped the back of her head as his mouth and tongue discovered her soft, secret places. Keeping it as light as he could, using every ounce of control he had, Gabe kissed this gorgeous woman as if *her* life depended on it, not his. This was about her and what she needed. Not him. *Liar.*

His tongue curled urgently around hers, in and out, exploring the heat and texture of her. Ali matched him, her hands reaching up to grab his shirt front. In a haze, he could feel her thighs grip his and pull him closer. Some remnant of sanity warned him that if their bodies touched, if he felt her heat against his straining body, all bets would be off. He'd lose control entirely and they'd be lucky to make it to the couch. *Hell,* his libido was yelling in his head, *just haul her up onto the counter – it would be the perfect height for you to lay her out and simply take her.*

But, no. Visions of her vulnerability earlier wouldn't disappear and he would absolutely *not* take advantage. *God,* his blood was racing, and it took a monumental effort to ease out of the kiss and pull back. Unable to pull away entirely, he rested his forehead on hers and tried to regulate his breathing. Her hands were still bunched in the fabric at his chest and he imagined she could feel every beat hammering against his skin.

"I definitely should *not* have done that, but I won't lie and say I am sorry." His voice sounded strained, even to his own ears. "And I had better go before I do it again."

He began to pull back, but Ali gripped him a second longer.

"Give me a minute," she said unsteadily. "I need to find my feet."

She let out a long breath and slipped down off the stool, bringing them flush against each other's bodies, and Gabe instantly put space between them. Ali let go of his shirt and gripped the top roll of her towel.

"Thanks for not apologising." She let her gaze fix on his. "That would have really pissed me off."

Gabe pressed his lips together to prevent a smile. *That was so typical.*

"Duly noted," he said and carried his empty glass to stack in the dishwasher. "Good luck this afternoon. I will see you at the filming tomorrow."

He walked unhurriedly to the door and let himself out.

Process. Process. Process. Ali paced the bathroom floor, her trembling fingers pressed to lips that still pulsed from the feel of his mouth. *What the actual fuck?* His kiss had seared her. Knifed into her like gutting a fish. Okay, maybe not that gruesome but, *God,* she'd felt it in every fibre of her body. She'd been telling the truth about finding her feet – she was afraid her knees would give way. And it hadn't even been a ravaging kiss, or one of monumental passion and energy. It had simply undone her in its directness, coupled with sweetness and a dash of tenderness. *And sparks. Lots of little sparks.* Tummy drops – they were there, too.

Aw, shit, who was she kidding? It had oozed passion.

Ali normally rated kissing as part of sex at a four out of ten, the odd time a five. She rarely kissed anyone unless it was part of sex. No dates with a kiss at the end of the night, leading to the anticipation of some heavy petting, followed several dates later with actual sex. *No. That wasn't her style.* If she wanted sex, she went for it – if the guy wasn't interested, so be it. She didn't do romance or relationships. It was a "use 'em and lose 'em" deal and it worked just fine for her. Kissing the Scot had *not* been in the plan.

Big, fat lie.

Of course it was in the plan – hadn't she been angling for that since Dev's wedding?

But she expected it to be of her time and her choosing, swiftly followed by time spent in the sheets and then an equally swift cheerio. But, she was slowly learning, things with this particular chap didn't fit the mould. And it both bugged her and intrigued her.

What now? Would he follow up with more? Did she want more? *Hell, yes.* But it was complicated – *yeah, that old adage.* Not only was he supposedly watching over her, but he was also a colleague of Flynn. And there was no way anyone who worked with Flynn would mess around with one of his sisters.

She didn't have time to think about it now. The crew were due to arrive and she needed to be on the ball. Not just for that, but in case her interviews had sparked any rumblings in the bad guys. *More time-will-tell shite.* Ali just wanted to take the bull by the horns and ask the competitor chefs what the fuck they were playing at.

After shrugging into jeans and a vest top with a large wool sweater, she wandered back out into her space. Turning slowly, she appraised all the work that had been done in a relatively short time. It was clean, freshly painted, well-laid-out and bright. It was a lovely kitchen setting and she was damn proud. The next bollocks who came and tried to mess up her space had better be ready for a little fish-gutting – and not in any "passion ripping through a body" way but a seriously mean and painful way. She placed the kiss firmly in the "do not disturb" box in her brain and took a deep, cleansing breath. She was ready.

By the time Gabe got back to his office to collect his various warrants, two for the specific premises and the other for the finances of one of the individuals, he'd had some measure of control. It had taken every ounce of training to make himself walk out of that door. *She'd tasted like . . . damn, every good thing, ever. Sweet, soft, lush, spice and pepper.* All the awareness that had flooded his senses had almost invaded his mind and body, but he'd held it back. It wasn't the time – it was *never* the time to "read" another person unless they were in danger. Ali hadn't been in danger – except maybe from him. And that was nothing to do with psychic ability – that was pure male lust.

He'd never let that side of his psyche open to invade a person's thoughts without their permission. And he wasn't about to start now. That mantra had been drummed into him when he'd first discovered the blasted "gift". How anyone could think feeling someone's anguish or sadness or fear was a present of some variety was beyond him. He knew, logically – although that word was rarely applied to his brand of detecting – that he'd helped countless people back to safety. He hadn't been able to save them all and those losses never went away, but they were his losses now – as much, if not more so, as the ones he'd saved. He'd learned, with time, how to compartmentalise the loss, the failures, but it never got easier. It was still, always, to his way of thinking, his fault. His burden to bear.

Striding to his desk, he rubbed a hand over his jaw, unintentionally touching his mouth. The mouth that had experienced the most memorable kiss he'd ever had. She'd felt like bone china under his fingers, delicate yet built to last, her skin almost vibrating with need. He loved that she'd kissed him back, been as affected as he was. He'd sincerely appreciated her desire for more when she'd attempted to pin him with her thighs.

It had almost killed him to walk away, but walk away he must. How he was going to face her later was beyond him. He ought to stay in his car all night and not knock on the door to let her know he was on watch duty. They needed some distance. Sure, Alex or Carlos could take the watch, they were excellent at their jobs and highly skilled, but he'd promised Flynn.

118

After collecting the warrants from Lorraine at the central desk, he powered up his computer and began to search. Money was a great and enduring temptation – up there with passion. He'd bet his considerable experience that this case was based on power and prestige – both of which would be attached to Ali's name shortly and not to the remaining competitors. Now, all he had to do was be sure which one of them needed one or other of those that would make a person so greedy for it that they'd cause damage.

Gabe was concerned that if the perpetrator didn't make a definite move this evening, he was likely to cause mayhem on the set when they were invited on. While it would be excellent to catch him with his hand in the cookie jar, pun intended, it may cause bad press for Ali. Mind you, social media being what it is, it was just as likely to send her ratings sky high. But if the chef concerned hadn't figured that out, he may still play the waiting game till his turn as a guest chef. And God knew what trick he might pull to have Ali disgraced or "shown up" on set, even if he were to get caught out. All Gabe could do, for now, was wait and try to figure out the end game.

Chapter 9

Lights! Camera! Action! Those exciting words would never get old, Ali mused as she waited on a stool while a make-up artist touched up her face. Each time she heard those words she now knew it meant dabbing on non-shine powder. Shiny faces were a big no-no on TV, it seemed. God forbid anyone's skin glinted onscreen. She'd barely slept and cursed her excitement about the "big day", and her reliving of a certain kiss over and over. She wasn't sure which she could blame more but figured both deserved some dubious credit.

Her working day had begun at 6 a.m., when she'd arrived to let in her crew. God, she loved saying that – *her* crew. What an extraordinary privilege she was living and she'd bloody well *not* take it for granted. Not for a second. She was determined to work hard and produce the goods, both literal and metaphorical.

As she'd swung her leg over the crossbar at five forty-five, the cool dawn barely hinted its presence. She was sure she saw Highlander's jeep parked opposite her doorway across the street. But before she could cycle over, the car took off and she was left doubting she'd even seen it.

It was nine thirty now and he was nowhere to be seen. So much for not letting her out of his sight. She sighed. Had she freaked him out yesterday? He'd certainly seemed his usual "odd as two left feet" self as he'd strolled out of her door the previous morning. *Cool as a breeze. Not a care in the world.* While *her* stomach had been a skipping rope and her skin had felt like it was the most tender thing about her.

So far so good with today's schedule, though, so Ali could begin to ease the tension in her shoulders a smidgeon. The contestants were a delight: four women and two men, ranging in age from twenty-three, one of the males, to a great-granny and self-confessed baking disaster in her early seventies. Mavis, the granny, was pure Dub. Her accent was so strong one of the production assistants posed the real possibility of having subtitles on the screen. *Jesus,* Ali hoped it wouldn't come to that as the inner-city Dublin vernacular was a charm all of its own. She'd already begun repeating anything Mavis said, as if the others hadn't heard her, so as not to embarrass the woman, but she couldn't do that for everything. Archie, the other man in the group, was the opposite end of the scale when it came to accents and sounded like he had several hot potatoes in his mouth while speaking. He also twirled his handlebar moustache like a fictitious army colonel. It was going to be fun, there was no doubt about that.

"You're on," called the assistant.

Ali thanked the make-up girl, put her apron back on and strolled back on the set. This was her milieu, her domain. She could bake with a blindfold on and loved showing others how to take the fear out of it.

"So," she began, gathering her "students" about her, "let's get back to scones."

Gabe watched. And was awed. She was a natural, no doubt about it. That Bewley man knew exactly what he was getting: TV gold. Gabe had slipped in between takes and stayed in the background. It was almost noon and he'd swung back to his flat early that morning after his shift, when he'd seen Ali leave for work. He'd crashed for a few hours, showered, grabbed some eggs and toast then come straight here. All had been quiet outside her home last night, but it had soothed him to be there. Knowing he was the one guarding her. Choosing not to analyse that little nugget of self-awareness any further, he neatly compartmentalised it in the "don't go there" file somewhere in his brain.

Ali moved about her television kitchen in the loft like she owned it, which of course she did. Her natural, friendly, cheeky way of dealing with her budding bakers was a winner. Her often irreverent humour was tempered slightly, never hurful or sharp – she was just being herself, minus the swearing. It amused him to see she could put together whole sections of conversation and not curse once. Maybe he did bring it out in her.

That Mavis character was a hoot and sure to be a public favourite. This show wasn't a contest – not as such – and none of these students would get the boot as the weeks progressed. But, like all good TV, there would be angst and joy, tears and laughter. That was a given.

Ali had shown him an outline of the first eight shows and how they were to be combined with inter-student competitions, the guest chefs doing their thing and the students judging *them*. Camera crews would also visit the students' homes and film them trying out their new skills in their own kitchens. There was plenty of opportunity for the viewers to garner favourites and there would be an overall baker gold star awarded at the end, based on fifty per cent Ali's decision and fifty per cent the public's.

Ali hadn't wanted that part. "What the fuck does the public know about the bakes? They can't taste or feel them," had been, not surprisingly, her immediate response. She'd had to compromise. Gabe wondered why anyone would "feel" baking. Ali had proceeded to explain. *See?* Even he was learning.

She was mesmerising. As she flitted from baker to baker, helping with the "crumbing" of butter and flour, she engaged with each person on set. She even threw laughing comments at the crew, making everyone else laugh and relax instantly. Definitely a star in the making. Gabe could only imagine what she must look like on the screen. To that end, he edged his way to where the show's director was set up, moving silently and slowly so as not to throw anyone off.

His height, an advantage for peering unobtrusively over an unsuspecting shoulder, was a pain in the rear when it came to discretion. Gabe had learned how to blend, to slump and disappear among others when he had to. And there she was. The small visible area of the monitor wasn't great from his perspective, but even he could see she lit up the screen. He felt a wholly unexpected burst of pride. *She was killing it.* He barely knew this woman, but he was already beyond invested. He really, really needed to be careful. With her. With himself.

They took a lunch break and after some huddled discussions among the producer and students, Ali broke away, turned her head casually about the loft space and, spying him, stilled for a second before sauntering in his direction. She wore a smirk and a raised eyebrow. It was enough to know she'd be full of snark and smartassy. Gabe could feel his mouth twitch in anticipation.

"Well, sleepyhead, you eventually got your fine ass out of bed and remembered your duty. I thought you were supposed to be watching over me?"

She looked different. More. A sharper version of herself.

He took his time, letting his gaze wander over her face and clothes. Her make-up was strong – camera-ready, he assumed. She didn't need it, but even he was aware enough to know that some women wore a ton of cosmetics just to ensure they looked like they weren't. Her gorgeous blue – *pure cornflower blue* – eyes were lined in black and they looked even more stunning than normal. Little sweeps flicked out from the corners and her pale pink lips were an unusual but oddly successful contrast.

She wore an oversized, crisp, plain white shirt with long tails and a pair of those black leggings he'd helped her to purchase, with simple shoes – those, he wouldn't even attempt to name, though they were probably a very "in" style. They were flat, had some kind of buckle and were . . . *ah, red.* The outfit was covered with what he assumed was an old-fashioned apron that had flowers splattered over it and some had definitely, at one time, been red. *A nice touch.* He brought his eyes back to hers. *Not a hard choice.*

"I was watching over you."

"Could have fooled me," she said, eyebrow still up. "No sign of you here this morning when I let myself in. Anyone could have jumped me. Should I tell my big brother you're not up for the long hours?"

"I *was* watching over you," he repeated quietly, "all night. And Alex took over, following you to this very place, where he relieved Carlos, who was stationed in the alley all night." He folded his arms across his chest and waited.

"Oh. I thought I saw you. But you just drove off before I could say hi. Seems a bit cavalier to me."

"My shift was over, but let me assure you, I take your safety very seriously. Not a cavalier bone in my body." He reached out and stroked a finger down her cheek. "You are safe, I promise."

She stood very still, her own hand going up to touch where his finger had been.

"I know – I'm just messing with you." But her voice sounded slightly unsure. "I thought you'd be here to see the start of the show, but no worries, you probably would have been bored anyway." She shrugged a shoulder negligently.

"I am of no use to you if I am running on empty. I needed to catch some sleep. But I have been watching you entrance these beginners into believing in themselves. That is some feat."

Her face changed in a flash. "Aren't they great?" she enthused. "So brave, so full of balls. Well, maybe not all of them, but Mavis has enough to go around."

He huffed out a laugh. "That Mavis is certainly viewing fodder," he said. "You handle her very well."

"Funny you should say that – she's cut out of my great-aunt Kathleen! Now there was a woman who could eat you up, spit you out and come back for more. And in a fun way, too." Ali shook her head. "She was a trip."

"Sounds like you have it all under control. Any word from your fellow chefs, those under suspicion, specifically?"

"Texts from them all, wishing me good luck, each more ass-licking than the next. They all want a slot on the show now that it's had some publicity. Even Mary, though she kept hers simple. Men are such shits, you know?" She paused. "I'm supposed to say present company excepted, aren't I? Well, the jury is still out on you, so don't get too complacent."

"I wouldn't *dream* of it," he assured her.

"Just because you can kiss like a dream doesn't give you a pass," she added as she turned when her name was called by the TV studio caterers to go and get the food laid out for lunch. "And don't get big for your boots with that compliment, either."

"Duly noted re the hung jury and I would never assume a pass."

She narrowed her eyes at him as he spoke.

"I understand I have my work cut out for me."

Her lips twitched, holding back a smile before she turned to walk away as he continued.

"I will try harder. Next time."

She stilled. Glancing back over her shoulder, she said, "Next time? Don't promise what you can't deliver, Highlander. I'll be expecting greatness now."

"Trust me," he said and had the satisfaction of seeing a slight flush on her cheeks right before she was grabbed by a production assistant and dragged off.

He was playing with fire. He knew it. It was wrong.

Somehow, he just didn't care.

Going home. What is it they always say? Is it that you can, or you can't? And whoever "they" are surely have it as a flexible maxim, because everyone knows it can vary from situation to situation, person to person, time to time. Ali opened the back door of her family home and kicked off her shoes in the mudroom, as they called it. It was such a clever term really, given it was for outdoor shoes and boots, an Americanism introduced to them all by Frankie when she first came to visit as a child. She pulled down the slippers always stashed in the wicker basket on the shelf and opened the door to the kitchen.

Yes, she thought, *you can definitely go home again.* Well, in this family you could. It smelled like . . . *coffee, Italian sauce and polish. Home.* She reached for the kettle, filled it and yelled out of the hallway door.

"I'm home. Kettle's on. Who wants tea?"

She pulled a selection of mugs off the dresser hook – all the fine bone china ones because, well, it's tea – and raided the biscuit tin. *Hmm. That was disappointing. Only digestives.* She'd been hoping for a Jersey Cream. *Now there was a thought.* She whipped out her notebook from her satchel and scribbled down a few thoughts on biscuit baking. *Who didn't love a home-made shortbread or lemon square?*

"Hi, darling," her mother said as she breezed in, a load of ironed napkins in her hands.

Jo Fitzgerald was in her mid sixties and kept herself trim and fit. Her lightly coloured hair was cut short and sassy with streaks of grey peeping through. She wore a pair of old jeans, a blue cardigan open over a white T-shirt and woolly socks. She dumped the cloth napkins on the kitchen table and reached for her middle daughter.

"Come here, you," she said, her voice warm, and wrapped her arms tightly about Ali, breathing her in. "You are the best of daughters," she continued, "and we are so proud of you."

"We are." Ali's dad strolled into the kitchen just then

and glided his hand gently over the top of her head. "Well done on your first day," he said.

"How do you know I did well?" Ali disentangled herself from Jo's embrace and began making tea.

"Because you do everything well," he said as if she'd asked a silly question.

"The others are coming for dinner in a bit," her mum intervened, "so not too many sweet things, please. That's directed at you, Patrick," she said as she saw him remove his hand from the tin, several digestives clutched in his palm.

He smiled at her benignly and took the tea from Ali. Unfazed by his wife's comments, he sat at the table and began dunking the crumbly offering in the hot liquid.

"Mum's right, Dad," Ali agreed with Jo. "I bet this isn't your first snack of the day. You've got to watch your figure."

Ignoring the intended barb at his slightly thickening waistline, Patrick just smiled. "So, tell us everything," he said.

Ali did. As she chatted, filling them in on the day's filming, she and her mum fell into a well-established routine. Ali laid the table using the fresh napkins, putting out a selection of colourful cutlery and table mats. She added the salad bowl from the fridge, topped up the dressing with some more extra olive oil and honey, and began slicing a stick of French bread. Jo busied herself taking out a large tray of lasagne and slicing it into sections. Then she grated Parmesan and chopped coriander, cucumbers and tomatoes to be added to the salad greens.

"Smells great, Mum," Ali said as she inhaled the aroma.

A door slammed down the hallway and a cacophony of voices drifted through.

"Oh, good, they're here. They didn't all reply to the

128

WhatsApp message, so I wasn't sure how many to expect," Jo said. "Darling, please do the drinks." She turned to her husband, but he was one step ahead, uncorking a Rioja and, naturally, sampling it.

He set it on the table to breathe as he uncorked a second. Ali grabbed a white Viognier from the fridge and poured a small amount into both her own and her mum's glass.

"Before the madness, can I just toast you two, please?" Ali spoke quickly. "I don't want a big fuss, but I do want to say thank you for believing in me. For always supporting me, even when I changed my career direction. It means a lot." She clinked glasses with her parents, two thoroughly decent adults who were everything to her.

"Ah, pet, you don't have to thank us! You're the one with all the talent and creativity. We'll always support you and believe in you." Her mum smiled and then headed to the door to let in the rest of the gang.

Ali took a sip of delicious cool wine and stamped down the tiny traitorous thoughts that often raised their ugly heads at the most inopportune moments. *They believed in her abilities, but would they have believed in her then? Back when she'd needed their support, their safety net. But, well, she'd never know, would she?*

Her sister Molly grabbed her in a big hug and promptly held out a glass for Patrick to fill with the now almost room-temperature red wine. Molly's hair was in a wild tangle about her head but held back with a paisley silk scarf. She was the epitome of the artist she was. Almost a year graduated from art school, she worked in a snazzy art gallery in the city centre and was always out, day or night, at shows and exhibitions, and seemed to be living the dream of the young artist about town.

PAMELA G. HOBBS

Her clothing was as eccentric as she was. Flowing skirts and tunics, colourful tights and boots, jackets garnered from vintage shops and scarves of all the colours and patterns of the spectrum. Despite her bright appearance, Molly was the quietest of the Fitzgerald gang and maybe, Ali often thought, her dress sense was her way of letting herself be heard.

Molly turned her aqua-coloured eyes on her older sister and grinned. "So, TV star, how do you feel now that you're on the rise to fame? Can I have your autograph so I can sell it on the internet in a few months?"

"Feck off," Ali replied, giving her a gentle shove. "I'm not letting you make money off me. Go make your own."

"Selfish as ever, I see." Dev reached around her shoulders and gave a squeeze. "Already a prima donna and the show not even a day old." He shook his head in mock disgust as he kissed her lightly on the cheek.

"You feck off as well," Ali replied, hugging him back. "Hi, Frankie," she added as the vision of beauty walked into the kitchen, unwrapping herself from her plum-coloured knitted coat.

Francesca Jones was a stunner. No one could or would argue that fact. She just was. Lithe and lean, with a cloud of short dark mink hair and amazing grey eyes, she had cheekbones that should be patented. The long, thin pale scar down one cheek did absolutely nothing to distract from her beauty and had been earned in a particularly nasty series of events the previous summer.

Now married to Dev, Frankie was official – she'd got her "wings", so to speak, the name Fitzgerald tagged onto her own. She'd been a "sort of" sister to them all from the age of ten, having spent every summer in the

130

Fitzgerald home after her mother was killed, and was Caro's best friend.

Ali hugged her now, the embrace warm and real. Maybe more so than it used to be. Now Caro was living in Rome, these last few months she and Frankie had grown closer. They'd never been at odds, just not the best buds that the older girls were. There was no jealousy there. But Ali harboured some wayward dark thoughts about Frankie, ones that could be potentially damaging to their present relationship should they ever come to light, so she made sure they didn't. And, truthfully, the circumstances of that hidden place were not of Frankie's doing, so Ali kept that door firmly locked.

She loved her new sister-in-law, and loved even more seeing how happy she and Dev made each other. Her once short-tempered, hot-headed brother had settled. Not settled down, *God, no*. But in himself. He was still easy to rouse to a healthy argy-bargy, but he had a peace about him now that in retrospect no one had known was really missing. It was the Frankie part of his heart. And he wore it well.

"Whoop-whoop!" Frankie squealed, releasing Ali from the hug. "Go you, Ali Fitzgerald, baking star. How did it feel under the lights? It's awful, right?"

She tugged Ali over to plonk beside her on a small two-seater against the back wall of the kitchen, shoving aside some knitting and a stack of magazines. Jo swooped in and grabbed the tangled wool and needles.

"Don't mess with my creations," she scolded and had the women groaning.

"Ah, Jaysus, Mum, not again." Ali heaved a large sigh. "You know you're crap at these craft things. Stop trying. And stick to what you're good at."

131

"It's never too late to learn," Jo replied, a stubborn tilt to her chin.

Patrick appeared at her side, an arm sneaking around her waist.

"Don't mind them, my Josephine, you're multitalented, in all the ways that count. Come, let me top up your wine."

He guided his wife away, but not before winking broadly at the two on the couch snorting with laughter.

"God, Dad's a hoot. He's so supportive, but I don't know how he puts up with all of her new projects." Ali sipped her wine and sat back against the cushions, relaxed and content, safe in her own home.

"I think Patrick's a darling," Frankie said wistfully, even a little proudly.

Ali was instantly reminded of Frankie's own very serious daddy issues that had almost ended in all kinds of tragedy not that long ago.

Frankie brushed her fingers lightly down her scar, straightened her shoulders and turned back to Ali. "Now, tell me *everything*. You know I love film-set gossip."

Once more, Ali recounted all about her day, the lights, cameras, action and all the anecdotes about the contestants. She was good at telling stories, had a sharp eye and a good ear for nuance and accents, so made them all laugh. As soon as she'd started on the retelling, both Molly and Dev had joined them. Molly dragged over one of the kitchen chairs and Dev had propped himself on the arm of the couch next to his wife.

Dev drank a craft beer straight from the bottle with one hand, the other resting along the top of Frankie's back, his long fingers lazily circling her bared skin at the

132

join between neck and shoulder. Even as she continued her often caustic recounting of her day, Ali felt a ripple of envy. Not for her brother – *ew, no, that would be just weird* – but for the odd yet lovely mixture of sizzle and serene these two brought out in each other.

It was extremely annoying. *Untrue. It was extremely misery-making.* To her. It was something she could never, ever have. She knew that deep in her gut and accepting it was fucking hard. Especially at times like this. But Ali was nothing if not realistic, so she told another story, slagging off both herself and her inexperience like she didn't have a care in the world. Armour in place, ready to roll.

Jo called them to the table and the ensuing mayhem and grab for chairs was ridiculous, because they always sat in the same spots. They each had their own napkin colours and even, for the more picky among them – looking at you, Molly Fitzgerald – specific cutlery.

"Where's Flynn?" Ali asked, noting the extra place settings. "And why is there an extra plate?"

"I added the extra," Jo said as the front door closed in the distance and footfall sounded on the tiled surface.

Voices rumbled, deep and indistinct. Ali felt a tingle creep along her arms and the back of her neck. *Fuck.* She knew.

"Sorry we're late," Flynn said as he entered the kitchen. "Work kept us." He walked straight to Jo, planted a soft kiss on her head, laid a hand on Patrick's shoulder and then ruffled Ali's hair. "Good job today, brat." He turned to the silent, tall dark-haired man who stepped into the kitchen behind him. "I think most of you met Gabe Mackenzie at the wedding, but just in case . . . everyone, this is the detective who's keeping a watchful eye on our baking queen as she deals with the latest break-in at the loft. I trust him with my life, hence he's the one I chose for Ali. Take a seat, Mac."

The Scot shook hands with both of her parents as Ali seethed quietly in her chair. *Well, hell.* Now, her food would churn in her belly. She wanted one, *just one fucking evening* where she didn't have to think about this damn man who insisted on invading her brain space at the oddest times. Her family was so boisterous she'd figured here would be perfect.

And yet *here* he was.

He took the chair beside her. *Good.* She wouldn't have to look at him and his smouldery, sexy, weird-as-shit green eyes.

"Breathe," he said softly next to her ear and placed a firm hand gently on her knee beneath the table.

That was when she realised she'd been holding her breath since the second he'd entered the room.

She whooshed out a breath and instantly dragged in another as the fingers on her leg, even through her jeans, felt like the best kind of heat her skin had ever felt.

She was royally screwed. *And, God, she wished she was, in all senses of the word.*

And there went her digestion.

Chapter 10

The food was delicious. The collective gang of Fitzgeralds were friendly, the conversation easy and fun. Gabe's stomach was tight, his chest even tighter. He could feel a hum, an undercurrent of all kinds of emotions flying around the room. Doing his best to switch off *that* part of him, he reached for the water pitcher and politely filled all the glasses as needed. It wasn't just Ali, though the tension rising from beside him was thick and palpable. It was the past and the present mingling together in this very room, and it felt . . . difficult. Challenging.

"This room is lovely, Mrs Fitzgerald," he said to his hostess, who instantly insisted he call her Jo. "It really feels like the centre of your home."

Jo smiled at him from one end of the table. "Everything worth anything happens here, Gabe. All the news, both good and bad, gets processed within these four walls. Let me think . . . " She paused, her eyes squinting in memory. "Some of the loveliest moments were the wedding chats before Christmas." She looked smilingly at the newlyweds. "But we've had some tough dealings here, too.

"Caro had her meltdown here around the same time, and of course there was the Toby incident, just last summer, along with all of Frankie's hard times and challenges, which were discussed around this very table."

She looked about at her family as they all added various scenarios with their ups and downs that were specific to them.

Gabe absorbed it all. *Meltdown? Ah!* He remembered something about Caro and her son, Toby, being targeted, and a dead ex-boyfriend to boot. This household seemed to attract all kinds of intrigue and mayhem.

But there was more. He looked up from his plate and caught Molly, the youngest, looking directly at him. She was still and tense. Her eyes, mirrors of her elder brother's, that pale aqua with a dark rim round the outside of the iris, didn't flinch from his. *She knows things*, he thought, *and she's not . . . content.*

Breathing deeply, he opened his mind, just a little, and offered support, understanding and peace. She blinked, startled, and pressed a hand to her chest. A slow smile spread across her face and she visibly relaxed. "Thank you," she mouthed, and he knew he was right. She was "aware". Maybe not to the extent he was, but she had the same uncanny "knowing" as Flynn – both of them had it in less intensity than his own, but it was there. *Interesting.*

"Stop staring at my baby sister, it's rude. And creepy."

An elbow to his arm, rather painfully, brought his attention back to his work in progress – the hot mess that was Ali Fitzgerald.

"I was merely offering her . . . calm."

"She's as touchy-feely as you, so you two are probably telepathically solving all the world's issues right now. God, you're so weird." Ali put down her fork, her plate still only half empty though everyone else was finished.

That was another thing he filed away. Ali was always involved with food – making it, serving it, talking about it – but she rarely ate even half a plateful. She certainly didn't seem to enjoy it that much. *Even more interesting.*

"We all have the capacity to understand another's pain or hurt. If we want to . . . " Gabe began, but Ali spun her head towards his, grabbing at his forearm.

"Shit, is Moll in pain? What happened? Tell me!" she hissed in a low tone.

"No. That is not what I meant."

"You always say what you mean!"

"Well, in this instance, perhaps I was unclear. Your sister is an empath, a person who can feel very deeply for others, or at least perceive it, and for herself. It appears to me that she has . . . much to ponder and just needs to take a step back. Regroup."

"You don't even know her! How can you make such a stupid statement? She's an artist, so of course she's an empath. Doesn't take rocket science to figure that out." Ali's tone was sneering, judgemental, albeit in a whisper.

"I disagree. Many artists, the truly passionate ones, are far from empathetic. In fact, they are blindingly selfish and self-centred. They have to be. They need headspace to create and mundane matters, like another's feelings or doing the dishes, is of no interest to them. It takes up room. I am not saying they shouldn't be like that. They need to be. What I am saying is, I do not believe your sister is a true artist, in that particular respect. And I think she knows it. And it's causing . . . concern."

Gabe took a drink of water, mildly angry with himself for his outburst, low-voiced though it was. He never got into these kinds of discussions. It was too tricky. Too difficult to manoeuvre his way through without giving away his skill set.

Ali sat back in her chair, arms folded tightly across her chest. She stared over at Molly, her eyes narrowed.

"Huh," she said. "I hate that you might be right. The last few months Moll has been tired and out of sorts. For her. She's usually the happy-go-lucky one. And, fuck, I didn't even notice."

"You have been rather busy yourself, Ali. Give yourself some slack," Gabe said quietly.

"No. No slack allowed in the sister department. Not ever."

Her voice was fierce and Gabe felt something shift inside. A wave of energy rippled through him as he watched Ali studying Molly. She has been the protector before and thinks she still should be. *I wonder why . . .*

Abruptly, Ali rose from the table, turning her back to the table, holding her plate, so her eagle-eyed mother wouldn't notice the food left uneaten, Gabe assumed.

"I've got to go. An early start with more filming."

She unobtrusively scraped her plate into the rubbish bin as several others also rose to begin gathering the dishes.

"Won't you stay for dessert, darling?" Jo asked her daughter. "I know it's not *your* standard, but it's the crumble you used love, rhubarb and strawberry."

"Not tonight, thanks, Mum. Freeze me a piece, please."

She walked to the end of the table and bent down to hug her mother, then proceeded to do the same for her father at the other end.

"Thank you for the delicious meal, Mrs Fi . . . I mean, Jo. It was kind of you to include me." Gabe stood and began shaking hands with all of the Fitzgeralds, bar Flynn, then pushed his chair in.

"Where do you think you're going?" Ali had the door to the mudroom open and was slipping her shoes on.

"With you. To do my job," Gabe replied calmly, closing the kitchen door and opening the outer back one.

"No need. I've my bike. I'm fine. I think Alex is on tonight, so no hassle."

She grabbed her jacket and slung it on. Gabe leaned into her and fixed the collar.

Pulling back, he said, "I will put your bike in the back of my jeep and there is no argument to be had. Your brother will have my head if I let you go home alone." He cocked an eyebrow at her. "Is that your plan?"

She stuck her tongue out at him. Huffing, she grunted out a "Fine," and collecting her bike, wheeled it round to the front of the house where his jeep was parked. He beeped it open and, stepping in front of her, easily swung it into the open back area where the seats had been laid flat then closed the boot door. He walked to the passenger side door and held it open.

"I'm not a frigging princess or Lady Muck, you know. I can open my own doors."

"I am well aware of all of those points. Nevertheless . . ."

With a grin tugging at his mouth to the dulcet sounds of her continued grumbles, he walked round to his own side, slid in and started the engine.

Sex. She wanted some hot, sweaty sex. Sure, her bedroom toys could scratch an itch, but she was restless for more. She hadn't had sex with an actual human being for months. A veritable dry spell. She liked her body to get a workout on a frequent basis and chose her play partners very specifically. No mess, no fuss. And absolutely no effing relationship nonsense. She often hooked up with a guy more than once – if they were a good fit between the sheets. But the last thing Ali wanted was romance and relationships. That ship had sailed, if indeed it had ever launched.

She turned her head in the darkening cab of the jeep and stared sightlessly out of the window. As April drew to a close the evenings were brighter, longer. She loved this time of year, and May and June definitely competed with September as her favourite months. All the gorgeous burgeoning of growth, the fresh sparkle of lime green as the leaves on the beech trees unfurled, the dappled hedgerows in the countryside filled with Queen Anne's Lace, making everything look like it was sprinkled with snow, in summer. Maybe she needed a trip west. Not on the cards at the moment, though. Not with the film schedule so tight. Still. She could *maybe* swing a weekend . . .

"Why did you kiss me?" Ali blurted, her mind catching up too late to stop her mouth from saying what her brain *really* wanted to know.

She could feel Highlander beside her, see his knuckles tighten on the wheel and then, after a moment, hear his sigh.

"Do we have to do this now?"

"We do."

"Because . . . ?" He spared her a quick glance.

"I like things in boxes. I like to know what things mean. I need to be able to differentiate between what's good for me and what's not. I . . . I haven't always been good at that, so I know it's what I need." She twisted in the seat and faced his profile in the dim light. "Was it pity?"

He let out a startled sound, between a huff and groan.

"No." His tone was emphatic. "I definitely do not pity you. Why would I? You are a strong, independent woman with a sharp, keen intellect and oodles of talent. No."

Oh. Well, that was certainly good to know. A keen intellect? Who knew her brain being sharp could turn him on so much? She squirmed a little as a rush of heat invaded her belly. And below. He thought she was smart. And talented.

"So why?"

Silence, then, "I find you irritatingly irresistible."

A huge grin split her face and she leaned over to poke him in the arm with a finger. "You do?"

"It is not funny," he grumbled. "In fact, it is extremely inconvenient."

She settled back against the leather, smirking. "I love being an inconvenience, it's my *raison d'être*."

He groaned. "I might have bloody known."

"You said bloody."

"That is not an actual curse."

"I bet it is in your book."

He drove the jeep into a parking space outside her flat and switched off the engine.

"Out," he ordered as he opened his own door. "No manners in the door-opening department for you any more. I wouldn't want to risk insulting you."

Surprised at herself for being peeved at this, she briefly thought she needed to reassess what she did and didn't want in the courtesy section of her life. *Shit,* maybe she was a big, fat – or in her case, skinny – fraud.

Ali climbed down from the jeep to find her bicycle already out and waiting for her, held at the handlebars by the man she really wanted to kiss. Just once more. *Fraudster.*

"Thanks," she said, leaning over to take hold of the frame.

A large, firm hand landed on her shoulder, stilling her.

"Kissing you, right now, is pretty much all I want to do. It has absolutely nothing to do with pity, just pure unadulterated want. However," he continued, "that is not going to happen. It was, in some respects, a mistake before and not one I can, duty-bound, repeat."

"Only in some respects?" *Yes,* she was a master at homing in on what she wanted to hear.

His mouth twitched and he hauled her into a tight hug. One arm braced along her shoulders, he rested his chin on top of her head.

"Ali Fitzgerald, you will be the death of me."

She felt the lightest kiss touch her hair, like a feather, and then gone.

"You know exactly what I mean. No, go inside and remember, I am at the end of the phone if you need anything."

Ali stepped back from him, oddly shaky from his tenderness, and tried for snark.

"Yeah, yeah, only call if I'm in danger, yadda yadda. I got it, Scotty."

She wheeled her bike up to the steps, lifted it easily up the short distance, unlocked the door and quickly entered, closing it behind her, leaving her bike leaning against the dado rail. *Why the fuck does that man affect me so much with his little kisses and his odd compliments? Damn!*

She literally shook herself, a good old waggle from top to toe, and headed to the kitchen. She wasn't getting any sex, sweaty or otherwise, tonight and she was just going to have to live with that. *Double damn.*

Sleep eluded him.

He paced, sat, paced some more.

The notes and printouts for Ali's case lay in a pattern on the coffee table. To an observer, there was no pattern – just odd placements of seemingly random scraps of paper – but Gabe knew his brain worked in a very specific mixture of visual and linear. He'd learned to trust his process, along with his overactive gut, a long time ago. He was now sure who the protagonist was, or at least the next link in the chain, but the why wasn't yet clear. And all good detectives know the why is of utmost importance. *Motive, motive, motive.*

His phone beeped. A text.

Ali: So, I was thinking . . .

Gabe chuckled. Of course she was. Her brain was as crazy as his – it never switched off.

S MacO: That sounds rather worrisome.
Ali: You'd better believe it.

More typing . . .

As he watched the dots indicating she was writing, Gabe wondered what would come next. One never knew with Ali Fitzgerald.

Ali: Could we just have sex? You could come over . . .

Whoa! He hadn't seen that one coming.

He was stymied. What the hell could he say? How could he possibly respond to that? Gabe put down his phone. He ran a hand over his face, inhaling a deep breath as he tried to shut down every blessed image that instantly played in his head at her words. He tried a rational response. Several times. But deleted each word. Finally, he wrote:

S MacO: Are you trying to drive me crazy? Or just ensure I get zero hours of sleep tonight?
Ali: Well, that depends. I quite like driving you crazy . . . for the right reasons.
S MacO: There are no right reasons for that.
Ali: Sure there are! In ALL the good ways. And if you get zero sleep because, a) you're with me having sex, that can only be a good reason. Or, b) if you're thinking about me as you pleasure yourself in the shower (or wherever, I'm not picky) then that, too, will work for me. And you too, obvs. So, you see? We are both winners here.

This was followed by several totally incomprehensible emojis, but definitely included an aubergine. And a . . . peach?

S MacO: I am not skilled in the hieroglyphics of texting, so all those emoticons are lost on me.
Ali: ALL of them??? I bet not.
S MacO: I am working.
Ali: On what? The "coming over to have sex with me" part? Or the self-pleasure part?
S MacO: Your case.

Dear God, Gabe thought, *the woman was relentless.* He

enjoyed that side of her crazy personality very much. Too much.

Ali: Can't you multitask?
Ali: I can.
Ali: I am.

Gabe dropped his head into his hands, groaning in sheer frustration. This woman was unreal. She'd genuinely be the death of him. He shouldn't ask. He couldn't. He was the older, wiser one in this situation. He needed to shut it down. He should shut it down.

S MacO: I don't want to know.

He typed words, delteted words, tried again, knowing he was in very dangerous territory.

S MacO: Tell me.
Ali: I'm baking and listening to music.

Gabe let out a laugh. An unusual sound in his silent living room. It echoed and made him realise just how quiet he liked things as he worked.

S MacO: You got me good. Congratulations.
Ali: I'm in my kitchen, clearly. You've been here so you can visualise it. I'm listening to 'Dancing Queen' and thinking of you. I'm not really baking – I'm cooking. Making pancakes, American-style. And thinking of you.
Ali: And I'm naked.

Ali: Well, except for my apron – I'm not totally daft. No burns for me.

Gabe stared at his phone. Stunned. *How could she do this?* Turn him into a randy boy with just a few typed words. This had to stop. He started to write again, paused, deleted text, thought about what he should say, what he wanted to say, what he shouldn't say. He gave up and thought about her safety.

S MacO: Are the blinds closed?
Ali: Seriously? That's all you have to say? You're worried about a peeping Tom?
S MacO: I don't want anyone to see you. I want to imagine you doing all that, by yourself, with only me to watch. And my, as it turns out, extremely VIVID imagination is doing that rather well.

Okay, maybe it wasn't just her safety that concerned him, that bothered him, in a *hot* and bothered way.

Ali: Come over.
S MacO: No.
Ali: I look cute.
S MacO: Of that I have no doubt. Although cute is not a word I would apply to this situation.
Ali: What, then? What word would you use?

Christ! she would try the patience of a saint. And right now it was far from saintly he was feeling. He felt *more.* So much more. And it had nothing to do with being canonised. It was the exact opposite.

S MacO: Tempting
S MacO: Outrageous
S MacO: Beautiful
S MacO: Desirable
S MacO: Unforgettable

He took a moment, his fingers paused over the phone screen. He tried several words. Deleted each one. Imagined Ali's face watching the typing indicator dots appearing and disappearing. Imagined her impatience. Her frustration. He let out a deep sigh. And typed.

S MacO: Mine

Gabe watched his phone, wishing he could take back the last text. She wasn't his. She'd never be his. Could never be his. For all the reasons. But right now, seeing her in his mind's eye, dancing naked to ABBA, was just making him wish for the impossible. That he could drive over there, wrap her in his arms. *Kiss her. Kiss her some more. Take her.* Take her to places only they would know together.

He wanted all that.

She was like a burr on his backside. Drove him crazy. Irritated him with her stubborn ways. Yet, what drew him so keenly was her mouth. *What came out of it. Irreverence. Cheek and snark. Kind and thoughtful comments to strangers. Helpful, encouraging words to those in need.* He'd been on both the receiving end and witness to it. She wasn't as tough as she pretended. He knew that as clear as he knew himself. She held many, many secrets. Dark ones. Just like him. All of that drew him in.

And back to her mouth.

The taste he now knew. *The softness, the hardness. The sensitive lips and probing tongue. Her smile and her grimace. Her gasps and her groans.* He wanted it all again. He wanted every bit of that mouth on every bit of him.

This could only end badly. He knew that. But maybe there was a way. He looked at his phone, saw Ali was typing. He held his breath.

Ali: I'm a little flustered here. All the pretty words. I didn't know you had a touch of the poet, Outlander. It's making my pulse race, just a bit. Okay, more than a bit.
Ali: My pancakes are done. But I'm no longer hungry. Or not for them, anyway.
S MacO: Please stop.
Ali: I don't need your consent for what I'm about to do.
S MacO: Fuck.
Ali: Ha! And my work here is done! Go play, Scotsman. Enjoy yourself. You know I will. I'll be thinking of you. Only you.

Gabe glared at his phone and threw it down on the couch. He'd let her get to him. He couldn't believe what he'd written. *What was wrong with him?* He'd never sent dirty, naughty texts to anyone in his life. And he'd never been so turned on by the written word. He ached. His cock was throbbing and he needed release or he'd embarrass himself even with no one to see.

Stripping off his clothes, he took yet another long shower, his head filled with images of Ali doing the equivalent of what his own hand was doing right now.

He wished it didn't feel so damn good.

Chapter 11

Two weeks. Two weeks of filming and prepping. Of creating and baking. *Bloody exhausting*, thought Ali as she wiped down the countertops in her loft now everyone had left. Everyone except her guard. Her Highlander. He was standing by the large window – one hand held a phone he was reading from rather intently, the other was propped on his hip, giving him a dashing air. That pose also brushed back his jacket, giving her a very fine view of a very fine rear.

The show was going well. Everyone said so. They'd air the first programme in a few days, even though they had a few more episodes to record. Bewley thought it would be better to get the public involved in the bakers' journey in real time – to create a buzz as it was happening, so the contestants-cum-participants could gather a following. It was all about the numbers, he'd said. She got that. Absolutely. But the tightened schedule meant she was running on empty. And getting antsy with it.

Two weeks.

The days were the same. The Outlander was with her most days, with Alex or Carlos or the others. During daylight hours they conducted a business relationship. Or, as she liked to think of it, an "Ali harassing Mac" relationship. She gave no quarter. Always pushing the limits of his professionalism. But never as much as late at night. Then, all rules were ditched.

They never discussed their night-time texting conversations in the day – it was like they were two separate things. Not related, in any way, to each other. He responded differently to her in the wee hours of the morning. More openly. Less secretive. Yes, she knew it was pot calling kettle – there was so much he'd never know about her – but she anticipated those night chats with a pleasure that was wholly new to her. It was a little intoxicating.

It wasn't always sexting. And initially it was Ali who texted first. About five days into their nightly routine, Ali had collapsed onto the bed and nodded off, stretched out face down, still fully dressed, when a beep sometime later roused her:

S MacO: Everything okay?
Ali: Wreck a girl's beauty sleep, why don't you.
S MacO: Apologies. Go back to sleep. I will see you in the morning. And you don't need it.
Ali: Not so fast, big guy. I'm awake now. What don't I need?
S MacO: Beauty sleep. As you are well aware.
Ali: Flatterer. But a girl likes to hear it all the same.

Ali was under no allusions about her looks. She had a certain gamine style, sure, but she was no beauty. Caro was beautiful in a classical way and Molly in an artistic Pre-Raphaelite way – and Frankie? Well, she was just darn gorgeous. No one was in her league. Ali knew her own cheekbones were a little too sharp, her chin a little too pointed. Plus, she was scrawny as hell. She was working on that. In progress, one might say. And thanks to her therapist, she was doing so much better. Every day.

Ali: Anyway, you woke me from a bad dream, so it's actually fine.

Shit. Shit. She shouldn't have mentioned bad dreams. Now he'd go all Dr Freud on her. *Shit.*

S Mac O: Do you have them often?

And there he was – Mr Concerned. She changed tack as quickly as possible.

Ali: On and off. Hey, I meant to ask you earlier – what's your favourite food?
S Mac O: Good deflection.
Ali: I want to know!
S Mac O: All right, I will play along.

And he did. *(No haggis, phew!) But braised venison, if you don't mind. Fancy.*
They'd texted back and forth. Night after night. Sometimes just chit-chat and sometimes, when she was feeling, she realised now, brave, she sent him flirty, suggestive, often dirty texts. He always played along, albeit in his own restrained way. She hadn't got him to curse again, but she was beginning to know what buttons to push, as well as storing up nuggets of information about all manner of things in his personality.
He was an only child. His father lived in Scotland, dividing his time between the Highlands where their main home was and Edinburgh where the town house was. She gave him a load of shit for that! He didn't even seem embarrassed by his background, but by the time

she'd finished slagging him off, he was sounding rather flustered. One for the win. He loved his granny. He didn't say it outright, but his tone changed when he spoke of her. And he cared deeply for his mum, who lived, most of the time, on a reservation in Oklahoma.

He was a good listener. And was non-judgemental. Open-minded. Except when it came to the law. They argued no end about the merits of the law, over justice and the moral high ground. They got nowhere – well, they both got hot under the collar. *Not true. Ali did. He stayed measured and controlled.* She started nicknaming him M and C, for measured and calm. None of the monikers she threw at him seemed to bother his cool. So she kept trying.

She threw the cloth into the sink and dropped heavily onto a stool at the main workspace. There were plenty of people to do the cleaning. And they had, after the set closed for the day, but Ali always liked to put her own stamp on things. She was raised better – if you make a mess, you clean it up. Yes, these people were paid to clean, but it felt . . . wrong. Like she was taking advantage.

She propped her chin in her hands and said, "Fuck it."

Within seconds, she could feel him at her side. He stood behind her and placed strong hands on her shoulders, massaging gently. It was the first time he'd touched her since their kiss and it felt . . . amazing. She moved beneath his fingers, savouring every touch, feeling the heat, feeling the pressure and the strength.

"God, that feels good," she groaned, rotating her aching shoulders and neck.

He continued to work her muscles, silently but with an air of tension about him. She turned her head and caught a fierce expression in his unguarded face.

"Hey," she blinked up at him. "What's up?"

He closed his eyes briefly as his mouth made a firm line. She twisted from his grasp and swivelled to face him, still sitting on the stool. She placed her hands on his arms, feeling the rigid biceps beneath. Not taking the time to admire his form, she repeated her question.

He shook his head slightly. She'd never seen him at a loss. It was unnerving. She reached up and stroked his cheek. A tic worked in his jaw as he heaved a sigh.

"You are wearing yourself out," he said gruffly, his own hand moving up to hold hers against his face. "It is . . . it is hard to watch."

"Big softie," she said, a smile in her voice at his attempt to hide his tenderness.

"I am serious. You need a break."

"No." She decided to take a chance. "I need something else. You."

And, *God*, she did. All the heated looks she'd caught as her gaze collided with his during filming, at odd moments when she'd turn his way and catch him watching her, studying her. Their banter during the long, lonely nights . . . his daily care of her. His attention towards her. She knew it was his job, but it didn't feel like that. Not any more. And she wanted him. Viscerally. With a longing she was unused to.

And she was afraid.

Afraid, for the first time in her adult life to make a move. To be rejected now, after the intimacy of their conversations, the fun, the sexy talk, the sharing. She'd never really engaged her mind in relationships with men before this man – it had always been her body's needs driving her decisions. But with him . . . with him it was so much more and she was afraid.

Grasping all of her courage in her hands, seeing his beautiful green eyes darken as he stared silently down at her, she stood and, reaching up, pressed her lips to his mouth.

The shock. The instant sizzle of lips to lips, almost drew her back. But he was faster. With lightning speed, he had her in his arms, his mouth returning the pressure and holding her branded to his chest. Within seconds his tongue was exploring and tasting. Sucking and tasting – and she went limp. She felt shivers through her whole body, a heat rising with such rapidity she was stunned she didn't spontaneously combust. *God, that mouth of his. It was thorough. It was demanding and unrelenting.* He kissed her like his life depended on it, like she and she alone could save him. It was glorious.

One of his hand's went up to cup the back of her neck, holding her in place, commanding her response. He didn't have to work hard for that. She was all in. His other hand slid up and down her back, moulding her to him. And when it slid lower and pulled her ass tight to his frame, she was left in no doubt that she wasn't the only one on fire. The man was rock-hard.

They kissed. Again and again. Open mouths and tongues vying for best position. She slipped her arms around him, tracing her hands over his back under his jacket, revelling in the hard planes of muscle she discovered there. She might have got to know his mind over these last few weeks, but she didn't know his body at all. That was about to change . . .

His phone pinged insistently and the spell was shattered. Breaking away and gasping for air, they stared at each other, breath heaving, blue eyes locked to green.

"Jesus," muttered Ali, too stunned to say more.

With shaking hands, he reached into his jacket pocket, his eyes going flat. He pulled away, looking at the screen.

"I've got to go," he said calmly.

Calm. The man went from a spiral of heat to calm. In a nanosecond. Stupid, she thought. *Why did I think this was going to be different?*

"Sure you do," she managed and stepped away, wrapping her arms about her chest.

She felt naked, exposed. A mess. And he was . . . calm.

Gathering his bag, he headed for the door. He paused, took a deep breath and, turning, stared straight at her, that direct gaze blazing again.

"I *will* be back. This isn't finished. We are not done."

And he was gone.

He broke the speed limit and for once he didn't give it a thought. He drove competently and quickly. When the lights changed against him he rolled down the window, attached a flashing light to his roof and blasted his siren. He knew he was behaving uncharacteristically but he didn't care. He had other things on his mind.

He'd just got a break on the case and he was going to blow it open, arrest the bastard, or at least one of them, who'd been causing havoc. And then . . . then he was handing in his resignation for this case and driving straight back to Ali's flat. They had business to attend to. To finish. *Hell, to start.*

Flynn was waiting at his desk, a look of expectation on his face. He spoke first.

"You sure?"

"Yes."

"Right. Let's go."

Flynn motioned for two uniformed gardaí to follow and the four of them headed out. He and Gabe rode together in an unmarked car, and the two officers, accompanied now by another two, followed in separate police vehicles. They drove at speed, anxious now that the suspect would somehow get wind of the investigation and flee.

The winding maze of streets that was part of Shankill – a suburb south of Dublin city – and its wider area could be a nightmare. Flynn had the GPS set up and it brought them unerringly to a small estate of houses about a half-mile from the village. It had once been well kept and reasonably attractive but had been neglected of late and many of the houses looked deserted. Few lights were on in the homes that were occupied, and Gabe spoke over their communication devices to the cars behind them to kill any lights and go in silent.

They pulled up outside number seventeen and closed their doors quietly as they exited the vehicles. Using hand movements to direct them, Flynn sent two uniforms round the back of the house as he and Gabe walked up the path, while motioning the remaining gardaí to wait at the gate.

Gabe rang the bell and stepped back to wait. A few moments later, the door opened to reveal a woman of uncertain years, perhaps from mid forties to anywhere in her late fifties. She had a cigarette in one hand and a can of Heineken lager in the other.

"What do you want?" she asked, her voice sharp and tinny.

"Good evening, might you be Anne Carney?"

"Who wants to know?"

God, thought Gabe, *he could have written this script himself*. She looked weary and grey-faced, and Gabe felt a strong sense of disappointment from her.

"I would like to speak with Mel, if he is home," Gabe stated politely, ignoring her question.

"Why? What's he done now? Mel!" she hollered behind her towards the interior of the house. "Some fellas are here to talk to you."

There was some shuffling and the sound of furniture moving, then a figure in a dressing gown sauntered down the hall into the light. The second he caught sight of Gabe he did an about-turn.

"Don't!" barked Gabe, pushing past the woman to grab Mel by the arm. "There is no point. There are uniformed officers outside your back door just hoping you will try it. And they were very bored today, so this would be a fun activity for them. Not, I might add, for you."

"I didn't do anything," Mel stuttered, sniffing inelegantly and rubbing his nose. "It wasn't me."

"What wasn't you?" Gabe asked in a deceptively mild tone. "We haven't said why we are here."

The colour drained visibly from Mel's face as, continuing to sniff, he looked beyond Gabe, to see not just the silent but stern figure of Flynn, but also the policemen and vehicles beyond.

"Would you like to answer a few questions here with your wife in the comfort of your own home? It would only take a couple of hours and the officers can stay near the cars, on guard." He paused to let that, and the reality of their personal business being aired publicly, sink in. "Or," Gabe continued, his voice pleasant yet matter-of-fact, "you can come to the station with us and no one need be any the wiser."

He didn't point out that in this estate there was probably a network of communication and everyone was already gaping out of their windows or doors, eager for a show.

Anne Carney turned on her husband, disgust written all over her face.

"You sad, pathetic excuse of a man," she sneered. "What mess have you got yourself into? Is gambling away our savings and snivelling over everyone else's success not enough for you? Take him," she said dismissively to Gabe. "I don't want him here. He's a useless piece of shit. I rue the day I ever took up with him."

She shrugged off Mel's attempts to stop her as she marched back down the hall and into what looked like the kitchen. She slammed the door, but not before they'd heard her berating the gardaí standing outside.

As they escorted Mel down the path, now in a jacket and trousers instead of his robe, Flynn said dryly, "Charming picture of marital bliss. I know I should feel mildly sorry for one or other of them, but I find I am loath to choose."

Gabe gave him a sardonic look. "Indeed. Let's get him to the interview room and get this tied up tonight."

"You're in a hurry. What's the rush, considering all the work and background checks you've done on this? Is there somewhere you'd rather be?"

Gabe didn't answer. He couldn't. What could he say? Yes, there is. I want to go and sleep with your sister? *No.*

Certainly not that. He tightened his mouth and spoke grimly.

"Let's just get this done."

And he opened the back door, placed a hand on Mel Carney's head and guided him into the car.

It took longer than it should. Mel didn't make it easy for them. He'd backtracked, diverted and did his best to sidestep every allegation Gabe had laid out. His alibi for the two trespassing and vandalism events was shot, thanks to Gabe and his sergeant's digging, along with unrelenting footwork and door-to-door canvassing. Once he had actual suspects, and photos of them, people in the loft's vicinity suddenly had clearer memories. And once seen, and remembered, Mel stood out as distinctive. As did the description of a smaller, darker man.

And then there was the damning evidence of the chisel. Thank goodness for a timely warrant that enabled a search on Mel's garden shed the previous day. The Carneys hadn't been home, but the warrant had given them access to search open premises and the chisel, hidden in plain sight, had matched the photo documentation taken of the sabotaged oak tables in Ali's place.

They couldn't pin the bike incident or car door scenario on Mel, but on further prompting Carney gave up the name of Juan Garcia as his accomplice then swore up and down he had no clue where the man lived. He was just a hired hand to help scare Ali. He refused to say more, refused to say how they'd met and called for his lawyer.

Gabe wasn't convinced of Mel's apparent ignorance of the bigger picture. Not convinced at all. And he absolutely didn't believe that this excuse of a man had come up with the plan himself – he was way too interested in his next fix to formulate a coherent structure of anything. But what Gabe needed was proof. And, at the moment, that eluded him.

It was nearing midnight when Gabe pulled up outside Ali's flat. He relieved the guard, still on duty while Garcia remained at large, explaining that he'd take over for the remainder of the shift. All about him it appeared to be an uneventful night. Still. His hands gripping the steering wheel, he took a long, hard look at himself . . . There was no going back from what he was about to do. Or what he hoped *they* were about to do.

On paper, he'd finished with the case. In practice, considering the recent guard swap, he wasn't letting Ali out of his purview till Garcia was also caught. Tonight was either going to be the worst decision of his life, or the best. And he knew, 100 per cent, that he was walking a very thin line where his job was concerned.

He climbed out of the jeep.

Chapter 12

"Jesus!" Ali shouted. "Keep your effing shirt on. I'm coming!"

She grabbed a cardigan as she headed to her front door, sweeping at her unruly short crop of hair, vaguely wondering if it was standing on end. She'd fallen asleep on the couch and the TV hummed quietly in the background. She adjusted her sleep shorts that she'd pulled on earlier and peeped through the spyhole. *Oh,* she thought and opened the door.

"What are you doing here?" She stood firmly in the doorway, arms across her chest.

"I said I would be back," he said quietly, his gaze burning into hers.

"I didn't realise you meant this evening," Ali stuttered, her throat suddenly dry.

God, he looked gorgeous. Tired, weary, dishevelled – for him – and yeah, gorgeous.

"I can go," he said simply.

Ali knew he was really asking her if what they'd started before, the fire they'd ignited between them, was about to be fanned into flames or covered with ash. He was giving her an out. All she had to say was yes, that would be wise, but screw wise. Wise wasn't going to make her body vibrate and her toes curl. Wise wouldn't kiss her senseless and then some. He was asking for consent. And he *would* go, without any questions or recriminations, she knew that, too. Without a doubt.

It took barely a second.

She stepped back and gestured him inside. His eyes glinted in the shadows cast from the street light outside and she closed the door firmly behind her, attaching the chain lock out of habit. She was about to turn, but he did it for her, spinning her to face him while at the same time backing her up against the closed door.

His mouth descended and devoured. She opened to him, instinctively, immediately, craving what only he could give. He pressed his body to hers, shoulder to hip, and rested his hands on the wood on either side of her face, pinning her with his mouth.

She felt it everywhere, just like before. From head to toe her body was buzzing, simmering, tingling. Her heart slammed in her chest as his tongue delved deeper, swirled, tasted and sucked. Heat raced through her and somewhere in the background she was aware of two things: his heart was slamming right back against hers, and one of them was making deep, sexy groaning sounds. It was him, she realised. She was making him crazy. *Her.* Skinny, sharp, smart-mouthed Ali Fitzgerald had the Highlander on the ropes. *Thank you, Jesus.*

He pulled back, panting, his breath uneven and out of control. He stroked his fingers down her cheek, across her swollen lips, and grimaced slightly.

"I know we need to talk – I have things to tell you, about the case. They can wait. And I didn't mean for *that* to happen. Well, not the kissing, that was definitely on the schedule, but the suddenness of it, that was rather crass of me. I am sorry."

"Hey, Ace, don't ever be sorry for sharing those kinds of kisses," Ali said, her voice breathy.

He arched a brow. "Ace? A new name?"

"Well, you're pretty fucking ace at using your mouth, so it's kind of suitable, don't you think?"

"I think we need to be extra sure." A sly smile tugged at the corner of his mouth. "Show me where we can practise more comfortably."

Grinning, she spun on her heel and, grabbing his hand, dragged him towards her bedroom. Her bed was made, the sheets clean. *Thank God for small delights.* Low lamplight filled the room with dips and shadows, creating softness and a warm welcome.

As she pulled down the duvet, he began taking off his jacket. He threw a strip of condoms down on the bed beside her as he continued to undress. Ali's breath caught.

"Pretty confident, Ace!"

"Prepared. And I am completely confident that I will bring you all kinds of pleasure, I was just hopeful I would get the chance to do exactly that."

Well. Now. Huh. Ali gulped, suddenly, most unusually for her, nervous. She turned to look at him, determined to take back the reins she felt slipping away. This wasn't how it worked for her. She was always in charge. *Always.* She had to be. And her pleasure was no one's responsibility but hers. That's how she rolled.

She watched as he pulled off his tie and unbuttoned his shirt. She'd seen his body that one time, had dreamed of that body since, and now here it was, being revealed to her by his own strong, tanned hands. The colour of his skin against his white shirt while he undid the buttons was unbearably erotic. She shook her head. *That was daft*. Undoing a shirt couldn't be sexy, but Christ, each ounce of skin revealed was a treat for the eyes and she was mesmerised. He shrugged out of the cotton and undid his belt, and then his trousers, removing his shoes and socks. He stood before her in boxers that were plainly too small. Her gaze was riveted to the large outline straining against the fabric.

"May I?" she asked, moving her hands to settle on the waistband.

His skin was warm to the touch, but she could see instant goose bumps appear as she slid her fingers testingly along the top of where a slight shadowing of dark hair dipped beneath his shorts below his belly button. He hissed in a breath. Her eyes flew to his. He looked pained.

"It has, ah, been a while," he said, a tinge of embarrassment to his tone. "I don't want to be . . . er, a disappointment, so to speak, so better not get too adventurous straight away."

Ali laughed, lightening the mood. "That just means I'll get a couple of rounds out of you before I throw you out." His eyes did that slow blink of his and she thought she might have offended him. Tossing her head towards the bed, she added, "Get in," as she pulled her cardigan off and reached for the lamp.

He made a sound of protest but broke it off when she cut him a look that said plainly, *don't mess with me – my house, my rules.* She tossed her vest top and PJ shorts on a chair and climbed in beside him, suddenly shy.

He lay propped on his side, one arm tucked up with his head on his hand. She lay down next to him and wondered where the fuck all her sass and mojo were right now. Fine time for those two constant companions to desert her. *Traitors*. But that line of thought was quickly banished as her gallant Scot took control.

In all the best ways.

Gabe was determined to go slow. To eke out every ounce of enjoyment from this unexpected happenstance. Unexpected because sleeping with Ali hadn't been on the cards. Not from the get-go. Imagining it? Sure. Fantasising about it? Absolutely. But time in her company had drained all of his reserve. All of his stubborn dedication to the case and to the job.

The last couple of weeks since he'd first kissed her had been a living hell. It had certainly propelled the case along – he knew he couldn't cross the line and sleep with his "client", but he also knew he couldn't not. So, he'd worked round the clock and called in a few favours. Not many of the gardaí in the station knew him that well, but they did know his reputation and were willing to put in overtime to work with him.

And now here she was, this gorgeous creature lying next to him, her skin a pale form in the slice of light from a crack in the curtain. He'd been surprised she'd switched out the light, hadn't expected reserve, but he knew how to use his hands as well as his mouth and figured he'd see her body just as well in the dark. He'd certainly feel it. *Every fine inch of it.*

He reached out and traced the dip in her collarbone with one finger. She shivered and turned slightly towards him. He hadn't said a word since he'd admitted to a lack of sex life in the recent past and he wasn't sure if she liked to talk during sex.

As if reading his mind, she spoke clearly into the dark.

"Jeez, you're not going to be all Chatty Cathy now, are you? All this chit-chat is driv—"

He moved to lie over her and silenced her with his mouth, kissing her with the same passion they'd shared earlier. The feel of her slim body beneath his was agonising. He wanted to take her this instant. To shove inside her and take and take. *But . . . no, another time, perhaps.* There'd be an opportunity later for speed, for a quick round of pure sex, but now she deserved care and attention.

So he kissed her some more, relishing the way she returned each and every caress with one of her own. She was making husky sounds, eager sounds, gasping and moaning, and all they were doing was kissing. Her hands slid down his back and he shivered reflexively. He could feel heat and passion in her, and he pressed his hips against her in response.

Gasping, she muttered, "These have to go," and tugged at his boxers.

With lithe dexterity, he removed them and, after ripping open a condom, he sheathed himself then returned to her arms. He let his mouth wander, delighting in the feel of her skin under his lips. *The taste of her, the smell of her, the feel of her, it was intoxicating. It was dangerous.* He licked around her nipple, its taut peak tempting and alluring. He kissed the skin surrounding her small, perfect breasts and as he finally took one nub into his mouth to suck deeply, his other hand tweaked its twin.

"Jesus," she moaned, arching into his touch. "Fuck, that's good."

Her hands gripped at his arms, curling around his biceps, digging in as she squirmed below him. He pressed his lower body into the curve of her belly, fitting himself between her legs as they spread open for him. He used tiny pulsing movements, sucking with his mouth, each hip movement a counteract to the pull of his lips, the flick of his thumb against her other nipple setting a slow rhythm as he moved effortlessly from one breast to the other. He could feel the jerk of her body's reaction, paying attention to what made her respond, made her moan, gasp.

He released her breast and kissed his way back up her body to her mouth, pressing kiss after kiss as his hand moved lower, skimming her belly and down through her curls. It was he who moaned now. *She was so wet, so hot, so slick.*

He almost lost it.

Using his long fingers, he traced her folds and learned her secret places. Dipping one finger inside, he could feel her inner walls clench and had the insane thought that he might just come if she did that again. *That was crazy.* He should not be this close to the edge. No matter how long it was since he'd had a woman's touch. *He wasn't even inside her yet . . .*

Inhaling a deep breath, flooding his senses with the fragrance of her, he focused on the pleasure he could bring. Curling his finger inside, he pressed firmly while sliding in and out, over and over as she whimpered at his mouth, her hands now twisting in the sheet. Feeling her muscles clench again and again, he slid his thumb up though her folds and finding her centre, he pressed there in tandem with his finger inside.

It was mere moments before she pulled her mouth from his, her head flailing on her pillow as she let out a low guttural sound.

"*Fuck*," she gasped, "holy fuck. I need . . . I just want . . ."

He kissed across her jaw as she rose to a peak and whispered in her ear, "I know . . . You're beautiful, so beautiful. You can do this, just let go."

Let go, he said. *Let go. Fuck,* she'd not only let go, but she'd also fallen from the bloody cliff. *And what a fall.* Her body still floating while her heart began to slow, she turned her head back to hold his eyes.

"You sure know a thing or two, don't you, Ace?"

He smiled. "I know plenty," he agreed with a smirk.

He licked along the seam of her lips, then pressed a long, hard kiss to her whole mouth while angling his lower body flush to hers. He was hard as steel and although she knew, theoretically, that it's what you did with it rather than the size, she was pretty darn happy with the feel of his length and girth. Heat infused her bones again and she shifted, rocking slightly up into him. He groaned.

"What are you waiting for?" she asked. "Get in me."

"Quite the romantic, Ms Fitzgerald." His voice was uneven as he echoed her slight shifts, driving them both mad with desire.

"I know what I want."

"Are you sure? That we continue, I mean, with this, now?"

Why did he have to be such a fecking gentleman?

Her throat tightened, knowing if she said no, now, even now feeling him against her, teasing him with her movements, he'd stop. She'd never trusted a man more than right now and that was a pretty damn scary notion. And so damn sexy.

"Yes," she insisted, opening her legs in invitation.

He needed nothing more. Raising himself on his elbows, he reached down and, gripping with one hand, slid himself up and down her heat, reigniting all of her senses. On a sharp intake of breath, he eased inside her. And stopped.

"Need a second," he hissed.

She rocked upwards again, changing the angle, and on an exhale, he slid home. All the way in – all the way . . .

Oh! holy fucking sleigh bells . . .

And then he started to move. Briefly, she remembered the dancing. At Dev and Frankie's wedding, when he'd surprised the hell out of her at how easily he'd glided and danced about the room, picking up cues from her family and making it all so effortless. Such style and finesse. Such rhythm.

It wasn't effortless now based on the grunts that he was making, but it sure had rhythm. Shifting to one elbow, he grasped her hip and pulled her leg up and over his own, throwing them both into a new position and . . . *Well, Christ*, Ali thought with whatever brain cells she had left, *here was style and finesse in spades.* He hit all the spots, all the right places, as he thrust in and out in long, even strokes, faster and faster. Another orgasm was building swiftly and as her own need raced to meet his, she arched her back, allowing her clitoris to rub against him in exactly the right way.

His continued friction and rhythm had her panting, beads of sweat pooling on her chest as he grabbed her chin, turning her face, her eyes locking on his. She was glad of the sliver of moonlight. His face was tight and intense, his mouth a firm line as his concentration intensified. It was powerful being the entire focus of his gaze, so powerful she couldn't look away. She felt seen, *known*, but in a good way. Because they weren't usually words she liked applied to her where men were concerned. Not ever.

His green eyes not leaving hers, he quickened the pace and, his voice rough, he groaned, "You feel so fucking good, Ali Fitzgerald. So. Fucking. Good."

The sound of him swearing as he pounded into her, obviously so close to the edge, was her undoing. She felt the heat spiral up and over and she convulsed beneath him.

"Jesus, Gabe, *holy frigging God*!"

And with another oath, he followed her to relief, collapsing on top of her, their hearts hammering in tandem.

"You swore. Lots," she whispered as she slowly got her breathing back in line.

"You called me by my name," he whispered back, easing out and off her but gathering her close to his side. "Thank you."

They did it again. And again.

Ali had reached over and slid her hand along the outline of his hip, tracing her fingers up and over his ribcage, feeling each muscle move and undulate at her touch. She pushed him onto his back and climbed up onto his thighs, reaching over to unfurl a condom down his pulsating length. She teased him, rubbing against him before he lost it. Gripping her hips, he lifted her and slid her down.

They both groaned and began to move in earnest. She reached back and braced herself on his hard thighs, moving, taking her pleasure as he reached forwards, rearing up from the bed to kiss her fiercely. He managed to slide a hand between them, where he circled and pressed her core till she cried out his name once more, both shattering as they tumbled over the edge. She fell forwards onto his chest and dozed off, her cheek resting over his heart.

Later still, he rolled her onto her side and slid back in. This time it was slow. Slow and easy – *slow and very, very thorough*. No hard thrusting, no mad dash. Just long, deep, intense kisses and equally long, deep, intense pulses inside her.

When Ali recovered her breath from the most perfect orgasm of her life, she was horrified to feel tears slip from the corners of her eyes. *Fuck. That wouldn't do.* She'd get up and send him packing. Get him out of her flat and, as she knew she must, out of her life. This man was dangerous. Dangerous to her in the ways that she feared most.

She stirred and he turned and spooned her, gathering her close in his arms, sighing contentedly into the nape of her neck, the curve of her shoulder. *See? Dangerous.* She'd sort him out in a moment. She'd just close her eyes for a few minutes to regain her equilibrium.

Coffee and bacon. Could there be better smells? Ali peeled her eyes open and shifted to grab her phone to check the time: *six bloody thirty. Who ate at that hour?* Turning over, the duvet tangled about her legs, she became aware of all kinds of unusual muscle aches.

And, *oh, my Lord*, a flash of memories!

She swung out of bed, pulled on her vest top and shorts, hopping to get her leg in, and practically raced to her kitchen. *There he was. Shit.* Gabe Mackenzie was seated, *fully dressed, the stealthy bastard*, at *her* table, eating bacon and scrambled eggs, a mug of steaming coffee before him. Seeing her skid to a halt at the doorway, he paused, a forkful of eggs halfway to his mouth. Putting the food back down, he stood up from the table.

"Good morning. I hope you don't mind me helping myself, but I didn't want to wake you."

Calm and measured. No surprise there.

"Were you going to skive off without saying goodbye?" she demanded, crossing her arms.

He blushed. *Oh, hell, he was embarrassed. Was it because of what they'd done last night? Or because he was caught, about to do a stealthy departure?* Neither of those reasons suited Ali one iota. Sure, they couldn't possibly do this again, the sex part, because – *well, they just couldn't.* Neither of them were relationship people and she knew he was only in Dublin temporarily, so there was no actual future for them even if they *did* want it. But, *damn*, she didn't relish feeling like a fool, like she was being wrongfooted or brushed aside.

"I know it is your day off and I thought you might need a lie-in."

She raised her eyebrows at his assumption that she was a lazy slugabed.

"And I left you bacon in the warming oven," he added. "Though not eggs, as they don't reheat well."

"I can cook my own damn breakfast," she snapped ungratefully.

"I was going to leave a note."

"A note!" she snorted. "Three bouts in the sack and I get a *note*?" She turned on her heel and marched back to her bedroom, calling over her shoulder, "Put your dishes in the dishwasher and don't slam the door when you leave."

She closed and locked her bedroom door. Throwing herself on the bed, she wondered why she felt like shit.

Gabe wrote a note anyway. He knew better than to try to talk to her again. He'd got to know her ways over the weeks they'd been thrown together and in a mood like this, it was best to leave well alone. That didn't mean he wouldn't be swinging by to see her later – he wanted to catch her up on all the news. He couldn't believe he hadn't got round to telling her all about Mel and his arrest. Or that she hadn't asked him about the case. She knew, he hoped, he wouldn't have slept with her while she was still under his protection. She hadn't even asked about her guard.

She hadn't, in fact, questioned his ethics last night and he hadn't told her he'd, more or less, resigned from her case and his ethics were intact. That her case was, in fact, over – for his part as lead, anyway. Sure, there were technical things to finalise and Juan Garcia to find, and he'd make sure to be included on that. But last night their inability to do anything but have hot, sweaty sex had kind of taken over. Even as Gabe scribbled a few lines on a notepad on her table, he felt his cheeks flush again like a callow youth as his body remembered all the ways they'd come together – and not just in the orgasmic sense.

She'd felt so right in his arms. So natural. It was slightly terrifying. He knew he was on a short-term contract. He knew, from all the times she'd slagged off men and relationships, that she absolutely didn't want anything serious, but . . . *Yes, but.*

He closed the door quietly behind him and drove carefully back to his apartment to shower and change. Work, lots of paperwork and processing, had to be done and although in some ways he felt more alert than he had in a long time, in other ways he felt unbearably tired.

He checked his watch. He'd meet Flynn in an hour at the station and, he realised, they'd also have to call Ali in at some stage to make a statement. He hoped that could happen at a point when he, Flynn and Ali were *not* all in the same room together.

Her brother was, unfortunately in this instance, a very good detective.

Chapter 13

Ali arrived at the station several hours and many, many cups of strong coffee later. Her mood had improved only marginally. A hot shower to ease some aches and her breakfast of reheated bacon along with muesli and fruit had also helped. Gabe had even drunk coffee, she remembered now. He must have been pretty damn tired to engage with actual caffeine.

Gabe.

That's how she thought of him now. *How could she not?* It suited him. Strong and wolflike. Maybe that was a bit of an exaggeration, since she'd never encountered a wolf in real life, but, hey, she could use her imagination. *Gabe. Sexy as fuck. A man who knew exactly what to do with his body. And hers.*

What a treat.

Ali was mostly used to directing operations or taking care of it herself, so giving up control was new. And strangely erotic. What a shame she couldn't explore it further. *Or not.* Ali didn't want to explore sex any more than her norm. She had her hard limits, but not in a BDSM way. There were just some things she would not, could not, partake of and so never, ever allowed a sexual encounter to develop to the stage where there were "expectations". *No point.* No regrets. No recriminations.

And then there was the note. The crumpled paper was

stuck in the back pocket of her jeans and she would throw it out. When she got to the station, she'd find a bin and toss it. *Definitely*. The bastard had written, in a bold script:

Ali, I am not good at this, at the words.
Know I leave you this morning with regret.
I will phone you later.
Gabe

He hadn't phoned. Flynn had, all business – come down to my office, we need to talk. There's been a development. *Well, fuck.*

"Hey," she said, strolling into Flynn's workspace. "What's up?"

Flynn pushed back from his desk and walked round to envelop her in a hug. Resisting, Ali leaned back, worried.

"You're freaking me out, bro, what the hell?"

He drew her in tight and placed a kiss on the top of her head.

"It's over. Well, almost. And at least one of the jerks is behind bars."

Ali stilled, letting his words sink in. *Safe. It was over.* The fucker who'd vandalised her place was caught.

"Who?" she ground out. "I want to know who and why. And then I want to meet him, face to face."

She pulled back from her brother, suddenly feeling a bit shaky at the knees. Dragging out his office visitor chair, she sank down and put her head between her knees. *Christ. It was almost over.* Righting herself after a few moments of Flynn rubbing her back in gentle strokes, she took the glass of water offered.

176

"Tell me everything."

It took a while and Ali threw question after question at him, which he answered patiently. She was righteously furious with Mel Carney, had considered him a decent bloke and colleague, if not a friend. Had given him a job when he'd asked. *The bastard.*

After a while, Flynn asked another officer to join them in the room and they took an official statement from Ali.

"Where's Gabe?" she finally asked.

"With Carney, tying up all the loose ends . . . wait, did you just refer to him by name?" Flynn stood alarmingly still as he stared intently at his sister.

"Why wouldn't I?" she tossed back hastily. "It's what he's called, isn't it?"

She could have kicked herself for that slip-up. Flynn was no fool. And he obviously wasn't buying it.

"What have you done?" he asked coolly.

"Done? Nothing. Why would we have *done* anything?" she protested.

Flynn groaned. "Shit, Ali. Seriously? What have you done? And I didn't ask what you, plural, had done, I asked *you*. And now I know I was right to be worried. Out with it."

"Fuck off, Flynn, you're not my keeper, even if you're his," she sneered.

"Who is my keeper?" A quiet, Gabe-sounding voice spoke behind her.

And there he was. *The note-leaver. In person.*

Gabe and Flynn exchanged some incomprehensible looks and neither of them appeared remotely happy about it.

Flynn grunted under his breath about ethics and

177

glared at Gabe, who simply said, "I was off the case. Zero conflict. No dice, Fitz." He then turned to Ali, acknowledging her for the first time, and said, "Would you like to come and talk to Carney? He is in lock-up and someone will be with you, but I think you might need to hear him out."

Ali so wanted to tell him to take a hike, but she *was* curious, *damn him*. And Gabe knew she wouldn't let it go till she discovered the reasons behind the destruction left in her precious space.

"Yeah, I do want to have a little chat with my former colleague. Just as well he wasn't due on-set till this week – now I don't have to deal with having given air time to a criminal." She rose from her chair and placed the glass on the table. She turned to Flynn. "How did you catch him?"

Flynn tossed his head in Gabe's direction. "Ask supersleuth here – he's the one who broke the case. Now, get out of my office, I've work to do. But, hey . . . " He glared at Gabe. "You and I need to talk."

Ali strode to the door. Turning, she said, "I'm an adult, Flynn. What I do, with whomever I choose to do it, is my own business, so back the hell off."

And she left the room, Gabe following.

"You may find this more difficult than you imagine, so I'm going to have Garda Bridget Lennon in the room with you. I believe you know each other a little," Gabe said in a low voice as they walked down the stairs to the lock-up and interrogation rooms.

"I don't need anyone," Ali replied, her tone short.

"I disagree. If you won't take Garda Lennon, please suggest someone else."

Ali glanced back up at him from the lower step. "No."

"This is not negotiable – it is either Garda Lennon or me. Take your pick."

He moved ahead of her to decode a door lock and pushed it open. It was a plain room with no windows, a table and several chairs the only furniture. Mel sat on one chair that appeared to be chained to the floor. Garda Lennon sat opposite Mel but stood when they walked into the small space. Some electronic equipment sat on the table and Mel's handcuffed wrists rested on the surface also.

"Hey, Bridge," Ali greeted the other woman, trying to remain casual so the importance of what she was about to do would seem normalised. "You don't have to stay. Mackenzie will be my bodyguard, though this piece of shit doesn't look like he's capable of harming me."

"It's not what you think, Ali!" Mel practically moaned. "They won't believe me. I did nothing, not really. And it wasn't my . . . " He stopped, took a breath, started again. "Just . . . " He lapsed into silence, shaking his head wearily, a hand rubbing his nose.

Sweat beaded on his forehead and he could definitely do with a shower.

Ali put out a hand, like a stop sign. "You know what, Mel? I couldn't give more shits that they don't believe you. Why should anyone believe you? No one believes a criminal. But here's what I'll do . . . " She pulled out a chair, turned it and sat, arms resting along the back like she didn't have a care in the world. "I'll listen to you. And if I believe you're telling me the truth, I'll talk to the boss upstairs and see what can be done, okay?"

She figured changing tack and becoming complacent,

understanding, would throw him off his stride and couldn't help but get her what she wanted.

She ignored the sound of protest from Garda Lennon and then realised that Gabe was showing her out with quiet mutterings between them. The door shut and she imagined he was propped with his back against it, standing guard. She wouldn't look. She didn't want to appear as if she needed back-up and she wanted Mel focused on her, believing in her, as he told his pathetic excuse of the truth.

"Go ahead, Mel, I'm listening." *Fuck,* she sounded like a therapist.

He was an excuse for a man. No other way to put it. He "married above himself", his words, and had spent the last three years trying to please the unpleasable, and drowning in debt to do it. It was his wife's fault, naturally, he'd whined, and all he'd been doing was trying to make her happy. And her idea of happiness, it turned out, was to be married to a celebrity.

He believed that he was next in line to be the chef, after Ali. She didn't bother explaining about it not being a proper competition because why should she? He managed to be a complete tool without her help, he didn't require additional material. Plus, he could bawl that out to the media when he got out on bail, as he surely would. She wouldn't give him any ammunition to hurt her any more.

"So, you thought it was okay to follow me, hurt me, push me down steps, knock me off my bike, destroy my property, my space, in order to push me out and ensure your wife was asked for a double-page spread in *VIP* magazine because she was married to you? The new chef. Is that correct?" Ali kept her tone cajoling and indulgent, reeling the fool in so he felt like she, of all people, would be sympathetic.

"But *I* never meant to hurt you, that wasn't *my* plan, that's on Juan," he'd insisted, all innocence, like she should be grateful to him. "*I'd* never *actually* hurt you. It was just supposed to be a little scare, a little shove here and there. Just enough to stop you from being ready for the show. Because then they'd pick me."

Ali rolled her eyes at his stupidity. "Yeah, yeah. Blah, blah. Is Juan the short guy who was with you at my loft? The fucker who shoved me down the steps? Where is he? I want a word with him."

"I don't know. Really. He was just someone, a guy who hooked me up with some . . . you know, stuff. He wasn't meant to hurt you – or least not badly. *I* wasn't going to hurt you at all."

She'd almost lost it at that, he was such a sanctimonious-sounding bastard, and had reared up from the chair, tossing it aside with a clang. Gabe didn't move from his post as she slammed her hands on the table and shoved her face into his. And then she really let fly.

She couldn't remember everything she'd yelled into his face, didn't need to, and she sighed in satisfaction as she held a cup of coffee, slightly trembling, in her hands a little while later. The canteen was almost empty and Gabe had pushed her, none too gently, into a chair and strode off to get her a drink. She took a sip and almost spat it out.

"Jesus! This tastes revolting. Did you sweeten it? Fuck, Scot, the coffee is gross enough here without that."

Gabe sat back opposite her at the small table and held his own mug of tea in his hands.

181

"You need the sugar. You are shaking like a leaf. I should *not* have let you go in unprepared. I am sorry."

He put the mug down and ran a hand over his head in frustration.

"You couldn't have stopped me," she said, her voice cool. "No one could have. It was my right to speak with him. I needed to hear him admit his crimes to my face. To know it was him. And is Juan my swarthy individual? I'd like to get him alone in a room." She took another sip. Grimaced but drank again before lowering it to the table. "Did you see Mel's expression when he asked if I could put in a word for him?" A grin, unexpected and as wide as a mile, split her face in half.

Gabe's lips twitched. And then he broke and a smile – the first real one she'd ever seen on him – spread across his face as a flash of white teeth appeared momentarily.

"And your response," he said, "was top-notch. 'I lied,' you said, keeping your tone majestic as you swept from the room. We have all eyes on the lookout for Juan Garcia, but with Carney in here, the chances are Garcia has fled. We now know from Carney that drugs, and a considerable amount of, have changed hands and Garcia seems to be the supplier. We will get him. Eventually. All I can say, Ali Fitzgerald, is congratulations. Well played. And well done." His face resumed its normal expression as he continued, toasting her with his mug. "Seriously, excellent interrogation skills. Are you sure you wouldn't like to join the force when you tire of baking and being a celebrity? I would take you on my team."

She caught his eyes, serious and grave as normal.

"Would you? Never mind . . . " She rose from her

chair, putting her cup down. "This celebrity chef is going home. I'm a bit wrecked, to be honest."

He moved to walk with her.

"Not much sleep last night?" he enquired, his hand moving to rest against her back as her steps faltered for a second.

"Going *there*, are we?"

"I hope so."

Christ. He knew how to stop a girl in her tracks.

"Are you saying you want a repeat of last night?"

He stopped and turned towards her, placing his hands on her shoulders, forcing her to still.

"Yes. I do. We were good together. I thought you enjoyed it as much as I did?"

"Well, yeah, we were. And I did. But . . . "

Ali was thrown. Completely thrown. She'd assumed it was a hook-up, plain and simple. *Nothing remotely plain or simple about what they did, though, nothing at all. What to do? What the fuck to do?* She gaped at him, knowing she looked moronic but unable to come up with a single reason why they shouldn't go back to her flat – *or his, she wasn't picky* – and bang each other's brains out. She tried to recall all the reasons it was a bad, very bad, idea. Her mind, *traitorous lump that it obviously was*, refused to cooperate.

He stood in front of her, waiting as she mulled things over. Mature fella that he was, he didn't break in with persuasive comments or worse, backtrack because of her hesitancy. He simply waited her out. *Smart, smart man.*

She smiled at him.

"Wait here," he said. "I need to swing by my office and then we will go."

He stared at her, his eyes darkening as they took in her now heated cheeks. He bent and kissed her, hard, on the mouth, gripping her behind her neck in a deliciously possessive manner. His mouth seared hers and desire flooded through her. He let her go.

Blinking in his way, he repeated, "Wait," and turned and strode from the canteen.

Shit, that man could turn her to mush.

This was probably the worst idea ever.

Gabe stuck his head in Flynn's office and said a brisk, "Not now," then moved on to his own space.

He gathered papers from his new case, packed them into a bag and left to collect Ali without a backwards glance. He heard Flynn calling his name in exasperation but kept walking. He knew this was monumentally stupid, what he was doing, but for once in his adult life he wanted to go with stupid. He was always on his game, always correct, always mindful.

Not this time.

No, he'd be mindful of Ali. He'd mind her *very* carefully.

Leaning against the door in the interrogation room, he'd felt powerful waves of anger and frustration emanating from her thin frame. He'd also felt, very keenly, a sense of loss. From her. He hadn't delved deeper. And he didn't intend to. He just knew, bone-deep knew, that she needed him and that she needed to be taken away from her headspace until she could adjust and make sense of what Mel Carney had done to her understanding of trust.

Gabe also knew that Ali wasn't able to trust well or

openly. It wasn't simply from the casual remarks she threw around regarding honesty, especially where men were concerned, but like her anger and her loss, he felt it deep in his gut. Taking her to bed wasn't the answer, for either of them, but it would help. It would hopefully sate his powerful attraction towards her and help him to put his burgeoning need to be with her to rest. And a good bout of sex was a great stress reliever. Everyone knew that. And despite his admittedly stupid choice, he was also perfectly happy to go with "everyone" in this instance.

She was standing where he'd left her, unnaturally still. Probably in a state of shock – not because of what they intended to do but because of what had happened earlier with Mel. Relief when something is over can be overwhelming and he was going to take care of her. In all the ways.

He took her hand and walked her to his jeep, strapped her in then headed back to his apartment. She may need somewhere different to process, he thought, and he had a wonderful deep bathtub where she could soak. She didn't speak and nor did he engage her in conversation while he drove. Instead, he kept her hand in his, his thumb absently stroking her skin.

Up in his apartment, he sat her on the leather couch as he ran a bath, adding herbs and oils from bottles his mother and grandmother had given him years ago. He rarely used them – but once or twice, when his body hurt from chasing criminals or he'd not been quick enough to dodge a bullet, literally, these herbs and oils had soothed his aching limbs. He knew Ali wasn't physically hurt – *though she could be tender from last night*, a thought that gave him pause regarding his intentions for later –

but pampering and minding should always begin with a bath.

She went with him willingly to the bathroom, which was beautifully scented with rosemary and jasmine. It shouldn't work, the easing of tension through the sense of smell, but even he recognised the power of a healing aroma. He stripped her of her clothing, efficient and tender, doing his best to keep all unnecessary touches at bay. *So hard to do.* Her skin was pale and velvety, smooth and delicate.

Usually none of those things in the cerebral sense, she let him hand her into the tub and as she sank down, he switched off the main light after lighting the selection of candles placed along a wooden ledge, throwing the room into soft, flickering shadow. It wasn't dark outside, so an interior bathroom had its uses. This quiet, restful place definitely had its uses, and Gabe was going to see that quiet and rest were exactly what Ali received.

Gabe left the door ajar so he could hear her if she called. He ordered a takeaway meal – a rarity for him, but he figured she needed all the calories and all convenience. He prepared a salad to go with the kebabs, rice and chips he'd ordered. When it comes to takeaway, several food groups should always be ordered and sampled and then, unethical as it was, either dumped or left for a very speedy if rather lard-laden breakfast.

He opened a bottle of Portuguese wine and left it to breathe. When the food arrived, he placed it in the oven to keep warm and peeped his head round the bathroom door to check on Ali. She lay there with her head back against the padded rubber cushion he'd left for her, her eyes closed.

Keeping them shut, she said, "I'm almost ready."

"No rush. There is a robe on the rail – it's clean. Throw that on and come into the living room when you feel like it." And he left her alone.

When Ali wandered into the large room lit by evening sun, Gabe looked up from the papers he was studying and his heart stuttered. She looked . . . The word "angelic" came to mind like before, but it still wasn't right. Ali Fitzgerald was no angel and nor would she appreciate being called one. *Nymph? Maybe.* Regardless, she set his blood on fire as the tousled hair was stuck up on end, freshly washed and glinting like icicles on a frosty day. The robe was huge, enveloping her tiny frame but managing to make her look sexy as hell. Gabe cleared his throat while she strolled towards him, hands lost in the deep pockets. He rose, papers set aside, and moved to stand in front of her.

"How do you feel?"

He did his best to keep his voice neutral. He deserved all the awards for his pretence at appearing untouched by her presence.

She smiled at him, a wide, natural, beautiful, open smile, and his heart stuttered some more.

"Great," she said. "I feel bloody marvellous. Are you a witch doctor, perchance?"

Gabe let out a laugh, pleased that his ministrations had helped. "That, I can assure you, is not on my list of credentials!"

"You are scarily in touch with your feminine side for a great big hulk of a man," she noted.

"You can thank the women in my life for that."

She raised her eyebrows.

"My mother and grandmother," he amended quickly before he tried her patience. "Sit." He indicated the table and chairs next to the window. "I'll bring you some food."

They ate. They talked. They even laughed. Gabe tried to do an impression of Ali berating Mel Carney that had her snorting and getting a coughing fit. She drank a glass of wine but refused another – he drank water. They discussed books and films. Switching on the TV to look for some comedy to watch, they argued vehemently over what *was* funny. Ali threw a cushion at him, lamenting his choice of *Dad's Army* while she voted for *The Office*. They watched *It Happened One Night*. Both agreed it was hard to beat Gable and Colbert.

"I know it's outdated and so not hashtag 'metoo', but I love it," Ali admitted as the credits rolled. "There's a cleverness to it that draws me in."

Gabe sat at one end of the couch with her feet on his lap while she lay back against a selection of cushions, a warm-coloured blanket tucked about her. He'd been massaging her feet, slowly and steadily, feeling her relax into his strong touch. He reached over, picked up the remote and switched off the TV.

Silence filled the darkened room. Blue eyes met green in the dusky space. Without taking his eyes from hers, Gabe rose from the couch, tossed aside the blanket and, gathering her up in his arms to the sound of her "oomph", walked purposefully to his bedroom. He could see her pulse beat rapidly in her neck and his own heart rate increased with each step.

"Are you sure?" he asked quietly, watching her eyes for any hint of demure.

She looked straight back at him, not breaking the spell of their locked eyes. She reached up her hand and slid her thumb across his lower lip. He barely controlled a groan as he inhaled a ragged breath.

"Yes, please, Gabe. I want this. I want it so much."

Relief surged through him and he rested his forehead on hers for a brief moment, letting out the breath he still held.

He kicked the door closed behind them.

Chapter 14

What to do, what to do? Ali soaped herself leisurely in Gabe's shower the following morning. He had all the products. Fancy names and high-end brands. Nothing girly and, she admitted ruefully, in another man, even that might have been a turn-off, but with him, it just came across as being sensible with his body. *And what a body! God, he was built – in shape – and sculpted like a frigging athlete.* His skin tone made her weak at the knees, literally. She'd practically swooned earlier when he'd pulled back the covers and rose from the bed to hit the shower. He was *café au lait* all over and barely a hair anywhere. Smooth and strong, he made her blood simmer with just a look.

He'd brought her coffee and explained that he needed to get to the office. Sunday was a workday like any other when he was on a case and in a way, she got that. She admired his commitment and attention to detail. When she was creating recipes, she never knew what day of the week it was so understood that side of things.

She was also painfully aware that baking and saving lives just *might* not be in the same league. She turned off the hot spray and wrapped herself in a huge towel then wandered through the apartment, drying her body as she peeped into all the different places she'd not seen before. She sat at the window, in the chair where she'd eaten supper, and stared unseeing through the, *damn it*, streak-free glass.

What to do . . . ?

He didn't have a schedule of his time in Dublin. Flynn had him "on loan" and it was up to the boss to decide how best to use this "natural" resource. Which meant she and, indeed, he had no clue how long he'd be in Dublin. *Did they start something casual, maybe hooking up regularly but with a no-strings clause?* She couldn't imagine dating anyone per se – she never did it and had no clue of the rules.

She smiled as she thought of the book series she enjoyed, set in the future about a dectective who was always wondering about the "rules" of being married and how crap Eve, the main character, was at it. It didn't hinder the situation that the fictional protagonist's hunky billionaire husband was tall, dark and Irish. But Lieutenant Dallas's problems weren't real . . . and Ali's present conundrum certainly was.

She drank the now cold coffee Gabe had left her and paced about his comfortable and styled living space. It told more about him, and he was only there temporarily, than hers did about her. She would talk to Caro about her sister's future plans and potential living arrangements next week when she flew home for her show's final episode and rap party.

As Ali dressed a little while later, she thought back on the word Gabe had uttered as he spent inside her. *Mine.* He'd said it before, or at least written it, and it should make her run for the hills. It really should. She'd think on that when she made pastry as prep for tomorrow's show.

She'd neatly avoided her "situational issues", as she called them, last night, but wondered, a frown deepening, how much longer that could last. Normal men would find her "wanting", that she knew for a certainty. But maybe Gabe was just left of normal enough not to mind. *Nah. Not a hope. He was a man first.* She'd take her pleasure where and *while* she could – and deal with the consequences later. Now, pastry-making awaited her.

On Tuesday, four days before they were to film the last show, they got the three other chefs to appear on the pastry episode and it was a great success. The others asked where Mel was, but Ali simply said he was detained elsewhere. She got a sharp glint of satisfaction saying that and hoping that the news of his arrest wouldn't be made public, she assumed that would be the end of things. The student bakers had great fun with the professional former competitors and they all unashamedly showed off how well they were doing. Ali was delighted. That would make great TV, she knew. Perhaps it didn't, after all, always have to be angst-ridden to gain viewers.

Gabe had come by her flat on Sunday about 10.30 p.m. He'd looked exhausted. He was working a high-profile but hush-hush case and it was draining his energy badly. He'd stayed for a cup of some flower-scented tea Ali had "accidentally" allowed to fall into her shopping basket before leaving. When he stood up to go, she'd been dismayed.

"You can stay here, you know. My sheets are as clean as yours."

She knew she'd sounded belligerent in tone and decided that was just too bad. He could suck it up.

"I'm not going home, Ali, I'm going back to the station."

God, he'd sounded so weary that she'd felt awful. And selfish.

They'd chatted for the half-hour he'd been on the couch and she'd made him smile by telling stories of the previous day's pastry attempts – hers – and about the expected guest trio arriving the next morning to ply theirs. Gabe had seemed more light-hearted as he'd teased her about her skills. He'd never heard of, let alone watched, *The Great British Bake Off*, so she'd shown him a few minutes of one of the shows on the iPlayer and, *what a charming man*, he told her she was better on the screen than any of them. Secretly pleased, she brushed it off and suggested a trip to Specsavers.

"Lock the door, Ali," he said as he wrapped his arms about her when they said goodnight.

"But I'm safe now. Mel's still locked up, right?" she'd protested.

He'd held her chin firmly and locked his eyes to hers. "But Garcia is not. Please do as I ask," he'd said.

And then he'd spoiled the bossy man part by kissing her so sweetly and tenderly that she'd felt tears rise and had to blink them back.

"Yeah, yeah, okay, Highlander, Mr Caveman, I'll lock up right and tight." She'd pulled back from him so she could see him properly. "But only if you promise not to spend the entire night working. Saviours of the weak and vulnerable need rest too, I've been reliably informed."

"Check your sources, Ms Fitzgerald, it's a myth." Then he'd placed another gentle kiss on her forehead and left.

Her back to the closed door, Ali had let herself breathe in the changes in their comings and goings. They hadn't ripped each other's clothes off like teenagers –

they'd talked. They hadn't had wild sex up against the wall before he left – they'd kissed. Soft and gentle. And yet here she was, her heart beating as if she'd just had an orgasm and was coming down from the high.

She *felt* like she was on a high.

She knew she was in deep, deep trouble.

Gabe closed the file and rubbed his eyes. He did some shoulder rolls and neck bends, side to side. This new case was the very worst kind. Alleged abuse of innocents, theoretically from a well-known person. Two women, both in their early twenties, had come forwards the previous week when an ex-priest, once a popular face on Irish TV, had returned from a sojourn in South America. He had, they accused, sexually abused them for two years when they were barely teenagers and he was at the height of his fame. They had, they said, told their parents, who had, in turn, told the bishop of the diocese.

Within a week of that conversation, the accused man had left the country. He'd since left the priesthood and made a career for himself in Buenos Aires, Argentina, as a youth counsellor. No gardaí had been involved back then, but the young women had seen a story about his return in a local paper in Wexford, their hometown, which was about two hours' drive south of Dublin. He'd been a parish priest there for a number of years, and they'd decided it was now time to tell their tale.

They'd approached the police and the inspector there had handed the case to Flynn, as the man had "got a feeling" things weren't quite as simple as all that. And knowing the ex-priest had been transferred down from Dublin, like a lot of accused clergy were, he became suspicious. Policemen and women the world over knew well to pay attention to "a feeling".

Flynn had been disgusted when trawling through the statements of the young women but had passed it to Gabe, murmuring something about conflict of interest, to liaise with the Wexford department. It wasn't pretty. None of it. And the more Gabe delved, the more he was uncovering.

It was a deep, dark hole.

And to make matters worse, something was nagging at him. Some small detail, one he believed vital, was just out of range in his brain and despite trying to let it in during the quiet headspace he tried to give himself each evening, it remained elusive. Gabe knew to let it go, for now, as experience taught him it would come. When he was ready.

He pushed up from his desk and checked his watch. It was Wednesday, mid-afternoon, and Ali and her crew were filming an outdoor segment in Dundrum centre. The students were showing off their wares to the public with demos and tasting. He needed a break so considered driving over and watching from afar, believing it to be as good a way to relax the building tension as any. At least that's what he was telling himself.

He missed her. He'd kissed her goodbye on Monday night and although they'd texted last night, he was definitely in dire need of a sighting. *God, he felt like a boy in his first flush of lust. It was exciting, exhausting and bloody nerve-racking.* He didn't remember being this wound up about a female in his entire life. That's because he'd never had the draw to another woman the way he had to her. It was like an invisible wire was attached to him and strung directly to her. He needed her in his orbit at all times.

And that was just fanciful. He knew that. But he left a message for anyone who needed him to call his mobile and exited the building with a spring in his step for the first time in days.

Dundrum was buzzing. All the bright young things out and about. Although spring was well under way, and some of the days even had the temptation of summer, Gabe shook his head at the clothing – or lack of it – on the young girls. *Teenagers*, he supposed. He was getting old if he was inwardly chastising them for their short skirts instead of appreciating them.

He spotted the camera crew and the set-up straight away in the outside area, where busy shoppers sauntered from one selection of emporiums to another. He held back, watching. There she was, behind the table, directing her class of learners. Karl, Mary and Blaine were there, too, getting as much from their few moments of fame as possible, Gabe supposed. And why wouldn't they? It was what Ali wanted for them, too. They and the students looked excited and happy, and Ali was laughing at something one of them said. He felt his heart knock in his chest and decided to let that be and not examine it. Not yet.

She wore one of her old-fashioned flowery aprons over her uniform of leggings and white shirt. *It was so Ali. Crisp and sharp yet with a hint of playfulness.* Her bright head of hair was styled to one side and it gave a sweeter look to her face. He'd better not say that, or she'd run her hand through it instantly, messing it up again. Her competence and professionalism were evident in every movement, every gesture. The director called "Action!" and Ali looked to the camera and began talking.

196

Gabe couldn't hear her words, but he watched the reactions of those around her. Her students visibly relaxed and the audience, gathering to a crowd as they realised what they were witnessing, were enchanted and laughing as she continued with her spiel and began offering samples. This was to be a teaser for the final show, rather than an episode itself. The rest were being aired starting with episode one this week, so the camera was on and off, not filming everything, just snippets. It was also sweeping the audience for their expressions and comments, both verbal and physical. Gabe leaned against a shop wall and watched.

After about half an hour studying the crowd, moving and changing but always thronging, Gabe decided he'd venture forth and surprise Ali by turning up at her table for one of the samples that were on offer. Before he could push himself away from the bricks, he felt the cold. Stilling, he let it flood him and he listened. The hairs on his arms and the back of his neck were raised and his heart had slowed to an unnatural pace as he let his senses do their thing.

Something was off. Was this what was bothering him earlier? No, it couldn't be. This was new. Different. Immediate.

Someone was in danger.

He studiously moved through the crowd, his eyes searching for the unusual, the odd, the out of place. *He was good at this*, he reminded himself as fears for Ali rose rather urgently in his chest. She looked up as he neared and smiled – her bright, "I'm so in charge here" smile – and he felt an absurd burst of anger that he was about to change that. Wipe that gorgeous berry-red smile right off her face.

Instead of smiling back, he gestured with his head for her to move to the side and when she glared at him, he did it again, more urgently. Sighing rather obviously, she whispered something to the students, who happily stepped into her place like the pros they were becoming, and walked over to the edge of the set, waiting for him.

"What the fuck, Outlander?" she said. "I'm kinda in the middle of something here, in case you hadn't noticed."

She stuck her hands on her hips, cross and irritated – such a 100 per cent turnabout from her expression mere moments before that Gabe hated what he was about to do.

"You need to shut this down," he said sternly. "Now."

She gaped at him. "Are you crazy? I can't do that! This is a *thing*. For the show. Jesus, Gabe, be serious. Time is money and all." She swung her arms about to indicate the display and the crowd as if he were blind to it.

"I am aware of that, but something is not right and I believe you are in danger."

Gabe was glancing about, eyes serious and intent as he continued to look for a clue to what may happen.

"Spidey senses kicking in?" Ali said, a whole lot of sneer loud and clear. "Look," she continued, "I know you believe you're all supernatural and ESP-ish but, seriously, I'm fine. I'm safe here. Fucking Mel is behind bars. And we're in a public place, so what could he do, anyway?"

"Nevertheless," Gabe said, taking her by the arm and practically dragging her over to the director and producer, "I'm shutting it down."

He ignored her protests and quietly spoke to the few crew members, giving out a simple story about Ali being needed at the station for another statement and that they should close up "shop".

"Righto," Len, the cameraman, said cheerfully, "we're all done now, anyway."

He grabbed another crew member and they began to dissemble all the equipment.

Gabe was carefully directing the bakers away from the set-up, when he noticed a rucksack behind the back leg of the table where Ali had been standing demonstrating. A chill went down his spine as he quickly ushered everyone away from the table, then he bent down and crawled underneath to reach for the bag.

"What's that?" Ali asked, crouching beside him. "It's not mine."

"Ali, get up slowly and walk away. If you see anyone else around this table, take them with you. Do it. Now!" he added as she kneeled beside him, her mouth slowly opening in shock as the meaning of his words sank in.

"Shit, Gabe, what is it? No, don't tell me, I can guess. There's tons of people milling around, how am I supposed to get them clear of here?"

"Figure it out. Now go, dammit."

Ali glared at him. Opened her mouth to protest. But seeing the look on his face, she thought better of it. Nodding briskly, she backed away from the table, stood and, using the megaphone for crowd control, politely asked everyone to move to the other side of the pond and fountain area. The crew needed to clean up, she said, and she'd happily sign autographs and hand out more samples. She began directing them off to the left, away from Gabe and his suspicious bag.

Putting her, and everyone else, out of his mind, Gabe reached over and very, very slowly opened the zipper. He could feel beads of sweat down his back, but he kept focused on the interior of the bag. *And there it was: a home-made rather crude pipe bomb.*

Small but big enough to do some damage.

Especially to the one person standing over it just a few short minutes ago.

He studied it. Eyes taking in every aspect. He wasn't an explosives expert by any means, but he'd been in not too dissimilar situations before and knew what to do. He leaned forwards, listening for any sound, anything telling. *There it was. A ticking.* If he hadn't been so focused he'd have smiled, grim though that might have been.

He felt like he was watching a vintage TV show. It had a timer, which was good. Okay, not good, but better than a remote control that used a mobile phone to trigger it. *And, there* . . . He gingerly moved some of the canvas fabric aside and saw the clock: thirty-seven seconds to blast-off. And counting.

Right.

With not a moment to spare, he grabbed the bag, surged to his feet and within seconds, had it tossed into the water a few metres behind him.

Grabbing his gun from the inside of his jacket, he fired into the ground, stunning everyone in the vicinity into complete silence, into which he shouted, "Everyone, get down, *now*!" And they did.

He threw himself to the paving slabs just as a loud explosion erupted from the fountain, showering anyone close enough with water and concrete debris.

Following the initial few seconds of silence, all hell broke loose and people started screaming and running. Shouting and calling the names of their loved ones.

Grimly, Gabe raised himself up onto one elbow,

wincing as bits of rubble fell off him. The main structure was still intact, which at least prevented all the water from spilling out, but much of the top capping of the surrounding low wall, especially on his side, was scattered around him.

He stood, reeled slightly, righted himself and looked about.

Ali came barrelling towards him, face as white as a sheet, and threw herself into his arms.

"I'm sorry, I'm sorry, I'm sorry," she gabbled over and over, hugging him tight.

"It's fine." Gabe held her close, one arm tight about her shaking frame. "I am fine." Kissing her head, he took a step back and blanched. There was blood on her face and neck, and he felt his insides freeze. "You're hurt," he gasped, running his hands over her.

"No," she said. "I didn't get hit at all."

At that, they both realised at the same time that it wasn't her blood.

It was his.

Chapter 15

Ali paced. She didn't realise she had pacing in her. But no, it seemed she'd become a pacer – and no bloody wonder. How did anyone stay still when all the worries, the fears, the anxieties, *for someone else*, swirled around one like a frigging cold fog? A restless energy that came from frustration and anger. That's exactly what she felt now. Someone's head would roll. She'd make fucking sure of that.

"Ali . . . "

Her brother's voice interrupted her traipsing. Flynn. Everything would be okay now – he always made everything better. He strode towards her, his tall, lanky frame the dearest sight in the world, and suddenly Ali was in his arms, shaking.

"He could have been killed, Flynn. He could have died."

Sobs broke free as Flynn wrapped his arms about her and let her weep. With a gentle hand at her back, he held her for a few more moments before handing her a handkerchief from his pocket.

Ali sniffled out a gasp. "You and Gabe always have these," she half laughed. "Is it a prerequisite for your job description?"

Flynn pulled her gently towards the plastic waiting area chairs as hospital people hurried back and forth. They were in the emergency department of St Vincent's hospital in Dublin and Gabe had been gone for ages.

She told Flynn that, but he just smiled kindly and said, "No, sis, not really. I gather he needs stitches and maybe some X-rays, so we need to be patient."

"How did you get that info? They won't tell me anything." Ali finished mopping her tears and blew her nose vigorously. "I suppose you have pull here, too? You seem to be able to get anyone to tell you anything. It's not fair," she whined.

"Unfortunately, the staff here in the A & E know me only too well. They understand that any garda or detective who comes through their doors in an emergency capacity gets reported to me. They're great here, totally professional, and will take good care of Mac. Now, come, sit," he said, pointing to two chairs.

Ali sat. She turned to look at her brother, who was as tranquil as a pool of water on the stillest day of the year. He stretched his long legs out in front, crossed at the ankles, and folded his arms across his chest.

"Aren't you worried?" Ali asked, her hands restless in her lap.

Flynn tilted his gaze in her direction. "About him?" He inclined his head towards the closed doors. "No," he said.

"Then why are you here?" she challenged.

"Because I thought you might be injured, too. The report was sketchy."

"Oh." She sighed. "I didn't mean to worry you with my garbled message from the ambulance, but when Gabe passed out, I panicked," she admitted in a small voice. "I'm sorry. I should have told you I was fine."

He uncrossed his arms and pulled her close to his side. "I wouldn't have believed you. And I'm glad I'm here. You're most likely in shock and may have a reaction later."

They sat in silence for a bit, the bustle of the busy A & E – nurses, orderlies, doctors, families – some distraught and anxious, some smiling and relieved – buzzing about them. All life surely passed through these corridors, and Ali and Flynn, a part of it now, sat and absorbed it all.

"Oh, shit!" Ali suddenly exclaimed. "I forgot. Jesus, Flynn, I completely forgot in the mad rush to the hospital. I saw him! I saw Garcia, or at least I think I did."

Alert, notepad whipped out from his pocket, Flynn asked, "Where? When? Details, please."

Ali rubbed a hand behind her neck, the strain of the last few hours showing and being felt. "It was when Gabe had me moving everyone back from the table area. I was giving it the once-over to make sure we were all safe and as Gabe shot his gun, I caught a glimpse of who I think was Juan Garcia. He was standing off to the side, near the McDonald's, and I spotted him because he stayed standing and everyone else was diving to the ground."

"What was he doing?"

"Nothing! Just watching. I'm sure it was him. Maybe someone else saw him, too. You should check, ask questions, talk to witnesses."

Flynn glanced up from his notebook and looked at her. "Oh, really? You think?"

Ali sighed. "Duh, of course. Sorry." She scrubbed her hand over her face, exhausted and worried. "I just thought you should know."

Flynn nudged her shoulder. "This is great. Thank you. I didn't mean to be sarcastic."

He pulled out his phone, tapped in a number and spoke briefly, giving Ali's account of events. He pocketed the phone and rested his hand gently over Ali's fidgeting fingers.

"You seem rather . . . concerned about Mac," Flynn said quietly after a while. "Is there something I should know?" He cocked an eyebrow at Ali, who felt her cheeks heat. "Other than that," he qualified dryly.

"He's . . . different. He cares. About me. I think."

She sounded muddled, she knew she did, but that was because she was muddled. When she'd heard the blast, even already understanding that it was some kind of device, her heart had simply stopped. The fear had been huge. Bigger than anything. Gabe might be hurt. When she saw him stand upright her heart had started beating again, only to be stilled once more at the sight of his blood. *On her. On him.* And when he passed out in the ambulance and the two paramedics had worked on him with all kinds of tubes and injections, she'd known a terror too large to contemplate.

"You don't have to care back, you know, just because he cares for you. It's not an obligation or a . . . or an expectation. I'm pretty sure that's a known fact." Flynn spoke quietly, not looking at her, just making a casual observance.

"Shit, I know that. But he makes me feel . . . I don't know how to describe it. I feel more myself with him than I ever thought I would with anyone outside our family. It scares me stupid. I don't do relationships and I'm pretty sure Gabe doesn't either, so I'm trying to stay cool about it all. And it's not just sex, you know, it—"

"Stop!" Flynn interjected urgently. "Stop right there. I really do *not* want to know anything about what my sister and my colleague are doing between the sheets.

Argh! Now I've said those words out loud. Dammit, Ali. Keep your thoughts to yourself or my ears will be sullied. I can't take it. I've enough on my plate."

His look of abject horror made Ali burst out laughing, the first tiny sensation of relief she'd felt in hours. She remembered something else.

"Hey, did you call or text Mum and Dad? I bet this is on the news already and they'll freak out."

"Taken care of," Flynn said. "And yes, it is all over social media, too. The joys of being a celebrity, however minor," he added with a wink.

She chuckled again, relieved she could.

A doctor walked towards them as Ali got herself under control.

"Fitzgerald?" the doctor asked curiously, looking about.

Both Ali and Flynn rose to their feet.

"Yes," they said simultaneously.

The doctor looked mildly amused and glanced down at her notes.

"Hmm, it seems I do need two of you." She turned to Flynn and said, "I need some forms filled in by you, if you're the Flynn Fitzgerald who's Detective Mackenzie's boss. And . . . " She studied her papers again. "If you're Ali . . . " She got no further before Ali grabbed her arm.

"Is he okay? Will he be okay?" she begged.

The doctor looked surprised. "Oh. Yes. Sorry. I should have said. He's going to be fine. In time. He's very lucky – a few centimetres to the left and I'd be telling you a different story."

"Does he need surgery?" Flynn asked.

"No. Or least nothing more than the minor stitching up we've already done."

Ali interrupted again. "Can I see him?"

"Yes, he's been asking after you. Go through those doors. He's in the second bed on the left."

With a grin at Flynn, Ali rushed off, pushing open the double doors as if she were Wonder Woman herself.

He looked dreadful. Pale, tired and uncomfortable. He was sitting on the side of the bed, grimacing. He was in his trousers, with a large bandage wrapped about his upper torso and over his left shoulder. His once white shirt lay in a bloodied mess on the floor.

"You scared the shit out of me," Ali said through gritted teeth as she strode towards him.

She wasn't really sure of the etiquette in these circumstances, not used to being either desirous of seeing someone who'd been hurt or of what to expect and how to act when that person was the one she'd been sleeping with. It was a conundrum.

Fortunately, Gabe was the sane one in the room and he said quietly, "Come here."

Within seconds, she was wrapped in his good arm and inhaling his very specific scent like sniffing out water in the dessert. Strangely, he seemed to be doing the same to her.

He spoke into her neck. "Thank God you're okay. I was worried sick. They told me you were in the ambulance but couldn't say if that was because you were hurt, too, or not."

She pulled away and sat on the side of the bed, careful not to jar the bandaged shoulder.

"Of course I was in the ambulance, you idiot," Ali snarled, her fear returning as she saw how weary he was. "You passed out as they were helping you in and there was no way I was letting them go without me. The fact that I had blood on me probably made them agree, in case it was mine." She traced her fingers gently over the bandage across his chest. "What did they do, the doctors, I mean?"

"A flying piece of sharp stone got embedded near my shoulder, which they removed and stitched. The rest," he indicated the expanse of white dressings, "these are just scratches they have cleaned and are keeping wrapped for now as a precaution."

"God, it could have been so much worse. I'm so glad you're okay. So fucking glad."

"Thank you." Gabe smiled slightly. "I would really like to go home now. If you could call a taxi, I would be most grateful."

"That won't be necessary," Flynn said, his head appearing round the curtain. "I'll be taking you," he paused, "but not to your flat. You'll be going to my parents' place."

His tone brooked no argument, but he got them – arguments. Loud and clear, from both Ali and Gabe. Protestations were useless. Flynn had that way. People just did what he said. Eventually.

"My mother will be eternally grateful. You saved her middle daughter, the current star in our family unit. Here." He picked up Gabe's jacket and helped him to get his arms inside then Ali buttoned it closed.

Flynn began gathering up Gabe's other belongings as the man in question stood with a bewildered look on his face. Ali, once she realised it was the Flynn way or no way, got on board and insisted she go, too.

"Mum will want to see I'm okay," she reasoned, not untruthfully.

The three of them headed out to Flynn's vehicle, some

nondescript SUV, with Gabe, protesting all the way, in a wheelchair.

As they piled into the car, Ali noticed Flynn had a smirk, *an actual smirk*, on his face and she knew she'd been played. She caught his eyes in the mirror as she settled into the back seat and stuck her tongue out, maturity personified. *He winked. The bastard brother winked.*

Ali flopped back against the leather and try as she might, she couldn't stop the smile sneaking across her face. *Bloody Flynn.* He knew she wouldn't have gone home to their parents, or anywhere, without Gabe, so he'd used the wounded man as bait to get her safely to their mum and dad, who must, she realised, be going crazy, as it was all over the news and social media already. *Clever.*

The sheets were cool and comfortable, and his pillow soft and pliable. Gabe knew he should be grateful for the care, but he was chomping at the bit, eager to get back to work and find out who the hell was responsible for the bomb. A knock at the door alerted him to his grumpiness and he settled his face to one of acceptance as he called a "Come in."

Jo Fitzgerald walked in carrying a tray and placed it on his bedside table.

"Gabe," she said pleasantly, "are you sure I can't call your parents? Either of them? They may have heard and will be worried sick, I'm sure. I know when it's Flynn," she continued, prattling on as she poured tea and arranged a napkin over his duvet-covered legs, "I'm an actual basket case till I hear from him." She smiled as she handed him the tea and placed a plate of home-made brown bread with butter and marmalade, her traditional cure-all, on his lap.

"No, thank you," he replied to her original question. "My parents are fine. They are used to me being in touch when I can and the silences when I can't. They will be fine. I promise to text both of them in a while," he added as he saw the "mum" look settle on her face. "Honestly."

It was a little after 8 a.m. and he'd slept, although fitfully and in some discomfort, since he'd been left alone at about 11.30 p.m. the previous night. He'd finally had to promise Ali to text her, down the hall, if she was needed. She'd been so pale, so exhausted, and by then swimming in an overload of hot, sweet tea, that she'd agreed. He obviously wasn't completely out of it, or maybe he was, because he could still feel her tender kiss as she bade him goodnight.

Flynn had left instructions, via the doctor, that he was not to move for twenty-four hours and he'd put his mother on duty. Gabe was silently furious but couldn't be rude to this lovely, kind woman, carefully fussing about the room as he tried to eat and settle himself more comfortably.

"How is your daughter this morning?" he enquired between bites.

He had to admit, the bread was delicious, the tea, the old-fashioned kind, hot and strong, and it felt . . . nice to be tended.

Jo walked back from the window and perched on the side of his bed.

"Sleeping like the dead. Oh, I suppose I shouldn't say that. But you know what I mean." She fussed with the blanket laid across the end of his bed, tying and untying the fringe. "I can't thank you enough. I was so worried when I heard the newsflash and remembered she'd been in Dundrum for the film thing. Of course we got a call from Flynn, so knew she was fine, but still. I . . . we . . . we're so incredibly grateful to you."

Jo smiled mistily at him and he could feel his cheeks colour under her scrutiny. *This was dreadful.* He hated this kind of attention at the best of times, but if they knew what he and Ali had been doing, well, they may not be so grateful then.

"Not at all," he said, clearing his throat when it came out rusty. "I am just sorry it happened. Flynn and I, we are not sure how it could have occurred, but we will be looking into it, I can assure you."

"Of course, dear," she said, patting the bedclothes where his legs were. "I have complete faith in you both. Now . . . " She stood, reaching for the empty plate and cup. "Get some rest and when Ali wakes and she's eaten, I'll send her up to you. Perhaps a game of Scrabble."

Without giving him time to answer, she sailed from the room, closing the door behind her. *A small but formidable force, that woman* – not in some ways like his own mother. Protective to the core yet loving. The very best kind.

He lay back against the pillows and closed his eyes to concentrate, letting his brain work its cogs and wheels as he tried to figure out just what had happened or, more importantly, *how.*

He reached for his phone, wincing as the stitches pulled and his scratched ribs protested. He got through to Flynn instantly and barked out, "Who let the ball drop?"

Flynn's voice was as irritated as his own as he went over some particulars with Gabe, the most worrying being that it couldn't have been Mel. He was well and truly alibied out. Seen and heard at his lawyer's office when the blast occurred. Both agreed, reluctantly, that even if he'd been in the vicinity, he didn't have the brain power, either, to make a bomb or hire someone to do it. And in truth, Gabe believed Mel when he'd sworn he'd not intended to harm Ali herself – just cause disruption.

There was that nagging in his brain again. Mel may not want to harm her, but . . . No, the thought was a whisper gone in the wind. *Damn.* Ali would be annoyed that Mel was even out on bail, but they had to follow the law and go through the procedures – he wasn't a flight risk and the pathetic man appeared to be devoted to his equally pathetic whining wife.

By the time he put down his phone his brain was whirring again. Someone, or rather, it seemed, Juan Garcia, was out to get Ali and this time he wasn't sure it was all baking-related. *Why would it be?* Mel wasn't going to be on the show now, so why would his one-time "partner in crime" want to continue the job? They were missing something. Something vital. Garcia definitely needed to be caught and questioned. But most worrying was the notion that someone else entirely was pulling the strings. And they hadn't a clue who that might be.

"It's not fair," Ali complained as Gabe scored another whopper on the board. She tallied up what was in front of her and didn't like it one bit. "You're only supposed to be smart in a couple of ways," she grumbled, "not *all* bloody ways."

Gabe looked smug as he eased himself back against the pile of cushions she'd procured for him in the hope of easing his discomfort.

212

"Years of time on my own doing crossword puzzles and playing chess," he supplied.

"Chess? What the hell has that to do with Scrabble?"

"Strategy," he said, "and thinking several steps ahead. And just genius, I guess."

There was a definite glint there now and Ali wished she could chuck something at him. *But, invalid and all that . . .* She cleared their game and set it up again. As she counted out tiles, she felt . . . *at ease. Comfortable. Relaxed.* Not feelings she was ever used to having around men. It was unnerving and yet, not. She felt herself, but more. So hard to define. Not that she should be defining anything, she admitted to herself. *That way was a crazy way. There was nothing to define, nothing to declare. And yet . . .*

"We need to talk." Gabe interrupted her musings with a hand on her wrist to pause her counting.

Ali snorted. "Ah, we're there already, are we? Well, you're off the hook. I've zero expectations."

Gabe looked at her, that gaze of his studying and intense, without blinking. "I am completely baffled by what you just said."

This time, Ali laughed. "You are, aren't you? That's a hoot. Maybe I got the wrong end of the stick. Explain." She tucked her feet up under her as she scooted back to the footboard, a scatter cushion at the small of her back.

Gabe took his time, his eyes shadowed and concerned. They seemed greener today, but that could be because his pupils were tiny owing to pain levels and exhaustion. He still looked hot as Hades. She really wished he didn't. Having half of his chest exposed wasn't helping. *Not. At. All.* Knowing he only had boxers on beneath the duvet and his long, muscular legs were just there for the stroking . . . *Not. Fair.*

"We need to talk about what happened. The device. The fact that Mel does not appear to be involved but Garcia does and what that means for you."

His voice was calm and measured, *no shock there*, but his eyes were fierce now and he was frowning. *He rarely frowned. That was an expression for people not in control.*

"Flynn already told me Mel couldn't have done it. At least not personally. A pity, in a way. It would have tied things up neatly."

"Don't make light of this, Ali. It is serious. It was a deliberate threat to you." He clenched his jaw, that muscle ticking away. "And although it may be Garcia, we don't know for sure who is behind it." His frustration obvious, Gabe closed his eyes briefly as he twisted to sit upright. "I need to get out of this damn bed," he muttered.

"Ooo, you said damn! I'm telling your mum!" Ali teased, doing her best to hide her own concern so he'd be less stressed.

Gabe smiled. *God, when he smiled it was like a present. A gift of the inner him to her, just her.* She felt her belly flutter and for once didn't try to dismiss it. She liked this guy. *Really* liked him. It was useless, she knew that. *But a little miniature fantasy was okay, wasn't it? A few minutes of pretence? A slice of normal.* A moment or two of we could become an "us". A couple. Be together . . . Gabe's phone rang, jolting her from her reverie, and she blinked away her dangerous, traitorous thoughts of being happy.

"Mackenzie," he barked into the phone without even looking at the screen.

See, thought Ali, *I even like the way he says his own name. Jesus, I have it bad.*

She'd wondered if there were certain words that brought out the Gaelic in him and certainly when he said his own name like that, all official, it was sooo obvious he was from Scotland. Normally he spoke in an incredibly neutral accent, even if his delivery was as odd, at times, as he was. The sound of his voice, though, that was enough to send shivers, the delicious kind, down her spine. Deep and quiet. Thoughtful. Measured. Ali would never have believed those traits would appeal to her – but, Christ, they did.

"Oh, hi, Dad." His tone changed in an instant. "Och, no, don't worry, I am fine, just a wee scrape."

Ali's mouth fell open. She didn't see that coming. He sounded gentle and reassuring. *All Scottish and "accenty".* That must happen when he spoke to family. Fucking adorable. Hearing this big, handsome man talk to his dad like that? Something melted in her chest, just a little.

"Yes, Mrs Fitzgerald is taking great care of me. Honestly, Dad, no," he said after a pause, "you don't need her address. I can write my own thank-you notes."

His eyes met Ali's and his cheeks flushed slightly at her hearing this obviously embarrassing conversation. He might have rolled his eyes, a quirk she'd have missed if she hadn't been glued to his face.

"Absolutely," he continued, his eyes not leaving hers. "I'll come see you soon. Aye, I promise. *Soraidh slàn.*"

He clicked off the phone and smiled at Ali. "I am not going to live this down, am I?"

"Hell, no," she agreed cheerily. "I've some serious mileage there!"

Ali hooted with glee as Gabe let his head fall back on the pillows with a groan. She proceeded to replay his conversation with the fakest of Scottish burrs and laughed outright at his horror.

After a few more moments of mirth, Gabe resumed speaking in his normal accent and said, "We do have to be serious for a bit, Ali. The Mel scenario is not over, unfortunately. I need to go back over your friends and acquaintances and relook at everyone who you have interacted with recently. Obviously, we have Garcia in the picture now, but I don't think either he or Mel are the masterminds. Can you think of anything else you may have found odd? Out of the ordinary?"

"No. We've been down this road, Gabe. There's nothing." Ali crossed her arms over her chest, a low twist beginning in her gut.

Gabe reached for his notebook on the bedside table and although Ali knew she should help, it was a much nicer sight to see all that gorgeous muscle and skin move and ripple in the cool afternoon light.

And then he asked the questions she'd dreaded but knew would come. If not today, then one day.

"What about before? Before your chef days, before your restaurant and your show. Is there anyone who might wish to cause you harm? To hurt you."

Was there? Oh, yeah. There was indeed. But that fucker had high-tailed it off to another continent many years ago and there was no way he'd show his face in polite company again. Not if he knew what was good for him. Not if he remembered her threats.

"No," she said firmly. "No one at all."

Chapter 16

The bomb and its fallout, literal and metaphorical, meant that filming of the last show was postponed for a few days while the crew settled. The contestants received counselling and were subjected to several lines of questioning as to whether or not they wanted to continue. All said yes. *They were troopers, each and every one*, Ali thought as she waited in Make-Up the following Friday.

It was the last show and she had very mixed feelings. The producers and directors were thrilled and the buzz from the advance viewings was so positive that a second season was already being muted. *Hmm*, Ali thought, *we'll see*. All the media circus around the bomb probably wouldn't affect the ratings, except to increase them, so in a way, whoever had it in for her or her show may have in fact given them a gift. *Silly feckers*.

Ali would be sad to see these contestants leave. They'd been a delight and so much fun onscreen. And they'd learned a hell of a lot, improving in leaps and bounds. Good for them and good for her teaching prowess, so win-win. She had some decisions to make regarding what was to come next, in the immediate future, but decided, perhaps, to take a few days away. Maybe head to Clifden to their holiday house. Or somewhere else.

She'd seen very little of Gabe since they'd left her parents' house and returned to their respective homes, but what she did see, *his gorgeous body over her, under her, next to her*, was pretty damn spectacular. *And oh, so satisfying.* Gabe had kissed her. Kissed her a lot. Kissed her deeply, lightly, with passion and – *dare she even think it?* – care. And that was so new for Ali, so scary and yet so delectably lovely. She hadn't yet taken to kissing him first, except when he'd been trapped in the bed in her parents' house. And that had been just a peck. It had embarrassed her a little – it had felt so "coupley" and they were not, *decidedly not*, a couple. As long as she kept telling herself that, all was good.

There was to be a short cast-and-crew celebration after filming later and Ali was looking forward to an actual "wrap party" – not words she ever imagined she'd apply to herself. *Life was a funny old journey*, she mused as she thanked the make-up assistants and headed over to her centre table, where the contestants were waiting excitedly.

Ali had bought personalised rolling pins as a thank you for each of them and would hand them out as a surprise before the credits *rolled*, pun intended. Later, she was going to her family home in Dalkey for a celebration party. Her parents were thrilled for her and wanted to toast her success. She was happy to let them. And happy to do something positive as she waited to hear more news of who might have wanted to harm her. Again. People needed to leave her the hell alone, that was for sure. Waiting for news of an arrest was . . . *frustrating*.

Gabe was invited to the family party, too – if he could, if work allowed. It was weird asking him. She almost chickened out. Three nights this week he'd come

218

to her bed, late and exhausted. Last night he'd flopped on her couch, a wry smile on his face.

"I seem to be making a habit of crashing at your place. I don't mean to assume and I am pretty sure you would kick me out if this was not okay."

Ali had climbed on his lap, facing him, her knees tucked by his thighs, and she'd leaned forwards to whisper in his ear.

"Damn straight, Scotty. If I didn't want you here, you wouldn't be here."

She'd reached for his tie and undone the silk knot as he'd let his head fall back wearily. She'd stroked a hand through his hair and he'd angled his head into her palm. She'd unbuttoned his shirt and opened the fabric, running her hand gently along his scar.

"It's healing really well," she'd said, surprised at the even colour and lack of puckering.

"A combination of excellent stitching and some of my special ointment."

"Ointment?" Ali had hooted. "No one uses that term any more! Next, you'll be telling me you have a home-made salve or poultice, as well."

There was silence. He'd cracked open one of his eyes, a slight twitch of his lips a true giveaway.

"You do. You bloody do. I might have known. Your granny probably sends it over."

Again, a twitch of his lips.

"Oh, you're a hopeless case."

She'd continued to run her hands lightly across his chest and Gabe had heaved a large, heavy sigh.

"Is it very rough, this latest case?" she'd asked quietly.

She didn't know the details of his case – he wouldn't

tell her, but it was wrecking him.

"Being with you makes it better," he'd said, and her heart had just about melted.

She'd moved slightly, but deliberately, on his lap. His eyes had cracked open. She could see the blaze even from beneath half-closed lids. She could feel his reaction elsewhere. She moved again.

"See what I mean?" he'd said, his voice a growl.

"If you're too tired . . . " she began but got no further.

His hand had grasped the back of her head, pulling her to him, and his mouth had devoured hers. Hungry, searching, demanding. *Yes,* she thought as her brain cells departed from her head, *this. Please.*

He broke the kiss, sliding his arms around her, and rose from the couch in one smooth move.

"Impressive," she'd muttered as she licked his neck, followed by a gentle nibble. "But watch your wound. I'd feel awful if you burst your stitches."

"I'm a quick healer. Always have been. It's genetic. Don't worry." He spoke in bursts as she'd tasted him and his breath had hitched as she'd discovered a very sensitive spot.

His groan was a rumble in his chest as he'd strode to her bedroom.

"I'll show you impressive," he'd promised and dropped her on the bed, stripping his jacket off as he followed her to the mattress. "I used to pride myself on finesse," he'd told her between kisses to her collarbone, exposed by a string top, "but you, you have bewitched me and all I can think of is having you."

It may not have been the most romantic of speeches, but it sure as hell worked for Ali. The kissing had continued. Slow and deep. Hot and urgent. On and on.

Experimenting. Changing. Testing. *It was so fucking erotic having him kiss her like that. As if he couldn't not pleasure her in all the ways.*

She'd had a moment of alarm later, when he'd kissed his way down her body, savouring each nipple with delicious attention to detail and making her writhe in anticipation of what was to come. Literally. He'd tasted her ribcage, her waistline. He'd kissed her belly and edged lower. Flutters of panic began, just a like a light breeze but there, felt. Definite.

She'd twisted in his grasp and hauled him back up towards her face. She could sense his puzzlement as she'd reached into her bedside table drawer for a condom. Quick thinking was usually her modus operandi but right then, with his skin gliding along hers, the heat of him scorching her as his hands touched just about everywhere, she'd almost forgotten her reasons. *Almost.* Because if he went *there*, then there were expectations.

Always the expectations. It was assumed. A given.

It was *not* going to happen.

She'd told him another time, "I just need you inside me now," and that had seemed to do the trick. *But for how long?* She was now on borrowed time.

Now, make-up on and hair styled, Ali chatted enthusiastically to her contestants, marvelling at her own ability to hold entire conversations while her headspace was elsewhere. Gabe had been respectful and hadn't pushed her last night, but doubts crept in, insidiously, as to how long that would last. He was, first and foremost, a man. And he'd want certain things. Things she wouldn't give him. *Couldn't* give him.

A part of her wanted him to leave. Go back to

Edinburgh or wherever his next placing would take him. And part of her, a small, scary part of her, wanted him to stay forever. Her only option was to end things. She knew that. And she'd do it. *Soon. In a while.* She would.

The celebrations at her loft space were great fun. Everyone was celebrating the end of a successful series and were delighted both with themselves and each other. A mutual admiration party – *was that what it was?* mused Ali as she took a taxi to Dalkey and her childhood home. There was no way she was fit for a bike ride – already, she'd had bubbles and nibbles and, yeah, more fizz. *And why not?* She was exhausted, though, and with still no word on who might be behind the blast the previous week, she had to admit, a little on edge.

Flynn had posted another guard on her 24/7, though not, for obvious reasons, Gabe. *Here we go again*, she thought as the taxi manoeuvred through the tight Dalkey main street. She turned and, sure enough, that unmarked car was right behind. *Bloody Juan Garcia and his effing bomb. It hadn't even been a very well-made bomb, according to those in the know.*

Why she couldn't have saved the fare and ridden with her protector she'd no clue, but it wasn't the thing, seemingly.

She hopped out of the taxi and paid her cheerful Egyptian driver who had, in fairness, kept her mightily entertained on the journey. She tipped him generously to thank him for his wonderful stories about his life in Cairo and, taking a card from him, promised to use his services in future.

The house was lit from within. It was nearly the

middle of May and the evenings were beautifully bright, but her home simply glowed like a warm sun as she crossed the gravel to the front door, which was wide open.

"Hey, I'm here," she called and walked down the chequered black-and-white tiled hall.

A huge bunch of flowers stood on the hall table, dripping in wisteria, fresh beech leaves and cow parsley. Her mum was great at making statement arrangements and this was a doozy. *Fair play to her.*

"We're in here, darling," her mother called from the large drawing room to the right of the stairs.

Ali walked in to cheers and hoots, as half the neighbourhood had gathered to toast her success. The lovely, graceful room was thronged. And the double doors to the dining room beyond were open with yet more people.

Ali walked straight to her mum, bent over to hug her and muttered, "I'll kill you, Mum! I thought it was just a few close friends. There's a fecking rent-a-crowd here!"

Her mother took her face in her hands and smiled mistily at her. "It's not every day we have a celebrity in the family."

"Eh, we do," Ali countered. "We have bloody Francesca Jones in our family. Where is she, by the way? And Dev?"

"Well, of course we have Frankie – she and your brother will be along shortly," her mum said, "but we've become so used to her fame it's kind of fun to have it all again with you." She beamed at Ali as if she'd just won the biggest of prizes. "Come eat, sweetheart, I've made tons of your favourites."

She led Ali by the arm and marched her about the

room, stopping to greet all the locals, neighbours from their road, pals from school, Jo and Patrick's friends, and a host of people Ali didn't even recognise. That wouldn't normally bother her, but lately . . . well, lately she was a bit on edge. She assumed her parents knew these guests. Though knowing someone, being their friend – that meant nothing, really. That was a fact Ali knew all too well.

"Your father's bridge club," Jo muttered sotto voce and reached out to hand Ali a plate of sausage rolls.

"Hey, sis." Molly hugged her tightly. "Well fecking done. Now that we have two bloody TV personalities in the family I'm never – you heard it here first – ever putting my head above that particular parapet."

Ali rolled her eyes at her younger sibling and hugged her back.

"It's not as easy as it looks, I'll have you know. And it seems we're a family of targets for weirdo loonies too, so definitely stay away from that selection of careers." She snatched a glass of champagne from a young person dressed in black and carrying a tray of flutes. Paranoia must be her new playmate, because her first instinct was to check the name badge in case she needed to identify him later – in case he meant her harm. *Christ!* She shook off the fear. This was her home. She was *safe* here. "What the fuck? Did the parents hire waiting staff? What world am I in?"

Molly laughed. "Leave off," she said. "They wanted to be able to celebrate you and your show without worrying about who had enough food or drink. I think it's a great idea. They're always entertaining and are excellent hosts but chose this time to enjoy your success without the hassle."

"Fair enough," Ali agreed as she looked over and saw

both of her parents relaxed and in conversation with sundry neighbours.

They did look happy. And worry-free. *Good for them*, she thought.

"Where's your hunky Scot?" Molly wanted to know and *oh, fuck*, Ali could feel herself blush.

That wouldn't do. Not at all.

"He's not *my* Scot, though I'll accept the hunky part. And I've no clue when or if he'll be here. I did mention it to him, but he's on a case at the moment that's pretty intense so, who knows?"

"Yeah, I hear you. At least we're all used to 'maybe' with Flynn, so it's not a shock if Mackenzie can't make it. So . . . " She nudged Ali in the arm. "Spill all the gory details. Are you two exclusive? I bet he's great in bed. He's got those amazing smouldery eyes. I bet he's got stamina."

Ali choked on her bubbly as Molly leered at her, flicking her eyebrows up and down à la Groucho Marx.

"Jesus, Moll, who made you the sex police? And yes . . . " She lowered her voice to a whisper but stiffened slightly as they heard a commotion in the hall. "Yes to all of that."

The noise from outside increased and Ali, who'd been staring intently at the door, relaxed her suddenly tense shoulders as she heard familiar laughter and squeals included in the cacophony. Then the door burst open and her darling nephew, Toby, barrelled in.

"Hi everyo—" He stopped on seeing the vast amount of people, his eyes scanning the room for someone familiar.

They landed on Ali and a smile lit his fourteen-year-old face. Within seconds he was wrapped in a big hug and kissing her on both cheeks. "Like the Italians," he said and then abandoned her to find his grandparents. Ali's grin was wide as she turned to embrace the young woman who'd entered the room more quietly behind her son.

"Caro." Ali breathed in the comforting scent of lilies from her older sister's perfume. "You came."

"Wild horses and all that," Caro said as she hugged Ali close. "I'm almost grateful your final show was postponed from last week or we'd not have been able to be here. Not the reason why, though," she added quickly. "I'm so glad you weren't hurt by that bomb. Mum texted me links from the TV reports. How horrible."

"Ha!" Ali snorted. "Don't think you and Frankie can be the only women in our family to court danger. All we have to do now is find the bastards and make sure Moll never meets nefarious assholes. Simple!"

"But, God, Ali, are you sure you're okay? All joking aside, that was bloody terrifying for you. An actual bomb. I mean . . . shit, we could have lost you." On that, she gathered Ali close again and squeezed tight.

"Softy," Ali said, a strange lump in her throat. "And sure, I had Outlander with me to save the day."

"Who?" Caro asked, bewildered.

"She means the hot, sexy Scot who Flynn has got protecting her. You know the one. I think you met him at the wedding," Molly interjected.

Caro wrinkled her nose in consternation. Then her eyes narrowed. "Not the guy you made a beeline for, the one you fancied? Jesus, Ali, seriously?"

"And," Molly continued before Ali could defend herself, "they're doing the 'down and dirty'. Regularly. Like dating," she smirked with a finish.

Caro looked aghast. "You're dating? The Scot? The

hot guy you accosted at the wedding? The one who's supposedly minding you? Ali!"

"Hey," Ali protested, "it's not like that. We're not dating. We're hooking up. A bit."

Molly raised an eyebrow.

"Okay, a lot. But he's not my bodyguard any more. He *recused* himself."

There was a moment's silence. Then Caro spoke slowly, ticking things off on her fingers, as was her way.

"So, let me get this straight, you fancy this Scot cop, he *was* guarding you but isn't any more because he opted out so he could sleep with you, you're *not* dating but you *are* hooking up on a regular basis, *and* he saved your life. Am I missing anything?"

Ali thought about it. It sounded about right. Less than what it was in so many ways but factually correct.

"No. That about covers it."

"He 'recused' himself," Molly repeated. "That means he really, really wants you, Ali – otherwise he'd just break the rules."

"Break the rules? Not a chance! Scotty MacScot is so rule-happy I'm surprised he doesn't come to bed with a notebook," Ali snorted.

"Does he need . . . direction?" Caro asked, a grin on her face. "Because I can send Nick, my *extremely* hot fiancé, to chat to him, if you like?"

"No direction needed. This guy knows *exactly* what he's doing."

All three sisters laughed and then Molly sighed.

"You two are all loved up and it's great but a bit nauseating, too. Keep your smugness to a minimum is all I ask."

"Don't worry," Ali said, reaching for another flute of champagne, "I'm not keeping him. We have an expiry date, that I can guarantee. He's too much. They're all too bloody much after a while. Hey, you . . . " She changed direction and faced Caro as she felt a wave of something unbearably like regret sweep across her chest. "Are you still bonkers in love with your hotelier, Mr Nick Sullivan?"

"Oh," said Caro, her cheeks turning a delicate pink. "Yes."

"Aww!" Ali and Molly said at exactly the same time and all three laughed again.

Gabe hesitated outside the drawing room door. He knew the layout of the home thanks to his 24-hour house arrest the previous week, so it wasn't that he didn't know where to go. The noise of merriment from within would have lured him to this door regardless of his knowledge. He paused because he figured Ali would have told her sisters about them. He had no way of knowing what they might think about that. He reckoned he'd be able to "read" Molly if she was here – not in an intrusive way but because she was exposed to him, emotionally.

He didn't know which of the other siblings would be inside. Childish of him maybe, but he hoped Flynn was delayed at the station. He and Ali hadn't been out together since they'd been seeing each other. Not on an actual date. Not like regular people dating. Since they'd been . . . He didn't know what to call it. Well, sex, obviously. But it was more than that. She drew him like a magnet. He wanted to know all of her. The harsh, hurt bits, the vulnerable, quiet bits. And he was already getting to know and need the siren part of her.

Her response to him in bed was like oil on a fire. They went up in flames together. The sound of her laugh, her griping to the director, the snort when she was trying not to giggle, they all made him ache. They all made him want. He didn't particularly like it and knew he had some serious analysing to do before long, but he kept putting it off and told himself he'd sort out the head from the heart soon. He'd figure it out. *They'd* figure it out.

Last night he'd felt her pull back a little and he was determined to find out why. It didn't matter to him if she had preferred sexual positions or ones she'd prefer not to do. As long as she was in his arms, he'd be satisfied. There was no pressure from his side. He just wanted to make her come, over and over, in any way he could. He wanted her saying *his* name as she let go. As she came apart. That was always the goal. That wouldn't change.

But he had a feeling, one of his slow-burn feelings, that all was not quite as it should be. Whether it was his new case or Ali-related, he couldn't tell. *Yet.* But something was off and he was taking time to allow his brain to catch up to his gut, so it would, in time, become clear. If he had to do some extra meditation and dream practice, well, he'd just suck it up and do it. What he wouldn't do is ignore it. *That never ended well. Not for him and not for the victim. See?* He was already accepting there *was* a victim – and maybe not only the ones already being questioned. Maybe he needed to shut off his libido and focus on what his senses were trying to tell him.

He didn't have the time to go and visit his mother and have a dream session with her, but he *could* go see his grandmother. Get a reading from her. Talk to her. Let her "see" him.

Maybe he'd ask Ali to go with him. He wondered if she'd ever been to Edinburgh. *Time to find out.*

On a deep breath, he opened the drawing room door and stepped inside.

Chapter 17

It was . . . a lot. A lot of noise – from people and music – a lot of food, a lot of drink, a lot of laughing. Some shrieking. A lot of excitement, that was for sure. Gabe let his gaze search for Ali but stopped on her parents first. *A lot of pride.* He caught Patrick's eye, who nodded his head in acknowledgement and then indicated the dining room through the open double doors with another nod.

Moving steadily through the throng, Gabe dodged several attempts to engage him in conversation. He passed a sideboard littered with framed photographs and paused, wondering what Ali had looked like as a child. He noticed one of the whole family and he picked it up, studying each face, naming them silently. He almost missed her. She looked . . . different. No hint of the cocky, confident woman she'd become. Her face was . . . The only word he could think of was *hollow*. She had a mass of chestnut hair streaming about her shoulders that swamped her narrow frame. Her eyes were unfocused and she wasn't smiling.

He studied it for a moment, trying to reconcile the Fitzgerald hair colouring with her present white-blonde spikes. He discovered he quite liked present-day white-blonde Ali with the various looks and styles she carried off with such aplomb. He returned the photograph to its place, took a flute of champagne from a waiter and continued walking, spying the three women out on the patio, which extended from the back of the house. Approaching Ali from behind, he laid a gentle hand on her neck and said softly, "Congratulations."

Ali stilled beneath his touch and then leaned back slightly into his hand. *He liked that.* It felt possessive and perhaps silly, but he wasn't going to think on that now.

"Good evening, ladies," he continued, remembering his manners. "Molly, nice to see you again, and I believe we have met briefly . . . " He turned to the dark-haired woman. "Caroline, isn't it?"

"Yes," she said and held out her hand.

He handed his glass to Ali and shook Caroline's hand.

"But, please, call me Caro."

She smiled and was transformed from an attractive woman to a beautiful one. The Fitzgerald women stood out from the norm in their different looks, one more intriguing than the other. He knew, abstractly, that Devlin and Flynn were handsome men and figured good genes had a strong grounding here.

Ali turned to look at him. "Why have you got champers? You don't drink."

"Not normally, no. But this is a special occasion. I thought I'd drink to you."

Ali's eyes locked on his, the cornflower blue deepening, a delicate pink flushing her cheeks. *God, she was gorgeous.* Vaguely aware that the two sisters were observing them blatantly, he realised he didn't care and bent and kissed Ali on the mouth. A light touch but one felt through his whole body. He was claiming her, here in her home, in front of everyone, and he was perfectly fine with it. *How bizarre. Definitely one to be pondered later.*

Ali took a sip from his glass and handed it back to him. "Go on, then. I think I'd like to see you with a few in you," she teased.

"That is unlikely," he replied with a smile but sipped the bubbles obligingly, his eyes never leaving hers. "It's good. A Bollinger?"

Ali gaped at him and then snorted in that ridiculously charming way of hers. "I can't believe it." She turned to her sisters. "This guy inhales weird tea all herby and naturey, eschews caffeine after 10 a.m. yet can spot a decent champagne. Go figure!" She shook her head in bemusement as Gabe leaned into her, nudging her shoulder a little.

"Eschews? Getting a bit big for our boots, Ms TV Star?"

"Who's too big for their boots?"

Their tête-à-tête was interrupted by a deep voice behind them.

"Dev!" squealed Ali, breaking away from Gabe and hugging her brother. "And Frankie. Oh, and Flynn." She beamed. "You're all here."

She continued hugging her family, who showered congratulations and praise for a job well done, and she glowed. Gabe watched her, a warm hum in his chest as she responded to all of their comments. She deserved this. She'd worked so hard, planning, practising, more planning and then, with apparent ease, making sure everyone was comfortable and relaxed. Gabe had been on-set. He knew it was tough. Hard graft, for sure. But he also knew she loved it.

"Ooo, everybody, it's about to start!" Jo called to the guests and then hushed them as they all clambered for a place to watch the large-screen TV and the first programme of *Ali Bakes*.

"Not so fast." Flynn spoke behind Gabe, resting a hand on his arm. "*We* need to talk."

"No, we do not. Or at least not now. I want to watch the show."

Flynn stared at him.

"You want to watch my sister on TV? You don't think you've been ogling her enough in real life already?" Flynn's voice was whip-sharp, low and intense.

"Back off, Fitzgerald. I am not assigned to her any more, so what we choose to do in our own time is none of your business."

"My family is *always* my business," came the short retort.

"Then why did you assign me to her in the first place? Never mind. I will not discuss this with you. Not now. Not at all." Gabe shook off the hand still gripping his arm.

Flynn sighed heavily but the sound was almost drowned out as a big cheer filled the room when TV Ali strode onto the set looking like the champ she was. She twisted in her seat to turn and lock her gaze with Gabe's as he stood at the back of the room. He raised his glass in salute and she was swallowed up in well-wishers again, but not before he saw a wide grin split her glowing face.

As if he hadn't just been giving Gabe the third-degree, Flynn said, "She's great, isn't she? A bloody natural. I hear they're already thinking of a second series and a companion book. I think that's what they call it." He took a drink of his straight Scotch and looked directly at Gabe. "Don't hurt her."

"It is not my intention."

"It's never anyone's intention, but yet . . . " He let the sentence hang. "How's it going with Neary? I know I shouldn't ask since I've had to take a step back, but I'm concerned."

Flynn's abrupt change of subject didn't bother Gabe. He welcomed it.

"I'll fill you in, the bare facts anyway, after the show. Now go elsewhere – I want to watch your sister shine, without you looking over my shoulder."

Flynn grunted, nodded and left Gabe to his own devices.

Gabe leaned back against the door frame leading into the drawing room and crossed one leg in front of the other. As the show progressed, only a half-hour in length, Ali's professional demeanour, coupled with her cheeky charm, had the contestants eating out of her hand. This really was her milieu. He'd seen the live recordings, the stopping and starting, the make-up touch-ups and the retakes. He'd give Marc Bewley his due – the episode was slick without being cheesy, and the warmth and earnest nervousness of the novice bakers was infectious.

But there was no doubt in anyone's mind at the end of the programme – Ali Fitzgerald stole the show.

Gabe had a bit of a catch-up with Flynn later, discussing the suspect Neary and the accusations against him. Gabe was looking into the veracity of the claims and so far, was unable to shake the young women's stories. Not that it was his intention to discredit them. Quite the opposite. He'd met Neary – and a shadier piece of work he'd yet to encounter. A smooth operator with all the charm offensive of flattery and cajoling, sincerity and trust oozing from every pore. Except that it was all a lie. Gabe could feel the evil emanating from his every pore. But feelings and even his famous gut instinct weren't enough. They needed actual proof. And the dates and places from the women's testimonies were sketchy at best. They needed a more credible witness. Not a more honest one – they weren't lying – but they just hadn't, not unnaturally, documented anything.

Gabe told Flynn he'd be out of town for a couple of nights but would stay in touch via email and text. Flynn was fine with that – considering he wasn't supposed to be in this particular loop – and Gabe shrugged to himself as he wandered out to the back garden, imagining that Flynn must at least be thinking that would mean Ali wasn't in the picture.

It wasn't, Gabe mused, his place to inform him otherwise. If his luck held, Ali would be right by his side. A shiver of anticipation ran through him. He'd never wanted to show a woman his hometown or introduce them to his family. Ali was beginning to find a place in his psyche and was getting rather comfortable there.

The garden looked magical. The light was fading, and fairy lights were strung from tree to tree and along the various poles and sculptures dotted around the space. The lawn stretched down to the rocky coastline and the view across to Dalkey Island was a treasure. Jo Fitzgerald was, by all accounts, an excellent and inventive gardener. The early summer colours of camassia, good old-fashioned wallflowers, rosemary and libertia filled the borders. A winding stone path took the walker though some low shrubs and soft grasses down to the gate that led to the dock. People in all stages of intoxication and, at this stage, undress were dotted about the garden and music flowed from speakers on the patio. Tables had been set up, placed at bends on the path and across the lawn, holding glasses and ice buckets.

No expense had been spared and the party feeling was evident everywhere one looked. Bursts of laughter and excited babble sporadically broke the lower murmur of chatter. Gabe caught a flash of movement by the dock and realised someone was taking a late-evening dip. He figured that lone soul would soon be joined by others as the alcohol emboldened them. The older generation had sauntered indoors and there was no sign of Jo or Patrick. He assumed they were entertaining within, and smiled as he thought of their obvious love and pride for their middle daughter on her special evening.

Sipping from his glass of ginger ale, the one glass of champagne long gone, Gabe wandered down to the group sitting round a wooden table and benches close to the shoreline. There was a low dry-stone wall dividing the lawn from the rocks and a few people were propped on the flatter stone slabs. Ali was squished on the wooden bench between her sisters, and Frankie and Dev were opposite them. Flynn wasn't there and Gabe felt a moment of relief.

He stopped behind the three women and rested one hand lightly on Ali's back. She angled her head back to look at him, a goofy smile on her face.

"Hey, you." Her slightly slurry voice was happy and relaxed. "I knew you were there. I felt you. Your Spidey senses must be rubbing off on me."

Gabe raised a quizzical brow at her.

"Oh, right, I forgot. You didn't get it the last time,

237

either – silly me. Your knowledge of pop culture is limited at best. Never mind – I think you are super cute." Ali laughed and, turning to her companions, said, "Can you believe this guy? He doesn't even know who Spiderman is! Go figure. Isn't that adorable?"

Her smile widened as she must surely have detected his slight blush. How this woman could make him feel a mixture of embarrassment, gaucheness and pure lust in a single shot, he just didn't know.

"May I borrow you for a moment?" He looked at her and then the other family members and their gathering of friends. "If you'll excuse us?"

Ali turned and scrambled off the bench, almost tripping but landing neatly in Gabe's arms.

"Falling for the Scot, Ali?" Dev called and her head spun to glare at him, then she ruined the effect by sticking out her tongue.

"Don't mind him – he's the idiot in the family. Whatcha want, anyway?"

Gabe directed her down the path and in the back door to the mudroom. It was blessedly quiet. And empty. He closed the door firmly and turned Ali in his arms, her back to the door.

"This," he growled and took her mouth in a searing kiss.

Yes was all he could think, feel, welcome. *This.* She tasted like champagne, sweet and tangy, sharp and delicious. She tasted like nectar. Like his elixir of life. He thrust his tongue inside her mouth, holding her face steady in his large hands as she gasped. The sound of her, coupled with her hot, eager mouth, had him as hard as a rock and he pressed himself to her body so she could feel just how much he wanted her.

Angling his mouth, he took the kiss deeper and heard a whimper, a moan, a groan, and couldn't honestly say it was coming from her. He kissed her hard, he kissed her deep, and as she let her small frame melt into him, he softened it all and kissed her long and slow.

Not touching anywhere but mouth and hips was strangely erotic. But it soon wasn't enough. Ali pulled her arms free from where they were flattened against the door behind her and wound them around his neck, pulling him impossibly closer. One of her hands clutched the back of his head while the other cupped his jaw, holding him to her. It was indescribably sexy to have this woman want him as much as he wanted her. He shifted his body against hers, angling his thigh between her legs and rocking into her.

Somewhere in the back of his brain he recognised that he was behaving like a randy teen or an animal – *maybe they were the same.* He didn't care. Except he did. He was devouring Ali in her own home, where any member of her family could walk in. *Christ.* He *was* an animal.

He eased back, dropping slow, gentle nibbles on her lips, soft kisses on her jaw and down her neck as their ragged breathing became the only sound in the small room. He kissed his way back to her mouth and pressed his lips firmly to hers once more before resting his forehead on hers as he caught his breath. Eyes closed, he took in the moment, feeling the rapid rise and fall of her chest as she, too, tried to regain her equilibrium.

"I missed you," he growled reluctantly.

"I've been here the whole time," she smiled up at him, her eyes large and dark in her small face.

"I know, it is just . . . "

"Shh." Ali placed her fingers to his lips. "Me too."

She was floating. Not actually up-in-the-air floating, but it felt like that. What she and Gabe had? It wasn't something she wanted or needed, this kind of scary. The good kind. The "oh my God, I think I'm falling for him" kind. Not on her schedule, her plan, her anything. She hadn't realised how much she needed him, his kiss, till he'd pinned her to the door in the mudroom. Kind of all alpha male and territorial. Kind of hot. He'd missed her. *Missed* her. That *had* to mean something, right?

As Ali returned to the garden from a bathroom break, her thoughts a complete muddle and all over the place, she considered grabbing her sisters and Frankie and doing some Gabe problem-solving. The main problem being her, unfortunately. None of the girls knew her issues. They'd never know. But she could dance around them and focus on what they thought it meant when Gabe had said that missed *her*, even though she was right there. *Fuck!* She sounded, even to her own ears, like a lovelorn dippy groupie – *that would never do.*

Straightening her shoulders and realising she should probably eat some nibbles before going for another drink, she strolled out onto the patio, snatching a handful of crackers with pâte as she passed the main table. Thank God her parents never got so above themselves in their entertaining that they forgot the sheer necessity of a decent salty biscuit.

"So, when's Nick coming over?" Molly was asking Caro when Ali arrived back at the bench set.

Ali noted that Gabe was nearby, chatting apparently easily with some neighbours from two doors up the road, towards Dalkey. Ali remembered they had a grown daughter living in Arizona in America, so she bet they were plying him for info on life across the pond.

"Soon, I hope," Caro replied, a sigh in her voice, and then she leaned in conspiratorially. "You know we were thinking of getting married next spring?"

They all nodded.

"Welll," she drawled, "we've decided we can't wait and intend to pick a date for a small gathering here as soon as possible."

There was a stunned silence and then Ali asked, "How soon? This autumn? This summer? More deets, sis."

Caro looked at them expectantly. "Late June, maybe. First week in July at the latest."

Gasps of shock followed by shouts of glee and excitement met that piece of news and all the women clamoured for specifics.

Caro brushed them aside. "I don't know yet. I thought I'd go and check at the parish and see what dates are vacant and then we can decide. It doesn't matter if it's a weekday – we're keeping it really small, just immediate family and a few close friends. Nick needs a date so he can book flights for his family in New York, so I have to get on to that asap. Toby and I are flying back to Rome on Wednesday, so I haven't much time."

"Are you determined to have a church wedding?" Frankie asked.

"I'd like to. I know I'm not the most religious of people, but I've always imagined it would be our local church. Silly, really, but we were all baptised there, made our communions and confirmations there. I just feel it would be a nice way to say goodbye to my old life."

"That's a nice concept," Molly agreed. "But Father Sloane is very busy. I'm not sure how many curates he has."

Ali turned to gape at her. "How do you know who the priest is or how many minions he has slaving for him? You don't still go to Mass, do you?"

Molly blushed but held her gaze steady. "I like Mass. Sometimes. I don't agree with a lot of what the Church says or even does, but I like the ritual. The continuity. The community feeling. People in our parish are very supportive of each other, you know."

If she sounded defensive, nobody mentioned it.

"Well, I think it's a load of shite," Ali declared. "But I'll put on another frock and stroll down the aisle for you, Caro, if it makes you happy."

Caro chuckled. "Manners to wait to be asked, smartypants." She took a sip of her wine and smiled at all three of her favourite people. "I hope you'll all be with me," she said, "and no fancy frocks or bridesmaid paraphernalia. You can all wear a nice summer outfit in, say a blue of your choice, and that'll be fine. If you have a dress in your wardrobe already, so much the better. I'm looking at you, Frankie Jones!"

"I just might have a blue dress or three in there. And seriously, Moll and Ali, don't go buying anything till you see what I have. You can borrow what you like."

Moll raised a sceptical eyebrow. "Yeah, 'cause we're sooo the same size."

Frankie nudged her gently. "I have a fabulous blue flowy maxi skirt that would be perfect for you. The top . . . " She looked down at her own small, and to her mind inadequate, chest and then at Molly's rather ample one. "Well, you're on your own for that, I'm afraid."

"And any dress you'd have would float on me." Ali stood to stretch her back as she sighed in regret. Sometimes being whippet-thin did one no favours, either. "Never mind, I might have a blue linen thing I can resurrect. Do the parents know your plans?"

"They do," Caro said, "and are happy to host a small reception right here. It'll be lovely. Now, if only I can get Father Sloane on board, all will be sorted."

Frankie sat forwards eagerly. "Hey, I've a great idea. You'll never guess who I bumped into in town the other day. Father Jack! Do you remember him from when we were teenagers? He could marry you both. He was often in this house when I was here back in the day. It'd be perfect."

"Really?" Caro asked. "I thought he was in Argentina or somewhere. And anyway, Father Jack is no more. I heard he left the priesthood."

"Yes," Molly agreed. "He has. No one knows why. I don't think he got married or anything."

Ali stepped back from the table. She could feel every ounce of her skin prickle. Every muscle in her belly spasm. Her throat was tight, dry. Her breathing . . . just stopped.

Her sisters and Frankie continued to talk about the encounter with Father Jack, oblivious.

"And then," Frankie went on blithely, turning to catch Ali's eye, "he was asking especially for you, Ali. Said to remember him particularly to you. That you were always his favourite." She paused, frowning. "Hey, are you okay? You look . . . "

Black. Everything faded to black. A loud whooshing noise thundered through her ears and Ali let go.

Something was wrong. Gabe felt his gut clench and the hairs on his arms lift as a whisper of fear curled about

243

him. Without being rude, he excused himself from the elderly pair and began sauntering towards the Fitzgerald group of women, drawn there by an invisible cord. Ali was standing to the end of the bench and looked . . . odd.

She was rigid and her hands formed bare-knuckled fists by her side. She was as still as stone. *Something was definitely wrong.* Even in the fading light of the early summer's evening, he could see she was the colour of parchment. He kicked up his speed and heard Frankie say something about favourites.

He caught her mere seconds before she hit the ground, holding her in his arms as her eyes rolled back in her head and her legs crumpled beneath her. The fear he'd felt moments before took on a whole new level as her body lay limp and floppy in a dead faint.

Amid the cries of anguish and shock at her collapse, he strode towards the house, ignoring everyone except to bark out the order for some brandy and water to be brought to Patrick's library.

With Molly scrambling in front of him to open the door, Gabe spotted the long leather couch and laid Ali down gently. Caro appeared with the requested drinks then both she and Frankie, who appeared with a blanket, stood hovering as Gabe checked her vitals. He reached over and took the blanket from Frankie's trembling hands then spoke over his shoulder.

"She will be fine. She just needs some air. Don't worry your parents. She will come round in a minute." He kept his voice even, steady, but all the while his pulse was clamouring with tension. "Knowing Ali, she hasn't eaten much all day and the strain of the last few weeks, added to an empty stomach, have finally taken their toll. Now, if you wouldn't mind, please excuse us."

His tone brooked no argument and although they hesitated, he kept his steady gaze on them, unrelenting, and they filed out, closing the door gently behind them.

He looked down at the pale creature lying inert on the couch. He stroked a finger over her clammy forehead and noticed beads of sweat on her upper lip.

"What the hell, Ali? Is it just lack of nourishment, or is there something you are not telling me?"

He didn't need her non-existent response to know the answer.

He'd seen, all too clearly, the look of abject terror on her face as she'd slid to the ground. And he'd do whatever it took to find out what, or who, put that look on her face.

And God help the person responsible.

Chapter 18

She'd never been to Scotland – it hadn't been on her radar – and yet as the plane descended towards Edinburgh Airport, Ali looked eagerly out of the window. It was delightful. All rolling hills and countryside. She turned to Gabe, sitting still and calm beside her. *No surprise there.*

"You might have been on to something, dragging me here," she conceded. "I just might need a break."

"There was no actual kicking and screaming, so I appreciate that. And I am glad you are with me," he added, catching her hand in his and rubbing his thumb slowly back and forth over the pad of hers. "My grandmother can be a bit of a handful but as it is her birthday, I promised I would visit. Your job is to distract her from any talk of my latest injuries. She is very protective."

Ali eyed him speculatively. "Your injury has healed just fine. You have ulterior motives, methinks." She waggled her eyebrows at him. "You want your merry way with me outside the purview of Flynn Fitzgerald!"

"Not that that isn't a side benefit – both of those things, in fact – but, truthfully, I honestly thought you simply might need a change of scenery. You have been working flat out, you have had several different traumas happen to you within a short space of time and now you have Caro's wedding to help organise. It's a lot."

246

She continued to study him, not at all convinced.

"Yeah, you see, I'm just not buying any of the 'granny needs me' shit. Nor am I a fecking wilting violet who can't handle a bit of drama in her life." She noticed his eyebrow heading to his hairline. "Okay, a lot of drama. But – and hear me out on this – I think you're worried the bomber guy isn't done and you're 'extracting me from the situation'." She air quoted the last bit as the plane landed smoothly on terra firma. "And I bet you're working on Flynn's orders, too."

She didn't add that that part of her theory kinda sucked. She didn't like the idea of Gabe doing anything for her based on job responsibilities. She'd been there and they'd both got the T-shirt.

Her feelings were entirely mixed on this whole Edinburgh jaunt. When Gabe had suggested it, not long after she'd come round from one of the most embarrassing moments in her life, she'd said no. Straight out no. And he'd left it at that, the crafty bugger. Then later, when her parents were clued in on her fainting scenario and they were all sipping brandy round the fire pit outside, and all the guests had finally gone, the bastard had brought it up again. *In front of everyone!* Getting all the sympathy votes for poor, worn-out, exhausted and traumatised Ali. *Sneaky Scot.*

Of course, all of them had jumped on the idea. Full of "Oh yes, she totally needs a break," and "That's exactly what she needs, a change of scenery," blah blah blah.

"*She* is sitting right here and needs no such thing," Ali had complained, but to no avail.

Lying in bed, unable to sleep – *no, terrified to sleep* – Ali had thought maybe, just maybe, a change would be good. She needed to be somewhere else. Somewhere away.

And going with the sexy Scot wasn't the worst idea. She'd punched her pillow into a better shape and thought that this could be their last fling. Whatever she felt before, when her head had known there would be an end date for them, now she knew, head *and* heart, that she must draw this "thing" with Gabe to a close. With that in mind, she'd plugged earphones in and listened to a podcast discussing the latest food science issues till her brain just gave up.

"I am not under anyone's orders," Gabe answered as he reached for their bags. "I merely thought you might like to meet my granny."

Ali's snort of incredulity was immediate. "Not buying it, Scotty, not buying it for one tiny second."

They took the tram into the city. Gabe said it would be a charming way to be introduced to his hometown and it was. They journeyed through the city to the last stop at York Place and then Gabe hailed a taxi.

"It's not far to the house, but we're both tired and we can always take a walk around the neighbourhood later."

Ali hadn't come down in the last rain shower and knew he meant "You're a wreck and could possibly faint on me again, so I'm taking no chances." But she didn't mind. It was all new and strangely exciting. Gabe had said his family home was in New Town, so her surprise was real when she realised that meant not, in fact, modern but new, relatively. As in new in the 1760s.

As the taxi wended its way through one more gorgeous row or square of houses after the next, Ali gaped in astonishment.

"These are amazing," she enthused. "Please don't tell me you live here?"

But live here he did.

"We are actually in the newer part of New Town," Gabe explained as the taxi entered Moray Place and pulled up in front of what Ali could only call a mansion. "These houses and the other circle, Ainslie, were built in the early 1800s, certainly after 1822, but they have a lovely vista, especially from the upper floors."

He paid the taxi driver and walked up to the front door of the large double-sided house. Then Gabe dug in his pocket for a key and pushed open the front door.

"Come on in and make yourself at home." He hesitated then, as if embarrassed, before saying, "We have housekeepers, I suppose you would call them, as it's important to keep the house lived in and warm. My father lives in the country at the main house. But they, the Macs, live here."

The hall was huge with a mixture of stone and marble, the staircase grand and curving upwards. Gabe threw his keys on the huge mahogany hallstand and called, "Mackie," before heading down the hall, gesturing for Ali to follow. "Mrs Mac?" he called again, and Ali realised with a sense of dawning horror that these Mackenzies did indeed have staff.

Holy fuck! she whispered to herself as she edged gingerly behind him. *I'm so out of my depth.*

Gabe smiled as he observed Ali slowly begin to relax. They were in the downstairs kitchen, a huge room kept cosy by a double range. Mrs Mac and her husband, Mackie, as they'd always been known, were sipping strong tea and entertaining Ali with stories from his childhood.

She looked enthralled.

It was most embarrassing. And he needed to put a stop to it sooner rather than later. He doubted she understood more than every third word as Mackie, in particular, had a strong Highland burr that even Gabe's ear needed adjusting to after a period away. The Macleans had been in service to the Mackenzies since Gabe had been about ten. They'd been as much a part of Gabe's upbringing as his own parents and still, at times, treated him as a child. He didn't mind. They were family, in their way.

"Your house is five stories high!" Ali announced in an accusatory tone as they climbed to the third floor. "*Five* fucking stories, Outlander. What's with that? Why does anyone need five different living spaces?"

And then she drew a sharp breath when he led her into the guest room overlooking the gardens below and she plonked herself down unceremoniously on the satin quilt.

"It's a four-poster!" she charged. "Am I in a Disney film?"

Gabe's lips twitched. It was funny to see her brain catch up with her mouth.

"Look, it's lovely and all but, like, seriously? It's a frigging mansion. No one needs to live in a house this big. Wait, how many of you *do* live here?"

"At the moment, just me and the Macs," he admitted, strolling to the window. His room was next door, so he knew this view as well as he knew the back of his own hand. "My father stays here when he is in town and we often have cousins come and visit. It is an open house, really, and the Macs are great at hosting when we are not here."

"Do you actually live here, when you're working in Edinburgh? Here in this actual house?" Ali's face was filled with a healthy dose of scepticism and disbelief with a good old dollop of "you've got to be kidding me".

"I do. It is my home."

"Your parents' home, you mean."

He could feel his cheeks warm. She studied him, understanding filtering in.

"Shit, it's *yours*?"

Gabe shoved his hands in his pockets, shrugging. How could he explain? He hadn't thought she'd be so shocked. But, he supposed reasonably, he hadn't really talked about his family. Or his heritage and circumstances.

Studying him, Ali's brows drew together. "Where *does* your father actually live, then? Do you have him tied up in a basement in a castle?"

"You *would* like me in the role of villain, wouldn't you?" Gabe reached over and took her hand. "Come with me."

He walked them out into the wide hall and turned left into the room next door. Without giving her a chance to take in the surroundings of his own fairly large master bedroom, he stopped in front of a painting on the wall. It was a huge oil in a heavy gilded frame, about a hundred and fifty years old, done by a famous artist of the time. It showed Mackenzie's Keep in all its castellated splendour.

Nestled at the edge of a lough, a forest behind, it was a pretty good depiction of his family's seat. It had changed over the years, of course – lots more modernisation and buildings added and changed – but

251

the guts of it were the same. Not huge but – as he'd heard it described by a socialite whom he'd squired about town for a bit in his youth – substantial.

"Fuck me."

He wasn't remotely surprised by her response and couldn't resist the grin her words elicited. Or the sudden heat that raced through his body at the actual meaning of her words, as opposed to her just gaping open-mouthed at his childhood home.

"About that," he growled, edging closer. "I think you need lots of distractions to help you relax and get your mind off things. Let me show you all the ways I can help with that."

He placed his hands on her shoulders, easing her gently back against his chest. He traced his tongue along the side of her neck, breathing her in, tasting her, nibbling her.

Ali shivered beneath his touch, sending darts of pleasure straight where he needed attention the most.

"Oh, I think I could manage a little distraction," she murmured, "but I'm pretty tired, so you might have to do all the work."

"That," he chuckled, scooping her up in his arms and tossing her on his huge bed, "can be arranged."

They ate at The Ivy on the Square, not a huge walk from Gabe's home. Ali really was tired but now it was also a satiated feeling – two pretty damn amazing orgasms followed by a hot shower could do that to a girl.

"I haven't any swanky clothes with me," she complained when he asked her to be ready by 7 p.m.

"It is fine," he'd said, "they know me."

And here they were. Dining at The Ivy. Ali wondered if she could chat with the chef later. It was all so posh. Hushed and discreet. In a fabulous setting overlooking St Andrew Square, the restaurant was small but very luxurious. It seemed like they had one waiting staff per guest, but that couldn't be the case.

Ali selected the duck and Gabe, sea bass. Their food was delicious, the wine sublime. Gabe even had a glass of white and Ali was impressed with what he chose. They talked about the city and Gabe explained about the competition for the building of New Town, the addition in the late 1820s of where he lived, and the old town and the Royal Mile itself. It was almost . . . *normal.*

Ali had dodged another bullet earlier. After he'd sent her flying with her first orgasm of the afternoon, she'd quickly taken over and clambered on top so she could have a vestige of control. *It wouldn't last. Time was definitely running out.* And with the return of the bastard, she was on borrowed time. She wasn't sure how long she could hold on to her little "Gabe-fest fantasy" where everything was all right. She felt like she was one of those wooden blocks in the game Jenga, where one false move – *hell, one twitch* – and her whole world could come tumbling down. She wasn't going to allow that to happen. Unless it was her doing the dislodging – on purpose.

They strolled back through the warm late May evening and Ali kept swivelling her head to catch different glimpses of the castle, high on its dominant perch. She'd seen photos and been made watch the Royal Edinburgh Military Tattoo by her granddad back in the day, but seeing it, backlit with the evening sun? *It was magical.* The local sandstone, used throughout New Town, gave a lovely soft feel to the city.

Gabe told her some of its history as they wandered through one square after another on their way back to Morlay Place. He made it interesting and human, mentioning various people, some she'd heard of, most not, who'd lived in the various extra-large versions of his own house. The flagstones in the main hall and the stone steps up to the third floor and her room fascinated her. No reason, just the simple charm of them.

She yawned spectacularly as they rounded the landing. "Sorry," she said, covering her mouth, "I'm zonked."

"*You* are sleeping in your own room. I have some work to do one floor down in my study and do not want to wake you later."

Gabe steered her through the door, flicking on a sidelamp, and with firm hands on her shoulders, sat her down on the mattress. He kissed the top of her head and stroked his fingers down the side of her face.

"*You* need some serious sleep and *I* am here to ensure you get it."

She was almost too tired to argue, but a worrisome shred of relief was also vying for attention at the knowledge that there would be one more reprieve.

"Yes, boss," she saluted and flopped backwards onto the soft fabric.

"That is too easy," Gabe commented as he reached down and started pulling off her ankle boots. "When you capitulate like that, I worry."

"Ha. I like to keep you guessing. On your toes, you know? Can't have you taking me for granted."

"There is no, absolutely no fear of that." He smiled as

he said it, setting her boots neatly next to the bed before turning and walking from the room, closing the door quietly behind him.

She'd been expecting him. It was no real surprise when he appeared. His face that same ruddy complexion she couldn't erase. Since Frankie had dropped her bombshell, Ali had blocked her mind – shut it down, gone on autopilot. She knew how – she'd practised enough over the years and used techniques to assist her. Taking a sleeping pill both nights since had helped, but she'd left them behind in her hurry to pack.

He touched her, lightly at first and then in that nasty, insistent way of his. Probing, shoving, hurting. She pushed at his big hands, tried to twist away, but he was too strong, too large to allow her any hold. His fingers hurt. They always hurt. She was just too little, too small.

"Oh no," he crooned, "no hiding now. You know what I want. You know what you have to do."

"No! I don't want to. I don't! Don't make me," she begged.

She tried not to beg. He liked that too much and drips of saliva would form on his wet lips as he made licking sounds. The sounds made her stomach turn, over and over.

"I can't," she gasped. "I'm going to be sick."

"Stop lying and do it!" His voice was angry, all attempts at cajoling gone. "Do it!"

"No, no, no, don't make me, no . . . please, no . . . "

Gabe felt it before he heard it. Sheer terror winding about him, making him gasp for air. He let his mind settle briefly to figure it out, but then he heard it – a low mumbling followed by a keening so pitiful it made his chest ache. Before either had even fully registered, he was on his feet, racing up the stairs to her room.

Her cries of "No, please, no . . . " had him fling open the door. What he saw had him stop in his footsteps and he had to force himself to breathe. Very softly, he walked to the bed, arm outstretched, ready to soothe.

Ali was kneeling in the centre of the bed, face ashen, eyes like dark pools, focused on something only she could see. Her sleep T-shirt was twisted in a knot at her waist, one hand turning it tighter and tighter, her other hand balled into a fist as she bit on it to stop herself from . . . *calling out?* She was rocking back and forth and completely oblivious to either the desperate eerie sounds escaping from her mouth or Gabe's presence.

"It's all right now," Gabe soothed as he stepped closer.

Silently and steadily, he reached the bed. She had no clue he was there. *She* wasn't there. He kneeled on the bed, twisting to sit next to her, and very, very slowly extended his arm to wrap it around her rigid shoulders. The rocking had stopped and some kind of gibberish was all he could hear. Nothing intelligible, just ramblings of fear, of pain.

"I've got you. You're safe with me. He's gone now. I've got you."

Gabe lowered her against his chest, took her fist in his hand and, gently kissing the knuckles, held it against her chest as he closed his arms about her. Teeth marks made ugly gashes on her skin and he blinked rapidly as he tried to deal with the enormity of what she must be feeling. He kept his words flowing, over and over, the same tone, the same rhythm, and gradually, so gradually it took him a minute to realise it, she relaxed into his embrace.

He rested his chin on top of her head, holding her in place. His fingers stroked her freezing arms, repeatedly, gently. As unremarkably as possible, he eased back to the top of the bed, resting his spine against the headboard. He reached for the covers and she clutched at him as he moved.

"It's okay, now. It's okay. I am just getting you nice and warm."

Shuddering, she sank against his body, trembles taking over from her previous rigidity. Using the heel of her hand, she swiped at her cheeks and he was appalled as he looked down at her to see tears tracking down her face. He'd never felt so helpless. Continuing to hold her, he began to hum. Where the melody came from, he could scarce remember. His maternal grandmother, perhaps. It was definitely tribal, and the repetitive air was calming and acted as a mild sedative.

Moments later, maybe longer, a husky, broken voice emanated from the area of his chest.

"I'll be okay now," she whispered. "You can go. Go back to work. It's over. I'll be okay."

Gabe ground his teeth together, his hold tightening marginally.

"I know you are okay, but I will just hang here a wee while. It has been a long day."

You may be okay, but I'm not. He didn't say the words out loud. She didn't need to feel responsible for his feelings. What she needed was unconditional support. That, he could do.

"Hum some more of that song," Ali said. "It sounds so restful."

He did.

Sometime later, when darkness had fallen completely, Gabe settled her down under the covers. He pulled off his clothes and in boxers and T-shirt, climbed in beside her. She turned, snuggling her back into the warmth of his large body, and he enclosed her in his arms. They slept.

Ali was mortified. Completely and utterly mortified. She'd fallen apart, or assumed she had when she woke just after dawn, to discover the hulking figure of Gabe Scotty MacScot and his delectable body flush against her back. Before she could analyse what he was doing there, she remembered the nightmare. It had been a big one and not unexpected. She'd hoped it hadn't been witnessed. *No such luck.* She didn't know how much of the spectacle he'd seen, but she imagined she'd soon find out.

Years ago, the first and only time she'd let a man sleep over, the nightmare had been pretty grim. Not last night grim, but not easy. Her potential boyfriend had been freaked out. Told her, as he hurriedly dressed in the dim early morning light, that he'd forgotten he had an early meeting. *Yeah, right. Sayonara, buddy. And good riddance.* It was never to happen again. Oh, not the nightmares, she wasn't *that* lucky, but the sleepovers? *They* weren't happening.

She thought she didn't mind. Genuinely believed it. And then, this. Gabe, his left leg hooked over hers, his left arm wrapped about her body, holding her. He was sleeping soundly – she could tell by his even breaths. But even in his sleep his fingers were lightly brushing the lower side of her breast. It felt so damn good. *So intimate. So wrong.* She began to ease away.

The arm tightened. "No," he growled, low and rusty, "stay."

Sighing, and deciding she could manage her fantasy a little longer, she wiggled back into him, causing a growl of a very different kind. *Christ, he was thick and hard against her bottom.* And even as that registered, his fingers moved upwards, a busy thumb sweeping across her instantly hardened nipple.

Licking her lips as heat coiled in her belly, she gasped as he flipped her onto her back, shoved up her T-shirt and sucked urgently on her tight buds, one after the other.

"Oh, fuck, that's good," she groaned and arched into his touch.

He continued to feast on her as she squirmed beneath him, feeling all kinds of heat build and simmer. Propping himself on one elbow, never taking his mouth from her breasts, he swept one hand down her side and peeled down her underwear. His hand was like a heat-seeking missile and found her centre within seconds, stroking and circling in all the needy places. She arched her hips this time, begging for more. His mouth finally left her breasts and headed down her belly, kissing and licking.

She tensed. *Ah, no. Not this.* She reached for his head to alter his course, to haul him back up, but he kept going. He was speaking, she realised, into her skin. Straining to hear, worry etching through her entire body, she caught some of the words. Among the "gorgeous" and "beautiful" was "taste".

"I just need to taste you," he groaned, his voice low and sexy as fuck.

It was so erotic, so unbelievably dirty and sexy and hot, that Ali threw metaphorical caution to wind and thought, *why the hell not?*

And then his tongue took over from his hands and *OMG!* that man displayed all of his kissing skills to this entirely new part of her body. He didn't just slide his tongue up and down in a random fashion. *No, this gentleman had superior skills. Licking. And sucking. And tasting. And kissing. And ooohhh, God! More sucking.*

Ali could feel her insides heat and crackles of tension wound their way through her belly. She could feel passion rise and soar and thought, in one last desperate attempt to keep sane, *I'm going to fall.* The two fingers Gabe slid inside her, curling upwards, along with the sudden pressure of his circling tongue, pushed her a step too far and down she went. *Spectacularly.*

Head pressed back on the pillow, her body shaking with the aftermath of such a huge release, Ali remembered she needed to do her bit. A cold hand slid over her insides. *But she was game. She'd give it a go. She could do this. She had to.* She raised her head to find Gabe climbing up the bed towards her. She opened her eyes, unaware till then that they'd been squeezed shut.

"Hey, come here," she said, disgusted with the slight tremor in her voice. "Let me."

To her surprise, Gabe twisted in the bed to go back to their original position, curling her into his chest. She twisted, looking over her shoulder.

"But what about you?" she asked. "Don't you want to . . . you know . . . finish?"

God, she was embarrassed. *This never happened. It was always quid pro quo.*

Gabe leaned down and pressed a kiss to her forehead. "I'm fine. I just wanted you to relax some more. Now go back to sleep."

"But . . . I can still feel you," she muttered, her cheeks heating.

He chuckled. "And I am not going to die of it." He kissed her again, settling his palm against her stomach, rubbing gently. "Get some sleep."

Huh, Ali thought. That was a new one on her. A man who put her needs ahead of his own. Without prompting. *He must be quite the rarity.* In her world, anyway.

Such a shame she had to give him back. That she had to return him to the general population. That he wouldn't be hers any more. A real damn shame.

Chapter 19

He was gone when she woke several hours later. A handwritten note lay on the pillow next to her:

I had to go to the station. Work-related. I didn't want to wake you – you were sleeping peacefully. Rest, explore, come and go as you please. I will be back this afternoon to take you to meet my grandmother.
MacScot

Ali stretched, twisting and reaching, and realised she felt . . . okay. Good, even. She'd slept deeply and dreamlessly for hours. She peeped at her watch. *Shit – it was after eleven.* She must have had about six straight. That was a champion sleep for her. Exhilarated, she threw back the covers, discovered her sleep shorts at the bottom of the bed and stopped still.

Oh, yeah. That.

Grabbing them, she tossed the offending article towards her suitcase and headed to the shower. She'd do the analysis later. Shower, coffee, food and . . . an important, badly needed phone call.

The Macs were a delight. The coffee was strong, and poached eggs, bacon and toasted home-made bread as good as her mum's – making her breakfast a treat. Mrs

Mac regaled her with stories of Gabe as a "wee chap", how independent and clever he was. How they missed him so much when he went to school or to the "Americas", as they so charmingly put it.

Ali was guarded in her questions. It wasn't her nature not to pry, but with Gabe, for some reason, each thing he told her about himself was like a trophy. It felt wrong to ask for details, badly though she wanted them, when he hadn't offered them himself. He was so private, so closed in many ways, that when he did reveal a memory or, even better, a feeling, she treasured it.

Dear God, she was turning into a complete sap.

She tried helping with the dishwasher but was shooed out, unceremoniously.

"Take a wee gander about the house and then the communal garden across the road. The key is on the hallstand. In fact, the back garden here, though smaller, of course, is pretty too, if you'd like a look?" Mackie was a gentle host, not pushing her but offering all the options.

"Thanks, but I've a phone call to make and then I'll probably explore the house. There are enough levels to keep me occupied for hours!"

"Aye," Mrs Mac agreed, "and don't forget the nursery on the fourth floor – there are lots of lovely wee toys and knick-knacks from the lad's childhood."

Ali thanked them and headed upstairs. She knew Gabe's office had a landline and her mobile signal was patchy at best. She didn't think he'd mind. The door was ajar, so not obviously housing any state secrets.

It was so him.

Old leather, book-lined, a large, heavy desk facing away from the window. *Typical – he wouldn't want to be distracted by the view to the gardens below.* This room faced the back of the house and was quiet and calm. *No surprise there, either.* She wandered the room, stroking her hand along the book-filled shelves. Alphabetised by category, of course, and some very interesting titles. *Well now, he even read thrillers. Was that for work?* she wondered. *Or pleasure?* Some classics, loads of history tomes, a ton of biographies and even old-fashioned detective ones. *And how had he missed Rankin and Rebus?* She'd definitiely give him more shit for that. She plonked herself in the old swing chair at his desk and spent a few moments twirling. Because she could. And for just a minute it felt *nice* to be carefree.

She was procrastinating. She knew it and didn't care. *Just a little longer.*

There was a desktop computer and a snazzy modern phone that looked like it had extensions on it. He probably had calls directed to his staff or whatever. A yellow legal notepad was neatly aligned to the desk edge with a fountain pen set precisely centred along the top.

Anal, much? Or was it simply a form of control, not unlike her own?

She certainly couldn't throw stones when it came to keeping her life compartmentalised. She was a fucking master at it.

The telephone stared back at her. Obviously, it didn't *stare* at her, but it sure gave off an accusatory vibe. *Fine,* she snapped, *just give me a second.*

She glanced around the room again.

Stalling.

From this vantage point the mid-grey walls had a nice slant of light on them from the two tall windows behind her. There were no photographs, just a few seascapes in the same old-master style and set in gilded frames. They were of mostly stormy seas and yet they were uncannily restful. She wondered, *did Gabe feel rested here, in this space?* Like she did in her loft. Or she used to. She wasn't sure how she felt there now. After everything. Time would tell.

Now the TV crews were gone she needed to readjust to her working day there. Writing recipes, planning her book for the show. Baking. Because of all the recent events and the repainting, with Gabe, the filming – often with him there watching – the practice bakes, she wondered how long it would take for her to be in her loft workspace alone and *not* feel his presence.

Oh, fuck it. The damn phone loomed silently.

Ali dialled and waited.

"Dr Hearne's office, how may I help you?"

"Hi, Michelle, it's Ali Fitzgerald. Is Dr H available? I really need to speak with her."

"Hi, Ali, she's with a client – oh, wait, they're just leaving. Hold on a moment and I'll see if she can talk now."

Ali was put on hold and listened to the dreary music that these places insisted on playing. Seconds passed. Ali's stomach was on full churn and her inner cheek had been bitten to a painful level.

"Ali!" Grace Hearne's professional and steady voice came through. "I have some time now. What's up?"

"Hey, Doc, it's . . . I'm a bit stressed." *Understatement of the century based on last night's nightmare.* "I just found out he's back – in Dublin – and I'm frozen in place."

"I was expecting to hear from you because of the bomb situation last week, but I wasn't expecting this. Can you come in?"

Ali huffed out a sort of laugh. "No. I'm in Edinburgh. I heard he was back on Friday night and I've been here ever since. But last night I had a whopper and I don't know how to move forwards. I don't know what to do."

There was silence for several beats. Then Dr Hearne spoke quietly but firmly.

"I think you do, Ali. I think you know exactly what to do. Cast your mind back to when you first started coming. Or rather, a few sessions in. What was the one thing you wanted more than any? What did you believe, in your heart, would make it better for you?"

Shit. This woman was tough.

It was both her strength and her most terrifying part. There was to be no soft sell, no "let's ease into this". Ali guessed that's why this psychologist was considered one of the best in her field. And it's why she'd placed the call. *Damn her.*

"I wanted to confront him. To challenge him and call him out?" Her voice was tentative, as if testing the validity of the statement. Making it a question, although she knew that wasn't what the doc wanted from her.

"Don't ask me," the doc confirmed. "What did *you* want? What *do* you want?"

What, indeed.

They talked some more. A lot more. After about ten minutes Dr Hearne put her on hold and moved an appointment back so they could continue the session. Because that's what it was now. This was work.

Ali had started seeing the renowned doctor in her

early twenties. It had been the result of an overheard conversation between two people on the DART train, sitting behind her discussing a scenario between them and praising a Dr Hearne to the hilt. Completely serendipitous for Ali, as she'd been struggling with her memories and knew she needed help but was too damn afraid to ask. It was the first time she'd ever told anyone what had happened to her. It had almost broken her. But Grace Hearne had listened. She'd listened and believed. And then she began helping.

In the beginning Ali had visited twice a week – simply to try it. It had taken nearly a month of complete ramblings and pain-filled rants before the whole story came out. Ali had slept for almost twenty-four hours straight after that last session. And not one nightmare had reared its head. The healing began that day. But it was a long, uphill struggle with many a slip.

This was normal, the doc reassured her. Three years had been taken from her – it would take more than a few months to get them back. If ever. Ali knew, intellectually knew, with the help of Dr Hearne, that she was entirely blameless in all that had happened. Only one person, one, was to blame.

Ali hadn't realised until her therapy sessions were well established how much she, herself, had blamed so many other people, as well. Or at least in the beginning. Her parents, primarily. How? she'd beseeched the doc. How could they not have known? Weren't they supposed to protect her? Where were they when she needed them the most? Dealing with a new member of the family, was where. So of course Frankie got the blame, too.

Her sister-in-law, the lovely kind and thoughtful,

charming and successful Frankie Jones had come into their lives as a bit of a tornado when Ali was only eight. She'd settled into the Fitzgerald routine but was so often the centre of attention. And with Frankie's mother dying so tragically when Frankie was only ten, Frankie got lots of exemptions for unruly behaviour. And lots of parental time was, naturally, Ali understood as a grown-up, spent on helping the grieving child.

Unfortunately, that meant what was happening to Ali went flying under the radar. For years, especially as a teenager, Ali resented Frankie and her blossoming looks – her talent, her grace, her everything. If Frankie hadn't been with them so much maybe her mum and dad would have *seen* Ali, Ali had reasoned.

The doc had been pretty direct in showing Ali that Frankie was in no way, absolutely none, to blame for Ali's trauma. That had been a hard truth to swallow at first. But she'd learned. And if Frankie didn't know or understand why Ali had, over the past few years, warmed to her, she didn't question it. Since Caro had moved to Rome and Frankie and Dev had become an item, Ali and Frankie had become much closer. *It felt good. Really good.*

She'd blamed her brothers, too. A bit. They were supposed to watch their sisters at all times. That was the house rule. The doc had put her straight on that one, too.

Of course, the person most to blame for all of it, in Ali's mind, was herself. What had *she* done to provoke, entice, enable the abuse? She must have *done* something. Everyone knew abuse was wrong, adults knew that, so it must have been her wild ways, her actions, her backchat that brought this upon herself.

But the healing and awareness that came with that

amount of guilt took a long time. Dr Hearne never let up, never gave up. She counselled Ali in such a tender, understanding and real way that Ali was able to heal. Not all the way, probably never all the way, but in so many good ways. She learned to believe in her gut – to *trust* her gut. She learned that *she* had power now. She could choose to use her power however she liked. No one, unless she let them, *and she fucking wouldn't*, could take that away from her.

What it boiled down to was the bare facts. No one was to blame for what happened to Ali, except the man himself.

As Ali and Dr Hearne talked, Ali remembered her wish. What the doc was referring to earlier. Her greatest desire had been to confront Father Jack. To go up to him as adult to adult and tell him exactly what she thought of him. Maybe now she had the opportunity. *Was she brave enough?*

"And remember, Ali," Dr Hearne said as they were finishing their talk. "*You* have *all* the power now. *He* is the criminal. The law states that. You know it and he knows it. What you do with your knowledge of his behaviour is up to you – and only you. You have some big decisions to make and all I want from you is your promise to think it through. What do you believe will make you feel better about your life right now? Keeping in mind that whatever you choose will have consequences. Not just for you but for those you love, and for him."

"No pressure, then?" Ali quipped as her stomach knotted in the total understanding of the massive burden if she took that path.

"I have the utmost faith and belief in your strength,

Ali. You're an amazing woman and you should be so proud of yourself. Let me know what you decide and call me, day or night, if the decision gets too big."

They hung up shortly after that and Ali collapsed back into Gabe's big comfy chair. *Wow. That had been . . . heavy. Scary – and thought-provoking, too.*

Could she actually do it?

Would she? Should she?

Argh!

Ali reared up from the chair, grabbed a book from the shelf that caught her interest and wandered up the stairs to the fourth floor. She opened several doors – rooms unused and with blobs of possible furniture draped in acres of white cloth. The last door on the garden side opened into a bright corner room, windows on two walls, and this one was still tended, with lots of care. Mrs Mac obviously had a soft spot for the nursery.

Ali didn't know what a traditional nursery was supposed to look like. She'd read about them in historical romance novels, but the reality was a bit different. Yes, there was the expected rocking horse, check, and a small table and chairs, check. A big old fireplace was against one wall and there were bookshelves upon bookshelves, all full to the brim. Perusing them, she saw that they were categorised by school year or age: baby, toddler, preschool, et cetera, right up to some college books. There was also a larger desk and chair, and an old desktop computer.

Gabe must have studied here even as a university student. How quaint.

She pulled out the chair and sat, loving the feel of the set-up. It was comfortable and modern. There was no feel of gloom and doom, or nasty nursemaids and cross governesses or tutors. It had a happy feel. She hoped Gabe had felt at ease in this room. Ali shook her head as she caught herself trying to imagine all the things young Gabe must have dreamed about, right here in this very chair.

She leaned forwards and picked up a framed photograph.

It took her a moment.

Oh. My. God.

Gabe would have been about sixteen and he looked every inch the young warrior. He wore what she imagined were called buckskin trousers. His torso was bare, his frame still narrow and a bit gangly. But his hair . . . *Christ!* He looked like a younger version of the movie star in "Last of the Mohicans".

Straight and silky, it fell halfway down his back and his arms, braced across his chest, gave him a proud stance. He wore some kind of bandana tied about his forehead and Ali knew, without doubt, that had she met teenage Gabe, she'd have fallen instantly in lust. Eyes staring straight into the camera. Not shy yet a certain reserve. A weird maturity for one so young. That shouldn't come as a shock. But teens were notoriously gauche and awkward. *Not this guy.*

Catching sight of a bunch of other photos on the wall next to the fireplace, Ali replaced the framed picture and walked over to investigate. They were split about half and half between American family groups and Scottish. There was a tall, straight-backed woman standing next to a younger Gabe, maybe thirteen, and she was pretty obviously his mother. *The same shape eyes, the same cheekbones. The same intense yet reserved look.*

271

Another showed a group of whom she assumed were native Osage Nation family members. Ali picked out what looked like his grandmother. It was fascinating, this glimpse into a whole other Gabe. *Oh, fuck!* One of Gabe on horseback, looking ridiculously hot – a bit older, late teens and still with the long hair. *Why had he cut it?*

She moved to study the Scottish groupings. *Ah! there was his dad. Wow. Gabe had absolutely nothing to worry about if he was to grow into a version of this silver fox. Tall, broad, wide-chested with a head of wild wavy brown hair.* Brawny was the word that popped into Ali's mind. And he was, *wait for it*, wearing a frigging kilt!

Ali put a hand to her chest as she was overcome with the urge to crack up laughing. This was all simply too weird. It was like she was watching someone's life unfold behind a secret door. Gabe in school uniform, long hair tied back in a ponytail. Gabe in jeans and T-shirt, hair braided, like in the movies.

Gabe in a kilt. *Wait* . . . She had to study that one again. *Gabe in a kilt.*

She took the photo off the wall and studied it closely in the light of the window.

Sweet divine. Scottish romance, anyone?

He was standing, legs slightly apart, in what looked like full Highland dress. His father was beside him, large hand resting on his son's shoulder. Other than the long hair and the skin colour, they looked the same. A slash of dark brows, firm mouth, strong chin. *Yup. They were family.*

His dad appeared to have light eyes too, so maybe Gabe got that unusual shade of green from him. His mum's folk all had a rich dark chocolate colour that looked so soft and strong at the same time. Ali ran her finger along the image of Gabe's face. He looked stern, calm, motionless. *Himself, in other words.* She sighed.

"What is the sigh for?" Gabe strolled into the nursery and stopped a few paces in front of her.

Ali had startled when she heard his voice. But that wasn't all she felt. A jump in her stomach and a kick in her chest made her most uncomfortable. It wasn't being found with his photograph clutched in her hands and a book tucked under her arm that brought these temporary side effects. It was him. *The sound of him. The presence of him.* She sighed again and handed over the photo for him to see.

"You are too cute too behold when wearing a skirt, MacScot," she said, her voice sounding cross. "Why can't you be normal?" She turned and waved a hand airily at the array of photographs on the wall. "Look at these," she declared. "Not. Normal."

Gabe hung the picture back in its space and shoved his hands in his pockets. "Explain."

"Okay, look at this one." Ali brushed past him, put the book down and picked up the desk photo. "I mean, *come on.* You look like a fucking movie star. Or a model. Where's the acne? The goofy 'not quite grown into himself' awkwardness? There's nothing in any of these photos that makes you human. Nothing." Ali shoved the picture at him, her finger jabbing at the young man he'd been. "And the hair? Christ Almighty, Gabe, did you have to? Did every single female in your vicinity, both here in bonny Scotland and in Oklahoma, collapse at your feet? Because this . . . " She swept her hand up and down the picture. "This is *hot.*"

Gabe stared at her. Doing his non-blinking thing. A

slight pink tinged his skin. *Oh, that was adorable! He was embarrassed.*

"You think I am hot?" Without warning, his hand enclosed the back of her neck and he pulled her to him.

"Well. You *were*," she gasped as his mouth landed kisses on her forehead and cheeks, one after the other. "Back then."

"And now?" He nuzzled her neck and bit lightly on her earlobe.

"Ah, emm," Ali said intelligently as she arched her neck to allow him better access when his other arm snaked around her back to hold her tight to his chest, the photograph hanging from her hand at her side.

"Or now?" He pulled on her lower lip, sucking the tender, delicate, sensitive skin.

Her groan seemed to give him the answer he needed, because his mouth stopped any and all teasing and got down to the business of making her feel all kinds of heat. *All over.*

Pulling back, he asked huskily, "Are you ready to come and meet my granny?"

"Seriously?" Ali snorted. "If I met your granny right this minute, she'd be able to see, gift of sight or not, that I'm about to spontaneously combust!"

Gabe quirked a brow. "That good, huh?"

She punched him on the arm as she pulled away, replacing the photo frame on his old desk.

"No need to get a big head along with everything else."

She grinned back at him, feeling refreshed and relaxed. *At home. Amazing what a really spectacular middle-of-the-day kiss can do for one's state of mind.* She wound her arm through his, happily feeling the strength and shape of his biceps. *So comforting in a sexy way. So not fair to other mere mortal me*n. She picked up the copy of *Killers of the Flower Moon* by David Grann she'd taken from his study and waved it at him.

"I'm borrowing this, by the way," she announced. "It looks pretty interesting." She tried for nonchalance but wasn't sure if it worked. She was intending to read a book about the Osage Nation during a particularly harrowing part of their history and wasn't sure if he thought that might be . . . invasive.

"It's neither relaxing nor pleasant reading, but I'd be interested to hear what you think when you finish it."

He spoke with a certain sadness and she immediately wanted to lighten his life, just a smidgen, if she could.

"Come on, Scotty MacHotness, let's go visit Granny. And, I want to hear all about the hair and why it's no longer flowing down your back in all its awesomeness."

Chapter 20

They walked. It was a warm evening and most of the business traffic was going in the opposite direction. Gabe kept his hands in his pockets as they strolled along the lovely squares and crescents to his grandmother's home. It was a breach of etiquette, he was well aware, but if his hands swung loose, one of them would inevitably end up grabbing Ali's hand and something told him she wasn't ready.

"So, why doesn't your granny live in your house?" Ali asked as she dragged a hand along the iron railings of an enclosed garden.

"It is not for want of asking," Gabe replied with a grimace. "Both my father and I are continually asking her to move in, but she is an independent soul. And a bit of a rebel."

Ali looked up at him, her expression curious.

"She thinks we are way too big for our boots, living in the 'fancy house', as she calls it. Her belief is that it was probably bought via ill-gotten gains and we should have more pride than to own it still."

"Is she right? And if she is right, just how ill-gotten are we talking? Smugglers? Crimes against the Crown? Bribery? Tell all!" she insisted, skipping along, rubbing her hands together in apparent glee.

"You look like a teenager." Gabe couldn't help smiling. "But you are correct. The story goes that smuggling was definitely – or probably, depending on who is recounting the story – an issue. Brandy from France, by all accounts. A lot of it. If we have time before we go tomorrow, I will show you the cellars. It is said that one reason this house suited was because of the sizable cellars. Cross here." He put his hand at her back, guiding her over the cobbled street.

"How far away is she?"

"Another minute or two. This area is at the edge of Dean, a neighbourhood that she likes and feels comfortable in. Her house is small – well, comparatively – and has a more manageable garden. She sometimes comes north to the Keep, but at her age she likes her own space and, though she doesn't say it, access to amenities like a hospital."

"I thought she was healthy?" Ali said, concern lacing her voice.

"As a horse. But she is . . . canny. She knows what she wants and is as stubborn as a mule. I swear if we moved her to the Keep, she would have a heart attack on purpose, to prove a point."

Ali skidded to a halt. "Shit!" She slapped her forehead. "I don't have anything to bring. Is there a shop nearby? Seriously, Gabe, I can't go visit your granny with my hands swinging. My mother would kill me."

"Your mother is not here."

"Ha. Easy for you to say. Hey, I seem to remember a phone call with your dad about thank-you notes?"

Gabe groaned.

"Yeah," she continued. "Don't think I forgot that little nugget. And Mum loved the one you sent, by the way."

Gabe obligingly changed direction and instead of

walking along the river on the nearside, he angled her down into a shopping area. They rounded a bend and a small row of shops opened up before them.

"Here," she said excitedly. "In here."

Inside the small local grocery shop, Ali mooched about, picking up and discarding various items. Gabe leaned against a stall, crossing one foot over the other, and watched. As a one-time chef, and now baker, Ali knew her produce. She sniffed and pressed, twirled and peered, finally selecting a few unwaxed lemons, a jar of local honey, some organic cane sugar and a small bottle of cloves. Her purchases paid for and neatly wrapped in a brown paper bag, they were on their way again.

"You should have brought a bottle of something. Or a cake." Ali prodded him in the arm as they rounded the corner up the hill to Ann Street.

"I had a basket delivered earlier. Reminding her we were coming for afternoon tea."

"I was just testing you." She sighed at this titbit of information and Gabe had a hard time figuring out quite how Ali Fitzgerald's mind worked.

He stopped outside a charming terraced house on a small curving street. It was like a gut punch every time Gabe came here. So many memories. So much learned, right here in this welcoming home. So different to the huge Moray Place house, this represented his grandmother to perfection.

He unlatched the gate and gestured to Ali to walk up the brick path.

"What a pretty garden she has, in such a small space." Ali stroked the petals of a rose-pink peony and bent down to inhale.

"Gabriel Andrew Lloyd Mackenzie. Right on time."

"Granny."

Gabe strode forwards, bending to capture the diminutive woman who'd spoken in an embrace. He wrapped his arms about her and lifted her clear off her feet as he twirled her round.

She bashed him on the arm in a futile attempt to get him to release her.

"You great oaf," she called, unable to hold her laughter in check. "Put me down or you'll break my ribs."

He did as she asked and, turning to Ali, took her hand and pulled her forwards.

"This is Fiona Duncan Mackenzie. Granny, meet Ali Fitzgerald."

Oh, fuck, thought Ali, *she hates me*. The older woman held herself straight as an arrow as her gaze travelled up and down Ali's entire body. Not a hint of a smile, no indication of welcome, Fiona Mackenzie simply studied her. Trying not to fidget or, as moments passed, flinch, Ali stood straighter. And stared right back. If they'd been men, it would have been like two alphas squaring up, vying for power. That's what it felt like. Ali knew she had no power over Gabe. No one did. Except maybe this woman.

"I'm right sorry for you, lass." A gnarled, arthritic hand grasped one of Ali's, drawing her forwards to wrap both of her old hands around Ali's. "He'll pay, you'll see."

Ali tried to pull away, a shiver of ice sliding along her skin at the words.

"Come in and have tea. And cake." She threw a smile at Gabe over her shoulder as she entered her home.

"We're in the parlour," she announced grandly, "and Marie has the kettle on."

Marie, it turned out, was a gem. A woman half as old as Mrs Mackenzie but almost twice her size bustled in and amid introductions (Ali) and hugs (Gabe), she unpacked a tea tray onto a small coffee table. The tea, when it arrived, was strong and full of flavour, and Ali raised an eyebrow as Gabe poured himself a cup as well as for the ladies.

"Rather daring, don't you think?" she teased. "Caffeine after eleven in the morning? You're pulling out all the stops. I hope Mrs Mackenzie appreciates your regime change."

Fiona Mackenzie laughed. A big sound from a tiny frame, she let go with verve.

"Och, dearie, isn't he a wee daftie with his silly nonsense and rules. Go on," she urged her grandson as his hand hesitated over a piece of white-iced walnut cake, "'twill do you no harm."

And to Ali's surprise, she turned and winked, just out of Gabe's range, and Ali relaxed. *It was going to be okay.* She and this elderly woman were totally on the same page when it came to slagging Gabe. *Excellent.* As long as she didn't dwell on the earlier weird remarks, she could do this.

"Granny, you are being a bit disingenuous. You are the one who insisted on rules and order in my life." Gabe took a bite of the cake and closed his eyes in apparent bliss.

"Hey, watch it, buddy." Ali reached over and snatched the piece of cake from his hand. "You're only allowed make that 'this is divine' look when you eat *my* cake."

Gabe caught her eye and his eyebrow raised, just a smidgen, as he let her dwell on her previous words.

She blushed. *Damn. She was off her game.* She hadn't even intended that double entendre, and certainly not in front of his grandmother, but a shimmer of heat slid into her belly as she instantly recalled exactly how he'd tasted her earlier this morning.

Time for a subject change.

"I brought you a small token." She handed over the brown paper bag and sat back as Fiona opened it.

"How thoughtful. The makings of a hot toddy. Minus the whisky."

"Yes, sorry about that," Ali mumbled, embarrassed. "There was no time to go to an off-licence."

"Dinna fash yourself, child. This is so kind. And the good Lord knows one particular cupboard in my kitchen has many a fine bottle. Marie!" She called for her companion, who appeared almost immediately. "A bottle of Cragganmore 29 for a toast, if you wouldn't mind."

"Bringing out the big guns?" Gabe asked with interest. "I am impressed."

"Don't act all surprised. Don't we always do this on our special day?" Fiona turned her gaze back to Ali. "My grandson probably didn't tell you—"

"Really, there's no—"

"But today is our day," she continued as if Gabe hadn't tried to intervene. "It's our common birthday."

Ali swung her head to meet Gabe's sheepish one. She punched him on the arm. Something she seemed to be doing rather a lot of late.

"Hey, why didn't you say something? I'd have given you a gift."

The second the words were out of her mouth, she could feel her stomach clench. *She could give him a gift. The one she knew he wanted.* He was no different than any of the others in that respect. *She would. She'd do it later.* She'd just close her eyes and think of taxes, or railway tracks or Lego houses, or some other inane, innocuous thing, and just do it.

She fake smiled at the big man beside her on the couch. "I'll give you a gift later," she promised.

She could see the light dawn on his face and a hint of a blush edged his cheekbones. He shifted slightly on the seat. *See? He wanted it.* They really were all the fucking same. She'd bring her A game. She'd promised.

Ali turned back to Fiona. "So, you two share the same birthdate. Have you always celebrated together?"

"Every year. As long as we're in the same time zone and Mr Hotshot Detective here hasn't a big case, then yes. Now, let's toast."

Ali had to chuckle as Fiona Mackenzie used a nickname that Ali herself would call Gabe. Maybe they had something in common, besides their care of this man. The older woman stood to her full height of five foot nothing and held out a tumbler for the amber liquid Marie put before them on yet another tray. Gabe poured a finger into each glass and handed one to Ali.

"Happy birthday, Granny," he said and they clinked glasses.

"Happy birthday to you, Gabriel," she returned and they clinked again.

She looked over at Ali. "He's a good boy. If a little strange," she added mischievously.

"Pot, kettle, Granny," he said. "Speaking of . . . " He

gave her an intense look before turning to Ali. "Would you mind waiting with Marie in the kitchen? I have to discuss a few business matters with my grandmother. It will be boring for you. I will only be a few minutes."

"Of course." Ali rose and gathered the empty cups and crumbed plates, stacking them expertly on the tray, but he stopped her from lifting it.

"I will bring that later," he said. "I won't be long," he repeated and opened the door for her.

She sailed past him as if not a care in the world.

"Take all the time you need. I'm sure I can find something to entertain me while you two discuss *business.*"

She closed the door with a nice heavy thud, right in his face – satisfied she'd made her point, though why she was suddenly feeling cross with him was beyond her.

No. It wasn't. She was well aware it was family business they were discussing. She wasn't a complete fool. It shouldn't hurt so much that she was being excluded but *damn, it stung.* She had no right. None. But who said logic had any say in the matter, anyway?

She turned towards the kitchen and the friendly face of Marie.

"So." Gabe paced the ancient wool carpet on the parlour floor. "What do you think?"

"Of the lassie?"

Gabe nodded.

His granny took a long time to answer, sipping her whisky and tilting her head from side to side.

"She's very . . . damaged," she said finally, and Gabe swung his head in her direction.

283

His immediate protest stayed on the tip of his tongue as she raised her hand in a silencing gesture.

"Not in a dangerous or disturbed way but . . . she's wary and afraid. Not of you." She looked at him tenderly. "Not at all of you. Or maybe a little, in how she feels about you. But you strengthen her. Ground her. Her fear remains, however, and you have a long road ahead if you want to keep her in your life. She's very close to flight."

Fiona stood and walked over to wrap her wiry arms about his waist. "Be careful, sweet man. She's filled with pain and *you* are going to have the overflow . . . soon, I think. Make sure, make damned sure you want it. That you'll keep it and her safe. Don't toy with her, Gabriel, she won't survive it."

Gabe returned his granny's hug. "I've got her, *mo seanmhair*," Gabe said, using the formal term for grandmother as befitted her place as head of their family and also because he was speaking of something so serious. "I won't let her down."

He disentangled himself from her embrace and took a sip of his now cold tea. He sat back down on the couch as she perched herself on the arm, her hand resting on his shoulder.

He reached up and, holding the weathered hand in his, asked, "Can you tell me anything specific I should be watching for? I know you've only just met her, but the aura is so strong, so fierce."

Fiona shut her eyes, breathing deeply. "So many barriers," she murmured, "so much hurt. So much . . . " She paused. "Why aren't you doing this yourself? You know so many more ways to dig deep than I do. Your mama taught you well in her ways, too." She took his chin in her grip and turned his face to hers. "Why, *balach*?"

When Fiona Mackenzie called him *boy*, he knew she was concerned. She was returning to the days when he'd been terrified by his own gifts. A double whammy from the Scottish "seeing" kind – both past and future – and his Osage heritage of just being able to "know" things about people: truth or lies, pain and hurt. Sometimes he'd walk into a room and be overwhelmed with feelings – all the bad and negative trauma that random people carried around and didn't process, he got hit with it. As a young boy he'd been completely unable to decipher or even compartmentalise it. Fiona had helped – showed him mind tricks and ways to harness and use his powers. Fortunately, all the summers he'd spent in Oklahoma with his mother and her family had been a huge blessing and he'd learned more of the same. He'd learned how to meditate and use dreams, how to let his mind conjure up certain scenes, certain things, and bypass others.

It had taken time. A lot of time and a lot of practice. And in order to practise the techniques, he'd had to allow the feelings in first. It had been hard. Often, he'd wanted to give up. To use drugs or mind-numbing pills to block it all out. And then he'd help someone to find a person, or help someone to focus on a past unremembered event that healed them, or had a vision of a place where someone was being held against their will – not necessarily captive but unhappy.

He began to work with the local police on the reservation where his Oklahoma family sometimes lived and since no one questioned his abilities there – they knew his ancestors – he began to earn respect and value his own capabilities. He soon realised, back in Scotland, that he could do the same. The locals up at the Keep knew his grandmother, knew of her powers, so didn't challenge his. In fact, they expected it. Respected it, too.

School had been different. There, he learned very quickly to keep all of himself tightly locked away.

"I promised, Granny. I promised Ali I wouldn't 'look' unless she asked," Gabe said quietly. "And I won't."

Fiona harrumphed. "Is it not a wee bit of cheating you're doing by asking me?"

Gabe had the grace to look embarrassed. "Aye," he said, "but I am worried for her safety – physically, not emotionally."

He told her all about the break-ins, Mel, Garcia and their part in vandalising Ali's property, and about the bomb. Fiona had known he'd been hurt in a recent event but hadn't realised till then it had concerned Ali.

"I will look, if I have to," he said. "Something is bothering me, something I am missing, and I feel there are connections just out of my grasp that need combining. A promise, however, is a promise. So, unless things get dangerous and her safety is compromised again, this is how it has to be."

His granny nodded sagely. "It's hard, isn't it, carrying what we know? Trying to juggle the truth and the perhaps and the maybe. Making that decision of when to intervene, when to hold back. When to walk away."

"I am *not* walking away." Gabe was determined. Deadly serious. "Even if I lose her trust, I will not walk away if she is in danger. That will *not* happen."

Fiona stood and Gabe rose from the couch to go with her.

"Come," she said. "We'll go and do a short meditation to help ease your mind, your heart. I'll just get a few herbs from my cupboard and I'll meet you in the library."

Gabe bent and kissed her on her silver hair. "Thank you, dear heart. I would appreciate the time spent with you. Perhaps just a few minutes, though – I don't want Marie to give away all of my secrets."

"Well, you shouldn't have sent the lassie to the kitchen, you oaf. Marie's not exactly known for her discretion."

She was still laughing as she went to her supply cupboard while Gabe took a left down the hall to the library.

The walk back was different. Ali was silent at first and Gabe was lost in his own thoughts. The evening was getting chilly as the late May sun set. After-dinner strollers meandered through the side streets, chatting and laughing among themselves.

Gabe cleared his throat. "I hope you don't mind that I told my grandmother about Carney, Garcia, the vandalism and the bomb scenario, too. I wasn't trying to violate your privacy." He dipped his head towards her. "And I realise I should have asked your permission first. So, in case it is necessary, I apologise."

Ali looked at him, puzzled. "But she already knew. She mentioned it when we arrived. She said 'he'll pay'."

Now it was Gabe's turn to look confused. "No, I just told her while you were with Marie. I didn't think you would want to be there, while I was telling her – it might have been . . . awkward for you."

"But . . . " Ali began then stopped as a chill swept through her body.

Shit. Fiona Mackenzie knew stuff. Knew her stuff.

This. Was. Not. Good.

Ali took a deep breath. "Did she make any comments? Have any pearls of wisdom?"

Gabe stilled beside her for a second – hardly at all – but Ali was watching closely so copped it.

"What?" she insisted. "What did she say?"

"Nothing," Gabe lied.

She knew in her gut he was lying and a little piece of her broke. She glared at him accusingly.

"Honestly, we talked about what happened and how hard it must have been for you. She was concerned. That is all."

Ali was shocked at how hurt she felt as they continued walking. *How could his lie hurt so much?* Maybe he thought he was protecting her but, shit, he should know her better than that by now. He should respect her need for truth. His granny knew something about her past – and whatever voodoo crap she called up to know it, Ali didn't care, she just knew that Mrs Mackenzie was tuned into her past in some way.

And Ali didn't like that one bit.

If Granny Mackenzie knew shit, then you could bet your life the "white-haired boy" knew it, too. *That would not do. Was that why he was so quiet? Was he in shock? Damn*, Ali wished she'd never left them alone. It was her own fault. This meant her decision time had just shortened dramatically. *It was so fucking unfair.*

They went to cross the street and a car accelerated as they were about halfway over. Gabe put his hand to her back and guided her to the pavement. As if on autopilot, he let it rest there, at the small of her back. *Protective. Caring. Aw, fuck.* Maybe she could get one more night. *Just one.*

Her heart hurt when she thought of what was to come. Not the activity she had in mind, but afterwards. When she proved to herself, one more time, that she could never truly be in a grown-up, adult relationship. It simply wasn't for her. The bastard had seen to that.

By the time they got to the house, by some unspoken agreement they headed upstairs to his room. Silently, Gabe reached for her and began unbuttoning her shirt as he edged her back towards the bed. Without a word, Ali pulled his jacket off his shoulders, tugging it down his arms. They broke away for a second, shrugging off their upper clothes, his clear green eyes never leaving her face, and then their mouths fused with a burning intensity.

Ali felt her body respond in an instant. Her skin felt every touch, every brush of fingertips, every taste of his tongue. She pulled back, gasping, wondering was she the only one who felt this rawness. This insane need to devour. Gabe's breathing was ragged, uneven. *And those eyes that had been clear mere seconds ago? Black pools of lust, with lids at half-mast.* He toppled her to the bed, reaching for a condom from the bedside table as she wriggled free from her underwear, the last bit of clothing she wore.

"Jesus," he groaned, "you are so fucking beautiful."

Ali's heart flipped right over, never to be settled again. The man who rarely swore, who never let go, he was coming undone because of her. It was both terrifying and sexy. So powerful. She climbed on top of him, thighs holding him close as she leaned down and sucked those sensitive brown nipples. She bit gently and he arched his back, gasping, eager for more. The sounds that escaped him made her so wet, so ready, she wondered would she even get to do it. To taste.

She took a deep breath. She'd made a promise to herself that she'd try and now was as good a time as any to screw it all up. Now, before he put the condom on. The one that sat next to her on the covers. Now.

She inched down, kissing his hot, silky skin, loving the texture beneath her lips, welcoming the feel of him – the saltiness of his own unique flavour under her tongue, the muskiness of his scent as she kissed her way down from his navel. Here, he had the barest line of hair, a small strip that led directly to a very large and ready cock. She took it in her hand, wrapping her fingers around him. The heated steel of it felt good and a tiny part of her relaxed. She could do this. She wasn't a complete freak. *Lego, railway tracks, taxes.* That's all she had to remember.

She bent forwards and put her trembling lips to the head, let the tip of her tongue brush lightly across the salty slit. *Lego, railway tracks, taxes.* Boring stuff. Inane stuff, stuff that didn't matter. Didn't matter at all.

Gabe let out a groan. It sounded like pleasure, but what did she know? He put his hand on her head, guiding her down. It *was* pleasure and he wanted more.

Oh. Fuck, no . . . Lego, railway tracks, taxes. Lego, railway tracks, taxes . . .

Gasping for air, her chest too tight – everything too tight. Ali reared back, unable to catch her breath. Everything too dark, too wavy, too much . . . everything . . . gone.

Chapter 21

When Gabe woke the following morning, he knew. She was gone. He could feel her absence as intensely as he felt her presence. He got up anyway, to go and check. To prove himself correct. One of the few times he wished to hell he was wrong. God, he was a fool. He should have seen it, known it.

He should have "looked".

Her bedroom was empty. Her suitcase gone.

Gabe strode to the window, leaning his hands against the side shutters as his head dropped forwards. *Fuck.* He allowed himself the curse because nothing else would do. After slamming one hand against the wood, he turned and went downstairs to interrogate Mrs Mac. It was as he suspected. Ali had left about six, booking an early flight online and taking the tram to the airport. She'd told the Macs that something had come up at home and he wasn't to be disturbed.

Disturbed. What an odd, completely inadequate word for what he felt now. Nothing to what he'd felt last night when she'd pretty much blacked out rather than go down on him. It wasn't an experience he'd ever had and certainly not one he wanted to repeat. He'd reared up from his prone position and gathered her in his arms. He'd had no idea what was wrong, but one thing was immediately sure, their sexplorations for the night were over.

He'd instinctively carried her to her own room and laid her carefully on the bed, offering water to her parched lips.

"No," she'd moaned, an agony of pain in her raspy voice. "Don't make me, please, no . . . I can't, it *hurts*."

That last one, *it hurts*, had Gabe's stomach roll as the awful possibilities flooded his brain one after the other. She'd been forced, at some stage. Forced to do something she clearly didn't want to do. Why the hell hadn't she told him? Why hadn't she just said no, I don't like that? He wasn't a monster. Surely she knew that wasn't an issue? *Surely?* Obviously not. What kind of man did she think him?

Gabe shook his head in disgust. Not at her but at himself for thinking this was about him. *It clearly wasn't.* The horrors of what might have happened to her played like a movie on slow via his way-too-functional imagination. He prayed it was recent – some bastard when she was in her twenties who needed an ego boost – but the other part of him, the part that knew things, totally disagreed. And that was a living nightmare.

Working on the Neary case had made him extra sensitive to what those young women had gone through as mere children and early teenagers. Their accounts were heartbreaking and Gabe shuddered to imagine anything like that happening to Ali.

When? How? What? Too many questions. Too many scenarios. Gabe needed to get to Dublin, confront her and find out what the hell happened. Not for his own sake but maybe, just maybe he could help. He'd stayed with her last night till she'd fully awoken, drank some more water, used the bathroom, though unsteadily, and crawled back into bed. They didn't talk about what happened – he'd sat next to her curled-up figure, stroking her back, talking quiet nonsense till he'd felt her breathing return to normal. Only then did he leave the room to go and put on some clothes. He'd gone down to his office, opened his drinks cabinet and pulled out a bottle of aged brandy.

Just because he rarely drank didn't mean he didn't know the good stuff, or not have a selection to offer guests. It didn't mean he didn't know its value and if ever an occasion or occurrence called for seriously strong alcohol, this was it. He poured a steep measure into the balloon goblet and downed it in one. He refilled but sipped it this time as he lowered himself into his leather chair and let his mind wander.

It wasn't the normal kind of wandering. This was the nasty, "violating a person's privacy" kind. He would "look". It was time to renege on his promise to her and open his mind to the potentially shocking prospects that lay within. It worked better when the person in question was there, but he could feel her – she was still here in her very essence – and that would have to do for now. When he saw her in Dublin, and he *would* "see" her, he'd look deeper.

And she need never know.

Ali took the bus to town from the airport, then the DART out to Dún Laoghaire. She climbed the steps to her hall door without even remembering getting there. *Autopilot was a good term*, she decided. If she could just go through life like that, all would be well. *No feelings, no mess, no shitstorm. No "unbe-fucking-lievably immense beyond belief" embarrassment.* No fainting while attempting oral sex. *Definitely not that.* She was *never* doing that again. If she couldn't manage a little sucking on a man she had the serious hots for, let alone some scarily deep feelings, what in the hell hope did she have?

Eh, that would be none.

She pushed open her bedroom door, face-planted on her bed and for the first time in years, she let proper, full-on tears fall. Out of nowhere, a huge lump in her throat had been building, ever since since hugging Mrs Mac goodbye. She'd appeared in the hall in a dressing gown, concern clear on her lined face. All the time on the plane when she'd sat with her teeth gritted and her jaw clenched. *All the way home.* Now, on her own bed, her own pillow tucked beneath her, the floodgates opened. She cried for the mess, for the pain, for the hurt. She cried for her past, for her present and for her future.

Ali realised, as she hauled another box of tissues to her bedside table, that she was crying for all the loss, all the potential of normality, all the natural order of things she should have experienced. She sobbed deeply for her parents and her own lack of faith in them. She cried for the young girl she'd been. *The innocent, violated beyond repair.* And then she cried for herself and the fucking misery her life was now.

Gabe, the one man she thought maybe, *just maybe,* could be in her life, was now so totally out of it, she felt her heart burst with sadness and she cried some more. It wasn't pretty. Loud, harsh, chest-racking sobs tore from her thin frame, wrecking her, exhausting her. She finally fell asleep, too drained even to kick off her shoes as she hauled a duvet up and over in a vain attempt at comfort.

God, her head hurt like a motherfucker.

She turned slightly but the hammering continued. Gingerly, she peeled open her eyes. *Shit. Bad decision.* They were trying their best to remain glued shut. *God love those poor orbs – they hadn't seen such action in forever.* A deep, shuddering sigh escaped and she swallowed. Not an easy task with a swollen throat and aching chest. *That term, feeling like you've been run over by a bus? Totally apt.*

I need drugs, Ali thought and crawled to a seated position. The room spun and the banging in her head took on a thumping, thudding quality. *Lots of drugs.*

Realisation dawned. *Ah, fuck,* someone was banging on the door. Her life had turned into a cliché.

"Knock it off," she growled. "I'm coming."

She hauled herself up from the bed, stumbled into the hall and yanked open the door. She really should have looked through the spyhole first.

"No," she said. "Just no."

She went to slam the door, but Gabe's foot stopped it and he simply looked at her, his face set in grim determination.

"Yes," he said. "We need to talk."

"We absolutely do not. There's nothing to say." Even to her own ears she sounded weary. Worn.

"Let me in, Ali. We *will* have this one conversation and then if you really want me to leave you alone, as I am assuming that is what this morning's behaviour was about, I will. Or at least I will try."

He added the last bit in a quieter tone and damn, if that didn't tug at her.

"Suit yourself," she said in as cool a tone as she could muster.

She walked into her kitchen to put on the kettle, letting him follow or not.

She heard the door close quietly behind her and set out two mugs, one tea bag with some smelly herby thing she'd deny till death that she'd bought just for him, and one with proper, normal-people tea. His large frame entered the kitchen and overwhelmed the space as he propped a shoulder on the door frame. He raised his eyebrow at the box of herbal tea and sensibly said nothing. She poured boiling water over both and got some milk for herself.

"So, talk," she said ungraciously.

He took his tea and headed back to the living room.

"We should sit for this," he said over his shoulder as she slouched in behind him and curled up in the large armchair, toeing off her shoes and tucking a rug about her knees.

He sat opposite on the small couch, his size dwarfing it, and sipped his tea. The silence lengthened but she'd be damned if she broke it first. He wasn't invited here.

He put his tea aside and leaned forwards, elbows on his knees. "I am so sorry," he said, his gaze intense. "So deeply sorry that I put you through that."

Wait. What? What had he to be sorry about? He'd done nothing but be kind. Supportive. Caring. This wasn't what she was expecting.

"Explain," she said, confused.

He cleared his throat and ran a hand over his face. "You never, ever have to do anything you don't want to with me," he began.

Ali could feel her cheeks heat in total mortification. "I . . . " she started but didn't know how to continue.

He wasn't finished, it seemed.

"Sex with you is, for me, and I thought for you,

296

something . . . something different. Something more. I felt the shock of you the moment our eyes met in that restaurant before Christmas. For your celebratory drinks," he clarified in case she'd forgotten.

She hadn't. She remembered every single encounter with this man. *Every. Single. One.*

She ducked her head. Warmth – unwanted but with him, it seemed, inevitable – spread through her at his words.

"Hey," he said, waiting till her eyes met his. "I mean it. You . . . Ali, you are special to me."

Ah, shit.

"I should never have made you feel you had to engage in sex acts that were distasteful to you," he said.

So, he wasn't letting that *elephant in the room go.*

"You didn't, I wanted to," she half-lied.

"Obviously that is not true, or things would not have developed the way they did."

He was like a fucking dog with a bone.

"Leave it," she mumbled, all the holes being dug in her imagination not remotely big enough for her and her mortification to fit.

"Not leaving it. Not till I know what the hell happened to you in the past to bring on such a . . . such a strong reaction."

"My dramatic blacking out, you mean? Let's call a spade a spade, shall we. I'm just weird, okay? I don't like oral sex, *okay?*"

He looked at her in his way. "That is not true. You are *not* weird. Well, not in the way you mean."

"Thanks," she said, loaded in sarcasm.

"And you liked it just fine when I tasted you. So, it is

297

not that you are . . . conservative in your tastes. You were . . . terrified."

"No—" Her protest was cut off with a single hand held up in that universal stop motion.

"Don't," he said firmly. "Don't lie to me. We have come too far for lies now. If it is me and doing that to me is what scares you, doing something you *don't* want, that is fine. You never have to do it again."

"Yeah, right. That's what they all say."

"They all?"

Ali squirmed in her chair. How could she not? This was a horrible conversation. This is where she said, "Don't let the door hit you on the way out," because he obviously hadn't got it yet.

"You're all the same," she grumbled. "You all say it doesn't matter, but it *does*! What kind of guy doesn't want their cock sucked? I mean, seriously?"

"A man who listens to the woman he cares about and understands it is *not* what she wants. That kind."

"Ha. You say that now, but in time, you'll change your mind. You'll want someone else. I tried it before and it doesn't fly."

"Do *not* insult me," he snapped. "You haven't tried it with me. I have told you I am fine with it. You are choosing not to believe me."

"Don't put this on me!"

"It *is* on you. You are choosing not to trust me and damn it, that hurts." Gabe rose and paced, his hand running through his hair. "Do you think I would force you? That I wouldn't listen to you saying no?"

He *must* have seen her face pale, because she could feel the colour draining from her skin as all the nos she'd uttered, cried and whispered over those years flooded her ears.

But still he continued.

"I *know* you are holding back. I know it because I heard you. Yes," he said as her head snapped back to his, a gasp in her throat. "I heard you beg to be left alone." He dropped to a crouch before her and pulled her clenched fists into his large, warm hands. "I heard you," he repeated. "I don't care if my cock never feels your mouth. Ever. But I do care that you are carrying hurt and pain and anger and you won't let me in. I care about that.

"I am not some green boy you can sleep with and toss aside when things get difficult. I am an adult who knows what he will and won't accept. I know what I can live with. And without. Trust *me*."

Ali looked at him. Saw those beautiful eyes, now filled with concern, with what looked like tenderness. If she told him . . . If she let him in? He'd never look at her the same way again. Never. He thought he was a mature adult, and he was exactly that, but nothing would or could change that bald fact that she was a complete fucking mess and not worthy of anyone's care. That was it, really. *In a nutshell.*

She was *not* worthy. Of anyone.

Christ, that truth sucked.

Ali inhaled, her breath catching in her throat. Could she tell him? Maybe that's what it would take for him to leave. It would be easier if he left. Much easier than trying to keep going. And failing spectacularly. Because even if he could live without specific intimacies – and she didn't really believe he'd want to – surely he wouldn't be able to live with her fallout. Her nightmares, her anxieties, her control issues. *She* could barely live with them, so there was no way she'd ever expect anyone else to. The horrible, unhappy reality was that Gabe was the first man ever to make her want to.

She inhaled again. Deeply. "I'm damaged," she whispered, unable to look him in the eye. "I'm broken into pieces, inside."

Her eyes remained downcast as she spoke, but he was having none of it. He placed a finger beneath her chin and raised it so she'd look at him.

"Not. True," he said. "You are strong and real. And we are all damaged in some way."

"Not this way," she barely whispered. "I'll never be fixed."

"You don't need fixing. You are in fine working order. But you do need help. If not mine," he added, talking over her instant protest, "then somebody else's. But let me be clear. I *am* here for you. Now. Tomorrow. The next day. And all the days."

Ali's eyes betrayed her, *the bastards*, and filled with tears. She wanted to believe him. She really did. A tear slid down her cheek. She wiped at it and clutched at his wrist, holding on as she let go.

"Of all the guys," she admitted, "you are the one who got *this* close." She pinched her thumb and forefinger together with only the barest of gaps. "Only you. But it's not enough. For me. Or you." She pulled away, let her hand drop as she wiped another tear.

"Why? Why can you not let me in? I want you, Ali. Like no other woman. And I want to help you. To be with you. The only reason that is not happening is because *you* are saying no. You. Not me." He rose from his crouch and sighed. "I will not *make* you tell me your story, share your pain. But I beg you to tell someone. It will not go away by itself."

"I've had therapy. I have told someone. I'm not stupid," she grumbled at his back as she followed him to the door.

He pulled it open and turned to face her. His hands cupped her face and his tired, worried eyes seemed to see right through her.

"It is not the same," he said and kissed her hard and fast on the mouth. "Tell someone who loves you."

And he was gone.

Caro hung up her phone, a worried frown in place. *That was weird.* Gabe Mackenzie had called and said Ali needed her. *What was that about?* If Ali wanted her for something, all she had to do was ask.

Caro was in town for another two days and had most of her wedding preparations well in hand. *Poor Nick*, she thought, feeling for her fiancé. She sure hoped he knew what being a member of the Fitzgeralds was going to be like. Well, that was silly. He couldn't *know*, not yet. But he would – and it couldn't come soon enough for Caro. And, she hoped, her son, Toby.

She put her car in gear and drove from the florist in Dalkey to her previous home in Dún Laoghaire where Ali now lived. She missed the flat, but not more than she wanted her new life with Nick and Toby in Rome. There was nothing she wanted more than that. And it was almost real. Almost hers.

She knocked on the door even as she used her old key, because, hey, sisters can do that.

"Ali? It's me. Just checking . . . " She paused, struck dumb by the sight of her younger sister curled up in the big armchair. "What the . . . ?"

Ali looked awful. Truly terrible. White as a ghost, huge dark circles under red-rimmed eyes. Her hair, always a bit squiffy, was a disaster. But it was the look of total grief that had Caro hurrying to her side and squatting next to her.

"What happened? Are you okay?"

Her sister glared at Caro through liquid eyes.

Okay? Duh! She was patently not okay.

"Are you in pain? Are you sick?"

Ali swallowed the lump in her throat. "No, no. Well, yes, kinda."

"Perfect sense, as usual. Wait here." Caro hauled herself up and rummaged in the kitchen cupboard for the brandy. She poured one large and one for herself – a finger's worth to keep her sister company. Drinking alone, even medicinally, was never good.

"Take this." She placed the glass in Ali's hand and sat back on the floor next to the chair. "Now, what's up?"

"Why are you here?" Ali countered.

"Gabe phoned me. He said you needed family. What did he do? Did he hurt you? Is that it?"

Caro was indignant. *What a cheek to call to have the sister clean up his mess! And here Caro was thinking he was a keeper.* Ali's lips trembled. *Oh, God. That isn't good.* She looked like she'd had a serious crying fest already and Ali never cried.

"He phoned you?" Ali asked, her voice quivering. "He shouldn't have – I'm fine."

Clearly not true, but Caro let it go.

"Tell me. What's up? What happened?"

Ali took a deep slug of the brandy, choked and took another.

"That bad, huh?" Caro rubbed the leg tucked under an old rug. "Come on, spill. I've nowhere to be till dinner with the parents tonight. Are you coming to that?"

"I'll see how I feel," Ali managed.

She closed her eyes and Caro watched, concern growing by the second.

"Gabe thinks I need help. That I need to tell someone something. But I don't want to. It *won't* help."

Yeah, that made no sense. Caro sipped her drink and reached out to hold Ali's hand.

"Did he say that because he cares or because he didn't want to deal with whatever the problem is?" Caro was nothing if not good at getting down to basics.

"He cares. I think. He wanted me to tell him. But I can't. He said tell someone who loves me. I don't think he was including himself in that. I think he meant you or Flynn or one of the others. Do you think Gabe meant himself, too?"

Dear God, the desperation in Ali's voice was tangible. *She must love Gabe a hell of a lot to feel this shitty about whatever was going on.*

"Are you in love with him?" Caro asked gently.

"No! No, no, I'm not. I can't be. Maybe a little. Maybe, yes." She blinked as tears slid down her face, bare tracks as all her mascara was now washed away.

"Oh, honey," Caro said, resting her face on Ali's knees. "I'm sorry you're hurting, but I think you'd better tell me what the hell is going on with you. It can't be as bad as you think. No one is going to judge you. I'm not.

303

And I'm right here." She gave Ali another squeeze. "It'll be okay."

Caro settled back down, leaning against the base of the chair, one arm raised and resting on Ali's covered legs. *I mean, how bad can it be?* Caro wondered.

One more drink of brandy and Caro discovered just how bad. Ali's words changed Caro's world of trust forever.

"When I was ten years old, Father Jack Neary sexually abused me. And it continued until I was thirteen. And I never told anyone." Her stricken face met Caro's horrified stare. "I'm damaged goods, Caro. No one will ever want me. No one."

Chapter 22

Ali stood in the mudroom, her mind a complete maelstrom. All she could think about was the kiss she and Gabe had shared here not that many days ago. And she was about to walk into her family's dining room and blow their lives apart. *Priorities, Ali, priorities.* She didn't know who'd be home, who she'd be facing, but she figured since the decision was made, there was no going back.

She thought back to her phone session with Dr Hearne and her comment on consequences. What did Ali want? What did she want to happen and if she followed through, who was really going to pay the price? *And what was the fucking price?* Hadn't she already paid it? In full?

So much responsibility. She was about to change everyone's life – in that room, because *he* had changed hers. Was it her right to do this? To upset her loved ones just because she'd been harmed? *Shit!* Her parents would be devastated. She knew that. *Yet, still.* Was she going to do this?

A light tap on the door from the kitchen side and Caro popped her head round. She was still in shock. Still bowled over by Ali's tale. And while the shaking and the rage had subsided, it was definitely simmering beneath the surface. Big-sister protectiveness was in full-on mode.

"You all right?" Caro asked carefully. "If you're not ready . . . You don't have to do this just because Gabe thinks you need to. He's not the boss of you."

Ali smiled. Albeit a wan one. "I know he's not and I do. Have to. It's time. I spoke to my therapist yesterday. Christ! yesterday – it feels like two lifetimes ago. Anyway, she said if I'm going to talk about it, I need to be aware of the possible repercussions. Not just for me or you or the family. But for my abuser. Plus, because he's a minor celebrity of sorts, the press could eat this up. We *all* have to be prepared. *I* have to be prepared. God, I feel sick."

She bent, dropped her head into her hands, elbows propping on her knees to breathe in air. *Perhaps now would be a good time for a paper bag and some swift gulps.* Maybe they only do that in the movies, but shit, she felt light-headed.

"We'll eat first, though I can't imagine putting a morsel in my mouth," Ali told Caro as she stood, and they made their way to the dining room. "I don't want the food to go to waste and Mum can freak out on a full stomach rather than an empty one. Dad, too." *Oh, God, what am I doing?*

"Hey, everyone," Caro called in only a slightly strangled voice, but the others were too busy filling plates to notice.

Jo had made two large dishes of shepherd's pie. Wielding the large serving spoon when they walked in, she explained that just because it was the end of May didn't mean summer was actually here and based on last week's run of chilly days, she thought they could all do with a nice warm dinner. Nobody argued. *Why would they?* A hot cooked meal was always welcome.

They all sat, and the usual racket of back-and-forth discussions went on around Ali, over her head and under her radar. She barely touched her food. Her stomach was already gearing up for what was to come and the acid churning away inside felt like it was doing serious erosion.

Caro reached for her hand under the table and squeezed. "Eat," she whispered, "just a little to settle you. Please."

"So, how was Edinburgh?" Flynn asked, eyeing her somewhat suspiciously over his water glass.

He must be going in to work after or he'd be sipping wine.

"Good. It was good. It's . . . good." *Ah, yes, Ali, the bright, intelligent human being that she was, bamboozling them with her wit and charm.*

"Good? That's it?" Flynn was sceptical. *Obviously.* "Mackenzie show you the sights?"

Was that a double entendre? She couldn't tell. Her mind was . . . elsewhere.

She glanced up from pushing her food around her plate to find several sets of eyes on her. *Shit. Speech was needed. Conversation.*

"He has a lovely home. Very grand. More so than you'd think by him and his weird ways. He has staff . . ." There were choked sounds at this, from both Flynn and Dev. "And his grandmother would have given Granny Flynn a run for her money. In fact, she'd have left Granny Flynn for dust."

Now *that* titbit caused quite the consternation. Granny Flynn had been known for her "attitude" – about *everything*. And they'd loved her for it.

"That I'd like to have seen," mumbled Patrick, stealing a cheeky peek at his wife, who rolled her eyes.

"Leave my sainted mother out of it," she said, and everyone laughed.

That was really stretching it. Whatever Granny Flynn had been, saintly was not among them.

Ali watched as her family ate. Her mum and dad still bickering and teasing in that way of long-married couples. Molly eating methodically in that serious way of hers, always thoughtful and careful. Frankie and Dev, in that obnoxious phase of loved-up honeymooners with all the touching and kissing – *yuck*. If it was anyone else it would have been gross, but they, *the jerks*, managed to get away with it.

Ali was glad Caro's Nick wasn't here – that would have pushed the lovefest off the scale. Toby was the real delight. Just turned fourteen and smart as a whip, he added so much to all the conversations. He had wisdom beyond his years – probably from so much drama in his life, over the last year in particular. Yet, he still looked out for his mama. Caro was so lucky. Not that she'd had it easy – she hadn't – but to be raising a son like Toby? Ali felt envy down to her marrow, as it was never to be in her own future.

And, damn, she'd forgotten about Toby in this mess that was about to go down. He couldn't hear this. Sure, he'd understand, but no way was she letting him have even more worries on his young shoulders.

She leaned over to Caro and spoke softly. "Toby. What are we going to do with Toby? I don't want him to know. Not yet, and not details."

Caro's mouth tightened to a flat line. "You're right. Give me a minute."

She excused herself from the table and a few minutes later returned with her phone still in her hand.

"Hey, kid, do you want to pop over to Gavin's after

dinner? To say goodbye till you see him at the wedding? His mum texted me to ask you and I forgot till now."

It was a gamble. Toby was unusually family-oriented and because he and Caro were mostly living in Rome, he treasured this family time.

"It can only be for an hour, as you've to get an early night."

Somehow, the limit was the deal-sealer. He'd be back before the others left, so all was well. Caro knew her boy.

"Cool," Toby said, folding his napkin and rising from the table. "Do you mind if I go now?" He was asking the whole table, not just his mum.

"Go for it," Dev said. "Tell Gavin not to hog the PlayStation. I remember what he used to be like."

"Have fun, kid," Flynn chipped in while Jo quickly wrapped two pieces of cake to take with him.

"One hour," Caro called as Toby shut the door behind him.

"Let's have dessert and coffee in the drawing room," Ali suggested. She might have to down a quick digestif to steady her nerves. "I've got something I need to tell you all and I'd prefer to talk in there."

Amid a bit of grumbling as people helped themselves to dessert and Molly ran out to the kitchen to put the kettle on for coffee, Ali did a bit of slow breathing. Her therapist had been adamant that, along with the self-defence classes, Ali also take yoga. Right now, she could kiss Dr Hearne and her forward-thinking.

It was showtime.

Ali sat on the arm of the big chair, as it was always called, the one facing into the room, and effectively blocked anyone else from grabbing it. She wanted to be able to see them. She needed that. The others scattered about, her parents taking two opposite armchairs, Molly one end of the couch with Frankie and Dev settled in at the other end. Flynn stood by the window, casually leaning back, arms crossed, eyes focused on her. *Did he know?* No, he couldn't, but he knew something serious was about to occur, his senses on high alert. *No wonder he and Gabe worked well together. Maybe they could start a TV duo: the Super Senses, here to save the day.*

Okay. Enough wool-gathering.

"This is hard to say and it's going to be hard for you all to hear. I know that but, on professional advice and my own judgement, I'm going to do it anyway. I want to apologise, even before I start, but I know I'm not supposed to do that. Because I'm not at fault." She looked about the room, gauging the expressions, and saw only interest and gathering concern.

"I know what I'm about to tell you will shock you, hurt some of you – especially you, Mum and Dad – and it will also have fallout, beyond this room, if I choose to follow through. But that's for later."

She hadn't realised Flynn had moved till she felt his hand on her shoulder, his rock-solid presence at her side as he spoke.

"Whatever it is, we're here for you. Just say it, Alison Jane, it'll be easier that way."

She reached up and held on to his hand, grateful beyond belief for his unconditional support.

Ali Fitzgerald told her family the truth. The nasty, horrible, awful truth. A truth she'd carried so long inside, as a protection against hurt for them. For her. Those days were now over.

When she stopped speaking, her voice getting threadier by the second, there was complete silence. She looked up, only then understanding that she hadn't in fact been able to look them in the eyes as she'd talked it out. It was odd – strangely like she'd been recounting a book or a film. That it wasn't her. A coping mechanism, she knew, and was glad of it.

Voices erupted as one.

"I'll kill him!" (Her father.)

"That bastard, I'll cut his balls off!" (Dev, always dramatic.)

"Oh, my poor baby!" (Her mother, with tears streaming down her face.)

"Why didn't you say something?" (Molly, in sheer bewilderment.)

"That's . . . that's just awful!" (Frankie, also in tears.)

Flynn squeezed her shoulder even as her parents rushed to hold and hug her.

"You should have told us, darling. We'd have stopped it immediately. Why didn't you tell us?"

The last bit was almost a wail and was the question Ali knew would be the toughest to answer. Thankfully, Ali didn't feel like crying – she felt like an onlooker and was happy enough with that status as she fielded more questions and hugs. And felt relief, dear God, the *relief* that no one doubted her.

It was Flynn, naturally, who asked the most important question – because, *yeah*, she hadn't told the whole truth. She hadn't named him. It was just "a man" and "he", but the jig was now up.

"*Who*, Ali, who did this to you? I can have him called in for questioning before this night is through! Who is it?"

"I didn't tell you his name while I told my story . . . " Ali looked about at her loving family. "Because you all know him. You like him. He was, *is*, your friend." She nodded her head in her parents' direction.

Their faces paled. They were seated again, hands clasped in each other's, offering mutual support. Ali supposed it was shocking enough that she'd been so abused, but to have it done by a trusted friend? This was going to slay them.

"Father Jack," she said. "Jack Neary abused me on a regular basis from the age of ten to thirteen. It only ended because he was sent to a different parish."

"*What?*" Her father reared from his seat. "Jack did *this*? *Jack* . . . hurt you and took advantage of you?" Her father's voice shook with rage. "Where is he? I want to put my hands round his neck and *kill* him!" He swung his head about the room as if looking for a weapon.

Shit, his colour wasn't good – he looked like he was about to explode.

"It's okay, Daddy." Ali moved to put her hand on his shoulder, to calm him.

"Okay? Are you out of your mind?" He was shouting now, incandescent. "It's so far from okay that if he were in this room right now, I'd kill him with my bare hands!"

"Dad," Dev said, for once the voice of reason. "You having a heart attack is not going to help Ali or get the bastard to pay. And he will pay, won't he, Ali?"

Ali wasn't sure now. She hadn't really thought through what she'd do with their reactions.

"Oh my God," Frankie murmured. "That's why you collapsed the other day, isn't it? Because I suggested him for Caro's wedding. Oh, God, I'm *so* sorry." Frankie took her in a hug and held her tight. "This is all my fault."

Jo held trembling hands to her mouth. "Oh, sweetheart, we failed you so badly, can you ever forgive us? What kind of a mother am I that I didn't see? That I didn't know. Darling, I'm so sorry." And she burst into tears.

See? This was one of the reasons Ali kept it to herself – everyone wanted to blame themselves. Everyone wanted to be the one to fix it, too. Neither of those scenarios could happen. No one was to blame but Jack and no one could fix it except Ali. The hard, inescapable truth was that in some weird and completely unfair way, Ali *had* blamed her parents. It was also true that she never wanted them to know that, so she'd deny it until her dying day.

"I *never* liked him," Molly said with such vehemence that several heads swung towards her. "I never trusted him for a second but didn't think I could say anything since everyone else seemed to think he was great."

"What? Why?"

Ali felt that like a punch. The sister she'd been protecting had been more aware than she? *Fuck that.*

"He had a vibe I didn't trust," Molly continued. "He'd look at me sometimes and I'd get a shiver. Goose bumps along the back of my neck. I knew even then to pay attention to my . . . *feels.*" She ducked her head, hating, as usual, to bring up her uncommon ability to be aware of certain things. "He asked me to go on a car trip with him – I must have been about nine . . . " She paused and stared right at Ali. "Almost the age he started on

313

you. I just said no and if he made me, I'd go and tell my parents he showed me his penis."

There was total shock in the room and then, strangely, a snort. Ali couldn't help it. Maybe it was the heightened tension in the air, but laughter, although theoretically inappropriate, sneaked out.

"And did he, you know, show you his penis?" Dev asked, his mouth doing its best not to break into a grin, despite the serious tension in the room.

"God, no! Yuck! The very thought. Oh, Jesus, sorry, Ali. I didn't—"

"Stop. Stop apologising. I'm so relieved you had more cop-on than me at that age. Good for you." She crossed to Molly and gave her a hug.

Once again it was Flynn, who'd remained gravely silent, who took matters in hand.

"What's next, Ali? You know he's in the country. What do you want to do? Do you want to accuse him? Confront him? I can help with both of those things."

Ali sighed. *This was it.* The moment of decision was upon her. *What to do? How to proceed, repercussions and all?*

"I'm not sure, to be honest. If I leave it with just telling you and I accidentally run into him in town, I genuinely don't know what I'd do. But I can't hide from the fact that he's back, local again. Frankie saw him by chance and the bastard asked after me. That's bold – daring, even. It says to me that he believes I'll never tell.

"He made me promise never to say anything and there were lots of believable scenarios he ran by me to convince me. To ten-year-old me, anyway. But I'm not a kid any more and I'm not afraid of him."

She sank down into the cushions, suddenly desperately weary. "What do you all think I should do? He was your college pal, Dad, that's a friendship of long-standing. He's been on TV, he's been in the papers, all with good causes, and he has a hell of a fan club. If I accuse him, does it have to be public?" This last question she directed at Flynn, who was tapping away on his phone.

"Not at first, it doesn't. But it would become a matter of public record."

Her father stood, walked to her and hauled her up from the chair into his strong arms. "You have to do what's right for you, my girl, and we'll support you all the way. But know this, regardless of what you decide, he and I *will* be having a conversation. Tomorrow."

"I'd like to be in on that chat, Dad," Dev said quietly.

"And me," Caro said.

"Me, too." Molly was definite in her delivery.

"You're not confronting that piece of filth without me, Patrick," Jo insisted as she joined in, hugging Ali. She ran a hand gently over her daughter's head. "I want to see his face when we tell him we know what he's done." She buried her face in Ali's neck, overcome once more.

Ali's heart was breaking for these fine people. Second-guessing herself over and over. Why did she not tell? Why did she believe Jack when he convinced her they'd never believe a child over a trusted adult friend? She had to believe none of that mattered now. But she knew, from her parent's worried frowns, that they'd be a long time forgiving themselves. Another chip at Ali's own hurt, her own pain. More burdens for her mum and dad and all her fault. This time she was choosing to cause them distress at the expense of her own continued denial.

Something had to give and maybe it just had.

"What would you like to do?" Flynn brought them back to the issue at hand. He'd put away his phone, but something about his demeanour bothered her.

Molly was quicker on the uptake. She jumped right in. "What are you *not* telling us, Flynn?"

Flynn rubbed a hand over his jaw as if considering something, maybe taking a moment to decide what he should and shouldn't say. He paced a bit and then turned and spoke directly to Ali, though for everyone to hear.

"Jack Neary was brought in for questioning a couple of weeks ago. He's suspected of child molestation in Wexford." He continued to speak over the gasps of shock. "Two women, a bit younger than you, have come forward with accusations and he's been in and out of the station, anonymously, for several sets of questioning."

"And?" Ali wanted to know, her heart kicking up a beat. "Did he admit it?"

"He denies everything. The women were eleven and twelve when the alleged abuse occurred and because they have no actual dates to confirm the accusations, he's going to be able to alibi himself if they pluck one from the calendar. He can just say if they can't remember a date or time that they must be manufacturing it, then he doesn't have to account for anything. Or he can fabricate an appointment in his diary.

"He has lawyered-up." Flynn mentioned a well-known senior counsel. "And, unfortunately, without corroborating evidence, he walks. His word against two women with no proof. And just so you are aware, I am telling you this in the strictest confidence – this information cannot leave this room."

There were murmurs of agreement as this new knowledge hit Ali.

"The bastard continued his reign of terror in Wexford! God, I should have said something. I should have told. It's my fault those girls were hurt."

Ali felt crushed. Devastated. She'd never thought he'd be doing it to others. She'd naïvely assumed it was because he had access to their house as a family friend. This new information rocked her mind. *Fuck. What if there were others, too? Before her. Was he a serial abuser?*

Mostly, she thought as she sat back in the chair, her hands covering her mouth to stop the howls from trying to escape, *she felt vindicated*. If there was more than just her, they *had* to be believed. *Right?* Reality struck again that she may have inadvertently caused those girls, and maybe others, to be harmed, too. Her belly hurt and as the feeling of nausea rose and threatened. She raced from the room, down the hall to the downstairs toilet, making it to the bowl with mere seconds to spare.

Chapter 23

Flynn Fitzgerald paced his office, head down, hands shoved into his pockets. He was in a predicament and was, unusually for him, unsure how to handle it. He paused and stared unseeing out of his window into the dark night sky. It was after 11 p.m. and the rest of the station was, at the moment, relatively quiet.

Christ! His sister had been through some dreadful stuff and he hadn't had a clue. He knew everyone in the family was feeling it, feeling the blame and the anger and the sheer bloody frustration that she'd said . . . *nothing*. *Why?* He was trying to understand but so far, he simply couldn't get his head around it, her conviction that their parents wouldn't have believed her. He was seven years older than Ali and had already left for college when it began, but that was no damn excuse. He'd been home for holidays and spent time with her as a family. He was supposed to be the one with intuition and he'd been as blind as the rest of them.

He'd stepped back from the Neary case because of the family connection and now he was kicking his own ass. Not that Gabe hadn't done a stellar job – *he had, of course* – but it was ongoing. And that brought him back to the problem at hand.

Gabe. Did he know?

Flynn got the feeling that Caro had been the only one

previously told, other than the therapist, and now he was going to have to tell Gabe as it was case-related. Or it might be, depending on what Ali decided. Flynn couldn't blame her for not wanting to have her dirty linen brought out into the public domain and with her own recent fame as the TV *chef du jour*, social media would be on it like a limpet.

Damn. He really didn't want his sister dragged through the mud but . . . *That bastard needed to pay.* And if she was to testify, those other two women could get justice, too. *And what if there were more?* Once Ali went public, they could, in theory, come out of the woodwork. If there *were* more.

Flynn banged his head several times against the window, frustration in every thud.

"You need to see me?"

Flynn turned at the sound of Gabe's voice, not really surprised that Gabe had just appeared in his office. It was what Gabe did. He was where he was wanted, when he was needed. It was uncanny. *Or peculiar.* Flynn hadn't decided.

"Sit down," Flynn said and moved to take his own chair as Gabe sat on the opposite one.

"Is she okay?" Gabe asked quietly.

Flynn shook his head. "Why am I not surprised that you'd ask that?" He reached for a bottle of water and took a long drink, wishing he was inhaling something a lot stronger. "What do you know?"

"Nothing. Officially."

"And unofficially?"

Gabe shifted in his chair, leaning forwards to rest his elbows on his knees. Then he sighed and spoke in a quiet tone.

"I know she was hurt. Badly. Over a period of time.

When she was a child." He swallowed and cleared his throat.

"Did she tell you?"

"No. Not in so many words. I . . . I put some things together and figured it out. I don't know who, but I've gathered the what. It's not pretty, Flynn – she went through hell."

Flynn squashed the plastic bottle into a ball and fired it across the room. "Well, I know who and I'll give you a guess. Think about what you've been working on these last few weeks . . . "

Gabe rose from his seat, the chair falling back with the suddenness of the movement. "Neary? The ex-priest? Your family *friend*?" He was incredulous. "What the hell, Fitz? How could you let that happen? How could you not have known? Not have seen something? For God's sake!" He slammed his fist on the table. "You're supposed to be the fucking best!"

Flynn winced at the justifiable anger pouring from his friend. *Gabe swearing*. That alone was indicative of the very fine hold he had on his temper.

"You aren't saying anything I haven't been telling myself since she told us at dinner this evening." Flynn sat forwards, his shoulders slumped. "I failed her. And I'll never forgive myself for that. I should have sensed something. Should have picked up on it. But I didn't. And *that's* on me."

Gabe drew in a breath. "I shouldn't have snapped. I apologise. I . . . I can only say it came from a place of . . . caring . . . for your sister."

Flynn's aqua gaze snapped on Gabe's steady eyes. Studied him. Awareness dawned.

"Oh, shit. You've done it, haven't you? You've bloody

fallen for her. Aw, fuck, Mac, I told you to keep your distance."

Gabe's cheeks reddened and Flynn could only gape in surprise. The big, quiet man was uncomfortable. Or something. *Huh.*

"Well," he continued, "what have you to say for yourself?"

"Nothing. It's none of your business. She's a grown woman and perfectly capable of making her own decisions." Gabe sat back in his chair.

"I figured you two were 'getting it together' – I just hadn't realised there were feelings involved. I hoped it was just sex. Why couldn't you have left it at that?"

"I repeat, none of your business. But to be clear, I would never have slept with your sister if it was only . . . physical. That would have been monumentally stupid."

"And falling for her isn't?"

"How could that be stupid? She's a woman of so many parts, so talented, clever, funny . . . " He stopped when he saw Flynn's face, eyebrows raised. "What? How can you not agree? You know her."

"Oh, I agree," Flynn said on a sigh. "It's because I know her, or thought I did, that I think it's stupid. Does she love you back?"

Gabe swallowed. "We haven't discussed it in so many words. And even if she was starting to reciprocate my feelings, I can be sure, when she knows what I've done, that I'm screwed. The worst part is, she told you anyway. I needn't have delved deeper at all."

Flynn glared at him. "What exactly *have* you done?"

Silence from Gabe confirmed his suspicion. "Shit, Mac. You did your mind games on her, didn't you?"

"They are not games! God, far from it."

Gabe sighed so deep and heavy that Flynn took his colleague's discomfort on board.

"But you did, as you just said, delve deep into her mind. Isn't that crossing a line?"

"Do you think I don't know that? I've ruined any chance of keeping her trust. I know that. But I also know she *needed* to talk about it. And her needs come first."

"You pushed her to it."

Gabe tilted his head at that.

"Caro told us you strongly recommended that Ali come clean. Don't know how long she would have continued to keep it to herself. All that pain, *shit*, Gabe. Something obviously happened between you two to bring this about."

Gabe shifted in his chair, uncomfortable.

Flynn continued, "Whatever it was, we owe you our thanks. Crap as all this is for us as a family, we all, every one of us, want to be here for Ali. From now on, whatever she decides."

"Decides?"

Flynn stood and, going to his cabinet, pulled out a bottle of Jameson and two glasses. It was time for the hard stuff. He poured a finger into each.

"I know it's not Scottish single malt or whatever you drink, but you might need this before we finish." He handed the glass to Gabe. "*Sláinte*."

They drank and Flynn set his glass down as Gabe continued to hold his.

"Decides what?" Gabe repeated.

"To confront Jack Neary. To accuse him officially. To testify. Any, one or none of the three. It's up to her."

Gabe groaned, running a hand over his jaw. "Has she proof? Wait . . . " he said as Flynn threw him a furious glare. "I know, without a shadow of doubt, it is true. But that is *not* enough. I know the two other women are telling the truth. They didn't have it as bad as Ali, but even so, they deserve justice. But there is nothing to substantiate their word. Without proof, we have nothing. He goes free."

"Right, well, just in case, gather everything you have. Let's put our heads together and go over every piece. Maybe you missed something."

Flynn was obviously tired and frustrated, as in the normal way of things he wouldn't *ever* assume Gabe had missed a blessed thing. But this was Ali. And he needed to fix it. In some way. Somehow.

"You are off this case, remember?" Gabe said as he rose from his chair and tossed back the last of his drink.

"Not any more. I'm in. I'll clear it with the boss. Neary is going down, one way or the other."

By the time Ali got to the station about nine thirty the following morning, she'd made up her mind. It had taken hours. Hours of soul-searching. Hours of actual searching. But she'd found what she needed both mentally and practically and was, she thought, as prepared as she could be. From today, her life would change. Sure, in theory it was from yesterday, when she told her family. But from today, when she made an official complaint, an accusation, there was no going back. There would be those dreaded but, she understood, necessary repercussions.

So many decisions.

She knew that once Gabe found out what had happened her, he'd never touch her again. And once it all went public, as it would, for several reasons, no man would want her, and her craziness, in their lives. She hoped she was okay with that. The path that would be a life of singledom. No kids. Well, maybe she could go the sperm donor route, but that was down the line. No man would want to father kids with her – she was too screwed up in every way you could think.

She made her way to the main desk, where she approached the duty sergeant, or "member in charge", as they were known.

"Good morning, Garda O'Neill. I'd like to make a formal complaint about a person. How do I go about that?"

Ali knew she could have phoned Flynn and told him she was coming in, but she wanted to do absolutely everything above board – nothing left to chance, to the dreaded loophole. To a procedure not followed.

"Ali?" Agnes O'Neill looked confused. "Is it Flynn you want to see?"

"Not unless he's specifically the one who can help me. It's a delicate matter and I'm unsure how to proceed. I want it to be done exactly by the book, so there will be zero room for error or complaint." She took a deep breath and felt like she was at her first victim-survivors meeting. "I was sexually abused from the age of ten to thirteen and I want to place charges against the man who did it."

She watched as Agnes's lips tightened into a flat line. The desk sergeant took her pad and pen and wrote down the date and time, Ali's name and what she'd just conveyed.

"The alleged abuser's name?" Her tone was clipped. Professional.

And blessedly steady.

Ali felt a strange comfort in that. It was procedure. She was doing this.

"Jack Neary."

There was a second's hesitation as Agnes looked at Ali, her sergeant's mask slipping for an instant. Then Agnes gathered her composure with a deep breath.

"You'll want to see Detective Inspector Gabe Mackenzie, Ali. He's the one in charge of this. I'll phone him and see if he can see you now."

Karma's a bitch, Ali thought as she reeled with the knowledge that she was going to have to spill her guts anyway, every last one of them, *to Gabe himself*. He would know all the details. All the pain, the dirt, the shame.

She turned to leave, but Agnes stopped her, saying, "He's in his office. Go on up. Second floor on the left."

Too late. He'd know she'd left because of him.

"Isn't there anyone else I could talk to?" Ali asked.

The sergeant looked askance at her. "But he's the best, Ali. Other than your brother, who recused himself from this, Mackenzie is the hotshot of the station. You want the best, don't you?"

"Yeah. Yeah, I do. Thanks, Agnes, I'll go up."

Damn, damn, damn.

And wouldn't you know it . . . but Flynn was in the office, too. She couldn't catch a break if she went around with an open pot of fresh honey.

Ali paused on the threshold of Gabe's office, leaning against the door frame as she studied the two men glued

325

to a large pedestal whiteboard. They were both in shirtsleeves, jackets hanging on a coat stand in the corner. Gabe's sleeves were folded over neatly, revealing those hypnotic tanned forearms, and his shirt and trousers were as fresh and pressed as always. Now that Ali knew first-hand just how well put together Gabe was, underneath his clothes, it was almost impossible to unsee. Not that she wanted to. That would be a pointless exercise in non-existent Gabe restraint.

Flynn dragged a hand over the crewcut on the top of his head and swore.

"Come in, Ali," Gabe said, scribbling a note on the board before looking round and meeting her gaze.

"How did y . . . never mind, Mac Oddball, you just sensed me, I get it."

She walked into the room, glancing about at the piles of folders on the desk and at the board itself. Jack Neary's name was written in block capitals across the top for all to see. This was the hub of his case and Ali knew she'd better get used to it.

"I've come to make a statement," she said, her voice hollow. "Agnes told me you're in charge. Have you been on this case for weeks? Is this the one you couldn't share? That had you drained?"

She met his eyes unflinchingly. She needed to know if he had something they could use. Hopefully, they wouldn't even need her added testimony.

Flynn walked over and gave her a hug, ignoring the questions she'd flung at Gabe.

"You're the best. I'm so proud of you for coming in. Take a seat."

Gabe threw him a look that definitely said, *offer seats*

in my office, why don't you, but just nodded. Ali sat, glad of it as her legs had chosen to play "jelly substance" charades today. She clutched her bag on her lap and waited as the two men exchanged knowing looks. Knowing for them, that is, not her.

Flynn cleared his throat, collected his jacket from the rack and slid his arms in the sleeves.

"I'll leave you to it," he said to Gabe and turned back to Ali. "Kid, take it slow. Take breaths. Drink water . . . " He indicated the glass carafe on the desk. "Ask for clarification if you don't understand the question. Tell him everything you remember, no matter how small . . . "

Gabe made a sound and Flynn halted in mid flow.

"Sorry. You're right. I . . . I'll go." He bent and kissed Ali on the top of her head. "I'll stay if you need me to . . . But I'm not sure I can . . . "

Ali heard the panic in his voice as clearly as if he'd said, *no, don't let me hear details of what the bastard did to my little sister – I won't be able to bear it.*

She took pity on him, though a part of her wished for his support.

Gabe intervened. "No, Fitz. You are out. It is *not* okay for you to hear this. Go."

Gabe pulled the door open wide and waited as Flynn left the room before closing it firmly behind him. He kept his eyes on Ali as he rounded the desk and pulled out his chair.

"Would you like another agent in here, too? To take notes. Or are you okay with me taping it?"

"Don't we have to go to the Interview Room or something? Like with Mel. Or in the movies."

Gabe's mouth twitched in a smile, but it didn't reach his eyes. *They remained shuttered, unreadable. Calm.*

"You are not a suspect, Ali, you have come with information. It is different." He indicated the hand-held taping device and raised his eyebrows.

"It's fine. Go ahead. And no, I don't want anyone else in here. God, no."

"All right, then. We will begin." He switched on the recorder, stated his name and rank, date and time, and Ali's full name, for the record. Then he turned and looked directly at her, asking, "Explain, for the record and in your own words, why you are here."

Ali told her story again. This time she referred to Jack Neary by name. Gabe interrupted her repeatedly, asking for clarification as to how she knew Mr Neary, why she would have been left with him and who else was aware of the alleged abuse. Ali bit the inside of her cheek each time the word *alleged* was used, but she understood the reasons why.

When it got to the details, the fine-tuned moments of the acts themselves, Ali found she couldn't look Gabe in the face any more. Whether it was to protect herself or him, she wasn't sure.

She knew she couldn't bear to see his expression when she explained that Jack Neary had forced his penis down her throat. Over and over. Time after time. Leaving her gagging, sick and broken. Terrified of its force and its pain. The feelings of complete helplessness, of shame and self-blame. Of feeling dirty and used. Of panic that it would happen again. Of abandonment when it did.

Twice, Gabe paused the recording and abruptly left the room. First, when she talked through the second time Neary had approached her to continue his abuse and her horror upon realising it was to happen again. And the second time when she explained how Neary *promised* her that as soon as she got her period and started to show budding breasts, he'd move on to Molly, who'd be exactly the right age for him.

When Gabe returned to the room the second time and restarted the interview, stating again for the record that he had left and re-entered the room, his tie was undone, pulled down from its usual perfect knot. He refilled the water bottle and drank a glass clear through to the bottom, topped up hers and sat back down.

"Continuing interview," he said, clipped and precise.

Ali kept her eyes lowered as she talked about how she'd assumed she'd got her period because there were blood spots in her underwear but then tracked back to Neary's assault from the previous day. His rough, blunt fingers tearing her tender skin. *Hurting. Invading.* She reached for the water, trying to control her trembling fingers. She needed two hands to hold the glass as she drank deeply.

She needed the moment.

She risked a look at Gabe and took a breath when she caught the flared nostrils and tight whiteness about his mouth. His jaw was so tightly locked that a tic worked endlessly on one side. She lowered her eyes again and kept going. *She had to*. If she stopped, took a break – though he asked her several times if she needed one – she may never start again. The realness of it all – the truth of it all – was almost more than she could bear. She'd borne it all once, as it happened, again as she'd had her sessions with Dr Hearne – but now she felt like she was reliving it through someone else's life. It wasn't a visual she ever wanted to see again.

She finished by speaking of Neary's transfer to Wexford – she named the date – and how she'd contemplated telling her parents. Neary's parting shot to her had been a threat. He'd promised her that if she told anyone what he'd done, he'd put it out that it was in fact her own father who'd "interfered" with her, as he'd so cleverly put it. It was the nail that locked that door of silence tightly shut. She'd sworn at him then, her one act of defiance, that she'd get even when she was grown up – that she'd tell the police and anyone else who'd listen, exactly what he'd done.

He'd laughed in her face.

Ali slumped back in her chair, her hands over her face. "I don't *ever* want to say all this again," she whispered hoarsely. "Can you make sure that doesn't happen?"

Gabe switched off the recording and cleared his throat. "I will do my best."

He got up from his chair, strode to the window and, propping a hand against the wall, stared out. He was silent for several moments and Ali began to wonder if she should leave. If they were done.

Then without turning, he said quietly, "What proof do you have that any of this happened?"

Ali stared at his strained back. Her mouth fell open in complete shock. She reared up from her seat and slammed her hands on the surface of his desk.

"Proof?" she snapped. "You want *proof*?" Her voice was rising, her breath catching as she gasped. "You *bastard*! Is it not enough that I spill my darkest, dirtiest moments out to you here, on record? Do you think I made this shit up?" She could barely contain her fury as she rounded the desk and stood in the centre of the room, hands balled into fists. "Was it not enough proof that I *fainted* while trying to be normal? For *you*. While trying to give you a blow job that every other woman would enjoy and I fucking collapse rather than carry it through. What more *fucking* proof do you need?"

"Christ, Ali." He was beside her in an instant, his hands gripping her shoulders, holding her steady, holding her upright. "*I* don't need proof. The case needs proof. Even if nothing had happened between us, I would believe you. I know it happened to you. I *knew* it." He paused until her eyes met his. "I just didn't know it was Neary."

She looked right back at him. Into those clear green eyes that saw everything.

"When? When did you know? Did Flynn tell you last night?"

This was it, then, Gabe thought. *This was going to finish any slim hope that they could salvage something from the mess. Salvage themselves.* Of course he could lie . . . he could say yes, that Flynn had told him everything last night. That would be the easy and probably sensible and – for them – safest thing to do. He could choose not to tell her that he'd gone deep into a meditative state, a trance almost, as he'd held her T-shirt to his nostrils and inhaled her scent. As he'd allowed himself to travel back in her shoes to a place so dark and distant and yet so raw and present that he thought he'd retch. When he'd let himself feel her emotions, see her visions, taste her despair.

He *had* retched. He'd woken from *her* nightmares and vomited at length, his skin pale and tacky, his heart hammering, legs shaky. He'd rested his head on the bowl for long moments, bringing himself back to reality.

Letting the cool porcelain soothe his forehead. His "dreams" always left him weak and unsteady, and he'd barely made it back to the couch before collapsing into a long, dreamless, comatose state.

Several litres of water upon waking helped, but he'd never not see or feel what Ali had been through, and that was a punishment he'd wear gladly if it was eventually to help her heal in some way. But he didn't think she needed to hear about *his* angst. This was *her* story and she had all the rights when it came to who knew and what truth she needed. It was time to man up.

"I looked," he said, keeping his voice steady and measured, wondering if she'd catch on.

"You *looked*? As in you did your secret voodoo shit and delved into my life? *My* memories?"

She tried to pull away from him but he held on.

"Yes," he said and waited for the onslaught.

Wrenching from his hold, she swung her arm and slapped him hard across the face. His head snapped back with the force, but he kept his eyes on her blazing ones.

"You complete shit! You promised me. You fucking promised you'd never do that without my permission! How could you *do* that?"

She wheeled about and with her back to him, covered her face in her hands. There were no tears, just pure shaking fury.

Nothing he didn't deserve, Gabe acknowledged silently.

"You knew when I came in here this morning? Everything I just put down on record, you already knew?" She rounded on him again, her arms now wrapped around her slim frame in that defiant way of hers.

"No. Of course not. It doesn't work like that. It is more a mixture of images and feelings. Not factual, minute-by-minute accounts."

"Why? Why did you do it?" Her shoulders dropped and she watched him, her gaze steady now and so damn frosty.

Understandably.

"I had no idea you would come in this morning. That you would choose to name Neary and tell your story. I wanted to see if there was anything you had experienced that could help me place time and dates with the two women already involved in the case. To see if there was some way I could move justice along. I should have waited. Or at the very least, I should have asked."

"You should have trusted me to do the right thing."

Silence greeted this cold, hard fact. Gabe was at a loss. *She was right.* He had, knowingly and willingly, violated her privacy. *And for what?* She'd shown up this morning and given him everything. She had more guts and bravery in her little finger than he'd ever have. He was never as ashamed of his supposed gifts than he was right now. He'd never wished for a "do-over" more than this moment. He wished he could go back and chose *not* to look into her mind. Too. Damn. Late.

"Yes," he sighed in agreement. "I should have trusted you."

Ali moved round him, brisk and focused. "And it was all for nothing anyway," she said. "Here." She rooted in her bag and pulled out a set of three small books. "These are my diaries from those years. The English isn't great, the spelling probably crap, but the content should keep Neary from ever doing it again. I wrote everything down – not at first but as it became apparent, even to me as a young kid, that this was now my life. A part of me knew that writing it down, no matter how crudely and inexpertly, would help. Help me." She shoved the small books at him and he took them wordlessly. "I'd no idea that they may help someone else one day. I hope they do."

She turned, took one more drink of water and left the room.

Gabe looked down at the proof of child abuse resting in his large hands. He walked to the window, flipped the top notebook open to a random page and read. Within seconds he could feel bile rising. He snapped it shut.

"Aw, Christ!" he muttered and slid to the floor, head braced on his knees as he tried to remember to breathe.

Chapter 24

The countertops gleamed. They felt so beautiful as Ali ran her hands along the golden wood. It was a task she didn't mind in the least. It was methodical and mind-bendingly numbing. Exactly what she needed. She put aside the mineral oil and cloth and sank to the stool. Her thoughts were everywhere and nowhere. How could she have been so unbelievably stupid? Was it not enough that she couldn't keep the man satisfied in bed, but that she had to bloody fall in love with him, as well?

For fuck's sake.

He was a brooder, a strong, silent type to her sarcastic, mouthy one. He rarely smiled and took everything so damn seriously. Lightening up was not in his play book. *So, what was it about him? And now?* Even now that the bastard had shattered all of her trust, she still felt drawn to making *him* feel better. Not right away, naturally – the man had to suffer a bit first.

After Ali had cycled back to the loft as if the hounds of hell were on her heels and downed two cups of coffee laced liberally with whiskey, she'd phoned Dr Hearne, who'd been as amazingly supportive, as usual. Ali explained that she'd felt broadsided by Gabe, without saying how exactly – she knew how to keep others' secrets, *unlike some people* – and the doc had talked her down by letting Ali talk it through. Effective and enlightening and food for further thought.

It seemed Ali wasn't quite as furious with Gabe as she'd first suspected and even, in a small way, understood why he'd done it. She just wished he'd told her first, so she could have been prepared, at least as much as one could be to letting someone invade their thoughts, their memories. She wished he'd told her he was going to delve into her psyche as opposed to barging in unannounced, so to speak.

A loud, insistent knock interrupted her musings and she hauled her exhausted body to the door, yanking it open expectantly. Caro, Frankie and Molly trooped in and set about disrupting her tentative peace. They dived into action, as sisters do. Caro switched on the kettle, Frankie pulled down mugs and Molly rummaged in the biscuit tin.

"Really?" Molly sniped, discovering the tin was completely empty. "The baker in the family has no goodies?"

"Top drawer to the left of the fridge," Ali said, a half-smile attempting to come out to play.

She watched as Molly sighed in deep pleasure on finding the selection of oatmeal and raisin cookies, baked fresh that morning before her foray into the station. Thank the Lord for baking. It was the one task guaranteed to relax Ali and nearly always took her to her happy place. Measurements, control, precision and time. All of her recipe decisions to make, to approve. The simple preparation of those early morning cookies had saved Ali's sanity before her trip to the police.

"Why are you here instead of at home?" Frankie asked as she took the kettle from Caro and poured the boiling water into a teapot with probably way more tea bags than strictly necessary.

It seemed this was to be a "strong tea and comfort" afternoon. *Fine by Ali.*

"Yeah," said Caro, looking expectantly at her younger sister. "Surely you've no work on at the moment?"

Ali stretched and readjusted her aching limbs. "No. Not really. I like it here. It feels . . . Safe. I wasn't sure it would after the break-ins but somehow it does. I've got to start on the book that's to follow the series, but I asked for a slight extension on the deadline. They were okay with that. I need some time. I'll probably head west this weekend just to, you know, be there."

The others nodded. They did know. The Fitzgerald home in Clifden, County Galway, was a treasured retreat for them all. Frankie had used it to escape the press *and* a rather dangerous individual just last summer. Over the years, that old house had seen many a broken heart, happy, wild parties, family holidays and the burgeoning of new love. The walls had a multitude of stories to tell and remained a welcome haven.

"Good plan," agreed Frankie. "It saved my life in so many ways last year. Not that you need saving," she hastily added as Ali's brows rose. "Sorry."

Ali gave her a pass. She wouldn't wish Frankie's drama on anyone. And that awesome woman had handled herself brilliantly. Not unlike Caro, a few short months ago. The women in the Fitzgerald clan were pretty badass. She needed to remind herself of that. *Today and every day.* She was a survivor, *fuck it*, and that was how she intended to live her life.

Ali straightened her shoulders. "I suppose you want chapter and verse from what went down at the station?"

"Well, yeah, obviously," Moll said, dunking a cookie in her tea.

The others nodded in accord.

"Flynn couldn't handle it and had to leave the room, like a big baby. Gabe was an asshole and I was incredible. That's it, in a nutshell."

Caro's mouth dropped open. "Wait, *Flynn* left the room?"

"Yup. Though in fairness, if the roles were reversed and I had to witness shit that happened to him, I'd back out, too. And also, in the interests of truth, I don't think he was allowed to be there – conflict of interest and all. But I sure as shit won't let him off the hook that easy." She smirked.

How could she smirk? How could she be making light of this?

She looked at the three unbelievably supportive and loving faces in front of her and relaxed. *That's how.*

"Why did you call Gabe an asshole?" Moll wanted to know. "I thought you and he were all snuggled up?" She furrowed her brow. "And *I* think he's nice."

There were murmurs of agreement from the other two hot-blooded women who began making "oooh, yeah" and "m-hmm" sounds.

Molly looked affronted. "Jesus, you two. You're both spoken for! Have some loyalty for the men in your lives."

"Come on, Moll," Caro laughed. "We're not blind and you've got to admit, he's one supreme specimen of manhood."

Ali snorted. "Specimen of manhood? Ha! You read too many regency romance novels, Caro. And just because he is, undeniably, gorgeous doesn't mean he can't multitask as an asshole." She glared them down. "He does *that* part very well."

"Spill," said Frankie, settling in with a cookie and a hot top-up of tea. She poured for the others, offered the baked goods around. "Start at the you being incredible bit."

She told them a lot. Not every detail. Facts and times and places. There was no need to distress them further. She'd gone through most of it last night anyway. They wanted to hear that Jack Neary would be arrested and Ali realised she'd left the station before finding out what would happen next.

They bounced scenarios back and forth, each devising sentences for Neary that were, by turns, more gruesome and grotesque than the next. Ali told them she'd felt hurt by Gabe, by his actions. She didn't go into too much detail there, either, but alluded to his weird qualities and explained it away by likening it to Molly and Flynn's unusual "sensing" of things, only more advanced. They were dubious when she admitted to feeling like she'd been violated by Gabe. Molly in particular was quite defensive of him.

"You can't blame him," she said. "He was only trying to help."

"But he promised he'd never do that without my knowledge," Ali insisted, getting all cross at him again. "You don't break promises to people you care about. Or say that you care about."

"Has he said that?" Caro was curious.

Ali sighed. "No. Yes. Kind of." She looked at the sceptical faces. "Okay, he hasn't declared undying devotion or anything, but he says he cares. He implied more. Whatever that means."

"And you? Do you care?"

"Oh, Frankie, I don't know."

"You do," Molly said firmly. "I know you do. Oh, not that kind of knowing," she grimaced at them. "You're different with him. I've seen it. You two have a connection. You watch each other when you aren't even aware of it. It's been that way since you met."

Ali stared at her, open-mouthed. "What do you mean?"

"I was there, remember? He walked into the restaurant with Flynn and your head just about swivelled off your neck, craning to see where he was the whole time. And *he* was as bad, only his behaviour was more subtle. I could feel the vibrations off him. And then there was Frankie and Dev's wedding."

"What?" Frankie was astounded. "What happened at our wedding? I don't remember meeting him."

"You were too loved-up to notice anything," Caro laughed. "I remember too, though. You hunted him down, didn't you?"

"Hunt is a strong word," Ali said sheepishly. "But yeah, I came on to him. I'd no idea what I was up against, though. He pushed me away and in hindsight, that was a good thing. Flynn would have killed him, as Gabe was there following a lead on some guy who'd seemingly crashed your reception as a way to hide out 'cause it was a big celebrity bash and the bad guy thought he'd lose himself in the crowd or something. I don't recall the details and it doesn't matter. But it wasn't my finest hour."

"Your finest hour was last night, telling us. We're so proud of you." Caro's voice wobbled and she blinked rapidly.

Molly handed her a Kleenex tissue.

"Now what? What happens next?" Frankie wanted to know.

Ali shrugged. "I haven't the faintest. I'll phone Flynn and ask. I'm not ready to ask Gabe. And even if he contacts me, there's . . . there's no point in communicating any more. We, whatever *we* were, it's over."

There was silence for a beat and then Molly asked, "Why?"

Ali closed her eyes briefly. She wasn't sure how much to share – how much would help and how much would just bring on a pity party from the others. That, she couldn't tolerate.

Molly continued before Ali could decide.

"I mean, you fancy him, he fancies you. What's not to like? Is there another problem? Is he a commitment-phobe?" She looked worried as she sat up straighter, as if girding herself for battle on Ali's behalf.

God, Ali loved these women. *All of them*. Even Frankie, the one who'd inadvertently changed the course of Ali's life. Ali could still see vividly, recount with awful accuracy, the conversations she'd attempted with her mother when things had first gone so spectacularly down the toilet. *Not now, darling, Frankie's having a meltdown about her mother.* Or, *Of course, pet, we'll chat as soon as I get Frankie off to sleep – she's emotionally drained. Can't your sisters help?*

No, they bloody couldn't. As it turned out, no one could. And as a fully fledged, therapied, mostly healed woman, Ali knew, really *knew*, that none of what happened had been Frankie's fault. Or her mother's. Any young girl whose mother had been killed in a dramatic car crash, its newsworthy content splashed all over the media for ages, would have a hard time doing normal daily things – eating properly, sleeping well, making friends. And grown Ali didn't begrudge her any of those things. Not one.

She smiled at the women watching her carefully. "Actually, that's more my line, *Ms* Commitment-Phobe," she said ruefully. "I'm not cut out for relationships."

"That's crap," Frankie said and folded her arms. "You're loyal, kind, helpful, generous, funny and talented."

Ali blinked at her, surprised. "Eh, thanks, I think, but that still doesn't make me a good life partner."

"What Frankie said," Caro chipped in, "those qualities are exactly what makes good relationships. Though I don't know how talented you need to be, unless . . . " She broke off, laughing. "Oh! you mean in the bedroom . . . "

Frankie and Caro high-fived each other, their twin grins as wide as a mile. Molly was smiling too, but she also had a pink flush on her soft round cheeks. *Interesting*.

It was Ali's non-reaction that brought the merriment to a halt.

"Shit!" Caro's hand flew to her mouth. "You can't be worried about sex, can you? You're the one who's given us all the advice and ass-kicking to go for it. You're our resident sex goddess!"

Alcohol. They needed wine or beer or brandy. Or at least Ali did. She got up from her stool and raided her wine rack, dragging out a good Rioja. She uncorked it adeptly, poured and handed glasses to her sisters as they looked on in bemusement.

"Full disclosure?" Ali took a large gulp.

Three heads nodded.

"I'm shite at sex."

Gabe read the diaries. Each one. Every page. Then he went to the bathroom and violently deposited any food that had ever lingered in his stomach. Wiping his hands on a paper towel, he studied himself in the mirror. *Yeah, he looked as desperate as he felt. Good. He needed to feel. To understand. To be furiously, indescribably angry.* And he needed a punching bag in the worst way. His stomach hurt and his chest felt tight, neither in any way related to his bathroom foray.

Tossing the scrunched-up wad in the bin, he then headed back to his office, gathered the three books and walked unhurriedly to speak to Flynn. He stopped by two desks on his way, asked for a meeting room for half an hour's time then paused at the water fountain to drink. And to regain composure. This was *not* going to be easy. Nor should it be. But Flynn had to be included, at least peripherally, if he so desired.

He rapped on the frame of the open office door and Flynn looked up from his computer. His shoulders sagged momentarily and then, drawing a deep breath, he shoved back from his desk and stood.

"Well?"

Gabe looked at him steadily and offered the diaries. Flynn flinched then reached for them.

"What are these?"

"They are evidence, now, from Ali."

Flynn's head shot up. He glared and looked back down at the three A5 books covered in worn velvet: one red, one blue, one purple. *Oh, fuck. They were Ali's diaries.* He remembered his sister walking about the house clutching one or other of them to her skinny chest.

His eyes met Gabe's. "She wrote everything down? Here?"

Gabe nodded.

"Is it enough?" he swallowed.

And as Gabe nodded again, he moved backwards, his hip hitting the desk. He propped himself there, holding the evidence in his hands as if they were made of broken glass.

"Unless you absolutely have to, do *not* read them," Gabe said quietly.

"Did you?"

"Yes. Every word." Gabe cleared his throat. "For one so young she had a very . . . vivid turn of phrase." It was his turn to swallow hard. "The entries are dated, some gaps, some mere allusions, but some . . . rather graphic. Simply and baldly stated, and more effective because of it." He shoved his hands in his pockets and rocked back on his heels. "I have made copies," he continued, "so keep these for now. I have arranged a room for a short meeting in . . . " He glanced at his watch. "Twenty minutes. Attend or not as you wish."

He turned to go but halted when Flynn said, "How was she?"

"Pissed. At me. And amazing. I expected nothing less."

"You have him, then? This will tie it up?"

"With a few more strands to entwine, yes. He will be arrested this evening."

Flynn heaved a sigh. "Go ahead," he said. "I'll be along when I can." And he walked back round to his chair, velvet secrets in his hands, and sat. "Close the door behind you, Gabe, I need a minute."

He needed more than that, Gabe knew as he pulled the door shut behind him. When Flynn's door was closed, nobody disturbed him unless there was an actual fire in the building, or life and limb were at stake. Gabe did *not* envy his colleague what he was never about to unsee again. His life would be forever altered.

Maybe that's what they all needed. Life-altering horrors to ensure they never stopped trying to help, never gave up.

There was a stunned silence as three mouths fell open. Three sets of eyes were glued to her face. Caro was the first to break the spell.

"But . . . " she sputtered. "But you're the one with all the experience! You told me to have sex with a virtual stranger! Granted, it turned out to be the best thing I ever did, sexually speaking, but still. I only did it 'cause you said!"

"And you, you've always said to us that you have loads of sex – first dates and everything. Even one-night hooks-ups!" Frankie added.

"Ah, the wonderful one-nighters," mused Ali, reminiscing. She glared back at them. "Give me a break! Yeah, I've had lots of sex. Why not? It's a good release and, with a half-decent partner, a good workout."

"So," Molly said slowly, "what you're saying is you have loads of experience but not great prowess?"

The others burst out laughing.

"Prowess? Feck, Moll, where did you get that word?" Caro held her stomach as she continued to laugh.

Molly squinted her eyes at her older sister. "What? What would you call it, then?"

"Technique?" Ali reached over and gave Molly's arm a squeeze. "I'm perfectly capable of reaching an orgasm, mostly with help from myself. I'm also more than capable of satisfying a man. I've discovered that most men are selfish lovers and as long as they *think* you're happy, they'll focus on themselves. I tend to gloss over certain aspects. And since I never have relationships, my lack in certain areas is less obvious."

"So, what makes you say you're shite? It sounds to me like you have it all figured out." Frankie was clearly puzzled.

"It's to do with *him*, isn't it?" Molly, as usual, cut to the chase. "What he made you do."

"Oh, darling." Caro's eyes filled with sudden tears.

Frankie copped it quicker than the others. "You don't perform oral sex," she stated, her voice carefully even. "You can't."

Ali looked at this woman. Francesca Jones, sister in name and now sister-in-law. Beloved friend. And in no way to blame for what happened to Ali, despite many teen years of resentment towards Frankie from Ali herself. She felt ashamed of the spite she'd heaped on Frankie, though much of it had been hidden inside. She felt a deep wave of shame sweep over her, clearly seeing, for the first time, the lost, heartbroken girl Frankie had been. Just as devastated and lost as Ali herself, though in a different way.

She stood, walked round the counter, wrapped her arms tight about Frankie and said, "Thank you for putting up with all of my shit. I'm really glad you're in our family."

Ali could feel her throat tighten as Frankie hugged her back, strong and sure, supportive and loving. *Like a sister.*

Ali wiped absently at her eyes and disentangling herself from a suspiciously silent Frankie, she sat back down on her stool.

"To be clear," Caro said, bringing them back to the sex discussion, "you're not shite at sex in general, just oral sex specifically. Correct?"

Ali couldn't help but laugh at Caro's practical turn of phrase. "Correct," she agreed.

"What's the problem, then? Or is there one? Don't do it if you don't like it. Simple," Molly said.

"Oh, honey, your inexperience is showing." Ali smiled patiently at her. "No man is going to want a life without oral sex. It's a truth universally acknowledged."

Molly blushed and looked for backing from her two supporters-in-arms. She got nothing.

"Really? You *have* to do oral sex?"

"Of course not," Caro rallied, but the pause had been significant. "No one *has* to do anything when it comes to sex. But it's kind of expected nowadays. Even kids use oral sex as a form of contraception. Or so I heard."

"Just because it's expected doesn't mean you have to do it. All the erotica novels have given women a sense that they must be all things to all men. They don't!" Molly was adamant. "It's all about consent these days."

"Go you, feminista girl!" Ali cheered. "I know, intellectually, that you're right, but men are . . . men. They want what they want. And in fairness, I'm not blaming them. I'm sure it's great." She hesitated, recalling the delicious feel of Gabe's mouth on her. "I *know* it's great," she amended. "But I can't satisfy a man in *that* way. I tried and it was a train wreck."

"What happened?" Caro asked.

"I fucking fainted."

Once again there was silence. The large, old-fashioned clock ticked away in the background. There was a snort. Then another. They could contain themselves no longer – four grown women, sisters by blood, bond and marriage, collapsed in whoops.

It was an unmitigated disaster. Or at least to Gabe's way of thinking it was. Jack Neary, ex-priest and one-time media darling, now a suspected felon, brought out the big guns. Gabe sent a detail of gardaí to bring him back in for further questioning and it didn't go to plan. How Neary had an inkling this might be occurring was something Gabe needed to investigate separately. He wondered, *was there someone at the station in Neary's pay?*

The man had amassed a bloody fortune while in South America and, by all accounts, wasn't shy about spending it. Gabe had access to his accounts – he knew his net worth. It was pretty damn huge. God knew what he'd been up to in those years abroad, but he was pretty darn certain it had involved no good.

Neary arrived at the station accompanied by his hotshot counsel. Gabe didn't blame the solicitor – he was simply doing the job he was paid for. Gabe ushered them into the interview room and asked two other gardaí to be in attendance.

He didn't trust himself to be alone with Neary, not with the heartbreaking words from the young, terrified girl still in neon lights in his brain. He could barely look at the man, and left him and his lawyer alone for ten minutes as he went outside to compose himself. He called on all of his meditative powers to reach a place of calm, of reason. He could rip this guy's head off in a second if he allowed his mind to venture into dark territory.

That would not do. This had to be handled professionally and procedurally. Nothing else was acceptable.

It took very little time for Neary to be released under house arrest. The hotshot was worthy of his stellar reputation. Although Ali's testimony was strong – they didn't use her name but indicated they had irrefutable evidence against him – they had to release the details of the years in question and copies of the diaries so Neary's man could begin to launch a defence.

Neary wasn't considered a flight risk – he was a well-known man, locally, anyway – but Gabe alerted all ports and borders just to be sure. He wanted the man watched 24/7. He wanted this man behind bars. And the key thrown as far away as possible. Above all, he wanted Ali safe. He wanted her to get justice – to get the satisfaction of seeing the look on Jack Neary's face as she handed him his life: going straight to hell. The place he deserved to be.

He hated watching the two men leave the station. His hands in fists at his sides, Gabe had to remind himself it was step-by-step process. A few more days of i-dotting and t-crossing and Neary *would* be arrested and held for trial. Gabe would make damn sure of it. At present, he had to be satisfied that Jack Neary would be sweating it out, wondering what was awaiting him. And Gabe had one more angle to check. Something had been bubbling away in the back of his mind and was slowly rising to the surface. And he needed another look at one of those accounts of Neary's. A bell was ringing, connecting some dots and pointing in a murky direction. He'd work on that, for now.

He was about to head upstairs, when Mel Carney and his lawyer walked by, Mel's face ashen. Carney was arguing with his counsel and the garda who was with them.

The garda called to Gabe, "Carney here wants to speak to you, Detective Mackenzie. He says he has information that you may need."

"I do," babbled Carney eagerly to Gabe. "That guy? The one who just left the building? I know him! I fucking know him. And what's more, I can tell you things about him. Big things. But you have to give me a deal. A sweet one."

Gabe eyed the former chef and let things shift about in his brain. *Was this the missing link? Were Carney and Neary connected?*

"I do *not* have to give you anything, Mr Carney. But I will listen to what you have to say. Who knows, you may turn out to be helpful, after all."

He indicated for the others to follow him as he changed direction and headed to an interview room, his mind calming as information and previously hidden pieces of the puzzle slotted into place.

Chapter 25

Ali heard nothing from Gabe. *Not a word.* It shouldn't make her so sad but, *fuck*, it did. She'd told him to go, or that had been the implication. But did he have to be so fecking honourable that he listened to her? *What was with that?* Why couldn't he just barge on back into her life and be here, where, she admitted, she really, really wanted him? But . . . *oh, well. Not to be. It was for the best.* But, *God*, she missed his steadiness. *His calm.* The very things she teased him about, the slagging she'd given him for his oddness – that's what she wanted, needed, right now.

Two days passed – two endless days of trying to write recipes and collate information. Two boring, lonely days. How could she miss him so much? What was it about him that tempted her? That made her *feel*. It wasn't comfortable, she didn't like it, but it was so. And nothing would ever come of it.

God, she was a sad sack.

The long evenings kept it still light at 9 p.m. The day had been warm and she'd thrown on a sky-blue T-shirt and lightweight beige linen trousers in an attempt at fashion and, more importantly, at trying a new, improved version of herself. A more feminine one. She was determined to find that girl she once was and if changing her wardrobe choices was only a small step, so be it. She did, however, wear her Doc Martens, because there was only so much diversity a girl could tackle in one go.

Ali got up from her stool in the loft and wandered to her large window. *Clean at last, not a streak in sight.* She rested her head against the cool glass and blew her breath to fog over the space. She drew a heart with her finger, sighed and scrubbed it away, messing up the glass again. Shit, she was an idiot.

She missed Caro, too. She'd left this morning, happy to be flying back to Nick. To her life there. Ali was happy for her. Unconditionally happy. Caro deserved her new life. She'd managed so beautifully being a single mum, working as an art history lecturer, keeping her shit together. Nick was a good man. He'd be good for Toby, too.

Gathering the recently purchased spray bottle and cloth from under the large Belfast sink, Ali methodically began to clean the glass, remembering Gabe doing this very task for her. She paused, closed her eyes and let her senses recall all the touches, the kisses, the tenderness. *The passion. The hunger. Christ!* she was getting hot and bothered just thinking about him and his magic fingers. Maybe she needed to go and take a cold shower – *wouldn't that be a hoot?* Or, better still, go and take care of business herself. Tried and trusted and nobody making unseemly demands. *Yeah, that might work.*

A knock on the door interrupted her wayward thoughts and her heart leaped. *Gabe. He'd come.* He'd tuned into her mad longings and come to her. *God*, she needed someone to hit her over the head, she was so obviously losing it. She put down her cleaning supplies and walked, as casually as she could manage, considering her heart was thumping erratically, to open the loft door.

352

Her heart stopped. Dead.

"Good evening, Alison," Jack Neary said, his voice as smooth and oily as her nightmares remembered. "I'm sure you've been expecting me."

Stunned, Ali could only stare. She couldn't breathe, couldn't speak. She didn't even blink as he shouldered his way inside and closed the door behind him. All she could do was gape, her mind and body completely numb. A roaring in her ears was the only clue reminding herself she was actually still alive.

This was not good. Hell was in her kitchen.

Well, that had been interesting. Thank goodness for serendipitous meetings in hallways. It transpired that Mel and Garcia had been taking orders from Jack Neary, of all people. Only Mel hadn't known his name. Hadn't known of his early connections to Ali in her childhood. Hadn't been interested in the whys and wherefores. All he'd been interested in was his next batch of cocaine and how soon he could get it. He'd simply met Neary at his car behind the Golden Goose pub, where he'd taken orders and received drugs. Or money. It had been Garcia who'd intoduced Mel to Neary on, it seemed now, Neary's orders, hoping to use Mel's penchant for sniffing money up his nose as a hook to get to Ali.

With Carney back in his cell, Gabe pulled out Neary's bank records and as he searched for specific names and dates in an obscure record, he could feel the hum of success in his veins. Moving his finger down the long list of transactions, Gabe found the links and it cemented his suspicions. This was worse than they thought. This brought the whole Neary investigation full circle. Right back to the initial attacks on Ali and her loft.

And why the hell hadn't he realised the man's involvement before? Mel Carney had, albeit unintentionally, pretty much tied everything together for Gabe. Had solved the case, in fact. Tied up so many loose ends in one fell swoop. There was no way Mel had ever been the ring leader. Gabe had known that. Had *felt* that. He should have pushed more when Mel was first detained. There was no way that excuse for a man had cooked up all the trail of events to get rid of Ali from hosting a baking programme – that excuse had never been valid.

But instead of heaving a sigh of relief at gleaning all this new information, Gabe felt an uncomfortable tingling on the back of his neck. Wearily, he rubbed a hand across his tight muscles, but it wasn't that kind of tingle.

It was the other kind.

None of what had happened to Ali was just to bunk her off the show, though it may have started that way.

It was way more serious than that now. Neary wanted her out of the picture. Permanently.

"Get out!" Ali said, breathing through the noise in her head.

She was over the initial shock and was now bloody furious. *How dare he! How* fucking *dare he come into her space!* She turned to the door to open it and before she could even reach for the handle, he spun her round, his large frame grasping her arms and walking her back towards the main cooking area.

"I like what you've done with the space," he said, snide and slick. "We can definitely make some good use of this amount of room."

His hands gripped her tightly and although she was surprised, she was *not* letting him overwhelm her. *Not. Ever. Again.* She let him manoeuvre her, let him walk her backwards, let him be in control. *For now.* Let him think he was in charge.

Ali wasn't a kid any more and there was no way, *no way in hell*, he was getting to her.

She gritted her teeth and spoke through them. "What do you want here, Neary? Haven't you an appointment with the guards?"

"Shut up," he snapped. "This is all *your* doing."

"This?" she asked. "This what? Oh, wait, you mean you being called out for the pathetic creep you are. That?"

Without warning, his hand flew out and slammed into her head. She stumbled forwards with a yelp of pain and grasped the edge of the stool for support.

"How dare you speak to me like that!" he roared, eerily echoing almost exactly what she'd been thinking about him.

Ali pulled herself upright, reminding herself to take it slow, keep him talking.

"You're in my space, I'll speak to you any way I like. Jesus, Jack, I'm not some vulnerable kid any more. Why are you even here? What the fuck do you want?"

His hand flew out again, but she was ready for him and ducked backwards. He growled. His tanned face was growing flushed. *Good*, she thought, *I need to keep him off his game.*

"You little bitch!" he snarled.

"Temper, temper," Ali taunted, her nerves settling.

Strange, that. She liked seeing him lose control, being out of his depth. She'd make use of that.

"Seriously, Flynn texted me you were under house arrest, so I can't imagine why you're here – or indeed how."

"How? Those idiots guards that Indian fella put on me were very easily fooled. I had one of my men set off a house alarm two doors down and they ran to check it. I was out the back door in an instant. So easy. As to why, I'm sure you know very well why."

"They won't be fooled for long and will figure out where you went. And he's part Native American, you ignoramus. Say your piece and get out."

She hoped her voice sounded steadier than she was now beginning to feel. Where did her previous bravado suddenly go?

Jack Neary was a big man, broad of shoulder and tall in height. He had a full head of hair, brushed back from his forehead, greying now, and she stared at his sagging face, not as ruddily strong as it used to be. He'd always been a vain man, snappily dressed and well groomed. He'd rarely worn the "collar" and liked his designer attire, though in hindsight, how he could have afforded them on his supposed cleric salary, she didn't know.

Tonight, he wore tailored trousers and a mint-green dress shirt, still veering towards snazzy. He was bronzed from years in the South American sun and it made him look like a fading movie idol from the 1940s. He'd even grown an Errol Flynn moustache and if Ali hadn't been so on edge, she may have laughed outright.

Now was not the time for levity.

"You've told me how you got here, now tell me why. What can you possibly want with me?"

"Want with you? Are you mad? I want to kill you!"

She blinked. Had he just said he wanted to kill her? *A figure of speech, surely?*

"Well. The feeling is entirely mutual, I assure you. I've wanted to kill you for years."

"You and your big mouth and your even bigger disaster of a bunch of diaries!"

Ali paled. He wasn't supposed to have known they were hers. *Shit.*

This was definitely *not good.*

She rallied, "I may have been vulnerable and innocent when you first laid your filthy paws on me, but I was never stupid. Of course I wrote everything down. Just wait till they're read out in court. I'm almost looking forward to it."

"No one will believe the ramblings of a little girl," he blustered, on edge.

"They don't have to be believed, not really, they just have to be heard. You're done, Jack Neary. You're finally going to get what you deserve."

She couldn't keep the satisfaction out of her voice. Truthfully, she didn't really try. But that tone of complacence pushed his buttons.

"No!" he roared. "No one will believe you! Do you know who I am? Do you know how many people owe me?"

He was losing it, she thought. *Better tread warily . . . Oh, fuck that!*

"Know who you are?" She gaped at him. "You're the *bastard* who stole my childhood from me. And from others like me, that's who the fuck you are." She pivoted away from him, needing air. Space.

She paced across the room, mind whirling. He followed closely. That was damn unnerving. She reminded herself to stay alert. To be aware.

She spun round and he was right there, hands in fists on his hips.

She drew in a deep breath. "And who the hell owes you? No one owes you shit."

His face florid, he practically spat at her, "There are many people of note who owe me a lot. You haven't a hope in hell, you little bitch. I'm a person of consequence."

Okay, now that made her laugh. Outright. In his face.

Big mistake.

His large hand flew out again and she toppled backwards, landing with a jolt against the corner of the counter. She yelled, rubbing her hip as pain seared through her. The pain in her head from his wallop was throbbing and she wondered how long she'd let him do this. How long she could wait. He was furious. And his temper was rising by the second. He paced to the large windows, slamming his hand against the surround, cursing fluently. How much more should she prod at him, egg him on?

"What do you want? The police have the diaries. It's too late to take them back. I've nothing you could want. Nothing," she hissed as her right hand rubbed her hip and came away with blood.

Blast it. But better still, she felt her phone in her back pocket. *Excellent.* She moved her hand backwards, pretending to rub her hip for relief in case he turned round and saw her. She needed to get that phone unlocked ASAP, so she dropped to the floor as if her hip had given out. She whipped out her phone, swiped, pressed the call icon and #1, and slid it under the stool.

Neary strode back and still swearing, he reached down

and grabbed her by the hair, hauling her to her feet.

"What do *I* want?" He prowled right up into her face.

Morsels of spit landed on her cheeks, but she refused to wince.

"I want to continue where we left off, little girl. And then I'm going to end it. For you."

Fuck. Not what she'd expected.

Concerned but furious with himself for not figuring it out sooner, he strode over to Flynn's office, a bundle of papers in his hand.

Flynn looked exhausted. His tie was gone and his shirtsleeves were rolled up, in a mirror image of Gabe himself. The circles under Flynn's eyes were deep and bruised. He was struggling with everything that had happened to Ali. Plus, an unhealthy dose of guilt and blame. Gabe didn't try to tell him he was wrong. Flynn was who he was and he'd work through this at his own pace.

"Take a look at this," Gabe said, placing the two sets of papers in front of Flynn.

The sigh said it all. Flynn picked one set up, rubbing a hand over his cropped hair.

"What am I looking at?"

Gabe pointed at two separate notations – the name of Mel's accomplice, Juan Garcia, and the damning bank statements tying them both to Neary. "Here and here."

Flynn studied the papers silently for a few moments, flicking through them competently and efficiently.

He looked up at Gabe. "Well, hell. The bastard has been involved from the get-go. Are you su . . . Never mind. Of course you're sure."

"That's not all – that is merely the paper trail. We

may have to do a deal for Mel Carney as he can positively identify Neary as the man who issued orders for Mel and Garcia to hurt Ali." Gabe sat and explained about his interaction earlier, but even as he spoke, his senses were on high alert, the tingle now flooding his entire body.

He felt cold and a stillness enveloped him as he suddenly felt all of Ali's pain resurface and make itself known with a severe tightening in his gut.

"Something is wrong," he said abruptly as he rose. "Ali needs me."

Before Flynn could respond, Gabe's phone rang. He pulled it from his trouser pocket, casting an impatient glance at the screen. Ali's name was displayed. *What? She never used the phone for calls. Only texts. Except . . .* He was on his feet, moving, fear lancing through him as his fears were confirmed.

"Grab your weapon," he called to Flynn as he headed to the door, phone to his ear. "She's in trouble."

She *had* to do something. *Now.* When Neary's words penetrated her sluggish, pain-filled brain, a trickle of unease began to fill her bones. There was no way she'd ever let him force her again. *No way.* She would, she knew, die fighting him off, if it came to that.

Not the vulnerable kid any more, Ali. You are strong and able. Remember your training.

Put him off guard, she told herself. *Throw him off balance, literally and figuratively.* She could do this. She would save herself. And if Gabe came along to help, so much the better. *If* he came. Would he remember what he'd told her? *Would he answer?*

Neary was smiling now. Confident and sure. A swagger back in his step as he prowled about her space again. As if he fucking owned it. Intruding and more unwanted than any person alive.

He was going to try to make her do it all again. Force her to her knees. Force her to take him in. *Force her.*

No. Not happening. And kill her? Let him bloody try.

She stared at him. Straight into his eyes. "No," she said firmly, "none of that will happen, Jack. I won't allow it. Get out. Keep walking. And maybe I won't tell the police about this little nocturnal foray."

He lunged. She was ready.

They tussled. If this were a scene on a TV show, the director would have called "cut" and had them redo it. But a real-life toss about was *not* elegant or stylish. Or co-ordinated. They fell to the floor, Ali beneath the weight of the large man, twisting and grappling for a hold. They rolled. And rolled again. She was strong now, not a child or defenceless. She would use her knowledge – but not just yet.

There was grunting and swearing, and Ali saw a gleam in Neary's eyes that made her go completely lax. *He was enjoying this. This was what he wanted.* He'd always loved power, used power, got off on power. Dr Hearne had told her that, but she'd already begun to understand before the therapy sessions just how screwed up he was. *That was not an excuse. There were none.* But she'd learned that what made some people turn vicious or depraved was *not* the same for everyone. She didn't care *why* this man was a paedophile, she simply wanted him gone.

They rolled again and Ali was face down. He grabbed her hands, hauling them backwards, and as she angled her head to see what he was doing, she was horrified to see him pull a garden cable tie from his pocket. Using it, he swiftly tied her hands together and let her flop back to the ground. *Shit.* This wasn't in her plan.

He yanked on her hair and pulled her over so she lay on her back. Straddling her, he fumbled at his zipper, saliva dribbling from his mouth, his eyes wild and unfocused.

He was going to do it. He was going to force her.

He pulled out his semi-erect penis and began stroking himself.

"Need some help at your age?" she gasped, determined not to lose her freaking mind.

She could feel her insides tighten and then an insistent shaking. Followed swiftly by a sort of paralysis. *No.* She couldn't let that happen. Freezing would hand him the power as a gift. *Not. Happening.* She'd use her brain and her brawn, thin though she may be. She'd learned shit. Those classes the doc had made her take? She was going to be a star pupil.

He slid forwards over her stomach, one hand going to her head as he pulled her hair. *God, that was sore.* Both of his hands now occupied, Ali knew she had to make a move. Otherwise . . . well, otherwise she might as well give up.

Quickly, she replayed some self-defence moves in her brain, only vaguely aware of the drivel of sex talk coming out of Neary's mouth. He sounded like an extra in a bad porn film. *He's pathetic,* she reminded herself as she geared up for some action.

Using every ounce of strength, she jackknifed her knees up and into the small of his back, giving his kidneys a good belt. Roaring, he toppled forwards just as Ali swung away and to the left, hefting him off and onto the floor. She scrambled to her feet as he screamed obscenities. He reached out with one hand, tugging on her ankle, but she kicked back and up, aiming for his kneecaps, knocking him away. She was never so grateful for her choice of footwear as she was in that moment. Docs rock.

Within seconds she was at the butcher's block next to the stove and using her mouth, pulled the cleaver free and dropped it on the countertop. Grabbing it, her wrists still bound, she angled it behind her and tried to cut open the hard plastic tie. *Bastard couldn't have used fabric? What were criminals coming to these days?* that's what Ali wanted to know. Well, at least she wanted to know that in one tiny part of her speeding brain. Mostly, she wanted to know what the feck her next move should be. She wanted to know if her phone, now slid somewhere under the table, was still on, recording everything. She wanted to know how long that disgraced piece of manhood would stay down.

Not long was the answer, as he stumbled to his feet. Clutching at his lower back, he started forwards. *Come on!* her brain screamed as she angled the knife against the plastic – up and down, up and down. Advancing on her with his body unprotected gave her one more option. Still keeping the knife between her trembling and probably bloody hands because this was *hard*, she kicked out, remembering skills, moves and actions she could use to protect herself in times of fear. *Times like this.*

She judged her aim, stepped forwards into him, which he obviously wasn't expecting, and, turning her leg at an angle, slammed her foot into his groin.

Yes. He fell forwards in agony, clutching his body as he wheezed out painful gasps. Ali danced out of his reach and continued cutting furiously.

Damn. She should have chosen a smaller knife, *a parer maybe.* But in that brief instant of decision, she'd just gone for what was biggest and easiest to grab with her teeth. She was stuck with the cleaver, and it had better fucking work or she was in deep shit.

And where the hell was the cavalry?

The cavalry, in the form of Gabe, Flynn and two gardaí, were approaching the perimeter of Ali's loft space. Gabe took the lead and using silent directions, motioned for Alex and Carlos to head round the back and secure the exits. There was an old-fashioned fire escape leading to the loft bathroom, odd though that was. He and Flynn crept noiselessly up the steps to the main door.

His ear to the wood, Gabe held up a hand in readiness to enter. Flynn handed him a lock-picking tool, but Gabe waved it away and used his own set. It had been the strangest moment, that second when he knew Ali was in danger. Not because of his so-called Spidey senses, as she called them, but because she'd trusted him, despite everything, to come to her. Her phone call proved that.

She'd remembered his words. *She was some woman.* He was *not* going to go in there and find her helpless, he knew that now as clear as he knew his own heart. The cold had left him, the sense of doom lessened considerably. He was merely the back-up. The clean-up. And he was never so happy to be put in that category. He knew his instincts were correct. He knew it in his bones.

Because he wasn't terrified for her. He trusted her as she trusted him.

"You took your fucking time," Ali grunted, sitting on top of Jack Neary's back, his arms bent back at an odd angle, a tea towel tied about his wrists in a tight knot.

She was sweating, her chest heaving from exertion and, *yeah*, she could admit it now, *sheer bloody panic*. There was blood. On him and her. Most of it was his, because the asshole came for her as her hands finally broke free from the tie and she'd used the knife on him. On his shoulder – a sharp jab, not remotely life-threatening but, she hoped, really sore and a bitch to heal. It had been enough of a shock to stop him in his tracks and enabled Ali to get the edge on him, attack from the front, twist him as he yelped and blood spurted, and tackle him to the ground. She kneeled on him, one knee to his already painful kidneys, the other keeping his thighs still. He was bellowing, *surprise, surprise*, and calling for his lawyer.

As Gabe and Flynn strolled into her loft, Neary lifted his head to shout at them. "This wild woman attacked me with a knife! I demand you arrest her! She's a lunatic. Not only besmirching my good name, but also physically threatening me! It's a disgrace. I'm suing."

"Besmirching? Your *good* name?" Flynn hitched his trousers and hunkered in front of Neary, whose head was still raised from the floor. "Oh, I think you'll find you managed that all by yourself." He turned to Ali. "Good work, kid, you took him down."

Ali could hear the pride from her brother's few words and a part of her warmed. She may be sweating, but a chill had started to form and her cramped hands were aching where they held the knot together.

Alex and Carlos came in through the bathroom, surveyed the scene and nodded to Ali.

"Well done, Ali. You did good. I can take over now," Alex said as he reached to check the knot and then for Ali's hand to help her up from her position on Neary's back.

"I've got this," Gabe interrupted and, bending, he picked Ali up in his arms and carried her to the large armchair in the corner. He put her down against soft cushions, pulled a rug from the back of the chair and tucked it about her trembling legs. He rested a hand briefly on her shoulder. "Wait here. Don't move until I say."

Christ! he was in bossy mode, Ali thought, her eyes following him as he reached for a glass, poured brandy, mumbled a few words to Flynn, who now had a loud, grumbling, properly handcuffed Neary on his feet, and came back to her.

"Drink," he said in that calm way.

He pulled a small stool over and sat next to her. He rested one large hand on her legs, the weight of it soothing her trembling limbs as she sipped her drink. She looked into that steady gaze, saw such emotion there, and almost closed her own eyes at the intensity. His eyes were blazing, on fire, but he was as still as a stone.

Overcome, tired, plain worn out, Ali said, "I fought back – this time I fought back." And the shakes started in earnest.

Gabe took the brandy from her hands, placed it on the floor, stood and gathered her up once more. This time he turned, sat down and snuggled her into his embrace, arms wrapped tightly about her shaking body as he held her close.

He spoke over her head to the other detective. "Get him out of here, Carlos. Call forensics for photos and clean-up" He turned his head to catch Flynn's eyes. "We'll see you at the station in a bit."

Flynn hesitated. Then, seeing something in Gabe's eyes, just nodded. He delivered orders to Alex and Carlos, who both held a more subdued Neary, then tied the tea towel around Neary's wound.

Flynn walked over to Ali, bent down and kissed her head. "See you in a bit, kiddo."

Phone to his ear, he followed the others from the room and closed the loft door behind them.

Ali didn't know what to say and then decided she didn't have to. She could feel the warmth of Gabe's chest, the steady rise and fall of it, his even, regular heartbeat, and let herself fall into it. She rested her head there, turning to feel his skin through the shirt he wore.

He changed the angle of his arms, one staying about her shoulders, the other cupping her head as she lay there.

"I'm so proud of you," he said quietly after a bit. "You held your own *and* you handed him his ass."

"Huh," she grunted then sighed. Being the woman of the hour was exhausting business. "You got my call, then?"

"Yes, sweetheart," he said, his hand stroking her back. "You remembered. I knew you were okay."

She turned to look up at him, partly in shock from the endearment, partly just to look at him.

"Not because of my heightened senses or any magical

powers," he added, his mouth twitching, "but because I believe in you. Though I admit I had a *feeling*, right before I got your call. You're strong and brave and you knew, deep inside, that once you named the whole thing publicly, it would come to this. Or a version of this. Personally, I'm glad it's this one. The you kicking ass version." He pressed a kiss to her head, just like Flynn.

Except, it didn't feel like Flynn's kiss. Not even a little.

She twisted to study his face. He was tired, his skin paler than its normal warm milky coffee.

"Can I ask you something?" She was taking a chance. A big one. But that *sweetheart* moments ago gave her confidence.

He nodded.

"Kiss me?"

Her voice was a whisper, but he heard. Lifting her slightly and lowering his head at the same time, he rested his lips on hers. Soft. Gentle. Light.

She sighed against his mouth. "More? I need . . . "

She got no further. He took her mouth in a devastating kiss. One meant to conquer. He invaded and vanquished her thoroughly. His tongue took possession of her mouth and as he angled her head to take more, they both groaned. She gave back, as much as she could, but was happy just to receive the heat, the passion, the sheer onslaught of tongue and lips. That man could do amazing things with his mouth and for once, Ali was content to be overpowered and not feel a competitive streak to match him.

She drank it in, the touches, the warmth. The closeness she'd never yearned for before. With him, it felt natural.

He shifted beneath her and she realised she wasn't the only one affected by the kiss. His body was rock-hard and yet he remained focused entirely on her mouth.

He finally drew away, kissing her jaw, moving down to her neck, nibbling a bit followed by the swirl of his tongue. She arched into him, offering more. He took and tasted. Their mingled breaths were unsteady and broken, and it felt so fucking sexy Ali thought she might come apart just from his kisses. *That was plain bonkers, obviously*, so she pulled back, gasping for air, and reached up to hold his face in her hands.

"Thank you," she said, soft and low. "I feel sooo much better."

The quick grin that split his face was reward enough, but then he rested his forehead against hers in such a tender gesture that her heart turned over.

"You don't ever have to ask me for kisses. They all belong to you now."

Chapter 26

Ali was pissed. *Seriously pissed.* And she wished she could use the term in the drunken sense. But no, she was totally pissed off. All the waiting, the hanging around. The processing. *That sucked, big time.* She felt dirty, tired and fed up. Her wrists hurt where the plastic had cut into her and some jabs from the cleaver knife where she'd tried to cut herself free were deep enough that they might leave scars. In a way, she hoped they did. *A little memento of her winning the battle.*

Her parents were due at any moment, and probably Moll, Dev and Frankie, too. Her family seemed to move in a pack and it was maddeningly comforting that they'd be here for her.

They burst into the hallway en masse, a garda scurrying along behind them.

"Darling," her mum cried as she saw her, came to a halt and slapped a hand to her mouth. "You're hurt! They didn't say you were hurt."

Ali looked down at herself, her T-shirt bloodstained and torn. *Ah, shit.* She'd forgotten they may not have been told what had actually happened.

"And you stink," Molly said, bypassing their mother and bringing Ali in for a hug.

"I'm not hurt. The blood, or this blood," she said, indicating her top, "isn't mine." She held up her wrists and patted at her hip. "These are superficial and will heal."

She returned Moll's hug and then stepped into her mother's arms. Her dad came in for the family hug special and Ali could feel tears prick behind her lashes. *Nope. Not crying here and now. And never again for that bastard.* Although, realistically, that could change.

"I'm fine," she said to the group of worried onlookers. "You should see the other guy," she joked. Badly.

"That is *exactly* what I want to do," her father interjected, grim and fierce. "I want a word with Jack Neary."

"Get in line, Dad," Dev added.

"You'll all get a turn." Flynn's voice cut through the general babbling. "If you want it." He walked over to the group, moving past each of them till he stood next to Ali. "I know Mac wouldn't let you shower earlier and I know that pissed you off. You know the reasons, so no whining over procedure. The last thing we need is the chain to be broken and Neary to have a gap, no matter how small, where he can elude us. That, well, *that* would really do you in. Not happening," he promised them all.

"Ali has been incredible and needs to take a breath. Neary is in questioning with a couple of our other senior detectives. Next up, he'll be charged. Ali . . . " He turned back to her, resting a hand on her back. "Do you want to talk to him? He'll be handcuffed and on a secured chair across from you. You don't have to. It's not a thing. But I can arrange it, if you want. If it will help."

She only needed a second. "Yeah, I want to have a chat with good ole Father Jack. Let's see how he feels now." She turned to a stern-faced Patrick Fitzgerald. "Dad, you don't have to see him. I'm not sure how it'll help."

"I'll see him," her dad insisted. "Make it happen, son."

Flynn nodded, directed Ali to the storeroom where clean clothes were available, and with a brief "Excuse me," headed back down the hall.

It took another half-hour, but Flynn returned to say Jack Neary had officially been charged with several counts of child abuse, along with other charges Flynn said he'd discuss later. Ali was puzzled by that but let her brother do his thing.

Her dad went in first, stayed a mere five minutes and came out grey-faced. He wrapped his arms tightly around Jo and they could all see how emotionally drained he was. He pulled away from his wife and went to stand in front of Ali.

"Can you ever forgive me?" His voice quivered as he stood forlornly, broken, before his middle daughter.

"Ah, Dad, stop." She touched his face, rubbing a tear from his cheek. "Stop, now. It's over. You didn't know. I didn't tell. The only one at fault is Jack."

They hugged, Ali welcoming her father's strong arms as they banded about her.

Jo stepped forwards and rested a hand on her husband's sleeve. "I have a suggestion," she said softly. "I know you're not one for therapy, Patrick, but I'd like us to go and see someone, as a family, at the very least us three, but also anyone else who needs to deal with blame and guilt. You and I certainly need that, my love." She stroked his arm tenderly, her own eyes full. "And we need to let Ali vent about us, to us, for our lack of care – our failure of duty as parents—"

"No, that's not what I think—" said Ali, but her mum shushed her.

"We need this, darling. And you do, too. I know you've seen someone and I'm grateful that you did. I'm not a psychologist, but even I know there's enough blame and recriminations whizzing around this family right now that we could have a miniseries written about us. A bestseller, naturally," she added with a wry smile.

Patrick nodded, his hand reaching to hold his wife's. "You are right, my Joesphine, that's exactly what we should do." He looked questioningly at the others.

"I could do a session with you," Dev said gruffly. "I feel shit that I was so wrapped up in myself that I saw nothing."

Ali smiled at him and nodded. "Okay, then, family therapy it is. But only those who want it. Moll, you were too little so no need for you to attend." *Please don't let her come*, Ali begged silently.

Molly looked pensive and made a non-committal sound.

"I'll arrange everything and keep you all in the loop via our WhatsApp group," Jo said. "Times and location, et cetera."

Garda Lennon poked her head around the corner. "We're ready for you, Ali," she said. "If you want."

Her smile was tight, her demeanour tense. *It must have been a tough session.*

Ali took a deep breath, exhaled slowly. Repeated. She needed this face to face. She needed him to see he hadn't broken her. *Not completely.* And even if she was never entirely whole again, she was fighting. Every inch of the way. And now she had the entire Fitzgerald family as back-up.

She felt like a warrior.

"Let's go."

The room was windowless, with one table and three chairs in the centre. A small table was against a side wall with what Ali assumed was recording equipment and another chair was next to it. It was almost a mirror of her time facing Mel, an eon ago. Her life was a HBO special at the very least, miniseries be damned.

A garda sat there, hands resting on the table, waiting. Another garda stood behind Jack Neary, who sat handcuffed on the single chair, his ankles loosely chained together underneath. It was attached to the floor. She knew, from Flynn, that this was normal, like before with Mel Carney, so the accused couldn't throw it at her. Or anyone else. It made her feel marginally safer.

Neary looked older. Greyer. Weaker. *Good*, she thought as she took a seat on the other side of the table. She'd agreed to have the conversation officially taped, though she reserved the right to have it used, or not, in court. There was no saying what he might reveal and she didn't want *all* of her business aired in public.

He glared at her, eyes bleak and steady. His hands, knotted together in front of him, were, however, white-knuckled.

"Your evidence won't stand up in a court of law," he spat. "No one will believe the ramblings of a child. You made everything up. I know it. You know it. You were just an attention-seeking junkie. Still are, by all accounts."

Ali sat, taking it all in. She wondered how to play this. How to get him to say, out loud, on tape, what he'd done. *He was clever, sharp, shrewd.* She decided to use some of the options Flynn had offered.

"Would you two please leave?" she asked both guards. "I'd like to talk to Mr Neary in private."

She deliberately didn't say "off the record" and specifically didn't ask for the tape to be turned off. She was hoping Neary would forget it was recording. She also knew that Flynn was listening from next door with a hidden audio feed to her ear and could be in the room within seconds if things went astray.

The guards argued for her safety, but she insisted and they left, leaving her alone with her abuser for the second time in as many days.

"So," she said, sitting forwards and bracing her arms on the table. "Why did you pick me? It's just us now, no one to impress with your righteous indignation. No one to lie to. Just me. The kid you shattered into tiny pieces. Again and again."

"You're delusional," he said coolly, like she'd offered him a coffee.

"Ah, you've memory loss," she said sadly. "That's rotten for you. I hadn't realised you'd aged so much, or so severely."

"There's nothing wrong with my memory. I'm as active as I ever was. I'm in perfect health!"

God, some men were such vain idiots.

"I did think so, when I saw you at my door earlier, but now? Now, I think you're a sad sack of shit."

He sneered. "You always had a potty mouth. I used like that about you."

375

"Oh yeah? What did I used to say?"

"Ha, you won't catch me out like that, missy. I'm way too smart to fall for your tricks."

"Was it when you made me repeat certain phrases? Like 'Please, Father Jack, let me suck your dick?' Or did you prefer it when I had to say, 'Your cock is so big, Father Jack, it'll never fit in my small mouth'?"

Ali removed her arms from the table and gripped her hands tightly beneath the smooth surface. She had to stop them from shaking or the whole table would rattle. She could feel her breath begin to hitch, so conjured up her "happy place" in her mind's eye, just like Dr Hearne had taught her, and relaxed her suddenly hunched shoulders.

"You were quite the smooth-talker, even back then."

"You were a fast learner," he whispered, leaning in. "Always a bright spark."

"Yeah, so you said. Many times. You were great with the praise, always trying to lure me, win me over. You liked how I picked up on your rules too, didn't you? How obedient I was. How did you know I'd never tell? How could you have trusted me? I genuinely want to know. It was pretty smart of you, I have to say, to choose me."

She leaned in too, like they were old buddies having a chat. She couldn't trust her hands yet, so kept them hidden.

He smiled, wide and easy. He'd been so handsome in his youth and his teeth were still white and even. *South America must have good dentistry*, she thought idly as she watched him lower his guard, bit by bit.

"You know why."

She swallowed. "Tell me." She hated that her voice had a wobble. "Tell me, like you used to."

He sat further forwards, his hands opening now, even within the confines of the cuffs.

"Let me hold your hand," he said, gruff and eager. "Let me *feel* you."

Ali held her breath. *No, no, no*, screamed in her head.

"Tell me first, tell me why you picked me." She was playing this game, making up the rules on the fly, and it was killing her.

Ali gripped the seat beneath the table, not allowing his voice to pull her back, to make her do as she was told, to obey.

He smiled again, with a touch of reminiscence. Honestly, someone meeting him for the first time would never see the monster beneath. *He was a fine actor, that was for sure.* She'd give him that, reluctantly.

"I preferred your long chestnut hair," he mused. "This bleached boy cut doesn't suit you at all. And though you're still thin, you finally grew some breasts and hips. Pity."

Ali's stomach contents swirled dangerously. That was his thing, young and prepubescent. *Gangly. Awkward.* She'd been an ideal candidate. In so many ways. Physically, she'd fitted his type perfectly. Emotionally, she'd been ripe and ready. She'd felt lost in those years, neglected. *Unheard.* And he'd offered time and an ear.

It had started out innocently enough. On her part, anyway. Extra chats and attention, special sweets that he knew were her favourite. Praise for all of her schoolwork. For how pretty she was in a specific dress.

She'd had a yearning for being noticed and he'd been a shark in shallow waters.

At first it had been jaunts with her and her sisters, then as Caro had other things on and Frankie became Caro's best friend, it was just Molly and her. But Molly never liked him, she now knew, nor trusted him, so had backed out of trips for ice cream or to the zoo or to see the latest cartoon film. Her parents had been long-time friends with him. *Trusted friends.* They'd never once doubted his sincerity. His offer to help out. She wondered now if they'd even noticed that the focus began to be solely on her.

He'd got more daring as the first year advanced to the second. He'd babysit for the whole gang. Dev would be upstairs doing homework, Caro in her room on the phone or sketching. Molly would go to bed, always a half-hour before Ali, and he'd take her hand and lead her to the drawing room.

Sometimes he'd sit in one of the armchairs and cradle her on his lap, his erection digging into her bottom as he'd fondled her tiny breast buds. Other times, horrible times, way too many times, he'd slide her to the floor and force her to unzip his pants and stroke him, her little hands crushed under his as he brought himself relief.

Then there were the worst times. By the time she was twelve, he'd wanted more.

Ali shook herself out of nightmare lane and refocused on her goal. She could do this – she just had to lock down her fear and power through. She was pretty shit at mentoring, even herself, because her fear was rising higher in her belly by the second.

She looked him in the eye. "I changed my hair the day you left for Wexford. I never wanted to be that girl again. I never will be."

He smirked. "You were already starting to turn when I left – started getting cramps, beginning to widen at the hips. I thought that would have happened earlier. You were a late bloomer."

No. She hadn't been. She'd got her first period at eleven, like most of her friends, but something Jack had said, in passing, had freaked her out and changed her forever.

"A real woman, even a teenager with all the physical accoutrements, was too much for you to handle," she said. "You needed us weak and small. Malleable and powerless. All to feed your giant ego and pathetic greed."

On firmer footing again, Ali sat back, resting her hands in her lap, all casual. As if her body wasn't a riotous mess of tight muscles and churning organs. As if she wasn't about to explode in remembered agony.

Neary sat back too, mirroring her calm. Maybe he was calm. Maybe he believed he still had a chance. She was going to shatter that calm.

She stood. Pushed her chair in and leaned forwards, hands gripping its back. "You really are a piece of shit, Jack Neary. I've gained some notoriety from being on TV and I'm going public with my story, so even if by some extreme circumstance you get off, I'll be badmouthing you till the day I die."

"And that can't come soon enough," he snarled. "You and your bloody show. Acting all queenlike, baking and teaching morons how to make pastry. Ha! A fool could do that."

"Aw, how sweet. You're a fan of my show. I'm flattered. I didn't realise you even knew about it. I thought you'd stay clear of anything to do with me. I can't believe you spoke to Frankie. It was like you were hoping for a confrontation.

"I'm not a kid or afraid of you, so you're the one who had something to lose. Oh, I get it!" She snapped her fingers. "You wanted to see if I'd blanked it all out or pretended it never happened. Wrong." She made a buzzer sound. "So wrong. I've been to therapy and if my diaries aren't enough, I'll allow Dr Hearne to release my files to the court. You're toast, Jack Neary."

"And you nearly were," he muttered angrily. "Stupid imbeciles can do nothing right."

"Excuse me?" Ali was confused. She must have misheard him. "What imbeciles? Doing what?"

"I knew, once I heard through the grapevine about the TV offer, that you'd be on air, gaining fame, that you'd think you were capable of ruining me. That you wouldn't stay quiet."

Ali was seething inside – *how could that bastard ever imagine that once she found out he was home, she wouldn't find him? Did he think she'd let him get away with it? Did he think she was that meek? Still?*

But she said, "When did you get back to Ireland, anyway? We heard you made Argentina your home. What brought you back?"

"Not that it's any of your business, but I came back late January. People here need my skills in PR – I have a great rapport with the public, you know. I have set up many charities in my time away. And it was noticed by the powers that be. I was *asked* back, for my expertise."

"God, people must be very hard up, asking for your help," she sneered. "And how many young kids in South America bore the brunt of your vile behaviour? How many lives did you ruin there?"

He smiled. An awful, sick kind of smile. "Those children were very . . . shall we say, grateful."

She braced her arms, trying to hold herself back from taking a swing at him. His assumption that she'd just lie down and let him swan around Dublin, free and clear, with no justice served, made her see red. And knowing he continued to abuse? More red and furious as hell. But not everything added up.

"What has my TV show got to do with anything?"

"I couldn't let you go on air. You'd got cocky, too big for your boots. Become a liability. Thought you knew it all. Capable of saying untruths about me once you knew I was back in Ireland. Back then you were just a girl, a slip of a thing. You knew who your betters were. You knew how to behave, how to please."

How to please? God, that hurt. It bruised her in so many ways, ruined her in so many others. She'd never fully please a man again. And that was on Jack Neary.

"You taught me that, didn't you, Jack? How to please you. But you were a poor teacher. I've learned so much more since then. Stuff you wouldn't believe. With way better teachers."

"That Indian bastard wouldn't know how to please a whore, so I bet you do all the work – you were good at that, weren't you, pet? You always knew how to please a man."

Ali bit the inside of her cheek. She wanted to wail and curse but gritted her teeth as he began to unravel before her eyes. *Just a bit more taunting needed.*

She walked round the table, swinging her slim hips as provocatively as she could.

"Still don't want a woman, Jack? Still not able to get it up for anyone but a child? Maybe if you show me the old ways, I could help you. You could pretend. Just close your eyes and think of all the times you made me kneel before you."

She swallowed hard against the bile threatening to overcome her. She gestured for him to swivel round in the chair, so he was sitting sideways on it, facing her. She dropped to her knees in front of him, resting her palms on his thighs as he inhaled sharply and sat back, his hands pulled up to his chest.

"Do you remember this, Jack, how I'd unzip you slowly and reach in to ease your distress, as you called it? Do you remember what I used say?" She softened her voice, made it breathy and high, childlike. "What do you need, Father Jack, how can I help you?" She returned to her normal voice though kept it light. "And you'd say . . . " She wriggled closer, lowering herself to sit back on her calves so she'd appear small. "You'd say, 'Take me in your mouth, little girl, and suck me hard.'"

"Take me in your mouth, little girl, and suck me hard," he rasped at exactly the same time.

His eyes had closed and he was smiling, his handcuffed hands now rubbing his erection as he sold himself up the river.

Ali stood abruptly. "Gotcha, you perverted piece of shit."

She backed away as his eyes shot open and he realised what he'd done.

His face grew purple, eyes bulging as he lunged for her.

"You bitch! You should have been done by now. Stupid people can't follow simple orders. And you should have died in that bomb! I wanted you to die!" he roared.

He'd forgotten his feet were also chained together and as she darted backwards from him, he toppled over, landing on the floor with a heavy thud.

"You tricked me," he shouted up at her. "It's entrapment. My lawyer will see to it. You'll see."

"Oh, grow up, you big baby. You didn't have to say a fucking word. No one held a gun to your head." She paused, his previous words sinking in. "Wait, bomb?" she stammered, her heart suddenly racing so fast she thought she might faint. "What do you know about the bomb? Do you know who set it?" She stopped, horrified, realisation dawning. "Did you do that? Did you try to kill me with a fucking *bomb*?"

"Ask the Indian," he sneered. "I suppose pillow talk isn't what it used to be."

The door burst open and Flynn, the two previous gardai and Gabe entered.

"It's over, Neary. You're done," Flynn said sharply as he hauled the man to his feet.

Ali was beginning to shake now the adrenalin was wearing off and she wrapped her arms about herself to ward off the tremors. It reminded her of one more thing she needed to say – her thin, narrow frame and lack of curves being the very things, the very features, that saved others.

"The only good thing to come out of this was that you didn't get to Molly. At least I did that."

"That little tub? Nah, I was fine with you. I wasn't *ever* going for her."

Ali was stunned. "I heard you! You *told* me if I didn't do what you said, or if I got my period, you'd try out Molly next. I *heard* you!"

Jack Neary, ex-priest and lowest of lowlife, laughed. "We'll never know, will we?"

And he was bundled out of the room.

There was silence as Gabe and Flynn stood by her side, neither reaching out to touch her. She was glad. She wasn't ready.

"What did you do?" Flynn asked finally. "You said, 'at least I did that'. What?"

She looked at him, her eyes blank with shock. She shook her head. "Nothing," she whispered, "nothing."

Gabe cleared his throat. "She starved herself. She stopped eating. It was the beginning of her eating disorder."

Flynn's head spun round like he'd been slapped. "What? What did you say? Ali, what did you do?" He reached out and placed his hands gently on her shoulders, bending his head to study her eyes.

Gabe continued, "And it is my guess she tried to fatten up Molly, gave her extras – desserts, sweets and so on. The thinner Ali got, the later her period would arrive, or at least be halted. The less she ate, the more she gave to Molly, thereby ensuring that Neary's focus remain on her. And Molly would be safe."

"No, baby," Flynn groaned. "Oh, *God*, no." And he drew his uncomplaining sister fully into his arms.

She let him. What else could she do? She was laid bare. Open and wounded to the quick. So hurt, so tired and worn to a frazzle. She knew she'd have loads more questions to ask, loads of background information to catch up on. Loads of answers from Gabe. She knew she should be furious with him – and she would be, just as soon as she got about three days' sleep. And a shower. A long, hot shower. One that would wash everything away: blood, dirt, pain, memories and Jack's particular smell. She'd thought she was going to gag when she got close to him earlier on the floor in her loft and again just now. But she'd gulped it back. Held on. Had to.

She lifted her head and met Flynn's steady eyes. He was the ballast in their family, always there for each of them, always the first to defend them. She knew he was hurt about her past but right now, she couldn't deal with anyone's hurt but her own.

"I need a shower," she said, her voice a rasp. "I want to go home. No," she said when he nodded, "not to Dalkey. To my flat. I need space and sleep and no fussing. Please," she added as he shook his head in instinctive denial of her wishes in his belief that he knew best.

Flynn sighed. "I'll get a car to take you home. Mum and the gang all came in one, so there probably isn't room, though Dev and Frankie could get a taxi . . . "

He trailed off as she just stared him down, her chin tilted in that determined way of hers. It was times like this she reminded him of Molly, the most innocently stubborn one of the lot. Butter wouldn't melt in Molly's mouth – until you crossed her.

"I'll take Ali home and see her safely inside," Gabe said, his tone even, steady.

Just like he always was, standing there like nothing of note had happened. Ali glanced at him, frowning suddenly. His eyes were dead. Cold. Not Gabe eyes at all. Maybe not so steady.

"I don't think . . . " Flynn began.

Ali pulled back from him, resigned. "It's fine," she said. "You know Bossy Boots will get his way, so I might as well just go. I haven't the energy nor inclination for a stand-off with MacScot right now. I just want to go home."

Shit. She could feel a pressure behind her eyes, a gritty, burning sensation, and she wasn't ready.

"Come on." She stepped towards the door, pulling off her hidden earpiece that had recorded the entire encounter with Neary. "Here, take this. Do what you want with it. I'll testify. But . . . " She turned back to her brother, her eyes fierce and unyielding. "If you *ever* tell Molly, or anyone, what Gabe said about why I got so thin or what Neary had me believe he'd do to Molly? I'll deny it to my dying day. And," she said, adding another bite, "I'll *never* forgive you."

Flynn clenched his jaw, paused, his eyes closing briefly, and nodded once. "Understood."

Chapter 27

There was total silence in the car. Ali sat with her body curved away from him, her head resting against the glass, eyes staring blankly. She didn't look at him at all. Not once.

Gabe held the steering wheel tighter, his knuckles looking stark in the weird interior light from the funky dashboard of his jeep. He made an effort to relax and breathe and not, absolutely not, howl in a cauldron of frustration, anger and helplessness. That, he knew well, would help precisely no one. And certainly not the brave and remarkable woman beside him.

He sighed. He had to get her back to her own home – shower and bed. He'd make her a special tea while she was in the bathroom and put proper salve on her wounds. He always had a small box of supplies in his car, wherever he went, for any eventuality. His mum had taught him that.

He pulled the car to a stop and switched off the engine. Neither stirred. Gabe let a few moments lapse as Ali remained still. Straightening his shoulders, he got out of the jeep and walked round to open the passenger door. The pale face that tilted back to meet his eyes almost broke him. She was dazed and clearly in shock.

"Oh, sweetheart," he muttered, reaching down to gather her in his arms.

She made a murmur of protest, which he ignored,

and, closing the door with his hip, he walked up to her front door.

"Keys?" he asked quietly.

She gestured vaguely to her jacket pocket and with a quiet "Excuse me," he dug inside and retrieved them, propping her on one raised knee as he opened the door.

Inside her home, he took her directly to the bathroom. After depositing her on the side of the bath, he began by taking off her jacket, then her shoes and socks. He hauled her up and undid her trousers, sliding them down her legs before setting her back on the bath.

"Up," he ordered, and she raised her arms as he pulled the oversized police-issue T-shirt over her head.

He stopped then, hesitant to put his hands on her more intimately. Her bra and pants were matching – white cotton with some kind of embroidery along the cup. She caught his gaze and her mouth twitched.

"Super sexy, eh? Go ahead, I don't have the energy even to unclasp the bra. Don't even know why I bother wearing one," she said with a certain amount of sadness.

Gabe groaned. "It's so men have something to do, unclasping them, to slow them down as their bodies react to the sight of covered breasts. We're animals, really, and trust me, the sight of breasts as beautiful as yours is enough to undo me. *I* need the time."

He reached round and undid the clasp. Letting the straps fall forwards, the simple garment came away in his hand. Her breasts were perfect. *Small. Pale.* He groaned. Straightened, his body feeling strained in particular areas. He needed to grow the hell up and focus.

"Up," he said again and as she clung to him, he slid off her underwear.

She stepped out of the scrap of cotton and simply leaned into him. He knew there was nothing remotely sexual in the gesture and that instinctive trust of hers, to lean on him, clutched at his chest.

He stretched across her, switched on the shower over the bath and pulled back the curtain.

"In," he said. "Do you need me to help?" he offered.

"I can manage. Thanks." Her voice was raw. Barely there at all.

"Okay. I'll leave some nightclothes on your bed. Climb in and when you're done, I'll bring you tea and toast. I've got something for these, too." He touched her hip gently then turned her wrists over and bent to place his lips on the broken skin.

"Why?" she whispered. "Why are you doing this? I'm still mad at you. When I've the energy, I'll be really angry, you know that."

"Even so," was all he could manage as he placed a large towel on the sink so she could reach it from the bath.

Gabe wasn't actually sure he could say much else. She was so broken, standing before him, every ounce of her screaming dejection. He knew it was the exhaustion and aftershock, he'd seen it many times.

But not on Ali.

He left the bathroom door ajar in case she called for him, remembering the last time she bathed at his apartment, and went into the kitchen to switch on the kettle. He hurried back out to his jeep, grabbed a box of supplies, locked it and went back inside. The shower was still running. *Good.* She needed this cleansing in more ways than usual.

He made his special tea, filled with herbs his ancestors had used to soothe both body and mind after a battle. He put some bread on to toast and lathered it with butter when it popped. He rummaged in his box for salve and gauze bandages then laid everything out together on a tray. And sat down, his bones suddenly weary.

Every joint aching, Ali climbed into bed. Her fresh clothes felt soft against her skin and she slid down beneath the duvet with a sigh. She reached for her phone and texted Gabe rather than call for him – she wasn't sure she trusted her voice:

Ready.

She heard his phone beep and seconds later his tall, dark form appeared in her doorway. He carried a tray and she hoisted herself back up the bed to receive it on her lap. Her stomach growled, loudly. The toast looked like the most appetising thing ever and a memory of Caro, in her hospital bed having just given birth to Toby all those years ago, assailed her. Caro inhaling tea and toast like it was gourmet fare. Trauma, even one that produces a child, changes how a person feels about toast.

"Thanks," she managed before stuffing a triangle of buttered bliss into her mouth.

Gabe sat on the bed, further down so as not to disturb the tray. He watched her eat, in silence, which she thought ought to be odd but somehow wasn't. She simply didn't care. Hunger was everything. She gobbled all three slices and lay back, content.

"Drink this," Gabe said, handing her a mug of

steaming liquid. "No," he added at her expression of distaste, "don't ask, just drink. It is an elixir, if you will. An ancient healing remedy from my mother's family. It will help."

Doubtful, she sniffed and recoiled. Not because it was horrible, but it was . . . *pungent. Strong. Acidic, maybe.* Her chef's nose began to itemise the ingredients, but she floundered.

"I'd really like to know what I'm taking," she said as she sipped the brew carefully. "It's, hmm, lemony. Ginger and cumin. Sage? How could I taste sage?"

She drank some more, finding the weird-tasting drink surprisingly easy to swallow. Before realising it, it was almost gone, and a warmth and easiness enveloped her body.

"You've drugged me," she slurred. Just a little, but she could hear her voice was off.

Gabe smiled as he reached for one wrist, angled it so he could smooth some ointment across her gashes.

Ali hadn't realised he'd been playing doctor while she drank her tea and was startled not long after when she discovered one wrist was already neatly bound in white bandages. She obediently switched her almost empty mug to her bound hand and offered the other for his ministrations.

"Where did you learn this skill?" she asked, resting the empty mug on her bedside table and sliding down under the covers.

He carefully pulled back the duvet and angled her sleep shorts discreetly so he could attend to the cut on her hip. He straightened and tucked her in.

Yup, she was definitely drugged. All about her seemed

kind of glowy and soft, as if she were watching life through a lens smoothed with Vaseline. It felt nice. *Comforting. Safe.*

"All done," Gabe said, collecting his bits and pieces and setting them back on the tray. "Do you need anything else?"

"I didn't brush my teeth," Ali tried to say, but it sounded awfully like "shush my meet", so she gave up on trying to make him understand.

"I think the world of dentistry will be fine with this one lapse. Comfortable?"

She was. So comfy and cosy and warm and comfy . . . *I'm blathering*, she thought, *and I don't care if Gabe thinks I've lost my mind. He made me drink drugs.* She giggled. *Drink drugs!* It sounded funny.

As her mind began to slip away, she struggled for a moment – *something important. Something to say. Oh, yeah.* She needed to say thank you to the man standing patiently by her bed as she snuggled under the covers.

"You're a very odd, sexy man," she said instead.

Oh, well. She'd fix that right up tomorrow when she remembered to be mad at him.

Gabe woke, uncomfortable and not well-rested. He'd gone back to the station for a few hours after Ali fell into a deep sleep, returning about 4 a.m. to check on her. By then he was drooping so took the couch. Not a good idea, but he didn't want to disturb her much-needed rest.

He glanced at his watch and, groaning, hauled himself to the bathroom. A quick shower helped and though he hated wearing the same shirt two days in a row, needs must. He moved about Ali's kitchen, finding what he needed, and thanked his lucky stars she was a chef first and baker second. He pulled out flour, eggs, milk and pure Canadian maple syrup then began by frying some decent bacon strips and putting some coffee on for them both.

He couldn't help the dip in his belly when he saw, next to her bags of coffee, a selection of his favourite herbal teas. She'd bought them for him, during those few precious weeks when they'd been a *thing*, whatever that was.

Seeing each other every day, wrapping each other up every night, or as near as . . .

It was, despite the worry and concern for Ali's safety, the happiest he'd been in years. *Or ever.* Their banter, their jibes, their talks – both heavy and light – had filled him with a scary mixture of joy and trepidation. She brought all the joy – him, not so much. He knew she didn't want anything serious. She told him, many times. Now he knew why, or thought he did.

But her reasons didn't compute with him. She believed she wasn't cut out for a long-term relationship. *Hell, who was until you were in one, with the right person?* He wouldn't have said that about himself either, till her and all of her complexities had invaded his life.

His gnawing gut would demand he ask himself if he was donning a hero complex, if he was in saviour mode. But his head said *no. She pretty much saved herself.* All of his "superpowers" and special senses hadn't, in the end, been worth a damn. She'd trusted him and, more importantly, herself. *Surely she knew that was huge?* If not, it was his job to tell her.

"Hey."

A groggy voice interrupted his musings as he whipped up a batch of batter, which he hoped would end in fluffy pancakes.

"Good morning." He turned to see a tousled Ali leaning against the door frame.

He swallowed hard as the sight of her sleep T-shirt hitched high on her thigh, exposing creamy silky skin, had his body tightening in response. He shifted uncomfortably and focused on her face. *Bad idea. She looked stunning.* Her blonde spikes were askew, her mouth was all pouty and soft. And her cornflower blue eyes looked fresh and alert and, *thank God*, clear and rested.

He quickly turned back to the heating pan to avoid staring like a loon.

Pouring the batter, he said, "Take a seat – this will be ready in a few moments."

Ali grunted and straightened a kitchen chair, the scrape on the tile loud in the sudden silence.

"The smell of bacon and coffee woke me," she said after a beat. "Thank you for this."

Gabe could hear drawers being opened and shut as she set the small table. He turned with his plated meals and set one down in front of her.

"Eat," he said and poured her a mug of her favourite brew.

She sat and took a long drink then sighed in apparent ecstasy.

"You've learned well, my son," she said in a Mr. Miyagi voice.

Even he'd seen *The Karate Kid* back in the day. He smiled and, to please her, gave a little bow.

She laughed and grinned at him. "Look at you, all twentieth-century TV reruns. I'm impressed." She smirked now, around a bite of pancake.

A dribble of syrup ran down her chin and his desire to lean over and lick it off was so intense he had to shake himself. Then she used her tongue to swipe it anyway and he was very glad he was sitting down with a napkin covering his crotch.

This was ridiculous. It had to stop. They had things to discuss. Misunderstandings to clear up.

She wasn't acting mad at him but knowing Ali, she was saving it up for a humdinger. He'd prefer to avoid that particular scenario. He pushed aside his plate, noticing she'd eaten at least half before putting her utensils down. *Good. She'd feel better with some carbs and protein.* He poured her a top-up, one for himself, despite her eyebrows raising, and cleared his throat.

"We have to talk about what happened," he said in his usual calm way.

"Which part?" Her sarcasm was back. "The abuse? The not telling? The shame and blame? Neary? The *fucking* bomb? You tell me, Hotshot Detective, which part do *you* want to talk about? Maybe start with the part you neglected to tell me." She sat back, arms folded, one leg crossed over the other, foot swinging. Waiting.

He was in deep trouble. That much was obvious.

"In my defence," he began to a loud "Ha!" from her. "In my defence," he repeated, "I only figured out the bomb connection to Neary at pretty much the same time he went round to you at the loft. I was packing up to come and tell you, when my phone, with your call, buzzed in my pocket.

395

"I had already sent a detail to collect him and only seconds before your call, I received word that he was missing. So, I *was* including you. And Flynn," he added, so she'd know he respected both the chain of command and her close family ties. He didn't intend to sound pleading but realised that was how it came out. "I was doing my job *and* keeping you in the loop."

"Yeah, yeah. I get that. What I want to know is how the hell did Neary get the skills to build a bomb? And why the fuck was he trying to kill me? I didn't even know he was back until Frankie said. I was no threat to him."

"That's not how he saw it," Gabe said quietly.

And he told her all he knew.

About when Mel was first arrested and several things he'd said, or indeed didn't say, had struck Gabe as odd. To start with, in no particular order, a) Mel genuinely didn't want to hurt Ali, b) was unhappy that she had been, c) was happy enough to give away his accomplice's name and location. Garcia hadn't been found until last night but thanks to the money trail, they were able to trace the card he used for withdrawals and found him holed up in a bar in the inner city. And, d) Mel was very obviously not smart enough to mastermind the whole thing.

Finally, Gabe told Ali about Mel recognising Neary as he left the police station and confessing to Gabe about the meetings outside the Golden Goose. About how he didn't know the name of the man in the swanky car, just that he was rich, powerful and dangerous. With that, he'd also surrendered Juan Garcia. The jig was definitely up. And with Neary in custody, Mel actually felt safer with both him and Garcia out of the way.

That information alone would have tied things up, though Mel wasn't, really, the most credible of witnesses. Gabe could have got a warrant for any CCTV in the area around the pub where they met, but so far, that wasn't necessary. It had also become clear to Gabe that Mel had a serious and long-term drug habit and that the whole ruse of his wife wanting him to be a star was just that – a ruse.

What Mel wanted was more cocaine. And he had very definitely drained his bank accounts buying what had already gone up his nose. Mel needed more money and more drugs, then one would lead to the other and of course cycle back again. It was Juan, Mel's Spanish-speaking sidekick, who drew the link to Neary. He wasn't, it turned out, Spanish but Argentinian. And had arrived in Ireland the same time as Jack Neary back in late January.

Gabe's team had discovered an account among Neary's bank statements that had transfers to another account called simply AF. Each of the amounts deposited into that account coincided with the dates of each of the attempts to hurt Ali on her bike and the break-ins. And the clincher? The day of the bomb. Sure, Mel was in the clear for that, but no surprise here, Juan wasn't. And the nail in the coffin? The only recipients to draw from that account were Mel Carney and Juan Garcia. Gabe sat back, sipped some cold coffee, grimaced and stood to take a drink of water.

"So, I'm assuming the account AF is my initials. And that Jack set this whole thing in motion months ago. Why? What was he hoping would happen? I don't get it." Ali was frustrated and puzzled.

"Neary was running scared. Because of his days in Irish TV before he went to South America, he had heard, though old pals, that you were going to be staring in a baking show. He watched the recordings of the afternoon slots you'd done previously and like anyone who saw them, knew you would make a great presenter. What that would give you, in his mind, was clout. Exposure. Fame. And he knew you would have a following," Gabe explained.

"But that doesn't explain why he would want me out of the picture. And why drag Mel into it?"

Gabe shoved his hand though his hair, tired and weary of the whole business. "The competition was a great way for Neary to get someone to do his dirty work for him. He studied each of the potential 'winners' and as you know, they didn't realise you already had it in the bag. He introduced Juan to Mel – already, it seems in the drug world, a known user, so an easy mark.

"Juan promised all manner of supplies if Mel would help him to get you off the show under the pretence that he simply wanted the fame. I don't know how hard Mel fought against the idea, but my guess is not very. Cocaine is a very powerful carrot and as long as Mel believed you'd just be frightened and feel unable to work, he was okay to participate."

"But the bomb? I mean, shit, Gabe, that's just bonkers." Ali sighed, unable to grasp the whole sorry mess.

"The bomb was cheaply and poorly made. According to Juan, who remains in custody, he figured it out via the internet and some self-confessed nefarious dealings he'd done back home in Argentina. Either way, if it had exploded right next to you, it may not have killed you but would certainly have put you out of action."

"Some comfort that is," Ali replied.

"I know," Gabe agreed. "And when that failed, Neary seems to have decided on the direct approach. Your show was now airing and already had a massive and growing fan base. He couldn't risk you having a platform where the public might believe you should you chose to call him out."

Ali folded her arms and said, thoughtfully, "I still feel sorry for Mary, Karl and Blaine. They were all part of this mess in one way or another and were duped. Yeah, I know I justified it before, but I'm the one with the positive career trajectory. I'm definitely including each of them with regular guest spots on season two. There's no reason, when Mel's tie to this debacle comes out, that they should in any way be tarred with the same brush."

"That's thoughtful of you but probably unnecessary. Don't they say all publicity is good publicity?"

She raised an eyebrow at him. "You're quoting PR propaganda now?"

Gabe shrugged. "I'm learning."

Ali tapped her fingers abstractedly on the table, having taken it all in. "Will the charges stick? Neary's, I mean?"

"They will," Gabe assured her.

When he'd returned to the station, Neary was a defeated, pathetic mess. Mel's testiomony against Neary was enough on its own without the bank trail of evidence, but it felt good to have all bases covered. Gabe had done another round of questions with him, along with another detective, while Flynn had stayed outside, listening via a feed. Neary had revealed how he'd been sure Ali's fame would give her a believable platform and with the confidence she'd gained from her show, he was scared she'd tell all. Whether it would have gone down like that, they'd never know. It was what it was.

"I thought Flynn would go for Neary last night," Ali said, reaching for her mug and turning it round in her hands.

Gabe winced. Hopefully, she'd never know that he and Flynn had been "given" private access to Jack Neary for ten minutes. They'd walked up to the front desk, officially signed off duty, so there could be no recriminations later, and headed back to the holding cell. The garda usually on duty outside was absent and Neary was, "strangely", alone within.

All sound was off, all cameras blind. No one disputed their right to it and no one questioned when Flynn had subsequently requested that a doctor attend Neary. Flynn and Gabe had closed the door behind the groaning man when they'd exited, both replacing their jackets, Flynn flexing his hand, Gabe wiping blood from his fingers with his handkerchief. It's amazing what pressure on an open wound can inflict.

"Flynn knows better than to leave a mark on a suspect," he said truthfully.

Both he and Flynn were experts in inflicting pain that didn't actually break bones. Maybe one day Gabe would regret what he'd done to Neary, but that day would be a long time coming.

"Will it all go to court? Will I have to testify? Because I *will*." Ali's tone was fierce, determined. "I'll do what it takes to put him away."

"I don't know," Gabe answered truthfully as he got

up to scrape their plates and load them into the dishwasher. "You'll need to check in with your solicitor."

"Dad's hired one for me. He didn't need to – I could have done it." She sounded petulant.

Gabe leaned down and rested his hand on her tapping fingers. "Let him do this for you. He believes in his heart that he's failed as a parent and if this helps him to heal his own wounds, be the bigger person."

She grunted. Sighed. Mumbled under her breath. But he knew she'd listened.

She got up, microwaved her coffee on medium for a few seconds and, back still to him, asked the question he was dreading.

"How did you know about the food? My eating problems." She whirled back to glare at him. "I don't have an eating disorder! I never did, not like some do. I just needed to help. I needed to do something to protect Molly."

"And then?" Gabe prodded gently.

Ali slumped down on her chair. "Then . . . then it became a habit. A way to prove I could save others. He could always come back for me then, not some other girl who'd have had her life taken from her."

"*Ali*," was all Gabe could say or his voice would give out.

"Don't feel sorry for me!" she snapped. "Don't you dare!"

He stayed silent. She wouldn't believe him if he said sorry was the farthest emotion he felt when summing her up in his head. *Brave, fearless, warrior.* Those words fit.

"Why did you choose food as a career?" he asked after a bit.

"I know!" she almost laughed. "Daft, wasn't it? I suppose I got pleasure from seeing others enjoy what I created. They were happy when they ate my food. I have a great palette. I'm good at flavours and balances. I can be inventive and diners seemed to enjoy my mixes. Then . . . " She rose and put her empty mug in the top rack of the dishwasher. "Then I wanted more. Sometimes cooking, which I believe is an art, felt a bit overwhelming, sort of a bit runaway. Damn! I'm not explaining myself well." She stopped, hoisted herself up onto the counter and swung her legs, looking at the floor.

"You switched to baking because it is a science. There are rules. Measures and weights. Known formulae. Control."

Her shoulders slumped. The swinging stopped.

"Do you have to be so smart? It took me months of therapy to wrap my head around that and you figure it out in weeks. *Grrr.* And in the interest of transparency, I did get help for my food control, too. In my early teens, after, well, *after.* I was so scared he'd come back and choose Molly that I threw up my dinner most nights.

"That went on for some time, but I started getting stomach aches. The beginnings of an ulcer, the doc said when Mum eventually took me to see a specialist. I was old enough to know that wasn't okay, so went back to tiny portions.

"By sixteen, I was doing better. We had a health thing at school and I knew I could still eat less, stay thin but be healthy, too. Veggies and shit." She smiled up at him, a glimmer of the sarky Ali he'd grown to know. "Yup, I was one of those obnoxious teens who avoided sugar like the plague. And yeah, I get the irony with me being a baker now. So, sue me. I like when people drown in sensation as one of my confections melt in their mouths. It's my happy place."

"When did your cycles become regular?" Gabe asked.

Ali's head snapped up. "Are you shitting me? You want to know when I got my period? No. No, MacScot, you don't get to know that. You're so fucking weird. Wait, why? *Why* would you want to know that?"

"I need to know you are okay, that your body is well. That the physical effects are not lasting." The second those words were out of his damn fool mouth he saw the crater he'd just dived into.

She gaped at him. She had every right to. He was a first-class idiot.

"Lasting effects? You want to know about any lingering physical effects? Okay, Doc, I get semi-regular periods." She spoke as if to an idiot. "Happy to hear my reproductive organs are in working order?"

"That's not wh—"

"And as for the other long-term effects, well, you've had first-hand experience of those, haven't you? Or let me clarify, you *haven't* had *any* experience of that. Hand or mouth. Jesus!" She jumped down from the counter and stormed past him. "You're an asshole. I'm going to take a shower. Be gone when I'm done."

Gabe watched her go and leaned his head on the door frame, banging that stupid brain of his over and over.

How dare he! Ali rinsed the shampoo from her hair, letting the hot water trail over her as she turned round under the shower. *How the fuck* dare *he!* He was the most irritating, ignorant, stupid, meddling, nosy piece of whatever she'd ever had the misfortune to know. *Does my body work? What the actual fuck?* She began soaping to shave her legs and as she drew the razor rhythmically up and down her long limbs, other words sneaked into her brain. Other words that also described Gabriel Mackenzie very well. Honest. Kind. Caring. Thoughtful. *Damn him.* Sexy as hell. Generous. Smart. *No one could say Mac wasn't smart.*

She'd have to delete ignorant and stupid from her previous medley of name-calling. A pox on him, anyway. Him and his wanting to be sure her health was okay. Because she knew now she'd calmed down that he was genuinely concerned that her body would function. With zero ulterior motive other than her well-being. He was that kind of man.

Turning off the water, she then reached for her towel and stepped from the bathtub. *Feck it!* She'd be the one having to apologise. But Ali was woman enough to speak up when she was in the wrong. She'd learned, the hard-knock way, that the truth will, in fact, set you free.

She'd find her phone and text him, or maybe she'd phone. *Nah, that would freak him* . . . She came to a halt in the living room. He was seated on her couch. He hadn't left. *Oh.* She wished her stomach would settle. It must be the pancakes and syrup. Too much sugar made her jumpy.

He looked up and she couldn't help but notice the quick appraisal he gave her towel-clad body. But he was a gentleman, through and through, and brought his eyes to hers pretty sharpish. They glowed, his pupils dark, like he'd seen the best chocolate cake ever. Or the most beautiful woman. He was staring at her, though. *Huh.*

He stood, made to step towards her and sat back down. *Abruptly.* Now, she was puzzled. Gabe was never unsure. Never *uneasy.* A shiver ran down her spine.

"What?" she said, worry etching her voice.

"I . . . please put some clothes on. We, I, need to talk. To you."

That did not bode well. But what was she expecting? She'd told him in no uncertain terms they were done. *Was this the official goodbye?*

Ali turned and went to her bedroom, gathering clothes. Her chest felt leaden. *Goodbyes sucked.* She dressed quickly, choosing jeans and a flannel shirt. Sure, it was summer, but she'd been through shit and if she needed flannel, so be it.

"What?" she asked again, returning to the living room and sitting on the large chair he'd once sprawled in, listening to jazz.

His hands were white-knuckled as they hung clenched between his knees where his elbows were propped.

"I think we should take a break," he said.

"A break?"

"From this. Us." He gestured between them.

"There is no us, Highlander. We had a fling. It's over. There's no break to take."

Ali was confused. She thought they were on the same page.

"No," he said steadily. "It is *not* over. Not for me. But I do think we need distance and I am prepared to give us that. If you are."

"Hold up." Ali raised both of her hands in that time-honoured fashion. "We're at cross purposes. We don't have an 'us'," she air quoted. "Ergo, no break needed.

No distance to be had. You'll hightail it off to bonny Scotland or sunny Oklahoma or wherever, and I'll work on my TV show and accompanying books. Simple."

Except it didn't feel simple. It felt like the hardest thing she was ever going to have to do. Say goodbye to this man. This one man who saw her before she saw herself. Who never made her feel less, though she knew she was.

"I know you have said all along you don't do relationships. I didn't, either. But what do you call what we have had? It is more than a fling. You know it and I know it. We are good together, Ali. Good for each other. I feel . . . I feel like you see me. That you *get* me. And you don't mind my . . . oddities."

Oh, shit. She was drowning. He shouldn't say things like that. It was all wrong. It's just . . . he was supposed to leave. Why did he have to say these lovely things? He *wasn't* helping! She looked at him helplessly. Unsure what to say, what to do. Ali hated being unsure.

"I *do* see you, Gabe, but it won't work. It can't. I can't. I'm too messed up. I'll never be normal."

"Normal is overrated, I should know." Gabe got to his feet, crossed the space between them and hunkered in front of her. "Ali." He took her face in his hands and kissed her.

Not a hot, burning Gabe special but one of his gentle "I care about you forever" kind. Gentle or not, she was breathless when he pulled away.

He kept his hands on her face, his thumbs feathering gently over her cheeks. "I am giving us a month," he said softly. "A month to see where we stand. You have been under incredible strain the last while, and I have been your official protector and your back-up. That is *not* real life. We need a chance at real life. At a proper non-Neary, non-coke-head Mel life. One that focuses on us.

"I believe we see something in each other that can allow that to happen. But I also think you and yes, maybe me, need the space to let the fracas settle and for us to find our respective feet again."

"And then?" Her voice was a mere whisper.

"And then I want to woo you," he declared as if swearing an oath to his liege.

She ruined the moment by snorting. "Woo me? Ah, Sir Scot, what makes you think you could pull that off? I'm not exactly wooing material."

"I will make it my mission to ensure you are."

She eyed him thoughtfully. "So, you're saying we part company for a month and then, what, date?"

"Precisely."

"But I'm still flawed. I still can't be what you need. Can't give you what you deserve." She did her best to hold off the wobble that came awfully close to the surface.

"I know what I need, Ali Fitzgerald. All I am asking is that you think about it. About us, in a relationship, lovers and friends, partners and supporters. Think about it and tell me your answer at Caro's wedding." He stood then and stepped back.

Had she missed something?

"Caro's wedding? You'll be there?"

"I have received an invitation. It seems to be becoming a habit attending your sisters' weddings. But this time, if you find me, I *will* kiss you. And I will *not* let you go."

407

"It's my decision, then? I get to say if we do this or not? Is that fair?"

"I know how I feel. It seems you need to figure out how you feel, so yes, it will be your decision." Gabe shoved his hands in his pockets.

"And you'll walk away if I say no, it won't work?" Ali didn't, for one second, believe Gabe Mackenzie had ever given up on anything. But she also knew, in her bones, he'd never force her.

"Ah, I didn't say that." He smiled. "Have we a deal? Will you give me your answer at the wedding?"

Ali thought about it. Ran through everything he'd said. Their forced relationship, flung together through dangerous and often scary circumstances. How quickly they'd become involved. How hot it had been between them. Until her "faults" had reared their heads. That wasn't going to change. Could her hang-up about it? Would she *let* herself be happy? *God! he was asking a lot.* She looked at him, his calm presence making her *want* as she never had with any other man. Could she simply pack that in? Or was she just too scared to take a chance?

Damn him and his month-apart theory. She'd have headspace and time to feel semi normal. He, too, would have time to see if he really wanted her and her suite of baggage.

"I'll agree to a month's distance if it works both ways," she said finally.

He cocked his brow as he stood.

"*You* have to give it some serious thought, too. If you don't come to the wedding, I'll know you've changed your mind. No hard feelings." *Did she just outright lie to him?* "And if you do, I'll find you, if I've changed mine. Correct?"

"I have told you how I feel," he said. "I will *not* change my mind."

"Actually," Ali said as she followed him to the door, "you haven't said how you feel."

He stilled and then turned back to her in the open doorway.

"You're right. I haven't." He looked right into her eyes, darkened green to bright blue. "I have fallen for you in every way imaginable," he said, his voice low, rough, hands braced on either side of the door frame as if stopping himself from grabbing her. "I think about you night and day. I fall asleep with your face for comfort, your words as balm to my ears. I want to be with you for every day that I live on this Earth and beyond. I am so in love with you there are times I can't even breathe." He blinked slowly then pulled away, turned and walked down the steps to his jeep.

He didn't look back.

Ali closed the door slowly as if in a dream. Wiping at her wet cheeks, she took a deep breath. Well, it wasn't every day a girl was left stunned. *Wow. Go, Gabe.*

Chapter 28

She got the first note three days into their "monthcation", as she was calling it. *So much for keeping his distance.*

Remember to eat – enjoy your own delicious creations.
Outlander.

It was handwritten on stiff white card and addressed in the same inky black scrawl. She'd been charmed.

A week later, another note followed:

Sex is a lot, but it isn't everything. You are everything.
Highlander.

Ah, come on! He was being ridiculous now.
And then another note:

Night and day, Ali. I think about you from dawn to dusk and on through the long summer nights. Only you.
MacScot.

He was wooing her. He wasn't waiting till the wedding and her decision. He'd begun his campaign. Now, when the post slid with a light thump to the floor from her letter box, her heart kicked up a little, in case it was another note.

She wasn't spending all of her time waiting. *Not her.*

She was a modern, busy woman with things to do, places to go. People to see.

She and her parents went to their first therapy session. It was hard. Brutal in ways. And they all needed space afterwards. But they went again. Still hard but less so. There were more scheduled and they'd go to those, too. It was helping, if slowly. Dev had joined them for the last half-hour of the second session and it nearly broke her in two to see his raw anguish as he faced his lack of awareness and took ownership of it. He'd agreed to the third session, too. Ali was becoming very proud of her family and that in itself was hugely healing.

She went alone to Dr Hearne, for a "clean-up", she called it. Tidy up the loose ends. She told the good doc that she really wanted to perform oral sex. Or at least she *wanted* to want to. The doc had some interesting suggestions, among which were eating an ice-cream cone with swirls of her tongue, eating an ice lolly very slowly – making sure to catch every drip – using her toys – with flavoured edible gel – if she preferred. And there was more. She was to use her vivid imagination. As the doc said, you've seen the goods for real, now see if you can enjoy them in your imagination.

She also reassured Ali, as much as she could, that not all men expected it. Or even wanted it. Just like not all women. Ali hadn't actually thought about it from the different gender perspective. What if Gabe couldn't, because of some previous trauma, go down on her? How would she have felt? Would she have felt cheated? Like they couldn't be a real couple?

That one took some really honest soul-searching and a Skype session with Caro and Frankie. The two women, from the angle of being in relationships with "hot-sex", both admitted they'd miss it, but it would *in no way* stop them from having awesome sex in so many other ways. If the guy treated you like you were everything to them, then the rest would follow. *"You are everything,"* he'd written. Had he ever made her feel less than that? *No. No, he hadn't.*

Ali also took time out to reassess her TV career. Where did she want to go? So many opportunities came her way, producers offering her a different take on what she'd already done. But none of them were quite right. Should she just sign on for a season two of her show? She worked on her book and secured Dev the deal of doing the photography. That project began the third week of their Gabe-enforced break and brought such joy. She and Dev, hamming it up in front of, and behind, the camera. Following on from the tough therapy session, it was wonderful to laugh and slag and just be themselves. If Dev gave her more hugs than usual, if Flynn, Frankie and Molly swung by more regularly, and if Caro texted her every second day, well, she took it. She even enjoyed it.

By the beginning of week four, wedding prep was in full Fitzgerald swing. Americans began arriving and needed housing. Ali took in Gia, Nick's younger sister, and they became instant friends. Gia was like a dark Italian version of herself and had almost as much of a potty mouth as Ali. Caro arrived home with Toby in tow, and Nick and his Italian entourage of Toby's grandparents – Valentina and Antonio di Luca – came, too. Nick's employees, Vito and Naomi, and his one-time young cousin and now displaced di Luca granddaughter, Mia, were all due two days before the ceremony. Despite the growing numbers descending on the Fitzgerald house, the ceremony and reception were to be "intimate". Nick's parents were staying in the family home with Jo and Patrick, but unfortunately, Nick's brother, Sal, and his brother's wife, Louise, couldn't travel for the big day.

As Ali tried on her dress with Caro, Frankie, Molly and Gia in attendance, the post arrived.

"I'll grab it," Molly said, now already in the hall.

Ali tried to stay still and let Frankie zip her up. Frankie was Caro's only bridesmaid, as Molly had, in the end, refused and Ali felt there was enough going on without getting involved in nuptial dramas, so she, too, had bowed out. Party frocks still had to be tried on and adjusted, shoes selected and hair discussed, though.

"Stand still, for God's sake," Frankie grumbled, inching the zip upwards. "You're like a cat on a griddle."

Molly came into the room, a bunch of envelopes in her hand. She tossed them on the small table in the living room, where they'd congregated in Ali's flat. A pristine white envelope, the size of a postcard, lay there, black ink, scrawl, stamp. Ali's heart started pounding. What had she become? In such a short space of time, she'd morphed into a dreamy, moonstruck idiot, that's who. But, *God*, her stomach was flipping just seeing his handwriting. Knowing he'd thought of something to say to her, something that couldn't wait. *Fuck*, she couldn't wait.

"Moll, can you hand me the top one, the smaller envelope?" She hoped her voice didn't sound as squeaky as it seemed to her ears.

"Looks like an invite," Molly said as she handed it over.

"It's not," Ali said quietly as she turned it over and

413

over in her hands. She was stalling, anticipating. *Nervous.*

"How d'ya know? Open it." Molly crunched into an apple and plonked down on the couch. She hated fittings and dress parades of any kind and was here on sufferance.

Ali slid her finger under the seal and broke it open. She pulled out the white card and, her hand instinctively against her heart, read the message to herself.

Sometimes I can barely breathe when I think of your smile. I will keep trying to catch my breath, if you keep sharing your smile with me.
S MacO.

Oh. My. Goodness. Her belly did a particularly lively somersault and a grin spread across her face.

"Who's it from?" Caro asked, trying to rewrite the order of seating in the church.

Frankie had told her no one used an order of seating, but Caro was getting jittery and needed a chore.

"It's from Gabe." Ali handed the note to Frankie, who'd come to stand beside her, dress now all done up.

"Oh, be still, my heart!" Frankie's eyes immediately filled and she read the words on the card for the other women out loud through a blur.

"Jeez!" Gia said. "I'll have me one of them. Where do I sign up?"

Everyone laughed, but the note was duly handed from one woman to another, and all the resulting sighs and hand-fanning finally got on Ali's already frayed nerves.

"It's just a stupid note," she murmured, embarrassed as well as pissed off.

She hated this new tingly feeling, the flutters, the heart speeding up, her own deep sighs as she read over each note, every night. *Damn that man. What was a girl to do?*

"I think it's lovely," Caro said for all of them.

"Is he handsome, this dude?" Gia asked.

"Not so much," Molly said, deadpan.

"So-so," Caro agreed.

"Meh," Frankie added.

Ali looked at them blankly. *Were they blind?*

She swung round to Gia. "He's bloody gorgeous. Tall, with amazing skin – he's mixed race, so it's that smooth *café au lait* colour. Green eyes that would drown you. The sexiest mouth in the universe. Hands that are both strong and gentle. Abs for days. And he's kind and thoughtful and dependable and smart and careful with me. And . . . " She stopped as the realisation that she was being played dawned on her.

"So, you're not that into him, then," Gia surmised dryly. "Good to know."

Ali burst out laughing, she couldn't help it. "Oh, fuck it, girls, I have it bad, don't I?"

"Yup," they all agreed unanimously, delighted.

"You are *so* screwed," Caro laughed.

"Jesus, Mac, can you not with the tapping?" Flynn glared at his colleague and friend and shook his head in exasperation.

Gabe stiffened. Stopped his fingers from dancing on the tabletop and shoved his hand in his pocket.

"Apologies," he said and grimaced.

They were out to lunch, eating in a nondescript restaurant on the north side of the city. The village of

Malahide was charming and sported many decent eating establishments, but they didn't suit the purpose of today's trip. It was a business lunch of sorts – they were going to meet an accounting forensic specialist they needed on a new case – and, well, it was nearly 2 p.m. and they were hungry. Two birds, one stone. They were nothing if not efficient.

Flynn put down his sandwich and wiped his mouth with a paper napkin. It wasn't bad, his classic toasted ham and cheese, but however much he liked his, Mackenzie hadn't touched his own food.

"Tuna melt not doing it for you today? Or is something on your mind?" Flynn liked the direct approach. Except when he didn't. He used what he could and was, thankfully, highly adaptable. "Spill." He took a bite and waited. He was good at that, too.

Gabe picked up his sandwich, studied it and put it back down. "I have . . . " He took a breath. "I have something I wish to discuss with you. Not case-related."

Flynn nodded around a mouthful and gestured, "Go on."

Gabe lifted his eyes from his plate to meet Flynn's direct gaze. "I am in love with your sister. As soon as she gives me the official go-ahead, we are going to be dating. Properly." He let out a breath he probably wasn't aware he'd been holding and determinedly took a bite of tuna melt.

Flynn thought about all the things he could say. The smart remarks, the jibes, the jokes, the slags. Nothing floated to the surface. He'd make those comments, of course he would. But not today.

"When is this official start date?" he asked, deciding

there was no point pretending he hadn't known something was up.

"Caro and Nick's wedding, on Friday."

"Romantic," Flynn said, surprised he liked the notion of another blossoming love story at Caro's big day.

Gabe shrugged. "It wasn't intended to be romantic – it was actually practical. I had been invited, I had taken the day and weekend off on leave, and it fitted into my timeline."

Flynn looked at him curiously. "Timeline? You gave my sister, Ali Fitzgerald, the biggest ball-buster there is, a timeline. And you're still upright? No hospitalisations? I'm impressed."

Gabe let out a short laugh. "She is tough, all right. But also, not. After everything, I felt we needed to slow it all down. Start fresh without Neary or Mel being the reason we were together. I wanted her to want *me*. Us. Not the guy who was forced into her life – by her brother, I might add." He paused to glare at Flynn. "I wanted her to take a breath, to begin to love her life, to be without fear.

"I know it is asking a lot and I certainly do *not* expect it to be sorted anytime soon. But I hope she will have begun those few steps towards finding the new her. The 'after Ali', not the scared, closed-off girl of before." Gabe rubbed his hand over his jaw, looking embarrassed. "Sorry, you don't need to hear all this."

Flynn sat back, interested. "Actually, I do. I do need to hear this. It's important to know what the hell is going on in your mind that might have accounted for the 'stick it up your ass' behaviour of the last few weeks. You've either been barking orders at minions or mooning off into space. I want the pre-Ali Mac back." He kept his face serious as he watched Gabe's expression change and harden. *Ha! Got him.*

"Not going to happen, Fitz," Gabe said evenly, his hand curled into a fist on the table. "If you do not like the way I am doing my job, we can talk about that. But my life before Ali does not exist any more. It is all about her from now on. Her needs, her happiness. I am going to do everything in my power to ensure she lives her best life possible. With me."

Flynn smiled. Big and wide. "Easy, Mac, I'm just messing with you. Your work is stellar, as per. The crew respect and admire you. I know we've talked about it before, but I hope you do put in for the transfer to Dublin, even in the short-term. I'd hate to see Ali go to Edinburgh. So would the parents – especially as, in a way, they feel they've just got her back."

"Already sent off the paperwork. We will see . . . Ali knows I get called to other places at the oddest times. She understands that . . . that side of me." He cleared his throat. "You don't ever have to worry about her safety again, Fitz. I've got her."

"I know you do. I appreciate it. But don't ever let her hear you do that caveman talk. She'll chop off your balls, no mercy."

"I am in love, Flynn, not lobotomised."

They both grinned at that.

Gabe excused himself to go to the men's room and Flynn sat back, pondering all he'd heard. It was no great surprise. He'd seen the sparks fly between the two of them from day one. He'd liked it. It had made him see his sister in a new way. Grown up and adult, all by herself. He'd never forgive himself for not being there when she needed him, but that was the past. What he could do now was pat himself on the back for selecting the exact right man to take her into the future.

Flynn looked at his watch as Kit Elliot walked into the restaurant. *Ah, right on time. The sign of a good numbers man. This should be interesting.* He waved the newcomer over and the meeting began as Gabe returned to the table.

The ceremony was beautiful. Caro had freaked out about using a priest based on recent events, but Ali had shut her up. Father Sloane had been too busy, but Father Guiney was a pet. Honest as the day was long. Funny, too. And he made the simple marriage rite both a joy and a holy sacrament.

Caro and Nick looked radiant. Her dress was like a Grace Kelly affair, wide collar across the shoulder, nipped in at the waist and full tea-length skirt. All in glazed cotton as a nod to the summer's warmth. Frankie was divine in moss green, and Ali knew her own figure-hugging French blue shift dress was both classy and sexy. To the knee, it appeared demure, but that was its clever, deceptive ruse. Boat-necked and low-backed, it hit all the sensual notes. She wore kitten heels in the same blue and carried a simple white shrug in case of chill.

Her parents shed happy tears, Toby stood up with Nick as his best "man", which was a generous gesture lost on no one, and all the Sullivans seemed to be fitting in with gracious ease.

There was no sign of Gabe.

Drinks at the house reception were of the sparkling variety, though not, Ali suspected, Bollinger this time, and light canapés were tasty and going down a storm, but she was dealing with a worsening pain in her gut. Gia, in a scarlet fitted dress, bumped her hip in a friendly gesture and pointed towards the garden as guests floated about, wandering around the lawn or strolling down to the sea. Everything looked perfect.

"Your family home is awesome, Ali. All the space and the yard and the ocean? It's fab!"

"It's a garden and a sea," corrected Ali irritably, sipping a Kir.

"Duh," agreed Gia, taking no offence. "Your little sis looks so cool in that colour, doesn't she? Purple on a redhead? My mom's probably having a fit!"

"Molly's not a redhead, she's warm chestnut." Ali's cross-o-meter was ratcheting up. "And she looks great in every colour! Excuse me."

She turned abruptly to walk indoors and bumped into Flynn, who was coming out.

"Out of my way," she snarled. "I need the loo."

And she left Flynn to manage their new "sort-of" sister.

"Sullivan," she heard him say coolly.

"Fitzgerald," was the frosty response.

Ah, shit, now what? Bloody cops and their pissing contests. She didn't have time for this. She had . . . she had things . . . things to do.

She made it to the bathroom before hunching over in pain. Her stomach was cramping and she was bloody furious. Bloody being the operative word. *Gah! Her cycle decided to be on time now? Now? Of all days? Fuck Gabe and his concern over her body's workings. He wasn't bloody here, was he?* She sorted herself out from the supplies from the cabinet, took a slurp of water from the tap and unlocked the door.

Gabe was there. *There*. Leaning against the wall, hands in pockets, feet crossed at the ankles, all casual, not a care in the world. He was wearing a navy suit, white shirt open at the neck, and he looked ridiculously edible. Ali was furious. Everything was his fault.

"Where have you been?" she demanded, poking him in the arm. "You're late! It's rude to be late to a wedding."

Gabe peeled himself from the wall and studied her. "Hi," he said softly, ignoring her outburst. "You look beautiful."

Oh.

"Thanks," she grunted, not letting him off the hook for making her feel . . . *So. Damn. Much.*

Suddenly she felt shy, awkward. *This was it.* Their month was up and she didn't know what to do, how to act. Should she throw herself at him now, slobber kisses all over his face? *Argh! This love stuff was hard.*

"Let's get a plate of food," Gabe said, tucking her hand into his arm and pulling her forwards. "The spread looks delicious."

"The caterers are friends of mine from culinary school," Ali told him apropos of nothing other than she suddenly felt totally out of her depth. At least she could hook onto the one subject that was her comfort zone.

She told him about all the choices, babbling on as if she were a gauche teenager instead of a woman on the verge of . . . *what? Falling in love? Too late. That ship had sailed.* She'd admitted her feelings after the first note but acknowledged she'd been falling long, long before then. Now, all she had to do was stop talking and tell him. That didn't make sense, physically or practically, but she was about to burst!

Gabe took charge, steering her to a table with other guests, sitting with plates of food and chatting as if he were Mr Sociable himself. *Where was* her *Gabe? Grumpy, taciturn MacScot.* She missed *him.* The young women, friends of Caro's from the university, seemed to like this Gabe very much. *Jealous now?* she thought. *Christ! I've reached a new low.*

As they spent the next two hours together with Gabe ensuring they were never alone, Ali began to panic. *Just because he was here didn't mean they were on, did it?* She couldn't remember the rules, *damn it.* She had to kiss him, she knew that, she *wanted* that, but it seemed to be the farthest thing from his mind. He laughed politely at something friend number one said and Ali was done.

There was a small dance floor set up on the lawn, where Nick and Caro were already wrapped around each other, swaying to their own love story. Before Ali could drag Gabe into a darkened room and kiss the hell out of him, he pulled her towards the makeshift wooden dance floor and tugged her close. He rested his head atop hers and seemed to breathe her in. He took one of her hands in his and held it against his chest, while the other he wrapped about her body, holding her close against his long, lean frame. Ali just about melted in a puddle at his feet. This. *This* was what she missed. This tingle down her spine, the heat pooling in her belly, the rapid bumping of her heart, the *rightness* of it all.

She sighed and let her head fall forwards, resting on his shoulder. Relaxing into him as if he were her lifeboat on a wild and stormy sea.

"Ali," he whispered into her hair.

And they danced. Slow and languid, their limbs moved sinuously as they swayed to the music. The tempo changed several times, their dance, as they continued to hold one another close, did not. It felt like neither could let go, not even for a second. Ali slowly became aware of the tension in Gabe's shoulders and she lifted her head to meet his eyes in the dusky glow.

"Are you okay?" *Shit, are* we *okay?* was what she really wanted to know.

He shifted slightly. "Ah, no, not really." His voice was strained, on edge. "Do you think we could go somewhere private?"

Now he wanted privacy? What the . . . ?

Oh!

But when he moved slightly and she felt him, all of him, pressing into her hip, she understood. *Oh, boy, did she understand. Thank God!*

"Absolutely," she tossed over her shoulder as she drew him along behind her through the hall and upstairs to her room.

She dragged him inside, closing and locking the door behind them.

They stared at each other, as if for the first time, and to Ali, in a way, this *was* new. She'd never been in a room, alone, with a man she knew she was irrevocably in love with. She didn't know the protocol, so she went on instinct.

"You were right," she said, trying to keep her breathing even so he wouldn't know what a train wreck she was inside. "I did need the time. Thank you."

Gabe took something from his pocket and handed it

to her. An envelope. Just her name on the front this time.

With trembling fingers, she opened the seal and pulled out the card. Her eyes flew to his, holding steady for a moment as she drank him in, what he looked like right now, before. Before everything might change.

She let her eyes fall to the bold words:

I will kiss you back. Every day of our lives. And every day after.
Gabe.

Her heart hammered and when she raised her drenched eyes to his, they could never tell afterwards who kissed whom first or who was kissing back. It really didn't matter. It was never going to matter again.

They both moved and mouths melded as if they'd never had a breath between them. It was a glorious kiss, at once gentle and fierce. Filled with both longing and promises. It said more than words ever could. But words were also necessary.

"Yes," Ali gasped as he trailed his mouth down her neck. "I want an 'us', I want to be with you. I want—"

"You," he groaned back, his voice coarse and rough and cracking. "I want you. All of you. In whatever way you can. Always. *God*, I missed you." And he had to kiss her again.

She drew away, for breath, eons later, and they stood, foreheads touching, gasping for air to bring their bodies some relief. His hands cupped her face and she held the front of his shirt secure in her fists. This man, this man loved her just the way she was. He knew all the ugly bits and still he came to claim her.

424

"Gabe," she began, gathering all of her courage, about to say words she'd never said before.

"Wait," he said and reached into his jacket pocket.

He pulled out a bar of her favourite dark mint chocolate and handed it to her. She stepped back and looked at it, puzzled.

"Because?" she asked, now unsure.

The note had been all she'd wanted. All she hadn't known she'd needed. Chocolate wasn't on her radar when this scenario had played out in her head. She glanced up at him. He was flustered, his cheeks a little pink. *What the . . . ?*

"I thought you might need the sugar. You know, because of . . . " And he gestured to her stomach.

She gaped. Mouth actually open gaped.

"You counted my cycle and brought me period-cramp chocolate?"

"Ah, yes. I know you get, you know . . . "

"Bitchy?" she supplied, her heart melting to mush.

"Sensitive, a little shaky," he amended with that gorgeous half-smile.

If Ali hadn't already fallen off the cliff in love with Gabe Mackenzie before, this kindness would have toppled her for sure. She ripped open the package, craving the sharp sweetness, and snapped off a chunk, offering it to him.

"No, sweetheart, it is all for you," he said, taking her hand and drawing her to the bed.

"Much as I love you, Outlander, there will be no sexy times tonight. I'm not that okay with sharing my body's cycle with you. Not yet." She turned to laugh at him as she fell to the bed, but he'd gone utterly still.

He cleared his throat. "Do you? Love me? Don't say it if you are not ready. I can wait. I am a patient man." He sounded gruff, his voice uneven.

Ali cursed fluently as only she knew how. She scrambled forwards on the bed to catch his hands and pull him to her.

"Ah, shit, I'm sorry. That didn't come out the way it should. I'm new to this. I'm a learner. I need massive L-plates attached to my back as I tread warily though this new world. Sit with me."

She tugged him down next to her and then, hitching her dress up her thighs, climbed to sit astride his legs so she could see him face to face, right into his eyes. Her heart was banging so hard in her chest, she wondered it couldn't be seen through the fabric of her dress.

"Oh, Gabe, I've fallen for you big time. All the way in time. I've never told anyone I loved them before and I'm not really sure how, but I'll try. Your notes showed me a softer side to you, a poetic side, like some of those night-time texts did – well, other than the super-hot, sexy ones – and I wish I could do the same.

"Maybe on our tenth anniversary I'll be competent enough to write a sonnet, but for now all I can say is this." She leaned in and kissed him softly, full on his firm lips. "You have become my world. You let me be myself, warts and all, and I never expected that from anyone, not since . . . since back then." She kissed him again, feeling his firm hands rest on her hips as he let her have her say. "I don't know exactly when I fell in love with you, I just know that I'm overflowing with it.

"You've filled up all of my empty spaces and it's the most magical, unbelievable feeling in the world. No one makes me feel the way you do, no one. When I'm with you, I'm the happiest me I can be. I want to hold that forever and I know I will, because I'll love you forever."

Gabe closed his eyes briefly and the blazing green gaze that was transfixed on her when he opened them again took her breath away.

"Ali," he whispered, "my heart is yours for the keeping. And I will hold yours and keep it safe and warm as it glows inside me from this moment forwards."

At one time a vow like that would have freaked her out and coming from someone else, it probably still would have. But this was Gabe, a man who was sometimes of another world, who would lay down his life for those he protected, who made her feel hot and twisty in the best ways when he used his hands and mouth on her – and the man who brought her period chocolate.

It was pretty damn fucking hard to beat that.

Epilogue

Huh. Who knew Hogmanay was a real thing?

Mackenzie's Keep was decked out in full festive array and the place was heaving with guests. People had travelled for miles, many of whom would overnight in the huge house. To Ali's eye, it was a castle, pure and simple. *It had actual castellated walls, for God's sake.* She'd been up on the ramparts earlier with Gabe and the view had been stunning. Even with the heavy falls of snow, the vista had been spectacular. Maybe because the snow had made it take on a fairy-tale quality.

If anyone knew fairy tales didn't exist, it was she. *But. Still. It was magical.* She'd snuggled into Gabe's welcoming arms and, while grateful for the down jacket, she really appreciated the heat that radiated from him. *It was so fucking bizarre seeing him here, in his family "seat".* This was his heritage, his to own eventually. The responsibility was immense and she was extremely thankful that his dad, the present laird, was hale and hearty.

Ian Mackenzie was a huge man, bigger and broader than Gabe. He had a booming voice and a loquacious personality, quite different from his more discerning son. But there was a strong bond between them all the same. It was tangible. Not just the obvious bear hug they exchanged upon arrival, but also the looks and smiles they shared. The conversations that appeared to be a continuation from another visit. Seamless and easy.

It was, however, pretty clear to Ali that the elder Mackenzie was baffled by his son on some level. Ian kept asking Gabe when he was going to pack in the detecting and get down to the business of landowning. The question was half-hearted and only partly serious. Gabe deflected well and shrugged it off. Ali wondered if this was Gabe's future. *Would he have to be laird some day? Christ! that was some burden. What if Gabe didn't want to? What if when it came to it,* she *didn't want to?*

She stood at the top of the grand staircase, waiting to descend into the throng of guests. Thank God Gabe had warned her it was formal. She wore a strapless taffeta gown in midnight blue, picked up in a second-hand shop in Edinburgh on their way through a few days before. It had been lovely to catch up with the Macs in Moray Place when they'd overnighted there and the drive up had been an eye-opener, in beautiful scenery.

Gabe joined her at the top step and she gaped. Stunned. He was in full Mackenzie dress and it was a . . . sight.

"You're giving Jamie Fraser a run for his money in that get-up," she said breathlessly, fanning herself for extra impact as her eyes skimmed the kilt and she wondered what everyone else would – did he or didn't he? She knew she'd find out later.

Gabe grinned at her. "Is he the *Outlander* chap or the *Highlander* one?"

Ali laughed. "Done your research, have you?"

"Trying to keep up with you, sweetheart." He took her hand and drew it to his lips to kiss her knuckles.

It got to her. Every time he did these little romantic gestures, the thoughtful extras. Not a month went by without dark mint choc being on her pillow on just the right day. He brewed her coffee in the morning just the way she liked it. And he cleaned the windows in her loft. It was worrying sometimes how in tune with her he was. And not in his "I'm in touch with my senses" way, just the "I care about you" way.

And what did she do for him?

That was the question.

Gabe noticed his mother across the large ballroom and sighed in relief. *Excellent. It was time.* She'd arrived that afternoon – later than expected owing to flight delays – but she was here. He'd let his parents meet each other and catch up, so hadn't actually seen her himself yet. He could breathe easy now. That was until he introduced the women in his life to each other. He had no idea what to expect. *None.*

He moved through the ballroom, Ali's hand clutched in his as seas of people parted and let them pass. He stopped before the dark-haired beauty standing next to a large sculpture, trying, unsuccessfully, to fade into the background. No one with her looks would ever fade anywhere, but she always tried. Her twice-yearly trip to Scotland was usually a bit fraught at first as she readjusted. Then, suddenly, the nervousness would be gone and she would flow into the Keep's way of life as if to the manner born.

"Mama," Gabe said, letting go of Ali and enveloping his mother in a hug.

He kissed both of her cheeks and held her back from

him to study her familiar face. The same deep, dark eyes, all-knowing, all-seeing. The high, wide cheekbones and soft, full mouth. Her hair was still dark with a few strands of grey filtering through and a few fine lines added gravitas to her skin. Still his mother, still the woman who meant so much to him, despite their years spent on opposite continents. That was just distance, miles. Nothing to do with closeness.

"Gabriel," she sighed. "My boy. You look . . . you look so well." There was surprise in her voice. *Wonder. Speculation.* Missing nothing, she angled behind him to see Ali. "This must be the reason," she added as she slid from his hold.

"Ali." Gabe turned back and took Ali's hand, drawing her forwards. "This is my mother, Neosha, or Neo. Mama, this is Ali Fitzgerald, my . . . my girlfriend."

The two women sized each other up, shaking hands but eyes riveted to each other's faces. Gabe could feel the electricity in the air as his mother held Ali's hand in both of hers and after a brief moment, she closed her eyes and began mouthing something. Ali turned and looked at him enquiringly, eyebrows raised. He smiled and nodded briefly – everything was okay.

"Leave her alone, Neo," a brisk voice interrupted as his grandmother barrelled in to join them. "She's grand, this lass, just a wee bit mixed up. But all right now, I think?" She took Ali's chin in her hand and glared at her. "Aye, all is well." She let go of Ali and breaking the clasped hands apart, leaned in and hugged Neo herself.

Gabe often wondered how the two older women had ever made their peace with each other. There was Granny Fiona, a feisty, tough-as-old-boots "seer" and matriarch of their branch of the Mackenzie clan, and Neosha, tall, reserved and self-composed Osage Nations daughter of a very high-up chief, the interloper at Mackenzie's Keep. Two women at home in their own worlds, revered and respected by their own people and sharing not one, but two men. And each with a turbulent history behind them that generations of strong, determined people like themselves had overcome.

Ali had now finished the book she'd borrowed from Gabe's shelf in his town house months ago and they'd had many discussions about its disturbing contents. He was touched she wanted to know more about his non-Scottish side and he fully intended to introduce her to his extended Osage family when he could.

Gabe's parents still saw each other several times a year – they just didn't live together. Both were committed to their respective bonds, both leaders in their respective communities. Neither could be without those ties for any length of time. They'd tried. Many times. Gabe had been born at the Keep and Neo had stayed for a few years, but by the third, she was failing in health, so took herself and her son to Oklahoma.

Ian followed, but a year later, his manager called him home to deal with some difficulties and he took Gabe with him. Back and forth they went. Gabe was shuffled between both places, usually with both parents. But when he turned ten, they made a new arrangement. And it had been that way ever since. Love crossed the ocean and the prairies, the Highlands and the cities. He knew his parents were as devoted to each other as they were to him. But they couldn't leave their respective people.

Gabe watched as the three women became

acquainted, in a new way. He didn't doubt Ali would handle herself, would hold her own. He just hoped the other women wouldn't overwhelm Ali with, as she called it, *woo-woo*. They'd reached a really good place in their relationship and he was relieved Ali's new season of the TV show gave her the time off so she could come with him now. Hogmanay was important to his family and their dependants, and he hoped Ali would enjoy herself. He also hoped she'd be amenable to his proposition later that evening, when he got her alone.

Ali danced – waltzed, jigged, reeled and yes, rock and rolled. The band was so versatile they put a spin, literally, on every tune. Well after midnight, she thanked her latest partner, the gillie from the Keep, and took a sneaky dash out onto the terrace. Yes, it was freezing, the sky an ominous odd light colour even at this late hour, but she needed some air. And a moment to gather her thoughts.

She'd danced with Gabe several times in the last six months – they'd had things to attend: events, parties and another wedding. But tonight, among his family, it felt different. And that needed a moment. *Or several.* She turned and leaned over the low terrace wall, her eyes sweeping down across the vast expanse of lawn that led, eventually, to a loch. *Yup. They had their very own lake. As you do.* Ali had been flabbergasted the first evening when Gabe had told her he'd see her at dinner as he was off to chat with the land steward.

"Ha ha," she'd said, "next you'll be telling me you dress for dinner!"

His stoic face had her groaning.

"Fuck. You do, don't you?"

"Only when we have company, as we do this weekend, for the festivities. Don't worry, no one will mind if you come as you are. You will outshine them all," he'd added gallantly.

Thank God. And Frankie had thrown in a bunch of easy-to-wear dresses, so she wasn't completely at a loss, but *come on!* What had she landed into?

Warm arms surrounded her and she didn't need a sixth sense to know Gabe had joined her on the terrace.

"You are chilled," he said and moved to shrug out of his jacket.

"No, just your arms about me is fine," Ali murmured. "It's a beautiful night, but the light is so peculiar."

"It is going to snow again," Gabe said. "Fairly soon, I would imagine. Are you okay? Not too overwhelmed by that lot inside?"

"I used wonder why you were so calm in among my family. Now I know. You've had *this* going on."

"Ah, but only a few times a year. My days, even weeks, were often very . . . " He paused to consider. "Solo. I loved these events as a child. I was allowed to stay up till the haggis had been piped in and the dancing began. Then my nanny would whisk me away.

"As I got older, I enjoyed it in a different way – the tradition of it, the continuity, the community, I suppose. And it was always so good to see my parents dancing together. I still enjoy that." He sounded almost sheepish as he admitted to that romantic failing.

"They make a very striking couple, that's for sure. Your mum's hair is incredible, falling down her back like that, and she has the grace of a queen."

"And yet, I'm sensing some . . . restraint . . . on your

part," Gabe said quietly, resting his chin on her head, his arms enclosing her.

Ali sighed and, turning, snuggled into his heat, resting her head against his chest as she pondered what to say. How to say it.

"It's a lot. All of . . . this." She gestured a hand towards the house and then back across the land. "So much responsibility. It's all on you, or it will be. How does that make you feel?"

"I think the question is how does it make *you* feel?"

"Scared shitless?" She posed it as a question and looked up at him, a slight smile taking the sting from the words.

"Understood." He loosened his arms from about her and held her face in his hands with such tenderness she felt her eyes well.

She had to speak, to stop him from saying whatever he was gearing up to say. *He looked so serious. So solemn. Shit, he was going to go all laird of the manor and tell her duty came before all, et cetera.* She could feel the waves of anxiety rolling from him. She'd felt his tension on the plane on the way over. And things had been so good between them . . .

He'd done as he'd said – he'd courted her. They'd gone on dates, old-fashioned ones. Walks, picnics, the theatre, movie nights – both outside and in. They'd gone ice skating and orienteering. It had been *fun*. They'd had amazing sex – tender and sweet, fast and heady. They'd dated, like a real honest-to-God couple. All so new to Ali she was still feeling the simple joy of him, of them. It didn't look like simple was going to cut it any more, if Gabe's face was anything to go by.

"I'm not sure—" she began, but he stopped her with a kiss.

"I know it is all a bit much. I get that. But I just want you to put it all on the back burner in that overactive brain of yours and listen to me. Just me."

He stroked her bottom lip with his thumb, causing a hive of activity in her belly.

"Being a Mackenzie does not have to mean not being anything else. My father is strong, healthy and able. He knows I am committed to the force for as long as I feel I can be of use. I know this place is here for me – is mine – but I have chosen to look on it as a boon, not a weight around my neck.

"Even if I never live here, long-term, people's livelihoods will thrive. I know this because the stewards we hire are excellent, honest and loyal. Equally, if I choose to come home, I will be the laird and all that implies. Overseeing the people and the land, making changes and decisions that affect hundreds of households. If I do choose that, I will commit to it with equal fervour. But that is a long way off." He took a breath, closing his eyes briefly.

She reached up and laid a hand gently against his smooth cheek. *God*, she loved this man. *His strength, his honour, his heart. All were for the use of others.* He never put himself first, never sulked or moaned, even when he had to do those mental gymnastics to help others in trouble. She'd seen all this over the last six months and all that had happened was she'd fallen deeper, harder, stronger. He wasn't a paragon. *Hell, no. That man couldn't caffeinate to save his life! He'd cleaned and swept floors like a champion, and that couldn't be healthy.* And until he met Ali, he'd never ever eaten ice cream straight from the tub!

But he was patient with her. Endlessly, heartbreakingly patient. She'd broken through some of her issues, thanks to Dr Hearne, Gabe and, she admitted, her own desires. The doc had reminded her that Gabe's body was a thing of beauty – *ain't that the truth* – and that she could touch and taste any part of it she wished – or not. He said the same. And when she thought about it like that, it all seemed so natural, so right. No more thinking of taxes or Lego. Just him and how she loved and trusted him. And how much pleasure she could give as well as receive. That was a whole new level of power control – one she could get on board with completely.

"Ali," Gabe said, his voice soft, "I am not asking you to make choices about any of this now. I just want you to know, they will be in my future and, hopefully, yours at some stage. I want to ask if you are ready for the next step. If you would move in with me. It doesn't have to be my place. It can be somewhere new, or I could move into yours. What do you think?"

He stopped speaking and Ali could see he was actually holding his breath.

Wow. He wanted them to live together. Be in a proper grown-up relationship.

She took a deep breath and let the idea settle for a moment. *How would it feel? Would it change things hugely?* They slept over in each other's places several nights a week as it was. *But to wake up to him every day? To go to sleep in his arms every night? Man, that was* big. *And wonderful. Incredible. Perfect.*

"Yes, please," she said. "But—"

The rest was cut off as he took her mouth in a searing kiss. He lifted her from the ground and spun her round, his mouth not leaving hers.

"Hey," she gasped, laughing as he let her go. "I just want to say that I'll move into yours. Your flat has so much light and I love the space flow. I can ask Molly if she'd like to take over Caro's as a sublet. I know she's been looking—"

"When?" Gabe demanded, kissing his way down her neck and along her jaw.

"You're distracting me. I can't think."

"As soon as we get back? I will arrange a removal van and—"

"Whoa!" Ali intervened. "I can do that. I'm not a helpless damsel, remember. Modern, independent woman and all."

Gabe grinned. "How could I forget? My parents are loving your new show. They are so impressed with your on-air professionalism – as well as your talents."

Ali's new show was a beaut. She was thrilled with the concept, keeping her busy and enthralled week by week. She'd sold the producers on the idea of themed careers, so each was different – one week there were a selection of plumbers, the following week doctors, the week after electricians and so on. It was a great mix of trade and craftspeople against the more "professional" academic slice of life, including the lawyers, teachers, scientists and researchers. They had so many applicants for the show they had a really hard time narrowing it down. And she'd kept her promise to have the three former competitors return on a regular basis – whether to show off their own expertise or help with the contestants.

The dénouement would be a bake-off between the best from the two sides. Viewers were already invested and the response was huge. This idea may get a whole other series, based on demand. But most of all, it was *hers*.

"We'll both get it put in motion when we get back to Dublin," Ali said, a glow spreading through her whole body, a warmth invading her in the best possible way.

This was going to happen – they were becoming an official "us"!

"Let's go back inside and say our goodnights. I want to take you to bed and do unspeakably delicious things to you." Gabe's eyes glowed in the eerie light as he gazed into hers, all the love in the world there for her to see.

No pretence, no games, no histrionics. Just the two of them. Loving each other.

The first flakes of snow fell as Gabe drew the heavy drapes closed against the chill. He turned and looked at Ali as she slid out of her ballgown. Her hair was awry, her eye make-up smudged, managing to make her beautiful eyes mesmerising. Her lipstick had already been kissed off and as she stood there in lace underwear, his heart hitched and he brought a hand to his chest to steady the beat.

She overwhelmed him sometimes. Just completely slew him. He'd asked her days ago what was her biggest hurdle in life so far when they'd been discussing one of his old cases that he'd admitted had been a real challenge. She'd thought about the question seriously for a moment and then, her eyes sad, said, "Telling my parents." She hadn't needed to explain further, but her answer floored him. Of all the truly awful things that had happened in her life, the most bothersome was the anguish of causing her parents distress. He'd been staggered by her care, her concern for them. He really shouldn't have been.

He moved across the room towards her, peeling off his shirt and tossing aside his kilt. Yes, he was indeed a traditional Scotsman, and she watched him appreciatively, her gaze heated and potent. She was everything to him now. Everything. He thought of the velvet box in the family safe in Edinburgh, the sapphire and diamond heirloom that he hoped one day would sparkle on her finger.

But he was getting ahead of himself. He had loving to do, promises of delicious things to deliver.

He didn't need any special powers for that – they created their own brand of magic in each other's arms. She lay stretched out on the bed, waiting just for him. The sight of her, unafraid, welcoming, *wanting*, never ceased to humble him.

His own sweetheart. His Ali. His warrior.

The End

www.ingramcontent.com/pod-product-compliance
Lightning Source LLC
Chambersburg PA
CBHW070613260626
47161CB00007B/2422